The Cornish Cream Tea Summer

Cressida McLaughlin

HarperCollins*Publishers*

HarperCollins*Publishers* Ltd
The News Building
1 London Bridge Street
London SE1 9GF

www.harpercollins.co.uk

This paperback original 2020

5

First published in Great Britain as four separate
ebooks in 2020 by HarperCollins*Publishers*

A catalogue record for this book
is available from the British Library

ISBN 978-0-00-833347-8

This novel is entirely a work of fiction.
The names, characters and incidents portrayed in it are
the work of the author's imagination. Any resemblance to
actual persons, living or dead, events or localities is
entirely coincidental.

Typeset in Birka by Palimpsest Book Production Ltd, Falkirk, Stirlingshire

Printed and bound in Great Britain by CPI Group (UK) Ltd, Croydon CR0 4YY

MIX
Paper from
responsible sources
FSC
www.fsc.org   FSC® C007454

This book is produced from independently certified FSC™ paper
to ensure responsible forest management.

For more information visit: www.harpercollins.co.uk/green

To the BookCampers

Part One

All You Knead Is Love

Chapter One

Delilah Forest crested the ridge of the hill, looked down at the picture-postcard village of Porthgolow, its beach alive with colour and movement that cut through the sombreness of the grey day, and decided that fate had brought her here.

Her old Volvo made a noise that she was sure wasn't healthy, so she lifted her foot off the brake pedal and sped up, hoping she was about to receive a welcome as warm as the pillar-box hue of her cousin Charlie's bus.

The Cornish Cream Tea Bus. She had laughed when her mum, Tabitha, had told her about it. 'You'll never guess what Charlie's gone and done, Lila,' she'd said, one day last spring. 'Started up some café on Hal's old wreck of a bus. Down in Cornwall, of all places! You should go and see her,' she had finished decisively, before sauntering off into the colourful kitchen of her North London flat.

Delilah hadn't come down to see her then, even though she and Charlie got on. Charlie was a couple of years older than her, and – as her mum continually reminded her – wiser, and they bounced off each other well. But Delilah had been busy at the time, with her own catering career. She pushed away a flicker of regret as she drove down the hill and into the village.

Despite it being the end of February and the sky a solid wall of cloud, the beach car park was close to full. The seafront was pretty and quaint, with a bed and breakfast, convenience store with hanging baskets sporting clouds of white snowdrops and pastel-hued hyacinths, and Victorian-style streetlights. Lila wasn't sure where Charlie lived, so she squeezed her estate car into a space in the corner of the car park, brushed her hands down her ripped jeans, and checked her reflection in the mirror.

She practised her widest, warmest smile, then sighed. The bus café had worked out, she now knew from Aunt Bonnie. Charlie was happy – successful, and in love, too, by all accounts – so would she be delighted to see her, however unannounced her visit was? Or would Lila find herself on the road back to London before the day was out?

She wondered, again, why firstly she had allowed her mum to talk her into this trip, and secondly why she had headed off without warning Charlie first. Was it because, as Lila suspected, Charlie would not welcome her with open arms, and Tabitha knew that as well as she did? But then a living, breathing cousin was harder to turn away than the thought of one.

Lila opened the car door. The wind was icy, the closeness to the sea adding an extra bite, and she shivered and dug around on the back seat for a cardigan. She found one; grey, woven through with silver thread, the holes in the wool and the wide sleeves making it more like a fishing net than a garment for warding off the cold. Still, it would add *some* warmth. As she tugged it on, her phone buzzed in her pocket.

She felt a jolt of hope, but when she checked it was a message from her mum, asking if she'd arrived safely. She replied quickly, then shoved her phone in her handbag, alongside a packet of coffee beans that she hadn't had the heart to remove.

Car locked, Lila turned in the direction of the beach and let her senses take everything in. Her nose instantly took the lead: the smells emanating from the trucks, vans and marquees were heady and intoxicating. She picked up spices, caramelized sugar, the richness of frying meat and, of course, the distinctive aroma of coffee. Her stomach grumbled, reminding her that she hadn't had anything to eat or drink since a limp sandwich and a latte at a service station on the M3. She licked her lips in anticipation, and climbed over the metal rail of the car park onto the sand.

She was soon lost amongst the crowd, surrounded by laughter and voices and movement. The hairs prickled on her arms and a smile tugged at her lips. She had spent far too much time in her tiny flat recently: it felt good to be among people again. She heard the roar of an engine and watched as a yellow inflatable speedboat left the jetty behind, waterproof-clad people on board, seemingly unafraid of the wind-chill factor.

'The best burger van in Cornwall is just beyond the sushi truck,' said a voice at her shoulder. 'They have a Porthgolow burger, which I helped create. It's the most delicious thing in the whole market.'

Lila turned, discovering the voice belonged to a boy who might be nudging towards his teenage years but was almost as tall as her. He had blond hair and intelligent eyes, and was giving her an unselfconscious grin.

'Is it now?' she said. 'I am pretty hungry. Where's the best place for coffee?'

'You've got the coffee van,' he replied, pointing to a minute silver Citroën van that was dwarfed by most of the other food trucks. 'They do three different types of roast, and have twelve flavoured syrups. Or you can go on Charlie's bus. She does great coffee, and cream teas, and has a daily cake special that always sells out. But if you go there, you can't forget about Benji's Burgers. He'll never forgive me if I lose him customers.'

'He won't?' Lila folded her arms over her chest. 'That sounds pretty harsh.'

The boy rolled his eyes. 'It's an expression, isn't it? I don't mean it *literally*.'

'Recently, when people have told me they'll never forgive me, I've believed them,' she confided. She turned away from him, Charlie's bus visible above the other vehicles a couple of rows away, but the boy wasn't finished.

'Oh, really?' he asked. 'Why's that, then? What have you done?'

'It's a very long and boring story, and I'm sure you don't want to hear it.'

'I'm Jonah.' The boy held out his hand. 'My mum and dad run SeaKing Safaris from the jetty.'

Surprised, Lila paused for a moment before shaking. 'I'm Delilah, but everyone calls me Lila. You know Charlie well?'

He nodded. 'We're great friends. I help out on the bus sometimes, when Benji doesn't need me.'

'You're in demand.' She couldn't help smiling. 'Fancy taking me to see Charlie and her bus?'

'I'm not surprised that's where you want to go,' Jonah said. 'Everyone's heard about the Cornish Cream Tea Bus. It's the most famous bus in Cornwall! And it's not just a café – it's so much more than that.'

6

'Excellent,' Lila murmured. Her mum had assured her that this break would be exactly what she needed, but if she was just going to be reminded of all Charlie's successes, putting into even sharper focus how much Lila had messed up, it wasn't likely to be the balm she'd been led to believe. 'Charlie and I go way back,' she said to Jonah.

'Oh?' His eyebrows rose towards his hairline. 'Come on, then.'

Lila followed him as he picked a path between food vans and people. The aromas of spice and salt wafted past on a wind that tugged at her hair, her cardigan scant protection against its icy chill.

They stopped in front of the gleaming bus, and through the window Lila saw people sitting at tables, an expensive coffee machine, huge muffins bursting with blueberries and, with a flash of red hair and even redder apron, her cousin, laughing and smiling and handing someone what looked like an old-fashioned bus ticket.

'Are you just going to peer through the window, or are you coming in?' Jonah said.

'You're very direct, for a boy.' Lila watched him bristle at her words, and laughed. 'I'm joking. I was having a look before I went on board, that's all.'

'Have you and Charlie had an argument?' Jonah asked, his irritation replaced by curiosity. 'In fact, you never said *how* you knew her. You're not enemies, are you? I haven't led you right to her? Is *she* the person who's never going to forgive you?' He looked horrified, as if he'd just realized he'd committed a crime against humanity.

Lila pushed her second wave of laughter back down. 'Nope. We're cousins. Besides, if I was looking to carry out some kind of vendetta, it's not like she'd be hard to miss, would she? Even without you, I would have been able to track her down. The bus does have a reputation, after all.'

Jonah nodded, his expression thoughtful. 'I can tell, Lila, that you're going to be a bit of a handful.'

This time she couldn't hold back her laughter. But as she followed the boy on board the double decker and waited to see Charlie's reaction, Lila had to admit that this young man had his finger on the pulse. He wasn't the first person who'd said that about her.

The Cornish Cream Tea Bus was beautiful, Lila had to concede as she stepped on board. Cosy but not too twee, fairy lights dancing a path round the top of the windows, the mugs and crockery all matching, the coffee machine gleaming from the kitchen area at the front of the vehicle. Charlie was deep in conversation with a couple sitting at one of the tables, and Lila could hear the excited chatter of children on the upper deck. She watched her cousin for a moment, recalling the last time she had seen her: it had been in Cheltenham, almost exactly a year ago, at Hal's funeral. She had only met Charlie's uncle Hal a couple of times at wider family gatherings – her mum and Charlie's mum were sisters, and she hadn't had much contact with Charlie's dad's side of the family – but she had known how close they were.

Then, Charlie had clearly been working hard to hold it together. Smiling and circulating with plates of perfect mini sandwiches and delicate cakes, greeting everyone with more warmth and graciousness than Lila could have mustered, had she been in the same situation. Their conversation then had been short and heartfelt, not like previous family gath-erings where they had found a spare bottle of wine and sneaked away to a corner of whatever function room Bonnie and Tabitha had chosen, and tried to put the world to rights.

Lila felt a swell of affection for Charlie as she watched her joking and laughing and scribbling something on her jotter pad. Now, it was obvious that she was flourishing. Her pale skin was as close to tanned as it was possible to get, and her smile was wide and unaffected. Lila had thought that running a café on a bus would be hard work, but it was clear that it was exactly where her cousin needed to be.

She hovered in the doorway, suddenly nervous, and waited for Charlie to notice her.

Jonah cleared his throat. Lila batted a hand at him. 'Shush, I don't want to—'

'Charlie,' the boy said loudly, cutting over the chatter, 'someone's here to see you.'

Lila would have pushed Jonah back onto the sand, except that it was too late now and her introduction had been made. Charlie looked up, confusion turning to comprehension.

'Delilah?' she screeched. 'Oh my God, you're here!' She rushed forwards and embraced her. She was several inches taller than Lila, and Lila found herself pressed into her cousin's neck and getting a heady waft of perfume. 'Why didn't you tell me you were coming?'

'I wanted it to be a surprise,' Lila said brightly. For a moment she had thought that her mum might have called ahead and smoothed things over, but that would have been too easy.

'How long are you on holiday for? Where are you staying?' Charlie pushed Lila away from her and looked her up and down. 'Jonah, this is my cousin Delilah.'

'I know,' Jonah said casually. 'I brought her here.' As if he'd orchestrated the whole thing, rather than simply accosting her on the beach.

'I could have found my own way,' Lila said defensively. How could Charlie be friends with someone so young and precocious? The exchange had also confirmed that her mum hadn't passed on Lila's latest news to Bonnie, who would, in turn, have passed it to Charlie. 'I'm not sure how long,' she said, in answer to Charlie's first question. 'Mum suggested it, thought that a bit of a breather from London, a bit of sea air, would do me good. She said you'd been doing so well down here – according to Aunt B, anyway – and that I could learn a thing or two.'

Charlie nodded, her eyes narrowing, and Lila silently cursed her for being so perceptive. But now, in the middle of a crowded café bus, which Charlie was presumably supposed to be running, was not the time to spill all her secrets. 'So you've nowhere booked?' Charlie asked.

'I thought I'd find somewhere fairly easily, seaside village in February and all that. I noticed there's a B&B right on the seafront.'

'You can stay with me,' Charlie said. 'I've got a spare room, and it's only had Mum and Dad in it so far. I'd love to make more use of it.'

'I wouldn't be cramping your style?' Lila thought of this gorgeous boyfriend that Charlie was supposed to have, and wondered how thin the walls were.

'Not at all,' Charlie said. 'It'll be lovely to have you here for a couple of weeks. You remember Juliette, and Lawrence?'

Lila nodded. She'd found Charlie's best friend a bit quiet on the few occasions she'd met her, but there wasn't anything wrong with that. She tried not to linger on Charlie's assumption that she was only planning on staying a couple of weeks. She might well be crawling up the cliff face with boredom after one.

'There's so much to show you, so many people to introduce you to,' Charlie continued, her voice rising with excitement. A bell sounded – a 'ding, ding', as if someone wanted to get off at the next stop – and Charlie looked around, but all the people at the downstairs tables seemed happy enough. 'I need to nip upstairs. Jonah, have you got time to show Lila round the food market?'

'It's OK – I'll have a wander by myself.'

'I'm due to help Benji in ten minutes.'

They spoke at the same time, and Charlie laughed. 'You're sure?' she said to Lila. 'Juliette's going to take over in a bit so I can have a break. Do you want to take Marmite with you? He'd love a walk.'

'Marmite?' Lila frowned, and then remembered Charlie's puppy. She'd told her about him at Hal's funeral, and Lila remembered thinking that she wished she'd sneaked him to it in her handbag, to cheer everyone up. Of course funerals were all about celebrating a life – *he would have wanted us to wear bright colours; he would have wanted us to laugh and think only of the good times, blah blah blah* – but they were always such sombre occasions, even if the guests tried to hold back their tears. All those false, thin-lipped smiles would have turned to genuine laughter if there had been a naughty, adorable puppy chasing down a few sausage rolls. Now, the puppy must be fully-grown.

Lila followed Charlie to the front of the bus, where a small, scruffy, tan and black dog sat on the driver's seat, looking up at her quizzically, one ear folded over. Her heart melted instantly. 'Oh my God, Charlie!'

'Don't let his looks deceive you, he's a total terror. This cuteness is all for show.' She waggled her finger and Marmite licked it. Lila laughed.

'I would *love* to take him for a walk,' she breathed, and found her arms full of warm, wriggling, soft-smelling dog. 'Aaah, Marmite. Hello, little bruiser.'

It was Charlie's turn to laugh. 'He's not much of a bruiser, compared to Jasper. But Jasper is as soft as a teddy bear and, unlike Marmite, well behaved.'

'Jasper?' Lila looked around, expecting another fur-baby to emerge from under the driver's seat.

'Jasper is Daniel's dog,' Charlie explained. 'He's a German shepherd, and I think he's given my Yorkipoo a bit of a size complex.'

'Ah, Daniel.' There was no mistaking the indulgent look on Charlie's face. Daniel was the new man. 'I'm really looking forward to meeting him, too.' She fluttered her heavily mascara'd lashes, and Charlie grinned.

'You will. Very soon. That's settled, then. Come back in half an hour and we can have a catch-up, then I'll give you the keys to the house so you can let yourself in and get sorted.'

'I really appreciate this, Charlie. Thank you.' She felt an unexpected swell of emotion and swallowed the lump in her throat. She was so relieved to have a warm welcome, even if Charlie wasn't yet in possession of all the facts. Lila wanted to hold on to it, to delay telling her about her most recent calamity.

'Will you never learn?' her mum had asked her, exasperation sharpening her tone. The implication being that, at twenty-six years of age, she really should be getting the hang of being a grown-up by now. Lila had wanted to tell her it wasn't as easy as that, that it was as if the adult setting had been missing when they made her, and she couldn't turn it on, however hard she tried.

'You all right, Lila?' Charlie asked, concern denting her pretty face.

'I'm fine!' Lila said perkily. 'It's so lovely to be here. I can't wait to hear all about you and your bus, and explore the village. It's beautiful.'

'It's a really special place,' Charlie said with feeling. 'I'm sure in a couple of days you'll be as captivated by it as I am.'

Lila smiled and nodded back. It was far away from London, and that alone made it special.

She left Charlie on the bus and stepped back into the cold, Marmite as keen to investigate the sounds and smells around them as she was. She knew she would have to tell Charlie everything, but for now she was going to let Porthgolow and its food market distract her. Life was too short to spend time wallowing, and it wasn't as if she could do anything about what had happened – as she'd already been told, she'd done more than enough. Lila had no option but to move on.

Chapter Two

Lila drove the gold Volvo slowly up the hill, Marmite on the front passenger seat, a vegetarian burrito on the dashboard, just out of reach of his snuffling nose. She couldn't deny that Charlie's food market was vibrant, with a much younger feel than she had expected. She had been imagining something old and staid, a few pensioners picking up bread and wonky homemade cakes, and a burger van where the patties were more grease than meat. But this was fresh and fun, full of all kinds of flavours and people. A few had looked at her curiously, as if visitors to the market quickly became regulars and she stood out as a newcomer, but maybe it was just that she was with Marmite who, if Charlie was an integral part of this place, must also be well known.

She checked the road-signs as she drove, looking for Coral Terrace, Charlie's keyring tinkling in the cup holder. Their catch-up had been brief, the flow of conversation constantly interrupted as Charlie introduced Lila to the vendors, and she took the offered samples, said 'hello' and 'thank you' and 'wonderful', as they told her about their businesses.

She had warmed immediately to Hugh, who sold his local ale close to the pub which, Lila found out, was also his. The Seven Stars looked welcoming, and she wondered if there were ever lock-ins. A proper lock-in in a traditional pub had been on her bucket list since she'd discovered the joys of beer. But her lack of conversation with Charlie was weighing on her; she hadn't even indicated that she might want to stay longer than a fortnight, and the thought of going into her cousin's home without laying all her cards on the table somehow seemed like a betrayal.

The houses were like rows of teeth; close together, slightly higgledy-piggledy as they followed the shape of the cliff they were built on. Charlie's Yorkipoo yipped and pressed his front paws against the window, peering out. When she found the road she was looking for, Lila turned the car into it and parked in the first available space. Charlie had told her the parking was tight, so she wasn't going to be picky.

She got out and pulled her zebra-print wheelie case out of the boot, put her burrito and keys in her handbag, and lifted Marmite off the passenger seat. She brought his face close to hers, and he licked her chin and buried his nose into her neck. Lila wondered whether, when she went back to London, she might get her own dog – if she could find a job that would allow her to work from home, or at least be flexible so she could look after one.

'You're not kidnapping Marmite, are you?'

Lila turned and found a very attractive man staring at her. Broad shoulders, dark hair, brown eyes dancing with amusement. 'No, I . . . Charlie asked me to bring him with me, to her house.'

'And you are?' He held his hand out, the gesture welcoming

but his tone slightly threatening. This, she realized as she shook his hand, must be Daniel. Marmite scrabbled in her arms, pawing at him, and Daniel ruffled the dog's ears affectionately.

'I'm Lila, Charlie's cousin. You're Daniel.'

'I am. You live in London, is that right?'

Lila nodded and said, 'So she's mentioned me, then?'

'Not a lot, but I've heard your name before.'

'It's Delilah officially, but Lila for short,' she explained.

'Charlie and her family all seem to have unusual names,' he smiled. 'Bonnie, Vince, Charlene – and now Delilah. It's nice to meet you. Charlie didn't mention you were coming to stay.'

'Charlie didn't know,' Lila admitted. 'But it's lovely to meet you, too. I've heard lots about you. All good things. My aunt Bonnie has a tendency to exaggerate, but on this occasion, she hasn't.'

'I'm not going to ask what that means, but shall we go in – if you're on your way to Charlie's?'

'Sure. I could make you a cup of tea.'

'Or I could make you one. You're the guest, after all.' He held out his hand, and after a second Lila realized he was offering to take her case. She handed it to him and stretched her fingers out – she hadn't realized she'd been gripping the handle so hard.

'Do you live with Charlie, then? How long have you been together, now?'

Daniel gave her a sideways glance as they walked along Coral Terrace. 'No, my house is behind us, a couple of roads further towards the beach. We've been together since August, so . . . six months.'

'And it's true love?' Lila asked. He turned to look at her,

16

almost tripping on a raised paving stone in the process, and she inwardly cursed herself for being so bold.

'Shouldn't you be having this conversation with Charlie? You're close, I assume, since you've come all this way to see her?'

He stopped at a pretty white terraced house with a bold red front door; a couple of pots of pink and blue flowers that Lila couldn't name stood on the windowsill. There was no front garden but then, with the beach so close, Lila wasn't sure she'd miss it. She couldn't remember the last time she'd lived somewhere with any kind of garden, and even the roof terrace of her mum's flat was only graced with their presence if they had a sudden desire to watch the sunset, or lie on loungers and drink wine when the weather was sunny enough.

Daniel opened the front door and looked at her expectantly. 'Oh,' she said, realizing she hadn't answered his question. 'We don't see each other that often, but we get along.'

'And this impromptu visit is because . . .?' He stepped into a tiny hallway at the bottom of a narrow flight of stairs, one doorway off it into the living room. She followed him into the bright, airy space. It had slightly scuffed wooden floors and white walls, with several framed photographs spaced sparingly along them. Lila stepped closer to examine them. They were local: of the food market, Charlie's bus, the beach at sunset. Daniel walked through the living room and into the kitchen. He filled the kettle and switched it on.

'They're Reenie's,' he said. 'Has Charlie told you about her?'

'No, we haven't had much of a chance to talk. She was busy on the bus, but she said I could get sorted in the spare room, and . . .' Marmite knocked against her leg. He was twisting his lead around his small body as if he wanted to wrap himself up in it. She crouched and untangled him, then unclipped his lead.

'Charlie's done amazing things with Gertie,' Daniel said.

Lila could hear the fridge door opening and closing, the sound of a teaspoon chinking against ceramic as she went to gaze at each photograph in turn, looking at the village in its different states: dark and moody, the clouds low over the choppy sea; peach and amber at sunset; everything awash with midday sunshine. She got a sense of Porthgolow's personality from these photos, almost as strongly as she had from walking along the seafront and visiting the market herself.

'Gertie? Oh, that was the name of Hal's bus, wasn't it? Now the Cornish Cream Tea Bus.'

'Milk? Sugar?'

'Milk and two sugars, please.'

Daniel handed her a mug and sat down, clasping his own cup in both hands.

Lila perched on the other sofa, so she was at right angles to him. Daniel leaned forwards expectantly, and she had the sense she was about to be interrogated.

'So you're Charlie's cousin – remind me which side of the family?'

'My mum, Tabitha, is Charlie's mum Bonnie's sister.'

Daniel nodded and rubbed his jaw. He had a confident swagger – understandable, Lila thought, given his good looks, even if they were a bit too classic for her tastes – but he also had an immediate warmth and kindness. She prided herself on being able to read people, and she decided that Charlie had found herself a good man. Before today, Lila couldn't remember the last time she'd *met* a good man, let alone been able to claim him.

'And you're here for a holiday, but you didn't check with Charlie that you could stay with her first.'

'She offered, when I saw her.'

Daniel laughed. 'Of course she did. She would probably offer her spare room to a stranger if they asked. But you're . . .' His words trailed away and he went completely still, and Lila realized this wasn't an interrogation. He didn't need her to contribute anything, he was simply figuring things out for himself. It made her restless.

'I should probably explain all this to Charlie when she's finished work.' She gestured to her wheelie case, now sitting in the corner of the room.

'You're not just here for a holiday, are you?'

Lila pressed her lips together, lifted her shoulders in a barely there shrug.

Daniel rolled his eyes, but he didn't look cross, just amused. 'So, Charlie's got herself a lodger.'

Lila hung her head. 'Look, it's . . . my mum said that Charlie was so happy here, she thought it might be good for me to have a complete break from everything. Job and friends and . . . London's a bit of a disaster zone for me, at the moment. The parts I know, anyway.'

When she forced herself to meet Daniel's gaze, there was compassion in his eyes. 'Talk to Charlie,' he said. 'I'm sure she'll be understanding. And Porthgolow is a better place than any to recharge your batteries.'

'You're not mad that I'm here?'

'What do I have to be mad about? I've only just met you, and if you and Charlie are close, then I'm looking forward to getting to know you.'

'I promise I won't get in the way.'

Daniel stood and, as he was passing, placed a hand on

her shoulder. 'I know you won't. Get settled in; Charlie will be back in a couple of hours. See you later, Lila.'

'Bye, Daniel. And thank you.'

When he was gone, she kicked off her shoes and put her feet up on the sofa, then lifted Marmite onto her lap. The dog wriggled for a moment and then settled, like a hot-water bottle, on her stomach. It had been a long drive and now, with the thought of having to tell Charlie what she had done, and that she wasn't exactly here for a holiday, the emotional exhaustion was almost worse than the physical. She closed her eyes, thankful for the chance to let everything – most of all her thoughts – rest for a moment.

'Lila. *Lila.*'

She was woken with a gentle shake, and blinked and pulled herself up to sitting. Charlie was peering down at her and Lila could see, beyond her, that the day had lost its light. She had a sudden yearning for the long, shimmering evenings of midsummer. The end of winter couldn't come soon enough.

'Sorry, I closed my eyes for a moment.'

'Don't worry about that. Have you settled in OK?'

Lila glanced guiltily at her suitcase, still exactly where she had left it when she'd walked in with Daniel. The bag containing her burrito sat on top. Her mouth watered: she was sure it would be delicious cold. 'Uhm.'

Charlie went into the kitchen and Lila pushed herself off the sofa and looked at her reflection in the mirror over the fireplace. Her long dark hair had mostly come loose from its ponytail, her mascara was smudged and her skin was pale, enhancing the spray of dark freckles across her nose and cheeks. She looked ghastly.

'Shall I go and unpack now?'

'I got us some Thai food,' Charlie said, 'so if you're happy to wait, we can have this while it's hot. You're still a veggie?'

'Yup. And that smells amazing.' She sent a silent apology to the discarded burrito, and sat at the small round table in the corner of the living room while Charlie plated up and uncorked a bottle of white wine.

'It's so lovely that you're here,' Charlie said, once they'd clinked glasses. 'I mean, unexpected, but in a good way. I thought we'd stay in tonight, let you catch up after the drive, and then tomorrow I can introduce you to everyone, maybe take you to the pub.'

'I met Daniel earlier. On my way here.'

'I know.' Charlie twirled her fork in her noodles, then looked straight at Lila. 'He said I should talk to you, about your . . . holiday plans.'

Lila slumped in her chair. 'It was – is . . . maybe he got the wrong idea, or—'

'How long do you want to stay, exactly?'

'I don't know,' Lila admitted. 'It might even be less than two weeks. I just . . . things have gone a bit wrong, in London. Mum said . . . well, she keeps getting updates from Aunt Bonnie, and going on about how fabulously you're doing, how Cornwall has been the making of you. She suggested I should come and see if it could sort me out, too.'

Charlie laughed. 'I'm not sure I needed "sorting out" when I came here. But it was exactly the right thing for me. And . . .' She chewed her lip, and Lila crossed her fingers under the table. 'I stayed with Juliette and Lawrence for a really long time before I got this place. But what are your plans? What do you want to do while you're here? And what happened in London? What are you running from? Surely you can't be avoiding the *entire* city? That's a huge-scale disaster, even for you.'

They exchanged a smile. Charlie was the one person who could say that without her taking offence. 'Not the whole of London, just the important bits. And I'm not sure what I'm going to do. I just – I *had* to get away, Charlie. I was going insane, going from my flat, to Mum's flat, to my flat. This endless, mind-numbing circle. I knew I needed to make a fresh start, but—'

'Fresh from what? I thought you were working in that posh coffee place.'

Lila pushed a cashew around until her fork finally speared it. 'There was this thing . . . But it's over now. Nobody died and we've all moved on, I just need to . . . reset.' She gave her cousin what she hoped was a winning smile.

Charlie didn't return it. 'If the best thing you can say about this . . . whatever it is, is that nobody died, then you probably need to tell me about it.'

'It's nothing. Really.'

'Yes, Lila. It's something. Come on. Spill the beans.'

Lila cringed at Charlie's words: she didn't realize how apt they were. 'I honestly—'

'You *have* to tell me, how about that? The price of you staying with me is that I get to know why you've come here in the first place.'

Lila glared, but Charlie was adamant. Adamant but, Lila could instantly see, sympathetic.

'Fine,' Lila muttered, 'but maybe we could . . .' she gestured towards the living area.

Charlie put their empty plates in the kitchen, took the bottle of wine and settled herself on a sofa. Lila sat at the opposite end and turned to face her.

'So,' Charlie prompted. 'London. New start.'

'Promise you won't make a big deal of it,' Lila said.

'Make a bag deal of *what*, Lila?' Charlie laughed. 'You can stall all you want, but until you tell me, I'm not going to have an opinion about it.'

'I lost Clara her job,' Lila rushed. 'I lost mine, too, but that's inconsequential. And she's never going to forgive me, apparently, so . . .' She shrugged and sipped her wine.

'Oh, Lila.' Charlie sat back. 'You and Clara? You've been best friends for ever! What happened, exactly?'

Lila tucked her legs under her, and Marmite jumped up and curled himself in the hole between them.

'Clara had just been promoted,' Lila said. 'She was in charge of events for this large corporate company, and she'd worked so hard to get there. She had a huge reception to plan, welcoming some business partners over from America, and I was working at The Espresso Lounge and we'd got this amazing portable coffee bar. Not just a machine, but a whole bar. It was so swanky, all chrome and polished black metal, and designed exactly for those sorts of events, not food markets like down on the beach today – nothing quite so fun.' She laughed. 'So, I suggested that she hire me for the evening, because we didn't just provide coffee, but a coffee *experience*.'

'That sounds perfectly reasonable,' Charlie said.

'I thought so too,' Lila agreed. 'But Clara was reluctant. She said she wanted to use tried-and-tested suppliers, to make sure everything went smoothly. There could be no mishaps – not with the US partners. I felt a bit miffed, to be honest. I thought, as best mates, she should trust me. And I know now that was wrong, that friendship and business are entirely separate things, and that just because we love each other it doesn't mean that she should hire me for her events. Obviously, it's brilliant to realize that *afterwards*.'

'You persuaded her?' Charlie asked.

'I think it was more like emotional blackmail,' Lila admitted. 'I wouldn't let it go.'

'So you got the gig, and took your coffee experience machine to her corporate event?'

Lila winced, remembering the apprehension she'd felt on entering that huge foyer, the champagne tower being set up, the oyster bar, the waiters all in white shirts and black waistcoats. It was as if she'd stepped into a different world – one she didn't have a passport for. 'I thought our coffee place was superior, but this was on another level. I wheeled in my trolley, Clara directed me to my spot, and I could see from the look in her eyes that she knew she'd made a mistake. But I had to try and do her proud.' She chewed her fingernail.

'You set it up?' Charlie prompted quietly.

'I set it up. And it was a clever contraption, this impressive coffee machine with its own minibar running along the front, slots for the custom-made espresso, latte and cappuccino cups, all glass so you could see the blends and colour transitions. It unpacked smoothly, and I thought I was doing fine. But it was a newer model than I was used to. My boss hadn't told me he'd upgraded. Everything else was the same – the bar, the cups, the assembly – but not the machine itself. But it didn't seem drastically different, so—'

'You couldn't make anyone a coffee?' Charlie asked, grimacing.

'I wish!' Lila took a big gulp of wine. 'This group of people came in, all smartly dressed, perfect hair and shiny teeth and golden skin. I could tell they were the Americans, not least because the other guests were fawning over them. I prayed they would head straight to the champagne bar, but they didn't. They came to me. They asked me about the display and the different roasts, and I was perfect – I can do all that in my sleep. And then I tried to make this man a coffee.' She closed her eyes at the memory. 'There was something wrong – I'd turned the pressure up, too high maybe. At first the machine just started fizzing a bit, and I thought I'd overfilled it with water. I thought that by a couple of macchiatos in I'd be laughing. But then it made this horrible sound. It was a wrenching, gurgling, dying monster noise, and then bits of it sort of *flew* off and hit the bar, and the American partner, and a couple of his colleagues, and me – we were all sprayed with coffee grounds and water. Quite a lot of it.' She put her head in her hands.

'Holy shit,' Charlie whispered. 'Lila, it was an accident.'

'Clara came over while I was trying to clean up the American. She took me aside and told me I had to go. I understood her anger, though she was reining it in then, because the event was still going on around all this mess. A couple of the waiters came to help me clean up as best I could, and then I packed away my luxury coffee bastard of a machine. I sneaked out of the foyer, where a couple of very senior-looking people were trying to calm down the American, whose face was no longer golden but purple. And that's when I found Clara. She was in a corridor by the lifts, being spoken to by someone I presumed was her boss.'

'They fired her.'

'He said, "Clean this up as best you can, get the event back on track, and then go and pack up your things. You're done."'

Charlie pressed her hands to her lips.

'So I stormed up to them and tried to fix it,' Lila continued.

'I told him it wasn't Clara's fault, it was mine, that I had persuaded her to let me be a part of it, that we were friends and . . . it had the opposite effect. It made him even angrier, and Clara – that last look she gave me as I carted the broken machine back to the van.' Lila shook her head. 'The next day, Giuliano fired me. Word had spread, of course, and I'd broken an expensive piece of equipment and damaged the reputation of The Espresso Lounge.'

'And Clara?' Charlie asked quietly. 'What did you do about her?'

Lila huffed. She hadn't anticipated that telling Charlie the whole story would be so energy-sapping. 'Clara and I aren't friends any more.'

'You didn't try to make it up with her?' Charlie asked. 'Lila—'

'Of course I did!' Lila shot back. 'Of course I bloody did. But she wasn't having any of it, and I . . .' She swallowed, remembering the last time she'd gone to Clara's flat. It must have been the fifth or sixth time she'd tried to apologize, tried a different tack, a different gift and set of words to make up for the harm she'd caused. But then Clara, after first refusing to open the door, had followed her out of the building and caught up with her on the street. At first Lila thought she had come to forgive her, to hug and make up. But it was as if she'd been storing up years of annoyance and issues with Lila, and let her have them all at once. Over a decade of friendship, reduced to all the ways that Lila had failed her, all the ways she was no good.

'It's over, that's all,' Lila said, cross that her voice chose that moment to wobble.

'There *has* to be a way you can make it up to her,' Charlie suggested. 'Your friendship is too important to lose.'

Lila folded her arms and shrugged. 'Not all friendships survive for ever. Ours was one that didn't.'

'Lila—'

'Can I still stay? Just for a bit. Until I decide what I want to do.'

'Of course you can,' Charlie said, rubbing her arm. 'And that sounds so tough. All of it. It wasn't really your fault.'

'It was. I forced Clara into hiring me. She knew what was best, but I wanted to help her with this new promotion. I got it wrong. Now I need to dust myself down and move on.' Charlie gave her a sceptical look, but Lila chose to ignore it. 'I could help you on the bus,' she said. 'You looked so busy today.'

'I know, but the food markets are only once a month until May, and Porthgolow's much quieter in the off-season. I only open a couple of days during the week, and then at weekends. I'm running these Cornish Cream Tea Tours too, but only every fortnight at the moment. So I—'

'But you need help with those, right? I would do anything. My coffee-making skills are going begging. What I don't know about an arabica bean or an Italian roast isn't worth knowing. Show me the ropes, at least. You must be dying for some time off.'

Charlie took a long sip of wine and sat back against the cushions. 'I honestly can't offer you many hours.'

Lila shook her head. 'Anything, Charlie. And you don't have to pay me. You're letting me stay here, for goodness' sake. Let me help you out? I could be a real asset, and it would give me some time to figure things out.' She drained her glass. 'After all, what's family for?'

'What about your flat? Don't you have rent, bills, back in London?'

Lila dropped her gaze. 'My flat's only on a short-term lease, and Mum said she'd help out for a couple of months, while I decide if I want to keep it. She's given me some holiday money for this trip, too, so I can help with groceries. I'm going to pay her back once I'm all sorted.'

Charlie nodded. 'OK. A trial run. I'll give you a crash course in Gertie on Monday, and you never know, someone else in the village might have some work for you. We can ask around – we're pretty close-knit.'

'I'm getting that feeling,' Lila said, relief making her giddy. 'And good work with Daniel, too. You didn't think about using your womanly rights on Leap Day and proposing?'

Charlie looked shocked. 'That's a bit old fashioned, isn't it?'

'Romantic though,' Lila said, looking dreamily up at the ceiling. Charlie threw a cushion at her. Marmite raised his nose and blinked, then returned to his snooze.

'In this day and age, women can propose to their men – or their women – whenever they want,' Charlie said. 'They don't need outdated traditions to limit them to the one day that only comes around every four years.'

'But you have thought about it, though?' Lila couldn't help pushing. 'I mean, a man like that, you *must* have considered spending the rest of your life with him.'

Charlie rolled her eyes, but she was smiling. 'Did your mum tell you about how we got together?'

'Something about a life-or-death rescue?' Lila asked. 'I didn't entirely believe it, because Mum overdramatizes everything, so I'm desperate to hear the truth – and I want *all* the delicious details, please.' She wriggled further into the sofa cushions and settled in for a good gossip with her cousin who, when they spent time together, made her feel as if she wasn't an only child.

Lila had told Charlie what had happened, and now she could put to the back of her mind the final, furious row with Clara. She had chosen not to examine her best friend's accusations too closely – she had been angry, justifiably so, and it had certainly drawn a line under the whole sorry situation. Now Lila could focus on what she was going to do next, and spending a few weeks working on board a café on a double-decker bus with her cousin, the beach just outside the window, seemed a good place to start.

Chapter Three

Over the next few days, Lila got to know Porthgolow.
Nobody she met had a bad word to say about it, and
a few – including pub landlord Hugh, and Jonah's mum,
Amanda Kerr, went as far as to say that Charlie had saved
it. Lila wasn't sure how one person could save a village, unless
Gertie the bus had magical sea-repelling skills and had
somehow prevented it being flooded in a storm. But she
bought in to the villagers' enthusiasm for the place, and it
certainly had a quaint, slightly worn charm about it, as if
every bit of faded paint was intentional.

On her first evening, Charlie had told her about her first few
months in the village, and how she had ended up with Daniel.
The dramatic rescue had, in fact, happened as Lila's mum had
said. Charlie played it down, but Lila had spotted all the signs;
the way she spoke quickly and breathlessly, her eyes bright.
It seemed Daniel really had been in trouble, with Charlie his
'knight in a gleaming bus'. It was almost as if she was some
kind of saint, and yet, as much as Lila usually hated people
who could do no wrong, it was impossible to dislike Charlie.

True to her word, Charlie had given her a Gertie crash-course on Monday morning, with an optimistic sun bouncing off the water, picking out all the details that made the bus special: the matching crockery, all reds and blues; the authentic-looking ticket machine; the cake stands that displayed Charlie's bakes to their best advantage. Lila was particularly impressed with the coffee machine, which she regarded as her area of expertise, despite recent events. It was a compact model, but a good make, and it made an excellent espresso, Americano and latte.

'It's all very straightforward,' Charlie had said, as she plated up two warm fruit scones for an older couple who had come on board the bus within five minutes of it being open.

'It's magnificent,' Lila had replied, running her hand along the kitchen counter. 'And this is all your vision, Charlie. You turned Gertie into this wondrous eating establishment. A bus, a café, a tour guide, a life-saver – is there anything you can't do together?'

'I'm not sure we'd win any surfing competitions,' Charlie had said wistfully, but Lila could tell she was pleased, and that she knew how much she'd accomplished.

'I'm so happy for you.' She had felt compelled to hug her cousin, her affection rising to the surface, complete with a flash of envy. Lila couldn't remember the last time she had achieved anything worthwhile. Notorious, certainly. Noteworthy, not so much. But that was all going to change.

She had taken about five minutes to become addicted to paddling on Porthgolow's beach. She had always loved the sea, the feel of it against her skin, so different to the stripped, chlorinated feel of a gym pool. It didn't matter that it was freezing – she looked forward to the warm towel and fluffy socks afterwards – and Marmite, she quickly discovered, was happy to be her partner in crime.

She was walking along the sea's edge, carrying her shoes, Marmite splashing happily at her feet, when she heard someone shouting from further up the beach. She thought it sounded like '*You*', but the wind carried it away on the breeze before she could make it out. She turned and saw an older woman, her grey hair curling around her ears, waving in her direction. She looked behind her, but there was only the churn of the waves, and so she stepped out of the water, sand sticking to the soles of her feet.

'Hello?' she called. 'Are you talking to me?'

The older woman shuffled towards her, and Lila saw her face was pinched, unsmiling. Had something happened to Charlie? She felt a jolt of panic and hurried up the beach.

'So you're her, then?' the woman said.

'I'm who?' Lila asked.

'Charlie's relative. Cousin, isn't it? You don't look very alike, I must say.'

'Yes, I'm Charlie's cousin. I think we've got the same eyes, actually, but then I suppose from just a quick glance we do look quite diff—'

'I don't care 'bout that, really. Just wanted a good look at you. I was away on Saturday, missed the food market, missed all your introductions. You met Reenie, my friend, coverin' the Pop-In for me over the weekend.'

'Ah,' Lila said, the pieces falling into place. So this was Myrtle, the owner of the Pop-in that Charlie had told her about, luring her away from her paddling purely so she didn't have to walk down to the water herself. 'Yes, I'm Lila. But I'm a person, not a zoo exhibit.'

'Pardon?' Myrtle's brow creased.

'You said you wanted to look at me. I would have thought it's a bit of an antichmax. I'm pretty ordinary looking. No horns, no tail. No mermaid scales.' She had heard about Reenie – who had taken the photos on Charlie's wall – and the rumours that Jonah had spread about her.

'You've got some front, girl,' Myrtle replied, shaking her head. 'And to think you're connected to Charlie by blood. I suppose this sort of attitude is all well an' good in London, but believe me, cheel, it won't work around here. Not if you want to make friends. I was just tryin' to be welcoming.' She turned away.

'You were?' Lila asked. Both Charlie and Daniel had assured her Myrtle's heart was in the right place, even if she sometimes came across as more bristles than feathers. 'I'm sorry, then. But you had me worried, calling me away from the beach like that. I thought something awful had happened.'

Myrtle nodded, her lips pressed together. 'Don't know what you're doin' in the water anyway, weather as chill as it is. It's only just March, you realize. Just because we're by the sea, doesn't mean the weather's always beach weather. You'd do well to remember that.'

Lila chewed the inside of her cheek. 'I will try my hardest to remember that, Myrtle. Nice to meet you.' She held her hand out.

Myrtle hesitated, as if it might be some kind of trap, then shook it briefly. Then she shuffled off in the direction of the Pop-In, leaving Lila and Marmite alone at the edge of the beach, Lila's bare feet turning to blocks of ice as the wind chilled her damp flesh.

By Thursday she felt she knew Gertie inside and out. She had even helped Charlie, the evening before, make a batch of scones in her kitchen at home, marvelling at the way her cousin managed to get flour onto every conceivable surface, including the cooker hood. There had been a lot of laughing, which had felt so good after all the anger, and subsequent wallowing, in London. Lila still couldn't believe she'd allowed herself to mope for as long as she had. There were much better things for her to be doing with her time.

'You getting on all right, then, Lila?' Amanda asked, wiping sea spray off her waterproof jacket while Lila frothed the milk for her latte.

'I love the bus,' she said, pouring the milk slowly onto the coffee and handing the mug to Amanda. 'I mean, who wouldn't?'

'You've trained her well,' Amanda said to Charlie, who was coming down the stairs with a tray full of crockery.

Charlie laughed. 'It's only been a few days, but it's good to be sharing the load, as light as it is at the moment.'

'Charlie's taken me under her wing,' Lila added. 'She's always been good at that. And I turned up unannounced, so . . .'

'And with a rather defeatist attitude,' Charlie said, placing the tray next to the sink and starting to load plates into the narrow dishwasher. 'You know, I'm sure all Clara needs is some time. If you try to talk to her again in a couple of weeks, you might see that she's come around.'

'Who's Clara?' Amanda asked.

'My ex-best friend,' Lila said. 'And I tried the whole "giving-her-space" thing. Nope. It's over. End of. Nothing to see here.'

Charlie shook her head, a flicker of frustration in her eyes.

'Ah,' Amanda said, giving Lila a sympathetic smile. 'The troubles of youth.'

'The troubles of epic, unforgivable stupidity,' Lila corrected, taking the last mug from the tray and adding it to the dishwasher.

'Epic,' Charlie said, 'is reserved for death-defying journeys that take years to complete, or action films with meteor strikes in them. And for something supposedly so epic, you seem remarkably matter-of-fact about it. You aren't showing any signs of falling apart.'

'Who's to say I haven't already? This might be phase one of my recovery.'

'Denial?' Charlie asked, and then sighed when Lila shot her a pointed look. 'Fine. *Fine*. You can't fall apart for the next three hours, anyway. I need to go into Truro to stock up on supplies. Daniel's lending me his car. I can't always trust the supermarket to get the delivery right, and they're more expensive for the quantities I need. The bus is yours.' She grinned.

'Mine?' Lila asked.

'Yes. You're in charge. Don't worry, I doubt there'll be a rush on.' She turned to the window, where the grey sky was darkening almost by the minute, a thunderous cloud hovering menacingly above the sea.

'You're letting me take control?' Lila ran her hands down her floral-print trousers. 'Of your Cornish Cream Tea Bus?'

'I'm on the end of the phone, and Daniel's up at the hotel. Look, if you crouch, you can see it on the cliff. Surely that's reassuring?'

'It would be more reassuring if you were staying here and I was going to spend the afternoon in that hot tub you keep mentioning. I haven't even seen it yet, and I reckon a good massage and some time in the Jacuzzi bubbles would help a lot.'

'We can go this evening,' Charlie said, untying her apron. 'Right now, you need to do this for me. A few hours in charge of the café. Everything's here, the menu's self-explanatory, and we've not run out of anything. How much more simple could it get?'

Lila caught Amanda peering at her over the top of her mug, quietly amused. 'That does sound *quite* simple, I suppose,' she admitted.

'There you go, then.' Charlie lifted Marmite out of the driver's cab and, tugging gently on Lila's hair – a gesture that gave her a flash of nostalgia – walked towards the door. 'Call me – for anything. However big or small, however stupid you think your question is. If you're worried then ask, OK?'

'OK!' Lila said. She watched Charlie walk in the direction of home, presumably to pick up Daniel's car.

'You'll be grand,' Amanda said. She raised her mug for a final swallow and patted Lila on the shoulder. 'I have total faith in you.'

'You hardly know me,' Lila replied.

'But Charlie has faith in you, and that's good enough for me.' Amanda walked down the aisle, hopped off the bus and strolled towards the SeaKing Safaris boat, her body hunched against the cold.

When no customers thronged immediately onto the bus, Lila started to enjoy herself. She opened all the cupboards in turn – not that there were many in such a small kitchen – then checked the stock in the fridge, ticking each item off against the printed menu, the lettering in pleasingly ornate, but legible, script. For anyone else, the coffee machine would be the most daunting item on board, and Lila drew confidence from the fact that she could use it with her eyes closed. *This* model, anyway. Compared to the one she'd taken to Clara's corporate event, this one was a cinch.

Leaning on the counter, she stared out to sea. Jonah had told her that they often saw dolphins on their SeaKing tours, sometimes even from the beach, and Lila hadn't ever seen one in real life. How great would it be if she could tell Charlie that not only had she looked after the bus successfully, but that she'd seen the famous dolphin pod, too? She wanted to make Charlie proud. One afternoon in charge of the Cornish Cream Tea Bus might go a small way to restoring her confidence.

That afternoon, visitors dripped in like a leaky tap, and just infrequently enough to be annoying. Not that Lila found people annoying. She could talk to anyone, never found herself shy around strangers; she only ever got tongue-tied with people she cared about – especially when she owed them an apology. But this was like water torture. She would daydream, staring out to sea, and then get interrupted, her mind having to switch from fantasy-mode to scone-warming practicalities in an instant. She had always thought she was adaptable, but maybe not.

'Do we go upstairs or downstairs, love?' asked a woman wearing a beautiful scarf with a peacock feather design.

'Wherever you'd like,' Lila replied. 'The best views are on the top deck, but the staircase is on the steep side, so it depends if you think it's worth the risk.' She raised her eyebrows. The woman looked concerned and, when she and her male companion shuffled towards a downstairs table, Lila decided she'd better tone down the dramatics.

She made sure she got Peacock Lady's order right, and even coaxed a smile from her when she made a quip about how she had only been in the bus a few days and had already fallen down the stairs. The scones came out of the oven plump and warm and delicious-smelling, not burnt like the toast she had popped out of Charlie's toaster that morning.

'It's a lovely spot, this,' Peacock Lady said. 'So picturesque. Does the bus travel around?'

'It does,' Lila replied, leaning against the table opposite theirs. 'My cousin, Charlie, who owns it, takes it along the coast on these tours – cakes and sightseeing sort of thing. They're very popular, and she's only got stuck down the Cornish roads a couple of times. Her boyfriend, Daniel, was telling me about this tour just before Christmas when . . .' She hesitated, the look of alarm on Peacock Lady's face reminding her that she was straying into unwanted territory again. People did not want excitement with their Cornish cream teas. 'When they went to this hidden cove and there was a rainbow, poised perfectly over the sea,' she continued. 'They'd travelled down these dark, tree-tunnel roads, so narrow and winding, and then the world opened up for them in this magnificent way. That's the thing about Cornwall, isn't it? So many hidden places, so many opportunities to be enchanted.'

'Oh,' the woman said, her scone hovering inches from her lips, 'yes, that does sound wonderful. You don't have any details about the tours, do you?'

'I surely do,' Lila said, skipping to the front of the bus and getting one of the postcards with all Gertie's information on. 'Here you go. Up-to-date tour dates are on the website, and you can always contact us here. I'll leave you to your scones.' She gave them a twinkly smile and retreated into the kitchen, deciding that she could reward herself with a cappuccino dusted with chocolate, maybe even a squirt of cream. She had never tried her hand at selling, but perhaps she was a natural. Perhaps *that* was where her future lay.

'No, I don't mind about that, Marcie, I just – we need to amp it up. Now that we're here. Do you see . . .' The voice behind Lila cut out in a loud sigh, and she pivoted to discover a man standing in the middle of the aisle, wearing a green puffa jacket, taking up the space with his brash voice and his looming presence, his tightly curled hair so pale that she couldn't tell whether it was blond or white. She huffed; how rude of him to come onto the bus when he was on the phone. '*No*, Marcie,' he continued, after a pause, 'but production starts in a couple of weeks, so we need to line everything up. Truly Cornish, that's what we've said, and at the moment we've got a few local suppliers, and Toby Welsh's great-aunt was born in Penzance or something.'

Lila's ears pricked up at the word 'production' and the mention of Toby Welsh. She knew him. He was an actor. A young, hot actor. He'd starred in an ITV drama about a psychopath stalking the wards of a Manchester hospital. She'd only caught the last episode, so hadn't entirely followed the plot, but she'd been mesmerized by his performance. And his dark curls and smouldering eyes, and the evidence of his in-shape body beneath that tight-fitting black outfit.

She leaned on the counter and watched Phone Man, silently praying, now, that he wouldn't walk off the bus. After all, he must have come on board for something. He caught her gaze, pointed at the phone and rolled his eyes. It was an apology of sorts, and Lila found herself smiling back, as if she understood exactly what was going on.

'Of course, Marcie,' he said placatingly, rubbing the bridge of his nose. 'We'll sort it later. When I'm back, yes. Of course. See you then.' He pressed the screen to end the call and gave Lila a world-weary smile that reached his grey eyes.

'That sounded intense,' she said. 'Coffee?'

'Please. Strong, milky Americano if you've got it. And sorry for . . .' He glanced behind him, to where Peacock Lady and her husband were staring unashamedly at him, disapproval etched on their faces. 'For broadcasting that. The line wasn't great so I had to shout.'

'Trouble with the production?' Lila asked meekly while she set about making his coffee.

'There are always teething problems,' he replied. 'It's the nature of the beast, but I've left myself – well, *set* myself some additional challenges this time round.'

'I couldn't help hearing you mention Toby Welsh. You're working with him?'

'Yeah, he's one of the male leads. Adds an extra level of pressure, but of course it's worth it for his performance, and the attention he'll bring. We're lucky to have him. It's all been charmed, so far. Casting and location-wise, anyway. It's just this additional . . .' He sighed again, and Lila had the sense that he would be talking even if she walked off the bus. He wasn't really speaking to her any more. He rubbed his jaw and gave her an apologetic smile. 'Sorry, a million things on my mind. Thank you,' he added, when she passed him his coffee. He didn't sit down, instead leaned against the counter that marked the space between the kitchen and the customer seating. Breaking the fourth wall already, Lila thought wryly.

'I've always got time to listen,' she said, 'if you want to offload. And how about a Cornish cream tea from the Cornish Cream Tea Bus?' She spread her arms wide, testing out her sales technique again, seeing if it would work on even the most distracted of customers.

The man opened his mouth to speak, and then shut it. He looked around him, then extended that into a slow circle, holding his mug close to his chest. When he'd finished, his eyes pinned Lila to the spot. 'The Cornish Cream Tea Bus,' he repeated. 'A café? On a bus? Based here?'

'All those things are correct,' Lila said, smiling. He was very intense, this man.

'Wow.' He rubbed his jaw. 'I guess I saw all that – I was

desperate for a coffee, which is why I came on here in the first place, but thinking about it, I might . . . I mean I could possibly . . . Did you say you had a moment to listen?'

'Sure.' Lila picked up her cappuccino and led him to the nearest table. Peacock Lady got up to pay, and Lila gave her and her husband a cheery goodbye, and then returned to where the intense man was sitting, tapping frantically on his iPhone. She sat opposite him, and he finished what he was doing and put his phone in his pocket.

'Winston Thorpe,' he said, holding out his hand. 'Producer for new historical drama series, *Estelle*. We're filming it for the BBC, starting the Cornwall location shoot in a couple of weeks.'

Lila was silent for a moment, wishing her résumé was even half as impressive. 'Delilah Forest,' she replied. 'Helping out with my cousin's Cornish Cream Tea Bus.'

'It's not yours?' he asked. 'The bus? So you don't have any sway, any control over it?'

Lila raised her shoulders. 'Charlie's put me in charge, so I've got the capacity to make executive decisions.' It sounded pompous, but she couldn't help it. She didn't want to tell him that she was inconsequential. Not when he knew Toby Welsh.

'Excellent.' He rubbed his hands together and took a sip of his drink, before levelling her with another direct stare, this time accompanied by a charming smile. 'Well, Delilah Forest, I might have a proposition for you and the Cornish Cream Tea Bus. Have a moment to hear me out?'

Lila grinned, her pulse suddenly racing. 'I do, indeed. What is your proposition, Winston Thorpe?'

Chapter Four

In hindsight, Lila realized that telling Charlie about her conversation with Winston Thorpe while they relaxed around the indoor swimming pool of Daniel's posh, cliff-top spa hotel hadn't been the best idea. She had thought that the calming atmosphere of Crystal Waters, all its elegant luxury (and it was one of the most luxurious places Lila had ever seen), along with the fact that they weren't entirely alone, would allow Charlie to absorb the news before reacting. Not to mention that it was where they had been heading anyway, the evening of Lila's first solo afternoon on the bus. But as Charlie screeched out '*What?*' and Lila had to listen to it echo around the tiled walls, she realized she had chosen the wrong setting.

'*What did you say?*' Charlie hissed it this time, and Lila glanced at the two blonde, preened women in the shallow end of the pool, who were taking great care to keep their coiffed up-dos above the water, while watching Charlie and Lila intently.

Lila rolled over, adjusting her bright blue bikini with

orange, Nemo-style fish on it, wishing she'd packed a subtle one-piece like Charlie's, and met her cousin head on.

'It is a *great* opportunity,' Lila pressed. 'You, me and Gertie on an actual television set, for a programme that's going to be shown on the BBC. Toby Welsh is going to be there. He's the star of the show. And the Cornish Cream Tea Bus, Charlie, an integral part of it.' She pointed a finger, hoping she was achieving a level of gravitas.

'It's a period drama, isn't it?' Charlie said, her face not yet relaxing into anything approaching calm. 'I know Gertie's a vintage bus, but nineteenth century is pushing it a bit.'

Lila started to laugh, and then realized Charlie wasn't joining in. 'You don't believe me. You think I would make something like this up? He wants Gertie to be part of the catering for the cast and crew. Well, the craft services. So we're always available, people can come to the bus whenever they're not busy filming or make-up-ing or directing, and get a coffee or a snack. It's separate from the catering team who provide the hot meals. Winston told me all about it.'

'I'm sure Winston did,' Charlie said shortly. 'That doesn't mean you had any right to offer Gertie to him. I have responsibilities – the food markets, tours, the day-to-day café in Porthgolow. What will the regulars do if we're not there? What will Jeremy and Delia do if they can't have their Cornish cream tea on a Friday morning?'

'Did you hear what I said?' Lila picked up her glass of water and took a long, cooling swig. It was deceptive, this beautiful swimming pool, which – she still couldn't quite believe – was owned by Charlie's boyfriend. The sky outside had turned tumultuous, pre-empting the pall of winter darkness due within the next hour, and yet the lighting and warmth in the pool room was cosy and – now Lila was

43

under intense scrutiny from her cousin – almost stifling. 'It's a TV set. It's going to be one of BBC One's flagship dramas.'

'Yes, but—'

'And you told me that the bus wasn't busy in the off-season. Winston said they'll be doing the location filming over the next few months, and we won't be needed for the interior shoots which are all happening in studios in Bristol. So it won't be all the time. Week-blocks, depending on when the locations are booked in. But it will mean Gertie gets all the prestige of being part of the set, and she – we – will get to travel to different parts of Cornwall, so she'll get noticed, too. And we might get to serve Toby Welsh.' She flapped her hand in front of her face, imagining those dark curls bobbing before her, his beautiful eyes finding hers. He definitely had good eyes – she didn't think you could be a successful actor without expressive eyes. And so what if he'd turned out to be the killer in that hospital drama he'd been in? That just proved how talented he was.

Charlie hadn't shot back another question, and Lila experienced a brief blossoming of hope. She knew, the moment she'd shaken hands with Winston, said 'great' when he'd told her he'd get his assistant Marcie to draw up a contract and get it sent over, that she had made a mistake. It wasn't her bus to offer, and she had known Charlie would take some persuading, to say the least. Now she had to practise that selling technique she had been limbering up on board the bus, and show Charlie how good an idea it was. If it was too late to backtrack – and she didn't want to incur the wrath of a powerful TV producer, even if it was unlikely she'd ever see him again – then she had to get Charlie to come round to her way of thinking.

'What is this *Estelle* about again?' Charlie asked, narrowing her eyes at Lila.

'It's an atmospheric gothic ghost story, about two brothers who inherit this big, spooky Cornish house and move in only to discover it's haunted by the spirit of one of the previous occupants, Estelle. They have to unravel why she's haunting it, and of course they get embroiled in all the local goings-on in the tiny Cornish village, and there's drama and romance and betrayal. Doesn't it sound *amazing?*' To be honest, Lila sometimes found it hard to see past the dodgy outfits and hats, or the curly wigs they all seemed to wear in period dramas, but any kind of TV set was bound to be an exciting place to work.

'It sounds interesting,' Charlie murmured, chewing her lip and then rolling on to her back to stare up at the ceiling.

'Doesn't it?' Lila said. 'And it's not just Toby Welsh starring in it, but Aria Lundberg, that impossibly beautiful American-Scandinavian actress. It's a big deal, Charlie. And we have a chance to be part of it. You never know, we might even get a chance to be *in* it! Like as an extra, or something.'

'And this producer person, Winston?' Charlie asked, ignoring her last comment. Lila nodded encouragingly. 'He said he'd do a press release about our involvement? It's not a secret?'

Lila shook her head. 'He said part of his ethos for this shoot is using as many local suppliers as possible, to make it a truly Cornish series – aside from the bits in Bristol, of course – but a lot of it's being shot down here, and he wants everyone to know that this is a production not just set in Cornwall, but about and *for* Cornwall.' She pressed her hand against her chest as she repeated his passionate statement.

Charlie snorted. 'You fell for that?'

'I believed him,' she said quietly, her hope fizzling to nothing. Clara's face popped into her head, the fury in her eyes matching her words. Lila pushed it out again.

Charlie sighed and rolled onto her stomach, resting her chin on her hands. 'You have to let me think about it. It's a big change for Gertie.'

'But it *could* be an amazing one,' Lila said, kicking a leg up into the air. 'And just imagine, when it's over you can come back to Porthgolow, do all the summer food markets with this under your belt. Think of all the stories you'll have to tell, the publicity that will continue even once filming has finished. I'm sure there'll be some restrictions on what we can add to the socials, but we can check that out with Winston. Gertie will *love* it.'

'Gertie's a bus,' Charlie said. 'She doesn't have the capacity for love.'

Lila gasped. 'Charlie, why would you say such a thing? She's your *beloved* bus!'

Charlie wrinkled her nose and looked at Lila, her expression softening ever so slightly. 'This is a crazy, *crazy* thing, Delilah. You do realize that, don't you?'

Lila nodded. She was holding her breath, crossing her fingers behind her back and sending a prayer to the gods of fate, which she did quite often, even though she didn't know exactly who they were.

'I mean,' Charlie continued, 'if anyone was going to get themselves embroiled in a TV production within days of arriving somewhere, it would be you. And in sleepy little Porthgolow, too. You're some kind of drama magnet, aren't you?'

'That's not always a good thing,' Lila said. 'But on this occasion, I think it really could be.'

'There will be loads of practicalities to sort out,' Charlie added. 'When exactly we're needed, where we'll be based, when I can fit my tours in around it. The food market can cope without Gertie, especially as it's only once a month at the moment, but when summer comes . . .'

'She'll be needed here. I totally get that. So?' Lila glanced up as the first raindrops hit the windows. It was properly dark outside now, and she thought that the inside, ironically, must look like a stage set to anyone looking in: they were lit up behind glass walls for all the world to see. She pictured a ghostly figure on the cliff top in the dark and the rain, only fragments of the moon appearing through the clouds to illuminate her. She shuddered. It was going to be an amazing drama, and now Lila knew about it, she desperately wanted to be part of it. 'What do you think?'

'I need to sleep on it,' Charlie said. 'And we've got massages booked. After this revelation I am sorely in need of one, and I'm sure you are, too.' She sat up and swung her legs over her lounger, then held out her hand to Lila. 'Television catering proposition aside, you did a great job of looking after Gertie today. You are a complete liability, obviously,' she added, smiling, 'but you're my liability. Let's go and get the stress pummelled out of us, and I'll think about it some more.'

Lila took Charlie's hand and let her pull her to her feet. She should be feeling relieved: Charlie could easily have said a point-blank 'no' and then Lila would have been in serious trouble. But she was hanging on by a thread. She had shaken Winston's hand, said it would be no problem, basically conveyed to him that it was a done deal. But if Charlie agreed to it, she wouldn't have to admit to her that that was what she'd done.

If she could manage both sides for a couple more days, then everything would be fine and Lila, Charlie and Gertie could embark on the adventure of their lives. The alternative wasn't worth thinking about, and so, Lila decided, as she shrugged on the impossibly soft robe and followed her cousin through the door that led to the spa, she wouldn't. It was much better to focus on the positives.

'Toby *Welsh*?' Juliette squealed, sending Marmite and Daniel's German shepherd, Jasper, into a frenzy. 'Come on, Char, you have to say yes! And you have to let me help out, too. I'm sure there's room for all three of us, and if it's busy, you'll need all hands on deck.' She elbowed Lila in the side and gave her a conspiratorial smile. Lila smiled back and picked up a stick from the damp sand, throwing it in the direction of the dogs, who had raced off to inspect an ugly mound of seaweed close to the water.

It was the day after her meeting with Winston Thorpe, the day after her admission to Charlie and, despite sleeping like a log after the session at the Crystal Waters Spa Hotel, including the best massage she'd ever had, Lila was worried. She'd had a text from Winston saying he was bringing a contract for her to sign that afternoon, which meant that Lila had to convince Charlie by then, and then somehow also convince her that the production team moved so quickly that they had magicked up a contract in only a couple of hours. Juliette, though, was doing a good job of helping her cause.

'It's a big change, Jules,' Charlie said. 'I feel like I've got a routine established with Gertie now, and I don't want to mess it about too much in case we lose all our regulars.'

'Think of it as a hiatus,' Juliette said. 'It's only for a few months, right, Lila? And then Gertie comes sailing back into Porthgolow, famous for being the only Cornish Cream Tea Bus in the world, *and* the star of a BBC production. OK, she's not going to star *in* the show, but she'll be on set, hobnobbing with the talent. It's a scintillating prospect.'

'Scintillating?' Lila asked.

Juliette shrugged. 'I'm trying to stop using the word "stupendous". I seem to say it all the time, after Jonah started using it to describe the Porthgolow burgers. Scintillating is a bit over the top, though.'

'I don't think it is,' Lila said. 'I think scintillating is the perfect description, Jules.'

Charlie had often pointed out their physical similarities. They were both dark-haired, petite, bright-eyed (Lila couldn't help adding 'bushy-tailed' to the end of that description) but where Juliette's skin caught the sun easily, perhaps thanks to her French roots, Lila was decidedly Celtic, with her patchwork of dark freckles and pale skin beneath. An old boyfriend had told her she was like Bambi, with big dark eyes, spots and gangly limbs, as if she was always on the verge of falling over. Lila hadn't believed him at the time, but if the falling over was more metaphorical than physical, then maybe he had a point.

She opened the dictionary app on her phone. '*Scintillating*,' she read aloud. '*Sparkling or shining brightly*. That is exactly what this opportunity is doing, Charlie. Shining brightly like a beacon in your and Gertie's future. Just think of the possibility, the fun, the celebrity selfie opportunities! We could serve a cream tea to Toby Welsh. And I bet he's not the only gorgeous actor in the cast – there are two brothers in the plot, for starters. I know you've got Daniel now, but think of me. Think of poor, single, lonely me. Except, obviously, it's not all about me – it's hardly about me at all. It's you, and Gertie, the future of the Cornish Cream Tea Bus.' She turned in a circle, arms stretched towards the sky, and tripped over Marmite as he came racing back to join the party, only just stopping herself from landing face-first in the shallow water.

Juliette let out a loud laugh and Lila caught Charlie's eye; she was smiling. Lila's heart lifted.

'Never mind Toby Welsh or Aria Lundberg,' Charlie said. 'It's you who should be on that television set.'

Lila pranced and did a ridiculous curtsey in response. 'So you think we should go? Let Gertie be part of the craft catering? Come on, Charlie, what's the worst that can happen?'

Charlie sighed, looked out to sea and then crouched to ruffle Marmite's damp fur. Lila fidgeted with impatience. Finally, she stood, walked up to Lila and took both her hands. 'OK, Lila. You, me and Gertie. We'll do this. But next time, please, *please* check with me before you commit us to anything. I know it's a great opportunity that I would regret turning down, but that doesn't mean I'm happy with the way it's been thrust upon us. OK? Spontaneity will only get you so far, and then it'll get you in trouble.'

'Says the woman who turned her uncle's bus into a café on a whim, and almost had a huge disaster at the fair on the field,' Juliette chimed in. Lila resisted the urge to hug her, and then she didn't. She embraced Charlie, and then Juliette, and then Marmite and Jasper, not caring that their noses were slick with sea water, and then when Daniel appeared at the edge of the beach wearing a smart shirt and trousers, she ran over to him and, without saying anything, hugged him, too.

They were going to be part of *Estelle*. Suddenly, coming to Cornwall felt as if it had been the best idea in the world, because that world was now opening up in front of her with endless, breathtaking possibility – and Lila wasn't just talking about the magnificent Cornish coastline.

Chapter Five

Once Charlie had decided they were committed to *Estelle,* their lives became one, never-ending to-do list. Lila shouldn't have been surprised, Charlie was nothing if not determined, but the level of thought she put into everything made Lila feel like a scatty adolescent.

'We can't just sign the contract Winston sent over,' Charlie said, the day after their beach walk with Juliette, while they were making a fresh batch of scones and some white chocolate and walnut cookies for the bus. Charlie had a habit of flinging her spatula around, and Marmite was sitting next to the fridge, waiting for any morsels of cake mix to come flying in his direction.

'Why not?' Lila asked. 'It'll have all the relevant details and clauses and whatnot, won't it?'

'Gertie's reputation relies on more than a few bits of whatnot,' Charlie said, using the spatula as a pointing finger. Lila wiped a splodge of mix off her nose and checked that her top had survived unscathed.

'So what do we need to check?'

'I've made a list. We need to see Winston.'

The list Charlie went through was long. Winston sat opposite them both, back on board Gertie, an early March rain pelting the windows as if it was desperate to get in out of the cold. Lila clasped her mug, enjoying the faint burning sensation of hot water through ceramic, and nibbled on a cookie while Charlie and Winston were locked in an intense discussion.

Charlie had thought of everything, ideas that hadn't even crossed Lila's mind when she was faced with the enticing prospect of entering the entertainment business, or in the days afterwards, when she'd had time to mull it over. Where would the bus be situated at each site, and what was the ground like? Charlie could guarantee it would be their biggest and heaviest food truck, even if it did have a winch. What were the hours, and would the bus be expected to stay on site for the duration of a particular location, or was there access for it to come and go? The price Winston was offering for several weeks' use of the bus seemed eye-wateringly high to Lila, but Charlie didn't bat an eyelid; instead she made a point of listing the regular events the bus would have to forgo while they were a part of the craft service.

By the end Lila felt entirely bamboozled, but Winston and Charlie shook hands, wearing matching, excited smiles. Winston agreed to amend the contract accordingly and said he'd post the copies, first class, the following day. They stepped down onto the sand, even though the rain was still falling, and waved a goodbye as he got back in his car and drove up the hill.

'Monday the sixteenth of March,' Charlie said. 'That's the first day at the first location, down near Cape Cornwall.' She gave a wistful sigh.

'It's beautiful, is it, Cape Cornwall?'

'The most.' Charlie whirled round, making Lila jump. 'Oh Lila, this is going to be *amazing!* Being on a television set on location in Cornwall. Do you think we'll get to watch a lot of the action? Just think, Toby Welsh coming on board little old Gertie, dressed as Henry Bramerton, asking for a cream tea or a cappuccino. Do you think we should make *Estelle*-themed cakes? Gingerbread ghosts? I still don't know which house they're using for the Bramerton brothers' new pile, do you?'

Lila shook her head slowly, not bothering to hide her amusement. 'It's a great opportunity, isn't it? A really brilliant, *really* exciting thing.'

Charlie gave her a sheepish look and then flung her arms around Lila's shoulders. 'It took me a while to get there, obviously, but what you've done is perfect, Lila! Gertie gets a whole new lease of life, and then will be back in Porthgolow in time for high season. You are a marvel!'

Lila waved her praise away, but her heart swelled. A marvel? She'd never been called that. Nobody had had a good word to say about her in such a long time, and those bad ones, those truly awful things that Clara had said to her, and which she fully deserved, followed her around like a cloak tied tightly around her neck.

'You really think so?' she asked.

'I know so. I do, Lila. You're brilliant. Thank you.'

They walked up the hill to Charlie's house, and it was a good thing the wind was strong and the rain, while no longer pelting, was still falling in steady, heavy drops, because Lila could use both of those as excuses for her watering eyes.

It was the morning of their first day, so early that it was still inky black outside, and Lila could not have slept for one more wink even if she'd started up her sleep stories app. They would be wearing aprons and have their hair tied back, and would most likely be almost invisible to the very busy cast and production team of *Estelle,* and yet the entire contents of Lila's wheelie suitcase lay draped over the bed, armchair and rug in Charlie's spare room. The wardrobe, inevitably, was empty.

Lila threw herself out of bed and, after a shower, began trying on clothes. If she'd had an inkling that this day was coming before she'd made the journey from London, the contents of her suitcase would have been very different. She tried on an emerald top over skinny, ripped jeans, then a sheer silver affair, then a tight crimson blouse with lace detail. Then she remembered that the aprons were the same colour as Gertie's paintwork. In the end she pulled on a tight black pullover with cut-outs in the sleeves and a low neckline, giving her ample scope to adorn herself with chunky silver necklaces and earrings. She tied her dark hair back in a high ponytail, and added a generous flick of eyeliner.

Charlie was waiting in the living room, her smile unable to disguise the nervous energy Lila knew was bubbling beneath the surface. She knew because she had it too. Gertie was fully stocked, and with a few new treats that hadn't, before today, been sold on the Cornish Cream Tea Bus. Gertie had also been given a wash in the car park of Daniel's hotel, a hose and a broom making quick – but very soggy – work of the acres of red paintwork. The bus was ready, and so were they. They were actually doing this.

It was still dark when they left. Once they got off the main route, the roads were tiny and perilous, so Charlie had to creep the bus along them as if she was sneaking up on an enemy. Lila sat at one of the downstairs tables with Marmite on her lap.

'Are you sure we're allowed to bring him?' she asked, pushing the dog's soft fur into a parting on his forehead and chuckling when he gave her a mournful look, as if he knew exactly what kind of ridicule she was subjecting him to.

'Winston said it was fine: apparently it's good to have mascots sometimes, and animals can be a calming influence on set, so long as you're not trying to make them behave on screen.'

'I'm happy you're not left out,' Lila cooed at Marmite. 'Who could possibly not want you? *Everyone* will want you. Who do you think we should make friends with first? Toby or Aria? You'll help, won't you, puppy?'

'My dog is not a dating accessory,' Charlie said, laughing.

'He's a good ice-breaker, though. I've loved getting to know him.' Lila stared out of the window, where a thin band of gold was slowly widening above the shadowy landscape. 'Thank you, Charlie, for letting me stay on.'

'I could hardly make you go home when you've got us into this, could I?'

'You could have done it by yourself – or brought Juliette. She was dying to come, I could tell.'

'Jules is busy with her own business. She's helped out with the Cornish Cream Tea Bus in the past, and I did talk to her about it, but she's got lots of marketing contracts at the moment. She's happy with photos and the odd titbit of gossip – of course without breaking any of Winston's rules.'

There was a long list of things they couldn't do once they were there: no photos of any of the cast on set or any of the location set-ups, and no sharing details – not even the tiniest morsel – of the plot that they gleaned along the way. It was restrictive, but Lila knew why. She'd seen enough long-lens photos of various dramas on the *Daily Mail* website, and she hated the thought of being one of those vultures, leeching all the information, and all the fun, out of it. If she happened to find out any plot details, she would keep them entirely to herself.

By the time they reached the turn-off, blocked by a man in a hi-vis jacket and a clipboard, the sun was hovering above the fields, a mist shrouding the Cornish countryside and the sea beyond in a low, glistening veil. It was breathtaking. Lila would have run up the stairs to get a better view, had she not been called on by Charlie to present herself to the guard ticking them off his list of authorized personnel. So far, so inconspicuous, but then Lila knew they wouldn't want a huge sign announcing them, that they would want to film in as much peace as possible. News was bound to get out about the production soon enough. She wondered if she'd have the opportunity to kick a few *Daily Mail* photographers, or perhaps throw jugs of water over them. She knew Gertie had a good stock of jugs – and teapots – on board.

As Charlie inched the bus down the hill towards the sea, the land dropping steeply ahead of them, Lila was reminded of country fairs, the times she'd taken short-cuts behind the trucks, generators pumping, metal coupling-heads sticking out. There were a lot of vans and lorries, people hurrying in different directions, the whole place a hive of activity. It didn't look disorganized, but it didn't scream of glamour, either. There was no area cordoned off that she could see, with cameras and bounce boards and preening actors, but it was still early.

'Do you think the starring actors have their own trailers?' Charlie asked. 'Huge ones with double beds and showers and kitchens, even though all the food is provided for them and they don't have to lift a finger?'

'Isn't that more in America?' Lila peered at a row of boxy vehicles over to the left. 'Maybe here they're more like luxury caravans?'

'There must be a catering area, though. Hang on.' She leaned out of the window and spoke to a young woman in a hi-vis coat, her hair frizzing around her temples in the damp air. 'Yup,' she said, putting Gertie in gear. 'Just down here and to the right.'

Charlie expertly parked the double-decker in the space she was directed to, and Lila stood up and surveyed their surroundings. They were next to a long white marquee with plastic windows, and a couple of smaller food trucks – one serving coffee, and one which displayed a selection of fruit, chocolate bars and packets of crisps. Ahead of the bus, the rows of trucks and vehicles continued, but between those, Lila caught glimpses of the sea, turning from grey to blue in the early morning light.

Charlie unlocked Gertie's door. The air smelled of damp vegetation, salt, and a comforting aroma that reminded Lila of stews at her grandparents' house during the winter.

'Cornwall isn't short of stunning views,' Charlie murmured, before walking back to the kitchen. 'Come on, let's get ready.'

Ten minutes later, scones were warming in the oven and the coffee machine was ready for action. Charlie was telling Lila – unnecessarily, because it was a trick she was well aware of – that she always made a coffee for herself first thing, not only so she had a caffeine hit, but also so the bus would smell enticing the moment anyone walked on board, when they were joined by a woman with short blonde hair, wearing jeans, a plaid shirt and a warm-looking gilet.

'Welcome to the Cornish Cream Tea Bus,' Lila said with a flourish. 'What can I get you?'

'I'm Em, the catering manager,' the woman replied, shaking Lila's hand and then Charlie's. 'Winston must have mentioned me?'

'Yes of course,' Charlie said. 'This all looks wonderful,' she added, gesturing out of the window. Lila wouldn't have described a catering tent and a coffee stop as 'wonderful', but she knew it was important to make a good impression.

Em nodded, glancing at the bus's tiny kitchen, and then at Marmite, who was sitting on the driver's seat. She folded her arms. 'It's great to have you here,' she said, without an ounce of enthusiasm. 'It is all a bit *unorthodox*, having you as well as the catering and craft services, but Winston was adamant you had to come, and it does fit in with our "keeping it local" ethos. I suppose he's told you how this all works?'

'We're here for today's filming, and we're to serve anyone who comes on board.'

'Winston said he'd agreed with you that you could go off site at the end of each day?' Em rubbed her forehead, and Lila wondered whether she was making a point of seeming anguished.

'He did,' Charlie said, slowly, 'but if that's going to be a problem . . .'

'We do like as little disruption as possible, once everyone's in place. If you have another way of getting here tomorrow, we can get a car to take you home tonight, and you can leave the bus on site.'

Lila bit back a gasp. No way would Charlie leave Gertie so far away.

'There's good security, I presume?' Charlie asked, and when Em nodded, her cousin's smile was wide. 'Then of course

59

that's fine. I've been through the schedule with Winston, and he knows the few days the bus is unavailable.'

'Excellent. Thank you for accommodating us.' She gave them both a small but genuine-seeming smile. 'If you've got a moment, I'd like you to meet the rest of the catering team.'

'Sure,' Charlie said and, making sure Marmite was secure in the bus's cab, followed Em off the bus. Lila took up the rear, wrapping her arms around her to try and shield herself from the biting, cliff-top wind.

Em led them into the large white marquee and began the introductions. It seemed as though there were hundreds of people, and Lila was worried she wouldn't remember any names, except for Mina, who was the head chef. She was as tall as Charlie and had plum-coloured hair and pale, ghostly lips, and laughed uproariously at almost anything. They all seemed friendly, and they were interested in the bus, asking how Charlie developed her recipes and about the pitfalls of working in such a tiny kitchen.

'I'm Max,' said a tall, slightly pudgy man in jeans and a black T-shirt. He wasn't wearing chefs' whites like several of the others, and he was only about Lila's age. 'This your first set?' he asked.

'Is it that obvious?' Lila replied, grinning at him. He seemed more nervous than she was, though he, too, had that same excited look in his blue eyes, as if he couldn't believe he was actually here. 'What about you?'

'Third,' he said. 'But it's by far the biggest. We catered for an episode of a countryside documentary last year, but the crew was much smaller, and then there was an indie film in Portreath, but it was only one scene, so that was a few days. This is massive by comparison.'

'What does your company do the rest of the time? Or are you a new member of staff?'

Max shrugged. He had very fair hair, and smile lines round his mouth and eyes that suggested he was often in a good mood. 'Corporate events, mostly. The set gigs are the best part, though. I can't believe Aria Lundberg's going to be here!'

'Or Toby Welsh,' Lila added. 'It's madness!'

'If you need any pointers, about what to do and what not to do – as I said, I'm not that much of an expert, but I'll help if I can.'

'Thanks, Max,' Lila said. 'That's very kind of you. I feel like a rabbit in the headlights, albeit a very happy one.'

They swapped smiles just as Charlie grabbed her arm. 'We can go and have a look at the kitchens,' she said in a stage whisper.

'Wow,' Lila replied, deadpan. 'The thrill.' She laughed when Charlie shot her a look. 'Kidding. Of course I want to see them. But we've only got a few minutes, or our scones will burn.'

'Two minutes,' Charlie said, holding her fingers up. 'This is so cool, Lila.'

'And we haven't even met any actors yet,' Lila added, as she waved goodbye to Max and Charlie dragged her towards a gap in the marquee wall. The comforting smell of stew was much stronger here, and Lila wondered if she'd be able to sneak a taste, just like she used to at her grandparents' house.

Once they were back on the bus, Lila wielded an oven glove and began moving the scones to the cooling rack. 'You're really OK about leaving Gertie here?'

'She'll probably be more secure here than she would be on Porthgolow beach. You don't need to worry about Gertie.

Be your sparkling, dynamic self and woo people on board to eat all our cakes.'

'That is exactly what I'm going to do,' Lila agreed. 'We don't want people visiting the coffee van, we want them all in here. Imagine if we get to meet Toby Welsh on our first day!'

Charlie clapped her hands together and gave a very girly squeak, and Lila decided, then and there, that as long as *someone* came on to the bus, she would count the day as a success.

An hour later, she, Charlie and Marmite had served three members of the catering team they had met earlier, and a group of exuberant runners who were all at least five years younger than Lila and who greeted them with vigorous handshakes, then made a huge dent in the tower of chocolate brownies.

''Em said we were a bit unorthodox, so maybe the cast are going with what they're familiar with,' Charlie said, readjusting a muffin on a paisley cake stand.

Lila glanced out of the window, to where a small queue had formed at the coffee van. None of them was wearing period clothing, as far as she could see.

'But surely the fact that we're unusual means we should have *more* custom,' Lila said. 'Don't you always investigate new things? Thinking about it, you *brought* new things to Porthgolow and revolutionized the village, so I'm asking the wrong person.' She started to make her third cappuccino.

'Revolutionized is a bit strong,' Charlie replied. 'Anyway, they're obviously just busy. You know, filming.'

'I want to meet them all, though. I want to know how it works – I want to see the scripts. I have so many questions! I wonder what scene they're filming right now? Someone striding through the water wearing knee-high leather boots and a tight, midnight-blue waistcoat, riding crop in hand.' Lila sighed dreamily.

'Would that someone you're imagining be Toby Welsh? And what time period do you think this is? Your vision sounds a bit S&M.'

'Midnight-blue waistcoats are *not* S&M,' Lila shot back, laughing. 'Not unless they're made of leather, have holes or spikes or metal rings, and are accompanied by a gimp mask . . .' Her words trailed off as Charlie's eyes widened and she clamped her lips shut, trying not to laugh. 'Let me guess,' Lila murmured, 'we have a customer?'

'Got it in one,' Charlie said, striding past her and holding out her hand. 'Welcome to the Cornish Cream Tea Bus. Would you like to take a seat?'

Lila spun round, wondering how scarlet her cheeks had gone, and drank in the sight of their visitors.

There were two of them, a man and a woman. They were both, she estimated, under thirty, and both eminently filmable. The woman was petite, with skin as pale as Lila's and hair that curled in delicate blonde wisps around her face. She had a cute snub nose and eyes of deep, pooling blue. The man was tall, perhaps six foot, and slender, but with strong-looking shoulders and an upright posture. His hair was the colour of wet sand, and he had strong features: a long, elegant nose and high cheekbones. The eyes that met hers above his warm smile were hazel, but on the side of brown, rather than green. Under the glimmer of the bus's fairy lights, they seemed almost golden.

Actors, Lila concluded. They were definitely actors. Even here, wearing casual clothes – jeans and jumpers – it was obvious. They were mesmerizing.

'We haven't got long,' the woman said, in a soft, dancing voice. 'But we thought we'd come and say hello. What a beautiful bus!'

'We didn't know you'd be here until a couple of days ago,' the man added, with a hint of an accent that Lila couldn't quite place. 'Winston said he was sourcing everything from nearby, and the Cornish Cream Tea Bus certainly fits the bill. I'm Sam.' He held out his hand to Lila.

'And I'm Keeley,' added the woman.

'Hello,' Charlie said. 'It's lovely to meet you. Are you . . . cast members?' She had obviously come to the same conclusion as Lila.

'We are,' Keeley replied. 'This is the younger Bramerton brother, Robert, and I play Estelle.' She smiled, her blue eyes bright.

'Ooh, you're the title character?' Lila asked. 'Wow! Charlie and I are very happy to meet you. I'm Delilah – Lila. And the bus is Gertie, and she – and we – are entirely at your service.' She resisted the urge to curtsey, but she couldn't deny that she was starstruck, even if she hadn't heard of Sam or Keeley before this moment.

Sam's laugh was a low rumble. 'If that's the case, then a black coffee wouldn't go amiss. Double shot, if possible.'

'Of course,' Lila said. 'What about you, Keeley?'

'Do you have green tea?'

'Coming right up,' Charlie replied. 'Can I tempt either of you to a pastry or a muffin? We've made breakfast muffins filled with fruit and seeds. They're lower carb and sugar than usual, and packed full of energy.'

Sam and Keeley eyed the cake stands longingly.

'Why don't you share one?' Lila said, and before either of them could respond she cut a muffin in half and put the portions in separate paper bags. 'You're going to be outside all day, and it's not the balmiest morning.' She gestured out of the window where the mist had lifted and the weak sun was hitting the water as if it couldn't quite be bothered.

Charlie folded her arms. 'I didn't know you had mothering instincts, Lila. But I approve.'

'So do I,' Sam said, taking his coffee and half a muffin, and nodding at Lila in thanks, his strangely glowing eyes holding hers. 'Mothering instincts *and* an in-depth knowledge of S&M. I'm intrigued.'

Lila's cheeks heated, and she could only stare as Sam gave her a final, slightly hesitant smile and walked off the bus.

'Thank you,' Keeley said. 'I'll definitely be back. I want to know more about the bus, and I'd love to meet that guy hiding up at the front.' She pointed at Marmite, who was sitting with his ear folded over, dark eyes trained on this new person as if she was the most fascinating thing he'd ever seen. Lila could sympathize.

'You're welcome – any time,' she gushed, and Charlie nodded her agreement.

Once they were alone, Lila bounded up to Charlie and raised her hand for a high-five. Charlie hit it with enthusiasm. '*Lead actors*, Charlie,' she said. 'Wow. Don't you think it went well?'

'S&M comment aside,' Charlie replied wryly, 'I think it was a total success.'

Chapter Six

People visited the bus in dribs and drabs throughout the rest of the day. It was mostly crew members, shivering in fingerless gloves and desperate for a coffee. Some asked questions about the bus, while others were so lost in their own worlds that they barely seemed to notice what they'd walked onto. Charlie and Lila were enthusiastic, suggesting cakes or pastries, and while a few left with paper bags full of treats, nobody stayed long enough to sit down, have a Cornish cream tea or chat about the production.

Lila shouldn't have been disappointed – they were working, after all, and it wasn't like the bus's usual occupation, catering to people on holiday or a day out. On this television set, Gertie was a utilitarian vehicle rather than a pleasure cruiser. But Charlie seemed upbeat, and as they were driven home in a luxurious Mercedes by Mike, one of the team's drivers, and then set about making cakes and sausage rolls, muffins made from ground almonds, catering to a more takeaway-orientated – and more health-conscious – clientele, Lila's mood improved.

It was only the first day – there was plenty of time for things to get more exciting.

The following morning, Lila drove them to set in her Volvo, and Gertie was safely in place when they arrived. They laid out their new offerings, put the radio on low and sang along quietly, not wanting to disturb anyone. The starts were earlier than Lila was used to, but the drive over Cornwall's patchwork-quilt landscape made it more than bearable.

The day was mist-free, the sky a glorious blue as nighttime receded. Lila wanted to ask someone how they got the scene continuity right when the weather was so changeable. If she was honest, she wanted to ask a hundred things of everyone on set: the make-up artists, the cameramen, the lighting director. She wanted to grill Keeley about whether the costumes were comfortable and how she channelled herself into the role of Estelle. She wanted to ask Sam what techniques he had for memorizing his lines, and how nervous he got before takes. It was like working in a chocolatiers without being able to try anything: it was all just out of reach.

Keeley and Sam reappeared that morning, and Lila felt herself blush as she recalled the S&M discussion and Sam's quiet amusement. She wondered why she couldn't just shrug the moment off, as she usually did. She didn't often feel so embarrassed. Keeley walked up to the cab and held her hand out to Marmite, who gladly allowed himself to be the centre of attention. Keeley sneezed once, twice, three times.

'Are you OK?' Charlie asked. 'All that sea air hasn't got to you already, has it?'

Keeley shook her head. 'I'm allergic to dogs.'

'Oh no! Then we should never—'

Keeley waved away Charlie's concern. 'I can't have one of my own, but the sneezing and itchy eyes are worth it occasionally, and especially with this fluffster. What's his name?'

'Marmite,' Charlie said. 'He's a Yorkipoo.'

'Not sure Gregor will be over the moon if you arrive on set with bloodshot eyes,' Sam said, thanking Lila as she handed him a black, double-shot Americano. One thing she was good at was remembering regular orders, especially when the regulars themselves were so memorable.

'It doesn't last long, and Perry will banish the redness in make-up,' Keeley replied.

'Do you have a whole trailer thing for make-up?' Lila asked, using their conversation as her way in.

'We do,' Sam confirmed. 'We're both due there after this. Speaking of which—'

'So do *you* have to wear a lot of it, too?' Lila cut in, peering at Sam's smooth skin. 'Like what?'

Sam ran his hand through his wet-sand hair. 'Powder, a bit of eye make-up. For the guys it's more about enhancing our features on screen, taking away any shine. It's not like this is *Lord of the Rings* or anything: I don't have to transform into an elf.'

'That's a pity,' Lila said. 'I think you'd look quite good as an elf. You have the right bone structure.' He gave her a bemused look, and Lila's cheeks heated for a second time. She wondered what was wrong with her. 'Sorry, I . . . would you like an almond muffin? Flour free, low carb.'

'We'll have to have one each,' Keeley said. 'You should have seen Sam's forlorn little face after he'd wolfed down his half in about three bites yesterday.'

'Forlorn is a *bit* of an exaggeration,' Sam grinned.

'Maybe,' Keeley replied, smiling. 'Look after this guy for

me, and I'll pick us one out each.' She lifted Marmite into Sam's arms, and sneezed four times in quick succession. Sam gave the dog an indulgent smile, and Marmite stared up at him, then pawed at his chin.

'All right, doggo,' he murmured. Lila busied herself at the coffee machine, trying not to let the sight of a seriously attractive man cuddling a cute dog turn her to mush. It would make a perfect Instagram photo, except she wasn't allowed to take photos of the cast and plaster them all over the internet.

When they'd gone, Lila popped a mini cheese and onion puff in her mouth, and let it dissolve on her tongue before she spoke. 'Neither of them seems to have any kind of ego, which is odd, for actors, isn't it?'

Charlie frowned. 'I don't think you have to have an ego to be an actor, just like you don't have to be an actor to have an ego. Look at Daniel,' she added, grinning. 'He's got enough confidence for most of Porthgolow. And neither of us recognized Sam or Keeley, so maybe they've not experienced the adoration that comes with being well known?'

'Maybe,' Lila mused. 'I'm going to ask Keeley when I get a chance. There's lots of waiting around on TV sets, isn't there? Hopefully she'll spend some time here.'

'And what about Sam?' Charlie asked, amusement in her voice.

Lila ignored it. 'He seems nice. A bit unsure of himself. Perhaps this is his first big role and he's extra nervous. Maybe he's—'

'Spent a lot of time thinking about him, have you?'

Lila rolled her eyes. 'I've thought about everyone, Charlie. The list of questions I have is longer than the list you had for Winston before we started this.'

'Fair point,' Charlie said, laughing. 'Just pick your moments. We don't want to get thrown off the set because you let your curiosity get the better of you.'

'Honestly, Charlie, you have no idea how hard I'm working to stop that from happening. Calamitous Delilah is firmly locked away and, for now, the key is nowhere to be found.'

All Lila's hard-fought professionalism nearly evaporated on Wednesday, when Toby Welsh and Aria Lundberg graced Gertie with their presence. She almost coughed up her mouthful of coffee when they stepped on board, and she heard Charlie squeak beside her.

If Lila thought Sam and Keeley were aesthetically impressive human beings, then Toby and Aria were in another league. They were both wearing their *Estelle* costumes, and Toby looked beyond dashing in inky-black breeches, waistcoat and coat, a snowy-white shirt and cravat, and black boots. His dark hair was curled expertly into lush, loose waves, and even with a visible coating of powder and what looked suspiciously like eyeliner, he was a perfect, masculine specimen.

Aria was, quite simply, a princess. Her black hair was piled beautifully on top of her head, and her smile was soft but dazzling. Her dress, in the palest pink, was straight out of an original Disney sketch of *Sleeping Beauty*.

'Can I, I mean . . . hello. How can I . . . what would you like?' Charlie stuttered.

Neither Toby nor Aria seemed to notice her fumble. Lila wondered if they'd been told to keep their expressions to a minimum between scenes so as not to crack the powder. But then Toby strode forward and held out his hand, his dark eyes warm.

'Hi, I'm Toby, and this is Aria. We've heard a lot about – Gertie, isn't it? And even more about your muffins.'

'Made with ground almonds,' Aria added, as if it was a magical ingredient. 'We have to try them.'

'Of course,' Charlie said, recovering her composure. 'Would you like any drinks to go with those?'

'Tea,' Aria replied, 'builders' please. Strong as you like.' Her accent was American, but with a Scandinavian lilt, and Lila added accent training to her list of questions.

'I'd love a cappuccino if poss,' Toby added, rubbing his hands together. 'Warm us up a bit before we head back out there.'

'Is it going well?' Lila asked.

'So far. It's always troublesome, working with outside elements that have no sympathy for what you're trying to achieve, but Cornwall's being a peach today. The sunshine is nice, but a bit misleading. I envy you, being tucked away in here with an endless supply of hot drinks and sausage rolls.'

'You're welcome any time, of course. Whenever you get a breather, we'll be waiting.' Lila smiled at him. This was Toby Welsh. *The* Toby Welsh, and she was talking to him. She wiped her palms surreptitiously down her apron.

'It's much more homely than the catering tent, where you can't escape the wind however hard you try. Sorry, I didn't catch your name?'

'I'm Lila, and this is my cousin Charlie.'

'Hello,' Charlie said. 'Drinks are coming up.'

'Gertie *is* a cosy bus,' Lila continued, imagining her and Toby snuggled up on a sofa together in front of a roaring fire. She was pretty sure she could make Toby feel cosy, if that was what he was after.

'With fairy lights, no less.' His eyes flashed with amusement, and Lila had the sense that he was letting her in on some conspiracy, that they were on the same side.

'I think she's beautiful,' Aria said, accepting her tea from Charlie and then pushing her full skirt beneath one of the tables and sitting down. Toby shrugged, and sat opposite her – there was no room alongside Aria's dress for anyone else.

Charlie and Lila exchanged a look. They had two of the country's best-known actors sitting at one of their tables. Charlie spent an inordinately long time arranging two muffins on plates, before placing them on the table.

'Thank you,' Aria said. 'It's lovely to have a break somewhere other than our trailers.'

'You're so welcome,' Charlie gushed.

'How did you end up running a café on a bus?' Aria asked, before tearing off a chunk of muffin and nibbling it daintily.

As Charlie gave her a potted version of how the Cornish Cream Tea Bus came into being – Lila wondered if she ever got bored of telling that story – Lila and Toby exchanged smiles.

'How much set work have you done?' he asked. 'I would have thought your bus would be a crowd-pleaser wherever you end up.'

'This is our first week of our first ever set. And I've actually only been working on Gertie a few weeks.'

Toby raised his eyebrows. 'Oh. So, not an old hand – not that old hand is something that could ever be said of you, regardless. Have you watched any of the filming?'

Lila shook her head. 'No, we've . . . we have to stay here, to serve anyone who comes on board.'

'You can't pass up the chance, though,' Toby said, mock sternly. 'Even I still get overawed by large-scale operations

72

like this, the work and effort that goes into making eight hours of drama. You have to get someone to give you a tour – to get a sense of the scale of it. And you must come and watch the filming. Take it in turns, sneak down to see it. If nobody's free to show you round, then explore by yourself. If anyone asks what you're doing, you can always say you're lost.' He shrugged, nonchalant, but Lila saw the glint of mischief in his eyes and felt a thrill of excitement.

'You're actively encouraging me to misbehave?' she asked. 'To leave my post and wander around, spying on everyone while they're hard at work?'

Toby laughed. 'Yes, I suppose I am. I think you'll have a lot more fun that way.'

'What about the scripts?' Lila said.

'What about them?'

'Can I see them?' She knew it was a bold move but she didn't care.

Toby gave her a steady stare. 'I might be able to get you one – you've signed the disclaimer, I presume?'

Lila nodded and held her hands up. 'Purely my own curiosity. I just want to know the story.'

'Good. Then I will actively encourage that, too. And maybe one day when I'm free, I can give you a tour and we can do some spying together.'

'I'm pretty sure you wouldn't get very far,' Lila countered. 'You're not exactly inconspicuous, seeing as how you're the star of the show.'

'One of them,' Toby said, holding a hand up. 'This is an ensemble cast, and I rather fear my younger, greener co-stars are going to act me out of the park. Keeley Klein and Sam Magee, sneaking up on the inside like the dark horses that they are.' He sat back, and then looked down at his muffin, as if he'd only just remembered it. He took a huge bite.

'Keeley and Sam are going to be wonderful,' Aria added. 'After only being in a couple of scenes with them, you just know, don't you, Toby?'

'But they need their earnestness knocking out of them,' Toby mumbled through his mouthful. 'Don't worry, I've got that in hand.' He put the last, giant piece of muffin in his mouth, and wiped his fingers on a napkin.

'We need to get back,' Aria said, sliding out from the bench and standing. Even with her huge skirts she was effortlessly elegant, as if she glided, rather than walked, everywhere.

'Lovely to meet you both,' Toby added. 'I'm sure we'll be back soon, and don't forget what I said, Lila. Don't stay cooped up in here the whole time – go and explore.' He gave her and then Charlie a quick peck on the cheek, filling Lila's senses with spicy male aftershave, then he and Aria said goodbye and walked off the bus.

'Oh my God, Charlie,' Lila said. 'Did that really just happen?'

'Sort of inevitable, considering where we are. But it is pretty special, isn't it? Rubbing shoulders with the stars.'

'Toby was amazing.' Lila grinned at her cousin and shimmied down the aisle of the bus, picking up empty mugs and plates as she went. This was exactly what she'd been hoping for.

The next day the bus remained Toby- and Aria-free, and even Sam and Keeley must have been too busy to come and see them. Crew members whizzed on board for takeaway coffees and sausage rolls, but none of them stayed, and Lila and

Charlie spent a lot of time chatting and cleaning, until their throats were hoarse and the inside of Gertie gleamed like a spaceship. It took all of Lila's willpower not to eat her way methodically through the bus's entire stock. She realized, at the end of their fourth day, that they had not made a single Cornish cream tea.

'Is this going as you'd hoped?' she asked Charlie, as they finished the close-down routine on Thursday night.

'I wasn't sure what to expect,' Charlie said after a moment's thought. 'And I know we've had quiet periods, but sometimes that isn't a bad thing. Money-wise, this gig is setting us up – you, me *and* Gertie – for a while, so we don't have to worry, and in some respects, it's money for nothing – money for barely anything, at least. So, what I've been thinking,' she placed a hand on Lila's arm, 'is that it doesn't need both of us. Not all the time.'

It took Lila a moment to reply. 'You don't need me? What am I meant to do?' She thought of Toby and all his enticing suggestions, Keeley and her soft spot for Marmite, Sam with his mesmerizing eyes. Things had just started to get interesting; she didn't want to leave the bus yet.

Charlie shook her head. 'I was thinking that *you* could be in charge of Gertie, while she's here. That would allow me to start planning some more tours, contact more vendors for the food markets, so that when we're finished here and summer comes around, everything is sorted. It makes so much sense, Lila. Why don't you do it alone tomorrow – Em said we could borrow one of the catering team if we need cover for lunch or breaks – and we can take the weekend to assess how it's gone? We'll get double the work done, and you'll have more opportunities to talk to the cast.'

'If they have time to come and see us,' she said grudgingly, but her stomach was doing somersaults. Gertie, the set and all within it would be hers for the conquering. Without Charlie's safe, watchful eye she might be able to sneak in some of her questions, maybe even take Toby up on his offer of a set tour. It would be her chance to shine.

The next day Lila was on the bus early, dressed in skinny black jeans, a coral-coloured blouse and sparkly Converse. The sun was only just rising above the distant horizon, and everything was a pale, silvery blue that made her catch her breath with wonder. The earth smelt sweet, the scent of early spring flowers reaching her through Gertie's open door, and she opened all the windows, filling the bus with fresh air.

She laid out stands of muffins, sausage and cheese rolls, mini *arancini* that she and Charlie had made the previous night; mushroom risotto balls filled with gooey mozzarella. They were bite-sized, so not even the most appearance-conscious actor could protest. She tried to pile them up like a tower of Ferrero Rocher, but the rice balls had other ideas, and she settled for a less dramatic presentation.

'Hello? Are you accepting visitors?'

Lila looked up to find Sam hovering in the doorway. She was reminded of his cute Marmite moment, and wished Charlie hadn't kept her dog with her in Porthgolow today.

'Of course,' she said, pushing a wayward strand of hair behind her ear. 'What would you like? Other than an *arancini*, because they're obligatory, not optional.'

Sam raised his eyebrows. 'You've progressed from mothering to force-feeding, now? Where's Charlie?'

'Charlie is working on summer plans for the Cornish Cream Tea Bus, back in Porthgolow. You're stuck with me, I'm afraid.'

'What a hardship,' Sam said lightly. Lila gave him a questioning look, but his expression gave nothing away. 'I was after a coffee, if possible.'

'One black, double-shot Americano coming up. What's your favourite bean?'

Sam leaned against a table. He was wearing a scruffy grey jumper with the neckline pulled out of shape, and dark jeans. His feet looked huge in rugged, tan-coloured boots, and in the early morning light his hair seemed to glisten.

'Favourite bean?' he asked. 'I quite like jelly beans, except the ones that taste like washing powder. Not a huge fan of baked beans, and I haven't really considered how I feel about borlotti beans. I've not had cause to, so far in my life. *Magic* beans, though. They're something else. I once played Jack in a stage version of *Jack and the Beanstalk*, and—'

'I meant coffee beans,' Lila said, laughing. 'But good to know you're ambivalent about borlotti beans. I am, too.' Their eyes held for a moment. Lila was the first to look away. 'It's a moot point anyway,' she continued, 'because Charlie only has arabica beans, and only one type of roast, but I'm going to order some other varieties in next week, maybe do a coffee tasting one day.' Now she was in charge, she had all these exciting plans.

'I'm not sure how much time we'll have for coffee tastings,' Sam admitted, taking an *arancini* when she held the plate out to him.

'No,' Lila said, deflating. 'I suppose not.'

'It must get a bit dull, waiting here for someone to turn up.'

She shrugged. 'It's taking a while to get used to it, but it feels like a privilege to be here, too. It's just a bit of an adjustment.'

77

Sam nodded. 'You're not the only one adjusting. This is my first lead role, and while I'm ready, I've been working up to it for a long time, to be honest . . . I'm bricking it.'

'Wow. You seem . . .' She couldn't say she had guessed as much, but she was touched that he'd chosen to confide in her. 'I mean, well done. Good luck! Shit, that all sounds so patronizing. Sorry. You're here, and you're doing it – and alongside Toby Welsh, no less! That's super impressive.'

He gave her a weary smile and picked up his coffee cup. 'I'd better be getting back. Thank you, though, for the good wishes. We're both new at all this, so let me extend my good wishes to you, too. You're certainly making breaks better than they might otherwise have been.'

'Thank you,' Lila said, unsure how to act in the face of his sudden formality.

'And I'm sure you'll find a way to make things more entertaining. I imagine that you can be very resourceful, when the need arises.'

She smiled, surprised that he'd already guessed that about her. 'Resourcefulness is one of my more useful skills.'

'I thought so. Have a good day.'

'You too, Sam.' She watched him walk off the bus, drawn to the way his hair tufted into a point at the back of his neck, and the tanned skin beneath.

At lunchtime, Max – the young, friendly man she had met in the catering tent on their first morning – took her place on board Gertie. Lila picked up an apple and a packet of Monster Munch from one of the other craft stalls and slipped away from the catering area.

The day was fresh and bright, but her blouse wasn't protection enough against the wind. She shivered as she wove between the parked vehicles, past a large trailer called the Video Village, and down towards where she could hear waves crashing against rocks. There were so many people milling about, so much activity outside the bus, that Lila found it hard to take in. She remembered what Toby had said about the scale of the operation needed for filming a few hours of drama, and she wanted to find that central hub, the Ground Zero of the *Estelle* juggernaut.

She picked up her pace, rounded the corner of a long vehicle with high, blind-covered windows and almost bumped into someone. Her apple and crisps fell to ground as she jolted back, and she let out a helpless squeak.

'Sorry,' said a deep, resonant voice, and Lila discovered it was attached to a tall man with a crop of reddish-brown hair and intelligent eyes behind frameless glasses. He gave her a curious look.

'I'm sorry too,' she said. 'I was going too fast.'

'You need a new apple.' He bent to pick it up, and then looked at it intently, as if it was something more impressive than a Royal Gala covered in dirt.

'I do,' Lila said, amused. 'Would you like this one? You seem very enamoured with it.'

The man laughed and held out his hand. 'It's given me an idea. I'm Gregor, the director. I don't recall having seen you before?'

'I'm Delilah – Lila,' she managed to say, though her pulse was suddenly racing. She'd almost bumped into the *director* while she was trying to spy on the filming. 'I'm running the Cornish Cream Tea Bus, the quirky addition to the craft services.'

'Ah yes,' Gregor said. 'Winston is very pleased with himself about that particular move. I should come and get a coffee. Have any interest in the filming, Lila?'

'Oh yes,' she said enthusiastically. 'I was actually hoping to find . . .'

She brought herself up short, and Gregor laughed. 'We're all on our way to the catering tent for lunch, so filming's on pause. But next time you get a chance, come and have a look. See what your culinary efforts are helping to fuel.'

'I'd love that! Thank you.' She resisted the urge to hug Gregor who, despite his strange fascination with her fallen apple, didn't seem too intimidating. He *wanted* her to go and watch the filming. She waited until he'd gone, then made her way back to Gertie, her stomach growling. She stepped back on board just as a young woman, mobile pressed to her ear, was collecting a coffee. Lila whispered a thank you to Max and set about rearranging her display, unable to help over-hearing the woman's conversation.

'Yes, tonight. A few of us are going. Not far, down at Portheras Cove.' Lila pricked her ears up as the woman continued, oblivious to her interest. 'I'm not really into all that equinox stuff, but it hasn't been too cold today, and it should be a bit of a laugh. Yeah, I'll see you then, OK? Cheers.' The woman ended her call and gave Lila a quick smile.

'*Arancini?*' Lila asked, holding out the plate.

'I've already had a couple, but what the heck! They're great.' She reached forward and selected two more, then strolled off the bus.

For the rest of that afternoon, Lila's thoughts kept returning to what she'd heard. She hadn't done much exploring since she'd been here, and a beach party – albeit one in March – would be the perfect way of celebrating her first week on set, especially if some of the crew were going to be there. It would be a chance to integrate more with the *Estelle* team away from Gertie.

Sam's words popped into her head: *I'm sure you'll find a way to make things more entertaining.* For some reason, she wanted to prove him right.

She heard shouting somewhere far away, a smattering of applause carried to her on the wind. They were all still working. She was supposed to stay later this evening, to be on hand when the actors had finished their twilight shoot – Charlie had pinned a schedule of their hours at this location to the wall before they'd even arrived – but it was already half past five, and surely everyone would want to get back to their accommodation when they were finished, to hot meals and glasses of wine or beer, not start their weekend off with a latte.

Lila did a quick search on her phone, found directions to Portheras Cove and started to shut down, checking everything was put away and switched off. When she was done, she jumped off the bus and locked the door. Nobody would notice she was missing, and if they did, by the time Monday morning rolled around, it would be forgotten about.

'Right,' she said, brushing away the niggle of unease that she was disobeying Charlie – and Winston's – orders. She hurried to her Volvo and slid into the driver's seat. She sent Charlie a quick message saying she would be out for the evening, but that she'd drive her back to set first thing in the morning so she could pick up Gertie and take her back to Porthgolow for the weekend. Then she put the car in gear, reversed out of the car park, waved goodnight to Claude on the gate and set off, the amber of a spectacular sunset pushing through the driver's window as she headed towards her destination. 'Spring equinox festival, here I come.'

Chapter Seven

There was no advertising, no large signs or people with fluorescent jackets. It was even more tucked away than the *Estelle* set. But Lila found it, a discreet wooden signpost with an arrow and the word 'Ostara', surrounded by flickering electric tea lights. Following the winding track, the hedges encroaching more with every passing moment, she felt a thrill of anticipation.

Lila had never shied away from a gathering. It was as if interacting with other people recharged her batteries and, for the last few months, without Clara in her life, and with her confidence dented after their last, awful meeting, she had been running on empty.

Being in Porthgolow with Charlie had helped. She enjoyed spending time with her and Daniel, Juliette and Lawrence, and she could feel the *Estelle* set starting to warm up. Word was getting around about the quality of Gertie's menu, and if she continued to take Toby's advice and leave the confines of the bus, she would start to widen her circle. And then there were serendipitous moments like this.

The road ahead dipped steeply, and then suddenly the sea

was churning ahead of her. The burning orange sun picked out white horses on the uneven surface, and large waves crashed, frothed and receded against the sand. She had always wanted to celebrate Ostara – the spring equinox – at Stonehenge, but having the ocean instead made it feel as special. She drove slowly down to a scruffy car park – already over half full – and climbed out into the evening air.

It was thick with the sea's salty scent, and the burn and crackle of a bonfire. Hefting her handbag on to her shoulder, Lila followed the sounds and smells, the ground softening under her feet as she found the sand.

It didn't look like a formal event, but one that had spread through word of mouth and, Lila thought wryly, overheard conversations. It was exactly her sort of thing.

'Welcome!' shouted a tall man with a mop of blond hair and an impressive, shaggy beard. He was holding a can of beer and standing close to the fire. A few other people turned as Lila approached, and she waved. She couldn't see the woman who had been on Gertie earlier, or anyone else she recognized from the set.

'I'm Lila,' she said, striding up to join them, sitting cross-legged in a gap that seemed made just for her. 'A visitor to Cornwall, but here to celebrate with you tonight.'

'Welcome, Lila,' several voices replied, and a man sitting beside her offered her a can.

She waved it away. 'I'm driving.'

'No worries,' he said, and the beer was retracted and replaced with a can of lemonade, which she took with a thank you. 'I'm Holden. What brings you down this way?'

'Tonight, or more generally?' She popped the can open and took a long sip. It was sweet, giving her an instant burst of energy.

'Let's go with more generally,' Holden said. 'Why did you come to Cornwall?' He was Australian, the twang in his voice unmistakable.

'Well, Holden,' she said wryly, 'it involves mistakes, recrimination and heartbreak, and I would much rather focus on the positives right now.'

'But this is the perfect time,' he replied. 'It's the equinox. Moving into a fresh season, out with the old and in with the new. Purge yourself, Lila. Get it all out there, and you'll feel reborn by the time the sun comes up.'

Lila kicked off her shoes, pulled her legs up and dug her toes into the sand. She rested her arms on her knees and looked at Holden. He was attractive, in a classically Australian way. Square jaw, mouth dented into a permanent smile. The firelight showed the definition of his muscles beneath a pale T-shirt, the curve of his biceps under tanned skin. He was far too obvious for her, really, but then she had come here tonight for an adventure. There was nothing stopping her.

She took another sip of her drink, and said, 'What you need to know about me is—'

'Lila, is that you? Oh my God, it is!'

Lila looked up to see a petite figure wearing cut-off jeans and a hoodie that swamped her, pale curls bobbing around her face. 'Keeley?' she smiled. She had hoped to see some familiar faces, but hadn't considered that Keeley might be spending her Friday night here. She wondered if Sam was somewhere on the beach, too. She scooted over, making room for the actress between her and Holden. He raised an eyebrow at the interruption and turned to talk to the person on his other side.

'I didn't think I'd see you here,' Lila said as Keeley plopped down beside her and reached for a can of lemonade.

'Sarah, who works on crew, told me this was happening,

and I thought it would be the perfect way to wind down after tonight's filming. I didn't realize you were going to be here either.' She gestured to where the woman from the bus was chatting to a group of people in the process of lighting a second bonfire.

'I'm actually only here because I overheard Sarah talking about it. I felt exactly the same – you can't come to Cornwall and not end up at a beach party.'

'But you left before filming ended,' Keeley said. 'Gregor was *not* impressed.'

Lila closed her eyes. 'Bollocks.'

'They were still going when I left, but when they were resetting the shot Gregor and Toby said they were going to get a sausage roll, and came back empty handed. Gregor said you'd shut up and gone home. His cheeks were redder than his hair, and his glare could have burnt the shrubbery.'

'Shit.' Lila felt a familiar churning in her stomach. 'I thought as it was so close to the end of the day, and I hadn't seen anyone for hours, that it wouldn't matter if I headed off. I thought everyone would be keen to leave.'

'It's the first evening shoot, and there's so much to deal with, so many problems with the lighting, the sound of the sea and the wind: they'd spent over an hour setting up before we were even called, and then . . .' She shrugged.

'I met Gregor earlier, and he was so nice. Now I'm firmly in his bad books.'

'I wouldn't worry,' Keeley said, nudging her shoulder. 'Gregor is quick to get angry and quick to get over it. You have to be pretty resilient in his job, and he won't hold a grudge, I'm sure.'

'Thank you,' Lila said. 'For making me feel better. I've been pretty good at putting my foot in things recently.'

'All you need to do is turn up on Monday, apologize to Gregor, and show him how indispensable you are.'

'I'm not sure I am, though.' She shrugged. 'I mean, great for coffee and snacks, but what Gertie's really good at, her signature dish, is a Cornish cream tea, and we haven't made a single one of those this week.'

Keeley laughed and held her hands out towards the crackling flames. 'You sound hurt on behalf of cream teas. What you have to realize is that you being there – the bus, I mean – isn't exactly the norm. The catering and craft service has been organized for months, everything has, because scheduling the locations and actors and equipment is always such a feat of logistics. You were an unexpected, last-minute addition, so it's not that surprising if you haven't quite found yourself fitting in.'

'I thought everyone would love Gertie, like they do when she's sitting on Porthgolow beach.'

'Everyone *does*,' Keeley confirmed. 'But you're still sort of in-between. We have the hot, sit-down meals, and then, other than that, it's usually grab and go, so it's not an easy sell. How about I come onto the bus on Monday, when I've got enough time, and have a cream tea? Then I can go on about it to everyone, be your personal publicity manager.'

'That,' Lila said, 'would be amazing, if you're sure you'll be able to stay? I'm so glad I came tonight, to have a chance to chat to you when you're not under any pressure.'

'What brought you here, all on your own? Why didn't Charlie come? You don't strike me as a loner – I don't mean that in a bad way, just that you're so . . . effervescent.' She laughed self-consciously.

'Effervescent!' Lila repeated. 'That's a lot better than some of the things I've been called recently.'

86

Keeley's eyes widened. 'By Charlie? Is that why she's not here?'

'No, Charlie's been brilliant. This was something that happened in London. It's why I came to Cornwall, actually.'

'Oh? What was that then?'

Lila glanced around her. She didn't want to fob Keeley off the same way she had done with Holden – she was sure she wouldn't see the Australian after tonight – but she didn't want to go through the whole story again. The sun had gone and everything was awash with moonlight, the cliffs on either side of the cove forming dark hulks of shadow stretching up to meet the midnight-blue sky.

'Just a mistake I made,' Lila said, reaching over to the pile of refreshments and taking a large bag of crisps. It wasn't the most spiritual snack, but she was suddenly starving. 'Something that happened between me and my best friend, Clara. Cornwall is a chance for me to get some space from it all.'

'Do you want to talk about it?' Keeley asked. 'You don't have to, but I know it sometimes helps to get it all out there.'

'That's exactly what Holden said,' Lila whispered.

'Who's Holden?'

Lila pointed behind Keeley, where Holden had his back to them, deep in conversation with the person beyond him. 'Beautiful Aussie,' she murmured. 'I was talking to him when you turned up.'

'So I've ruined your chance at happiness with a beautiful Australian?' Keeley said, matching Lila's quiet tone.

'I don't think we were destined to be. And I'd much rather talk to you.'

'About what happened in London?'

Lila shook her head. 'Not right now. Let's just say that

even matching unicorn tattoos aren't a guarantee of ever-lasting friendship.'

'You and your friend – Clara, is it? – have matching unicorn tattoos?' Keeley's eyes widened.

Lila grinned and leaned to the side, pushing down her jeans to reveal the multicoloured illustration on her hip. It was small, but beautiful. She didn't regret it, because it tied her and Clara together.

Keeley leaned in close. 'That is ridiculous. But also pretty awesome.'

'Kitsch is cool.'

'But despite your matching tattoos, you think your friend-ship is over?'

Lila wanted more than anything to mend her friendship with Clara, but she knew a lost cause when she met one, and that day, standing on the pavement flinging insults at each other, had felt like the very definition of a lost cause. But tonight was not the night to go over it; she didn't want to rake over it again with Keeley just as they were getting to know each other.

'It's all a bit complicated. I'm giving Clara – both of us – some space. Anyway, I want to hear what it's like being an actress, working with Toby and Aria – and Sam, of course.'

'Ah, Sam,' Keeley said, her lips tugging up at the corners. 'We're like this.' She crossed her fingers to demonstrate. 'We're the newbies, learning the ropes, falling over our feet and spending half our time in astounded wonder that we're actu-ally here. We've both done smaller roles, of course – we've each been in an episode of *Doctors*, though not the *same* episode. We've done adverts, I had a small part in a BBC3 series, and Sam has had several theatre gigs. But for both of us it's our first time in lead roles, and in a drama of this size.'

'Are you together?' Lila shifted her position, the sand beneath her suddenly uncomfortable.

'Oh no,' Keeley laughed, 'not like that. I've left the love of my life, Jordan, up in Derbyshire. That's been the hardest part of this.'

'Is he going to come and visit the set?'

'Oh sure – he can't wait! But we both think it's best if I get a few weeks under my belt. We talk all the time. And of course this is my dream part, but it's also a bit bewildering. Foreign territory. I shouldn't moan, but . . . this, tonight, it's great.' She gave Lila the full force of her beautiful smile. She would, Lila knew, light up the screen. 'I've been so inside the character, which sounds strange when you're playing a ghost, but the whole point is that she was this young woman who had everything ahead of her, and then died tragically. I'm absorbed in it, which is a wonderful place to be, but . . .'

'You don't feel like you, quite,' Lila finished.

'Exactly. And I know it's something I have to get used to. And I *will*, because you can't turn down chances like this, or run away the moment it feels difficult. But nights off like tonight – it's all about balance. And Sam, too, helps me keep things in perspective. He's like my big brother. He's very funny.'

'Is he?' Lila was surprised. 'He comes across as a bit . . . awkward. Which seems strange for an actor.'

'He's not like that at all,' Keeley said. 'Once you get to know him, you'll see. And all of us, although it sounds a bit poncy to say, if we come onto the bus and we've just finished on set, our heads might still be in the character. I'll bring Sam on board with me for that cream tea, if you like.'

'That would be perfect,' Lila said enthusiastically. 'Having two of *Estelle*'s stars, including Estelle herself, on the Cornish

Cream Tea Bus for a whole cream tea will make a huge difference. If I'm still there on Monday, and Winston hasn't kicked me off set for absconding.'

'He won't, I promise. Oooh look, something's happening.'

The people around the fire were getting up and walking across the sand to gather around the second bonfire. 'It must be some sort of solstice ritual. I love all that stuff – chanting and symbols and spiritualism.'

'What about spirits? Are ghost stories your thing?'

'They are when they're set in Cornwall and have bus cafés as part of their catering team,' Lila said. 'Let's go and get in the thick of it.' They got to their feet and went to join the others. Holden greeted them with an unabashed smile that displayed, even in the moonlight, pearly white teeth.

The blond man Lila had met on arrival handed out candles, and everyone faced away from the sea, in the direction the sun was due to rise, cupping their flames with their hands to shield them from the wind. He recited a poem, his deep voice carrying over the sound of the waves, and Lila shivered when he talked about light and dark being equal, about shedding your old skin in preparation for the new season. He finished by getting everyone to make a silent wish, and Lila wished that she could find the strength to make amends for her mistakes, to learn from what Clara had said and step into spring a better, wiser person.

After that, the night slipped away from them, the anticipated daybreak making its slow, golden appearance behind the cliffs, so that the beach and water were cast in a strange yellow light long before the sun itself was visible.

'I should get back,' Keeley said, handing Lila a bottle of water. 'I promised Sam I'd rehearse with him this morning.'

'You don't get any rest, even on Saturdays?'

'We do, but we're both aiming to be pitch perfect, and weekends are our chance. What about you? Is Gertie back in the village?'

Lila nodded. 'I need to go and pick up Charlie, so she can drive the bus back to Porthgolow for a Saturday on the beach.'

'She knows you were out here?' Keeley asked.

'I messaged her to tell her I was celebrating the equinox. I didn't mention I left the set early, though.' She made a face. 'Do you need a lift back?'

'It's fine, Sarah will take me. Have a good weekend, Lila. I'll see you on Monday.'

'Don't forget about that cream tea! I'm counting on you and Sam to give Gertie your undivided attention for half an hour, minimum.'

'I'll be there.' She gave Lila a quick hug and went to join Sarah.

Lila watched her go, then turned away from the beach and the dying embers of the fires.

She'd had fun with Keeley and, while she wasn't entirely sure she believed wholly in the power of the equinox festival, she couldn't deny that she felt lighter, freer somehow. The sea sparkled behind her, the golden, glowing sun of a new season was ahead of her, and Lila realized that she could use her time on *Estelle* to step out of the shadow of Clara's condemnations and rebuild her confidence. As long as Winston let her stay, she would work hard, stick to the rules, and show that she was capable and trustworthy – all the things that had been called into question in her old life.

She had to show Charlie and Winston, Gregor, Keeley and Sam that she could do this. Most of all, she had to prove it to herself. Lila was starting again, and there wasn't a moment to lose.

Chapter Eight

'You cannot do that, Delilah. Not under any circum-stances.'

She was leaning against Gertie's kitchen counter and Winston was standing in the middle of the aisle, filling the bus with his curly hair and his anger. The bounciness Lila had been feeling over the weekend had evaporated, and she'd only been back on board an hour. But she had known this was coming, at least. Keeley's warning meant that she was prepared for the dressing-down.

'I'm so sorry, Winston. It won't happen again.'

'You're here for the cast and crew, whenever they need you. That's the nature of the work.'

'I do understand.' She found she was clasping her hands together in front of her, pious. After spending time with Keeley on Friday night, she knew that she didn't want to lose this job. She had realized just how much she wanted to be here, right after doing something that could take it away from her. This was typical Lila behaviour. 'Can you put it down to inexperience – to idiocy, if you like – and give me one final chance?'

Winston ran his hand through his pale curls, and they sprang back into place. He was wearing a heavy wax coat, and Lila thought a couple of lurchers at his heels would complete the image. 'We don't want to lose you,' he said after a moment. 'You're good for our Cornish image and, aside from what happened on Friday night, I've heard nothing but good things about your refreshments. *Excellent* things from some quarters, in fact.'

The relief was instant. Lila grinned. 'How about I treat you to a coffee and a sausage roll now? They're fresh.'

She and Charlie had spent Sunday evening baking, and Charlie had driven the fully replenished bus back this morning, Lila following in her Volvo, and then caught a lift into Truro with Juliette. Lila had mentioned how ridiculous it was to have to do a three-car convoy to get everyone where they needed to be, but Charlie had reminded her it was only at the beginning and end of each week, and with her having time to set everything up for the summer, it would be worth it.

'To make up for Friday?' Winston asked, but the anger had gone from his eyes. 'Sure.'

Lila obliged, drinking in the invigorating aroma of the coffee as she made it, knowing she had got off lightly.

Once Winston had gone, satisfied and placated with his flaky pastry sausage roll and a steaming latte, Lila sagged against the counter. She hoped Winston would pass on her apology to Gregor. She was safe, and she wanted to stay that way. She took one of Charlie's notebooks out of a drawer and started making a list. Coffee was the one thing she could bring to the Cornish Cream Tea Bus – her time at The Espresso Lounge had taught her to turn coffee into more than just a caffeine hit, and she wanted to use those skills.

She was so absorbed in her notes that she jumped when

a familiar male voice said, 'Sam Magee and Keeley Klein, reporting for cream tea duty, ma'am.'

Lila looked up and, for a moment, couldn't speak.

Up until now she had only seen Sam and Keeley off duty, but today they were dressed as their characters. Keeley's Estelle outfit was a simple white gown with hardly any decoration, almost like an old-fashioned nightgown. But then, Lila thought, Keeley didn't need any embellishments – she looked startlingly beautiful. And Sam. *Sam.* His lean frame and subtly tanned skin carried off the white shirt and breeches well. His waistcoat was a deep burgundy, with a design of twisting golden foliage, and his hair had been artfully ruffled by something other than the coastal wind. She flashed a quick glance at his knee-high, polished boots, then quickly looked away.

'Well,' she said, but it came out more like a heavy breath.

'How are you?' Keeley asked. 'After Winston?'

'Surviving!' Lila said. 'I've got a second chance and I plan to make the most of it, starting with two of Gertie's famous-all-over-Cornwall cream teas. You both look amazing, by the way.' Her eyes flickered to Sam and then back to Keeley, who was somehow easier to focus on. 'Take a seat.'

They sat at the table closest to the kitchen, next to each other so that they both faced Lila while she worked.

'I heard all about the solstice festival,' Sam said. 'I was tucked up safely in my digs while you were partying on the beach. I can't believe neither of you invited me.'

'It was a coincidence that we ended up there together,' Keeley said, as Lila put a teapot and two mugs on the table.

'Well, not really, because I overheard Sarah, one of the crew, talking about it,' Lila added. 'But I do sort of feel it was meant to happen.'

'Fate, you mean?' Sam said. 'You believe in fate, then?'

'Don't you?' Lila asked.

He leaned back in his chair. 'I kind of hope that the decisions I make have consequences, that I'm – at least partly – in charge of my own future.'

Lila wrinkled her nose. She opened the oven door and, after stepping back from the initial blast of heat, pushed her finger against one of the scones. It needed a couple more minutes. 'Well, of course,' she said. 'But when things work out so well, and so unexpectedly, don't you ever wonder whether there's something else at play? I feel like it was fate that I ended up in Porthgolow, looking after the bus when Winston came on board, and we got the gig to be here.'

'You and the bus being here is certainly a bonus,' he said, smiling. 'But do you let divine intervention explain away your whole life? That seems like a . . . well, a bit of a cheat, really.'

'If it was divine then my life would have been a lot smoother than it has been up to this point.'

'But you allow it to account for what happens to you?' Sam poured the tea, his concentration on the task in hand, and Lila felt both relieved and disappointed that his gaze had left hers.

She shrugged. 'Not all of it. I am wholly, entirely responsible for the mistakes I make.'

Sam looked up at that, his lips tugging up in amusement.

'But then I feel like fate, *something*, puts me back on track,' she continued. 'Takes my fuck-ups and puts a positive spin on them.'

'That's even worse,' Sam said loudly, laughing. The hint of an accent she'd noticed when she'd first met him was suddenly stronger, giving itself away. It was Irish. God, she loved an Irish accent. She wondered whether, if she asked nicely, he would speak to her in a full Irish brogue.

'Why is that worse?' She took the scones out of the oven and put them on the cooling rack, then filled two earthenware pots with dollops of local strawberry jam.

'Because it means you're giving yourself credit for all the bad stuff and none of the good. Do you really have that low an opinion of yourself?' He said it lightly, but she could tell he was genuinely curious.

Lila paused, a large blob of clotted cream hovering above its pot. 'I don't think I do. I just know when I've got things wrong.'

'But you palm off all your victories to some invisible deity, or fate, or whatever?' Sam seemed annoyed suddenly, all his levity gone. She'd never seen him look anything other than placid, and his handsome features cast so severely made him seem stern and commanding. She went quickly back to her cream tea assembly.

'Sam,' Keeley murmured, and Lila saw her put a hand on his arm. His shoulders dropped and he sat back in his chair.

'Sorry, Lila, I just—'

'He stood up for you, you know,' Keeley cut in.

Now it was Sam's turn to whisper to Keeley. He kept his voice low, but Lila still heard it: '*There's no need to tell her.*'

Keeley carried on as if he hadn't spoken. 'When Winston was on his way to see you this morning, hopping mad after Gregor told him what had happened on Friday night, Sam did this whole speech about how much you and Gertie added to the craft service, how it wasn't just great coffee, health-conscious muffins and occasional indulgent treats, but it was a lovely place to come and relax, and how nice you and

Charlie were. He stood there, dressed as Robert Bramerton, and made your case. It was . . . stirring.'

Lila's stomach flipped as she brought the scones over to the table, then went back for the pots of jam and cream. 'That was very nice of you,' she said. It sounded strangled, ungrateful, which was not how she'd meant it at all. She couldn't seem to act normally around him, his presence sending everything slightly off-kilter. When she glanced up, Sam had a flush of pink across his cheekbones. She thought they must be mirroring each other.

'It's all true,' he said. 'Not that Keeley needed to give me away. But I'd miss you, if you weren't here. Gertie, I mean. The coffee, the muffins. But you too obviously.' He lifted his hand to his forehead, as if to run it through his hair, and then stopped. He noticed her watching him. 'Can't mess it up, or I'm back to the hair and make-up trailer for more poking about.'

'Ah, of course,' Lila said. 'It looks beautifully tousled. I can see why you're not allowed to touch it.'

'Thank you so much for this,' Keeley said, digging her knife into the pot of cream.

'No!' Lila shouted, louder than she'd meant to. Keeley froze. 'God, sorry. Ignore me. I'm being an idiot.'

'You were about to serve us poisoned scones, and now you've realized you actually quite like us and want to spare our lives?' Sam's smile broke the tension.

Lila laughed, her composure returning. 'No, I quite liked you from day one, actually.' And just like that, it was gone again. She swallowed. 'I shouted because Keeley was about to make a *Devon* cream tea. You can't put the cream on the scone first or you'll be hounded out of Cornwall.'

'We will?'

'If anyone else sees, you might be. But honestly, it doesn't matter, I've just had it drummed into me by Charlie. Whenever a customer asks for the scones to be loaded up, I have to do the jam first. I thought I'd leave you to add your own toppings, seeing as how you're so conscious about what you eat and fitting into corsets and uhm . . . tight breeches.' She cleared her throat. 'But maybe that was a mistake, and allowing you to put it together yourself has left you exposed. It's a dangerous thing, this cream tea business. You have to get it right.'

'OK,' Sam said, matching her faux seriousness. 'So. Jam first. Understood.' He added jam and cream to his scone, his movements slow and deliberate. Lila watched for a moment, and then made herself a coffee, smiling at their appreciative groans.

'Oh wow,' Keeley said. 'This is amazing.'

'Bloody gorgeous,' Sam agreed.

Lila sipped her drink and felt a swell of accomplishment. As long as she turned up on time and stayed until she was supposed to, as long as she continued to offer delicious refreshments to the cast and crew, then she would stay out of trouble. It was straightforward and, while Charlie busied herself with summer plans, it was hers.

Warmth pooled in her stomach as she watched Keeley take small but committed bites of the scone, and Sam, elbows on the table, looking happy and relaxed despite his formal attire. She still had so many questions: what scene were they filming next, where did it come in the story, were those clothes comfortable or itchy, what were their trailers like? But they had come here for a break, not an inquisition, and Keeley was doing her a favour.

And, it seemed as if she wasn't the only one who had Lila's back.

Had Sam really said those things to Winston, or had Keeley been exaggerating? She wanted, suddenly, to see him in action. She wanted to watch Robert Bramerton striding across the beach or along the cliffs in his shiny boots, hair tugged out of its artful shape by a merciless Cornish wind.

Lila restacked the mugs, trying to picture Toby and Aria, and how beautiful they had been. She could remember their visit, of course – it had only been a couple of days ago – but she didn't feel the same flush of heat at the thought of Toby in all his magnificence as she did when she thought of Sam. And looking at him set off all kinds of strange sensations inside her.

Sam Magee, actor – soon to be incredibly famous actor, if *Estelle* was as big as they were predicting – not a believer in fate but kind, honest, and looks great with a puppy. Looks especially incredible in a crisp white shirt and skintight breeches. She spent an indulgent moment imagining him in his current outfit while also cuddling Marmite. She would have to bring Charlie's dog back on set.

But no. *No.* She couldn't have these thoughts. She didn't know Sam, and she had just promised herself that she was going to be fully committed to the Cornish Cream Tea Bus. One thing that always, *always always,* resulted in disaster, was mixing business and romance. Granted, it hadn't been the cause of her latest calamity, but that didn't mean she could get away with it while she was here. Though it was his fault for turning up looking roguishly handsome and also, apparently, saying nice things about her. But she would not trust her feelings today, when she'd just survived the wrath of Winston and had been given a second chance. It was just endorphins, or something similar. Tomorrow, her emotions and her mindset would be firmly back in place, wholly focused on her job.

'We've run out of time,' Keeley said, draining the last of her tea and standing. 'But I can safely say that was the best cream tea I've had, and I will be shouting about it to everyone. Be prepared to get busy, Lila.' Sam stood too, slipping out from behind the table to let Keeley past. Keeley walked to the door while Sam hovered, uncertain, before approaching Lila. She held her breath. The modern surroundings did nothing to dampen the effect of his outfit.

'That was delicious,' he said. 'And all your own work, as far as I can see. No fairies or angels hovering over your shoulder.'

'No.' Lila smiled. 'But Charlie made the scones.'

He rolled his eyes. 'You're great, Lila. Believe it.' He squeezed her arm, his fingers warm. He smelt fresh and woody, a lingering hint of some scent that had mostly been obliterated by the brisk wind.

'See you tomorrow?'

'There'll be no keeping me away, now. Not with cream teas like that, I mean,' he clarified, his cheeks flushing.

'You're Irish,' she blurted as he started to walk away from her.

He turned around. 'I am, on my dad's side. But we moved away when I was three.'

'Will you speak to me in a proper Irish accent sometime?'

Sam grinned. 'I would say I'm not a performing monkey, but actually, that is pretty much what I am. Maybe, Delilah. *One day*.' He said the last two words in an Irish lilt, and she laughed.

Sam and Keeley left the bus together, waving their good-byes, leaving Lila wondering at the wisdom of asking Sam to reveal more of himself to her. She was treading into dangerous territory, because surely if she asked that of him

100

and he obliged, she would have to give him something in return. In the face of his kindness and his warmth, his apparent complete lack of starriness, and despite her claim that she didn't have a low opinion of herself, she was pretty sure she would be found wanting.

Chapter Nine

By the time Lila locked up the Cornish Cream Tea Bus – and it was well after seven when Catering Manager Em came to tell her that filming had finished for the day – she was more than ready for home. Keeley and Sam had worked their magic, and while nobody else took the time to sit down on board Gertie, several crew members, as well as the actor who was playing the country estate's grizzly groundsman, asked for a Cornish cream tea to go. Lila was glad Charlie hadn't been there to watch her mashing the jam- and cream-filled scones together and putting them in a paper bag; it upset *her* sensibilities, so she could just imagine how Charlie would have reacted.

As she drove back to Porthgolow, the sunset was partially hidden by a fractured wall of cloud, peaches and pinks cracking through the grey and turning the water to fire. She approached the village from the south, slowing around Crumbling Cliff, the verge marked by a sturdy-looking barrier that stopped people getting too close to the edge. She knew, now, why that had been put up.

As she parked outside Charlie's house, she saw that the window was aglow, and she put her key in the lock with a weary triumph.

'Hello?' she called. 'Charlie, are you here?'

'Lila, hi.' Daniel greeted her, holding out a glass of red wine while Marmite and Jasper snuffled at her feet. She held the wine above her head and crouched, making a fuss of the dogs, resisting when the Yorkipoo tried to scrabble onto her knees.

'Give her a minute,' Daniel said, lifting Marmite up. She found it endearing that he spoke to the dogs as if they could understand him perfectly.

'I'm sorry,' she said. 'I didn't realize you and Charlie were having a night in. Do you want me to go to the pub?'

'Of course not,' Charlie cut in, appearing in the doorway. 'I wanted you both here.' She took Daniel's hand, the gesture somehow significant.

Lila's insides lurched but she kept quiet, waiting for her cousin to continue.

'How was your day?' Charlie asked. 'Eventful? Had any run-ins with any producers?'

Lila winced and sank onto the sofa. 'You know?'

Charlie nodded. 'I had to call him about something, so . . . but it looks like you're a hit, despite disappearing on Friday night. Why didn't you tell me you'd left the set early to go to the party? Anyway, Winston was very complimentary. He said some of the cast were big fans already.'

'*We're* a hit, Charlie. It's your bus. I'm just tagging along for the ride.' She watched as Daniel and Charlie exchanged a look, and then Daniel sat next to her, and Charlie went into the kitchen and started lifting pan lids. The whole place smelled delicious, but suddenly she wasn't hungry. 'What?' she asked Daniel. 'What was that look for?'

'Lila,' Daniel started, just as Jasper nosed his knee, spilling his wine. He hadn't changed out of his work clothes, she noticed. 'Shit! Jasper.' He shook his head, chiding the dog gently, and then followed Charlie into the kitchen, where they started up a whispered conversation that Lila couldn't hear.

She thought about her comment that she was just tagging along, and the *look*, and knew exactly why Charlie wanted to talk to her. She hid her face in her hands, knowing that in a few moments she would be told she'd outstayed her welcome, that Charlie wanted her spare room back. She pictured Gertie, sitting proudly on the *Estelle* set, and tried to imagine not seeing Keeley, or Sam, or Toby again. What would it be like, returning to London, but without the promise of her best friend to spend time with whenever she wanted?

She joined the others in the kitchen. 'I can find somewhere to rent. I bet there are houses in this area on short-term lease – a few months, maybe. I'm not ready to go back to London.'

'Who said anything about London?' Charlie asked. 'Do you want to go back? What about *Estelle*?' She looked alarmed, and Lila tried to untangle the knots in her brain.

'You aren't kicking me out?'

Charlie put down her serving spoon. 'Of course not. What made you think that?'

'I just . . . you said that . . . I don't know.' She shrugged.

'The reason we wanted to talk to you is pretty much the opposite of that. Let's get dinner on the table and I'll explain everything.'

Lila set the table while Charlie served up bowls of steaming vegetable bolognese, covered liberally with parmesan, and Daniel topped up their wine glasses. They all dug into the food, and Lila tried to pace herself and not tip the whole, delicious thing into her mouth.

'This is just what I needed,' she said.

'It went OK today, on Gertie?' Charlie asked. Lila thought there was a hint of longing in her voice. 'Despite everything with Winston?'

'He told me off,' Lila said, 'but it was no more than I deserved. He was actually quite lovely after that, and then Keeley and Sam had a full, sit-down cream tea, then spread the word around set, so I was busier than ever this afternoon.'

'That's great,' Charlie said. 'I'm so pleased it's working out.'

Lila chewed her nail. It didn't taste as nice as the bolognese. 'So am I. I know I shouldn't have left early on Friday, but I've made a promise to myself, to everyone, that I am fully, one-hundred-per-cent committed to this. Gertie and *Estelle*. A match made in heaven.'

Her cousin let out a sigh. 'That is excellent news. Because we have something to ask you.'

'OK.' Lila looked between her and Daniel.

He spoke next, resting his elbows on the table. 'I've been offered a place on a course for hoteliers, about turning Crystal Waters into an eco-hotel. It's something I've been thinking about for a while, and this course is hugely popular, so getting a spot is a big deal. Not something to be turned down.'

'That's great,' Lila said. 'Reducing your carbon footprint is the thing these days, isn't it? And you've got enough sun hitting Crystal Waters that solar panels are a no-brainer—'

'The thing is, Lila,' Charlie cut in, 'the course is in San Francisco.'

'Oh. Wow! Well, then . . .' She twirled spaghetti round her fork, wondering what any of this had to do with her.

'And I want to go with him.'

Lila stopped twirling. Charlie looked anxious. Daniel's expression was inscrutable. She wanted to chisel away that blank, handsome layer and find some real emotion underneath. But that wasn't the pressing issue. 'For how long? When? What about . . . what about Gertie?'

'That's the thing,' Charlie said. 'You're here now, and so I thought . . .'

'We'll be away for four weeks,' Daniel added, 'from next week. We'd like to travel a bit, make a holiday of it. Obviously flying to America isn't the most eco-friendly thing – the irony is not lost on me – so we want to fit in more than just the course. What Charlie's trying to ask is, would you be happy to run Gertie alone for the next month, take Marmite with you, and look after him?'

Lila glanced at the dogs lying prone in front of the fireplace.

'What about Jasper?'

'My neighbour Lily is happy to look after him during the day, but if you could have him with you in the evenings, we'd really appreciate it. He's usually very well behaved, as you've seen. He's certainly a lot better behaved than Marmite.'

'Hey!' Charlie said.

Lila smiled at Daniel, and he returned it. She saw it then, the hint of uncertainty. He'd put his offer on the table in his usual no-nonsense way, but he wasn't as confident as he was making out. He obviously really wanted this; the course to improve his hotel, and the chance to be with Charlie for a whole month with no spa or bus responsibilities.

'I suppose you don't get much of a chance at holidays, running the sort of businesses you do,' Lila said.

'The only reason I have the faintest glimmer of hope at

going with Daniel is because you're here,' Charlie rushed. 'I know it's a big ask, leaving you in sole charge of Gertie, looking after Marmite, and Jasper too. Winston said the catering team would support you, and I'm going to ask Amanda if she can pitch in with the baking, so you don't have to cover that as well as being on set every day, but even so, it's a lot. I'd love to go with Daniel, and then when we come back, we'll have the summer together. You can stay as long as you want, Lila. Porthgolow in summer is really special. But . . .'

'But I'd be in charge for four whole weeks, by myself!'

She thought how many opportunities that would give her to get things wrong. And then she thought of Sam telling her that she was great, his hand wrapped around her arm, his amber eyes holding hers. Winston had given her another chance. He saw something in her, too. And Charlie and Daniel . . . Charlie, especially, was putting her life in Lila's hands, despite what had happened in London. Her beautiful bus, her home, her adorable dog. She wouldn't risk that if she didn't think Lila could do it.

'You'd be great,' Charlie said. She was leaning over the table, as if trying to reason with a distracted child. 'You've been there on your own now—'

'For two days. And on one of those, I nearly got us kicked off the set.'

'You've got your mistakes out of the way early,' Daniel cut in smoothly. 'As a business strategy, it's not too bad.'

'Daniel—'

'And as Charlie says, you'll be great. You've got the energy, the enthusiasm. Everything else you can work on.'

'I don't have a licence to drive the bus. You've shown me how to drive it, and I managed to get it round an empty

107

car park without crashing into a barrier, but I can't *legally* drive it.'

'You won't need to drive the bus,' Charlie said. 'The production is moving to St Eval next week, and there are a couple of other locations while I'm away, but when I spoke to Winston he said Mike or Claude would be able to drive Gertie – they're both qualified. We've got everything covered. We'll be at the end of the phone whenever you need us, even if the time zones make things a bit awkward. Juliette and Lawrence are here, and Jules knows Gertie like the back of her hand. You could take her with you for a day or two if she's not too busy. You wouldn't be alone.'

Lila nodded. 'OK. It's . . . a lot to take in. I'm going to be in charge. Me. Of Gertie and Marmite. I'll be holding your reputation in these hands, Charlie.' She lifted her hands and cupped them together in front of her, as if Charlie's reputation was a pile of sand that could, so easily, slip through her fingers.

Charlie grasped them. 'Does that mean you'll do it? You don't want time to think?'

'Charlie,' Daniel murmured, 'don't try and talk her out of it. Lila.' He gave her a steady stare. 'We know how much we're asking, and that, if you agree to this, we will be in your debt. But it would mean a lot, to Charlie and to me . . .' His words trailed off as Lila shook her head. 'You're not . . .?'

'I am,' Lila said. 'I will be in charge of Gertie, look after Marmite – and Jasper – take care of your cosy little house, and make sure everything is just as you left it when you get back.'

'But you were shaking your head,' Charlie said.

'Because you won't be in my debt,' Lila replied, a laugh escaping. 'You've let me stay with you for a whole month.

You didn't go nuts – or not as nuts as I thought you would – when I got us involved with *Estelle* and forced you to change all your plans. You've both looked after me, and now you're letting me look after the Cornish Cream Tea Bus. I promise I won't let you down. Go and have an amazing time! Learn how to be the eco-king, Daniel.'

'Oh Lila! Thank you!' Charlie came around the table and wrapped Lila in a hug. When she'd finally let her go, it was Daniel's turn. His embrace was brief, but no less warm.

'Thank you for doing this,' he said.

'It's no problem. No problem at all.'

She basked in the glow of contentment, of being able to do something for Charlie, who had already done so much for her.

They finished their food and moved to the sofa, and Lila clutched her wine glass, feeling the tug of sleep. Daniel and Charlie had both visibly relaxed, and she sensed they were eager to talk about their upcoming trip, to enjoy the excited anticipation, to plan all the places they wanted to visit together.

'I'm off to bed,' she said.

'Night, Lila,' Daniel replied. 'And thank you, again.'

'You are, without a doubt, the *best*.' Charlie gave her another hug, and Lila left them to it, smiling as Marmite bounded up the stairs behind her, hoping for a soft spot to sleep on at the end of Lila's duvet. She welcomed the warm bundle of fur, the fact that, even though it was a dog rather than a man, she wouldn't be alone in bed that night. She wondered if Charlie would return from America with a sparkly ring as well as a holiday tan. She and Daniel were clearly meant to be together, and Lila turning up had given them the chance to have this wonderful, romantic trip together. Another mark in fate's favour.

Thinking about fate led her on to Sam, and she realized that he hadn't been far away for the entire evening, hovering in her thoughts in his white shirt and waistcoat, his sculpted hair and his half-smile. But he was a distraction, albeit a beautiful one. She was committed now, responsible for protecting the reputation of the Cornish Cream Tea Bus and making its time with *Estelle* a success. She could not allow herself to give in to beautiful distractions.

Lila cleaned her teeth, put on her pyjamas and got into bed, pulling the duvet up to her chin. Marmite settled on her feet, and she closed her eyes, deciding that if it wasn't fate, then it was some other kind of divine intervention that had led her here, to Porthgolow and Charlie, Marmite and *Estelle*. She had a chance to redeem herself, and that was exactly what she intended to do.

Part Two

Beauty and the Yeast

Chapter Ten

The sky was a muted grey, the wind tugging at the grass that edged the cliff top, the sound of crashing waves far below them distant, but still foreboding. Robert Bramerton strode forwards and then stopped, his handsome brow creasing, lips parting. Confusion and intrigue painted his features while the woman watched on, her dress twisting around her legs, her bare feet dusted with dirt. Her hand flickered up to her throat, the pale curls and skin making her seem almost translucent against the washed-out sky. But even from here, Delilah Forest could see the blue of her eyes.

Mesmerizing. The whole thing was mesmerizing.

'Estelle?' Robert Bramerton said, somehow managing to make it both a question and a statement. It was the moment, Lila knew, when he'd figured out who the spectre was, the presence who he'd been seeing, sensing, since he and his brother had moved to Cornwall, to the huge, crumbling house they'd inherited. His hand reached out slowly, reverently, to the woman clad in white, and then Gregor, the director, shouted, 'Cut!' breaking the spell.

Lila blinked and realized her heart was thumping, that she had been wholly engrossed in the moment, even though it was two people standing on a cliff top, saying hardly anything to each other. This time, she hadn't even glanced between the action and the monitor she was lurking behind. She had wanted to see it live, to stamp it into her memory: to be able to say she had been there when Keeley Klein and Sam Magee starred together in *Estelle*, thus securing their respective roads to superstardom.

She slipped away from the crowd of people – there was always a huge crowd hovering close to the action – and hurried back to the Cornish Cream Tea Bus, where she had left a tray of cherry scones on the cooling rack. Amanda had brought them round to Charlie's house yesterday evening, one of a number of different cakes and pastries she had baked, helping Lila out while she was in sole charge of the bus.

'Hello, Marmite,' Lila said as she checked on him. The Yorkipoo yapped in approval and turned around twice before settling back down on the driver's seat. It was still early, but Gregor had wanted the pure, post-dawn light for that scene, and Lila had to admit it had made everything look ghostly, almost magical.

She prodded her scones and surveyed her tiny kingdom, a smile on her face.

Charlie and Daniel had been gone for five days. Lila had waved them off from the doorway of Charlie's house, her cousin giddy with excitement about their American trip, Daniel not that much more composed. Their happiness had made Lila happy, but then she'd spent the evening in a state of pure terror, sitting on the sofa with Marmite on one side of her, and Jasper, Daniel's German shepherd, on the other, even though she was sure Charlie would have frowned at the large dog denting her sofa cushions.

She was responsible for Gertie, the dogs, and Charlie's house, which seemed like a *lot*. But when she had turned up at work the day after Charlie's departure, Keeley had bounded on board and given her a wordless hug, and Lila had known everything would be OK.

'Coffee machine ready and raring?' asked a voice, and Lila blinked herself back to the present.

'Of course,' she said to the imposing man with a salt and pepper beard, shock of dark hair and the most expressive eyebrows she had ever seen. 'What would you like? Arabica or robusta beans? Light or dark roast? Latte, flat white, Americano, espresso?'

'Good God, girl! Are you attempting to befuddle me with your barista wizardry *again*?'

Lila laughed. 'Arabica bean Americano with a splash of hot milk, then.'

'Indeed.'

Lila set about making it while Bert stared out of the window. Lila had only met Bertrand Harridge on Friday, as he hadn't been needed for the first two weeks of filming. Playing a judge, and distant relative of the Bramerton brothers in the production, he was everything Lila had expected of an older actor, even though most of those expectations had been clichés. Bert unapologetically fitted every one. He was loud, extremely posh, and entirely lacking in subtlety, and within five minutes of meeting him, Lila adored him.

'Saw you watching the action,' he said mildly, his gaze still fixed on the scene beyond the window.

'I may have sneaked away for ten minutes,' Lila admitted, heating the milk for his coffee. 'It was beautiful.'

'Everything about *Estelle* is. This director, Gregor Whatnot, is supposedly a visionary. I'm impressed so far, though the proof of the pudding will be in the rushes.'

'Are you filming today?'

'You think I hang around places like this for the fun of it?'

'Silly question,' Lila said, grinning. 'Here's your coffee. Muffin, sausage roll, cheese and spinach pie?' She gestured to the impressive display, and Bert's eyes lit up.

'Cheese and spinach, eh? Did you nab these from Gregg's on your way in?' He gave her a twinkly smile and took one. 'Much obliged, Delilah. No doubt I'll be seeing you later.' He held up the pie in thanks and sauntered off the bus.

She wished he could remember to call her Lila. Her full name made her feel told off, and reminded her of the song, the mantra she'd chided herself with on too many occasions. The famous Tom Jones song that included the words 'why' and 'Delilah'.

But not now. Now, she was triumphing, even if she was more exhausted than she'd ever been.

'Did you really make all of these?' Lila turned to find Keeley, no longer in her white dress, but wearing jeans and an oversized green sweater.

'Some of them,' Lila said. 'But Charlie's enlisted the help of Amanda, her friend in Porthgolow, to do a lot of the baking while I'm here, and it's making things easier. I don't know how Charlie found the time to run the bus and do all the baking for it, too, before I turned up. But she's a pro. You were *amazing*, by the way. You and Sam.'

'When?' Keeley's fingers danced over the cake stands, playing Eenie Meenie Miney Mo.

'Just now. That scene, when Robert calls Estelle by her name for the first time; when he's done research into the previous occupants of the house and realized who she is. *Estelle*,' she said, dipping her voice and holding her hand out just as he had. 'I was gripped, and I was standing behind Gregor and all the millions of cameramen and lighting crew. When people are watching it on a forty-inch flat screen they'll be in awe.'

Keeley pressed her lips together, her blue eyes large.

'What?' Lila asked. 'I shouldn't *technically* have been watching, but Toby has sneakily given me some scripts, and this scene was one I really wanted to—'

'It's not that,' Keeley cut in. 'You really think it was good? I mean, Sam is undeniably brilliant. He doesn't need to say anything to convey a whole world of emotion, but I feel like a sack of potatoes. It's easier when there's dialogue.'

'What's easier?' Lila asked her, softly. 'You're a wonderful actor. You're not having a crisis of confidence, are you?'

Keeley gave her a wobbly smile. 'Low blood sugar. What's this?'

'Mozzarella and tomato slice. I can warm one up for you.'

'That sounds like bliss.'

Lila got to work while Keeley sat down, her hands hidden inside the sleeves of her sweatshirt. She was fidgeting, and Lila thought she looked uncomfortable, disquieted. With nobody else on the bus, Lila lifted Marmite out of the cab and put him on Keeley's lap. Keeley sneezed, then smiled.

'Aaah, Marmite, how are you?' Marmite barked, and Keeley laughed and hugged him.

When they were ready, Lila brought over a coffee and the warmed-up slice. 'Are you sure you're OK?'

'I'm fine,' Keeley said. 'Except that I had a fight with Jordan last night. I hate phone fights, where you can't see each other and words get distorted and there's no . . . touching or hugging or twitching lips, when you're trying not to laugh and you know it'll all be OK.'

Lila slipped into the seat opposite her. 'Was it a big fight?'

'He's busy at work, so he can't make it down here for another couple of weeks. He works a lot of weekends, so there's no point in me going home either – we'd have about half an hour together, which would just make things worse.'

'Have you heard from him this morning?'

'We always speak first thing, and we did, but there was some lingering frostiness.'

'That'll thaw,' Lila said. 'You love each other, don't you? You're soul mates, and you're both finding it tough to be apart for this long. But that's completely understandable, and you'll get through it.'

Keeley wiped a dribble of tomato juice off her chin. 'Why is it that we're always so wise about other people's relationships, but not our own?'

'Detachment,' Lila said immediately. 'We can look at it objectively, without emotion.'

'So true,' Keeley sighed. 'What about your love life? Anyone waiting for you in London?'

'Nope,' she said, reaching over to take Marmite, who was intent on helping Keeley finish her pastry. 'There hasn't been anyone for a while. The last boy, Nathaniel – and he was a Nathaniel, not a Nate or a Nathan – said I was too unpredictable. But he ironed his boxer shorts and had his alarm turned on at six o'clock at weekends. Needless to say it didn't last long, which is pretty much the story of my life.'

'Isn't unpredictable good in a relationship? If boyfriends came with a blurb and an instruction leaflet then things would be dull.'

Lila shrugged. 'It wasn't his fault. We just weren't a great match, despite the initial attraction.'

118

'What about that Ozzie guy at the equinox festival? Did you get his number?'

'Holden? No, I didn't talk to him again after you appeared. Besides, he was far too full of himself for my liking. All white teeth and arrogant, lazy grins. I bet underneath he was as shallow as a paddling pool – not that there's anything wrong with that, it's just not for me, the same way as I'm not everyone's cup of tea. I'm not neat or organized, I like adventure, so sue me.' She shrugged. 'Speaking of which, are you free at lunchtime? Em, the catering manager, makes sure someone from the team gives me a break every day now that Charlie's not here. I'm going to walk Marmite along the cliff, if you fancy it?'

'I am entirely at your service,' Keeley said. 'I'd love to go for a walk with the puppy.'

'Listen to that, Marmite,' Lila said. 'Keeley thinks you're still a pup. What a compliment.' Marmite snuffled his nose into Lila's apron, which was adorable until she realized she'd probably dropped some cream or sugar down it, and he was simply helping himself.

'Thank you for the refreshments and the chat,' Keeley said. 'What time are we puppy walking?'

'About one thirty?'

'Perfect. I'll see you then.'

The coastline around St Eval was the most impressive that Lila had ever seen, which was probably why they'd picked it as a prime filming location. The sea was wild and raw ahead of them, and the cliffs stretched for miles in both directions. It was the first time Lila felt she could really *see* the world, how it was shaped and put together, and that if she ever went into space, she would be able to look down and find this exact spot. She breathed in the sea salt and the icy clarity of the wind, along with this new perspective.

Marmite scuffled in the grass, his lead wound three times round her hand so that he couldn't stray too far towards the edge. She imagined that on a normal day it would be busy with hikers walking the path, instead of this strange, put-together community. The crash of the waves couldn't disguise the sounds of the set, the shouts and bangs, people and trucks and moving equipment, even though there was a good distance between the soft ground along the cliff top and the heavy vehicles. The contrast between the wildness of the landscape and the hive of human activity was startling.

'Have you ever seen anything like it?' Lila asked.

Keeley shook her head. 'It's all so vast. And it's nice not being quite so close to the edge, on this occasion.'

'Does Gregor push you? Not literally, I mean – wrong choice of words.' She grinned. 'I meant does he encourage you to get closer?'

'He wants the shot to feel precarious to the audience,' Keeley explained. 'For them to have that sense of jeopardy, that Robert is risking his life by following Estelle towards danger. Did you see us setting up this morning?' She crouched, peering at some pink flowers beginning to bud beneath their feet.

Lila shook her head. 'I only arrived once you were shooting.'

'He'd set out our marks, and Sam's was on this jut of rock that was just sort of . . . hovering above the water. It was like something out of Indiana Jones. You should have seen Sam's face when Gregor showed him.' Keeley laughed. 'He's such a mild-mannered person, but he looked as if he wanted to kill Gregor, and then he told him he had to be fucking kidding. The assistant director, Beth, had to persuade Gregor to move it in at the risk of losing one of his lead actors.'

'What did Gregor say? Art requires sacrifice,' Lila suggested in a dramatic voice. 'Either Sam survives, or he is lost to us forever and we reach a new level of authenticity!' She gestured wildly, doing a half-pirouette that almost sent her tripping over Marmite's lead and straight over the edge.

'Shit, Lila!' Keeley grabbed her sleeve, laughing. 'Don't be such an idiot. And no, Gregor did not say that. He said "you're probably right", and changed the set-up.'

'Ah, shame,' Lila said. 'And was Sam OK after that? He calmed down?'

She tried to keep her voice level. He had been on the bus almost every day, sometimes dressed as Robert Bramerton, sometimes as himself. But those amber eyes were always the same, and his deep voice with a hint of an Irish accent reverberated somewhere deep inside her. Not to mention that he was kind, warm, humble. She sometimes wished he had an actor's ego, that he was bold and brash and utterly self-absorbed, that he knew how gorgeous he was so she wouldn't waste any time thinking it, too. But nothing about him said look at me, and so, of course, Lila looked.

'He was fine,' Keeley said. 'You know Sam – he's so professional. Stepped on his new mark, rolled his shoulders, became Robert Bramerton.'

'And there's romance ahead for Robert Bramerton.' She knew this already, but she wanted to hear it from Keeley.

'There most definitely is. It's one of the reasons the brothers wage war with each other later on in the series.'

'Aria's character, Marianne?'

'The very same,' Keeley said. 'Things are going to get very tangled. You know, though? You said Toby had given you some scripts? I'm pretty sure he's not allowed to do that.'

'He's not,' Lila replied, 'but I was desperate to find out

what the plot was, and it does get boring sometimes, when there are no customers to serve – I know some of the scenes off by heart. But he's sort of drip-feeding them to me, which is pretty cruel when you think about it. You're not filming the scenes in order, but he's letting me see them episode by episode.' She huffed, and Keeley laughed.

'Everyone else will have to watch it in episode instalments. That's the point.'

'Yes, but I'm an insider,' Lila said. 'I shouldn't have to wait. I love reading it, but I also love sneaking down to see you in action, to see the words coming alive. I've just got to a bit with Robert and Marianne,' she added, trying to sound nonchalant.

'I think they're filming one of those big scenes later this week, actually.'

Lila nodded. Aria would look extra beautiful alongside Sam. Individually they were both impressive human beings, but together, they might work even better than Aria and Toby, because of their contrasting colouring – Aria was dark haired and pale skinned, whereas everything about Sam was dusty gold and bronzed. Lila decided she wouldn't go and watch that scene: not if it was the one that ended with Robert Bramerton and Marianne kissing.

'Why *don't* you film the scenes in order?' she asked, trying to take her mind off it. 'Doesn't it get confusing?'

'Not really,' Keeley said. 'We've read all the scripts – unlike you,' she added, grinning, 'and the filming schedule is based on location and actor availability. Imagine if there was a five-minute scene out here, and then a long scene inside the big house – which will be filmed on set in Bristol – then another one out here. That would make zero logistical sense.'

'I hadn't thought about it like that,' Lila said, as they began making their way back to the sprawling backstage village. 'But isn't it strange, if your character's got close to another character, to be doing the later scenes and then going back and filming encounters where you barely know each other?'

'But we're actors,' Keeley replied. 'It's our job to be good at that stuff!' Her eyes were dancing, and Lila noticed she looked much happier than she had earlier that day. She didn't mind if her ignorance was helping her friend feel better.

'And you are,' Lila said. 'Very good – brilliant, in fact.'

Keeley laughed and rolled her eyes, turning sideways as three runners carried what looked like a piece of scaffolding in the direction they had just come from. Lila hoped that wasn't another of Gregor's methods for giving the audience a sense of danger. She couldn't imagine any of the actors would be happy to wobble on that while it was balanced over the water.

'Ooh, I meant to tell you,' Keeley said, 'a few of the cast are getting together on Friday evening for some drinks. We're not sure where yet, but when I find out, do you want to come?'

Lila hesitated. 'If it's just the cast, then—'

'But I want you there. And you know Sam, and Aria a little. And you must be getting on with Toby if he's giving you scripts.'

'And Bert,' Lila added, grinning. 'Bert's great fun. I would love to come.' She wondered if she could ask Daniel's neighbour, Lily, to hold on to Jasper until later on.

'It's settled then,' Keeley said. 'I'll let you know as soon as we've got a destination.'

Chapter Eleven

Friday turned out to be beautiful, and as Lila drove from Porthgolow to St Eval, the sun was already making an appearance, shining in the window of the Volvo as if reminding her it still existed. She arrived on set and climbed out of the car, instinctively zipping up her maroon leather biker's jacket, only to discover that it was warmer than it looked. The spring in her step was mirrored by Marmite, who bounded beside her as she passed the make-up trailer and made her way to the catering area, and Gertie.

She was already bubbling with excitement about that evening, looking forward to spending time away from the set with some of the cast, soaking up their thespian vibes and hearing their stories. It was exactly the kind of thing she'd imagined doing when Winston had first appeared on the Cornish Cream Tea Bus and suggested they could be a part of *Estelle*. Lily had been happy to look after Jasper until Saturday morning, and Marmite could join in the fun – he was already popular with Sam and Keeley. She unlocked the bus, put the boxes of fresh scones and cakes on the counter, and turned on the coffee machine.

From that moment, everything went wrong.

Em was the first to appear, telling her that a lorry had spilled its load on the A39 and some of the crew were stuck en route from their accommodation. Em sighed, tapping distractedly on her clipboard, and then, without an explanation as to why that might affect Lila, left again, leaving her to look at Marmite in puzzlement.

Regulars came in for their coffees, and Lila's new halloumi bites were an instant hit, but everyone had a harried, impatient air.

'What's happening, Bert?' she asked, when he sauntered onto the bus, togged up in his nineteenth-century finery.

'It's all gone to hell in a handcart,' he declared, putting his nose close to Lila's new selection of bakes. 'Pret today, was it? These are rather more upper-class than your usual fare.'

'Yup, Pret A Manger gave me a job lot this morning, and they're only just out of date, so you shouldn't get *too* sick. Why's it gone to hell in a handcart?' She started making his coffee, writing his name in a swirling script on the takeaway cup with a purple sharpie.

'Because,' Bert said, sighing dramatically, 'Gregor is trapped in this pile-up of seashells, or whatever it is that's currently covering Cornwall's western artery, so nothing can begin. We have the actors,' he swept his arms wide, 'and most of the crew. We could start, were it not that our fearless leader is stuck in his Land Rover five miles away. Why he can't start walking is beyond me.'

'And you've got a heavy schedule today?'

'Made even more crucial by the weather; the light is on point, and it's a crying shame to lose any hours while it's quite literally smiling down on us.'

'Have a cake while you're waiting. Or a savoury. Halloumi

bite? Sausage roll? What about some of my *arancini*? They're one of my biggest hits. Or, if you've got loads of time, how about a cream tea? I know it's early yet, but—' Bert held up a finger, silencing her.

Lila hovered, feeling ridiculous.

'Things are afoot,' he said. 'I'll have to go and see what's happening.'

'Don't you get called if you're needed?' Lila asked, pouring hot milk into his coffee and putting the lid on.

'Sometimes,' he said, 'nobody knows I'm needed until I get there.' He gave her a devilish grin and swept off the bus. Lila thought he should have a cloak, to make the effect even more dramatic. She wondered if he'd ever played Dracula, and took out her phone to look him up on IMDb.

After that, all Lila's customers weren't just harried, but harassed. Sarah, who had accompanied Keeley to the equinox festival, told Lila that Gregor had eventually turned up, but he was in a foul mood because of the delay, and was shouting all kinds of insults about Cornwall and how backwards it was which, given the amount of local people working on set, wasn't a good look.

'So then Winston – because of *course* he's here today – got a face like thunder,' Sarah explained, popping a halloumi bite in her mouth, 'and started snapping at everyone, and now the whole place is on the verge of exploding. Which is *not* good, especially when we're filming one of the biggies today – the first clinch between Sam and Aria.'

Lila chewed the inside of her cheek. She wished Sarah had said 'the first clinch between *Robert* and *Marianne*'. 'That does all sound a bit fraught,' she admitted.

'Fraught isn't the word, my love. I'd better get back. See what firefighting needs to be done.' She took her hot chocolate, and another couple of halloumi bites, and left the bus.

Lila rested her head against the wall. 'Oh Marmite,' she said. 'Why do I care? I don't even know him, and he's so out of my league.'

Marmite barked as if in agreement, which she felt was a little mean.

She spent the time in between customers scribbling new cake and pastry ideas in her notebook, and trying not to read the Robert and Marianne scene over and over again in her pilfered script. She sent Charlie photographic proof of her industriousness, and asked how their holiday was going, hoping for some photos of blue skies and San Francisco landmarks in return. She didn't want to disturb them too much, but despite all the excitement of being on set, she was missing her cousin.

As the official wrap time approached, Em came on board, looking contrite. 'We're going to overrun this evening by at least an hour. You happy to hang on? I expect coffee will be needed.'

'Sure,' she said, and felt her hopes of some downtime with the cast slipping away. It had sounded too good to be true in the first place.

The sun was setting; with nothing else to distract her, the noises Lila had started to associate with the workings of a TV set – distant chatter, laughter, the constant slamming of trailer and truck doors – came into focus. She could hear the sea, but only as an undercurrent, like the rush of wind.

She wondered where exactly they were filming, what Sam and Aria were doing at this very moment. Were their lips locked together? Hands tight on waists, bodies pressed close? Their clinch wasn't real, and even if it was, she had no claim on him. He was just an almost-friend, someone she admired and got on with.

But she couldn't help wondering if, when they kissed, Sam and Aria would find that elusive connection that meant they were the new Charlie and Daniel, destined to be together forever, their personalities perfectly complementing each other. So many actors ended up in relationships. It made sense – it was an unusual, demanding job, surely helped by having someone who understood what you went through on a daily basis, the perks and pitfalls of fame.

Marmite yelped and put his front paws on the back of the driver's seat.

'Are any of these thoughts useful?' she asked, scooping him into her arms. Despite his small size he was heavy and solid, his fur softer than it looked. 'You know Marmite,' she added, 'if I didn't have you, then I don't know what—'

'We need your bus.'

Lila spun round and found Toby Welsh in the doorway, dressed in an approximation of his Henry Bramerton outfit, though the waistcoat and top few buttons of the shirt were undone, the frock coat nowhere to be seen.

'You do?' Lila asked.

'We're running so late, by the time we make it to the pub it'll be near closing, even if the road's been cleared by now. Keeley said you were up for tonight, so—'

'I am, but what has Gertie got to do with it?'

'Sly and Claude, on night security, said they would turn a blind eye if the bus left its position this evening, as long as it's back by morning. Apparently there's a secluded cove a couple of miles away, and with your cakes and a few bottles that can be provided, the pub idea pales into insignificance anyway.'

Lila chewed her lip. Toby Welsh wanted to turn Gertie

into a party bus, with her as the host. Except it wasn't her bus, and the reason the Routemaster would be staying on set over the weekend and not taking up its usual spot on the beach in Porthgolow was because Lila couldn't drive it there. She didn't have a licence. She had promised herself she'd be responsible.

'Toby—'

'It's been a tough day,' he continued. 'Gregor's put us through the wringer. Sam and Aria especially. I suppose we could go back to digs, there's a scruffy little local in the village, but . . .' he let his words trail away, his dark eyes holding hers.

Lila thought of Sam and Aria cosying up to each other in a quaint pub in front of a roaring fire, commiserating over their hard day, perhaps practising for another clinch later on in the story. She might not have a licence, but she knew *how* to drive Gertie, and Toby had said the beach was only a couple of miles down the coast.

'What's your answer, Lila?' Toby gave her what had to be a practised, charming grin.

'You know what my answer is.' She returned his smile, ignoring the prickle of heat on her palms.

'Excellent. Give us five minutes, and we'll be on board. Aria can direct you.'

'I'll be waiting.'

When Toby had gone, white shirt flapping in the evening breeze, she did a little dance. 'Ready for a night of fun, Marmite? I'm not going to kill the entire cast of *Estelle*, am I?' The dog cocked his head to the side and looked up at her, considering. She pushed down the swell of panic and went to check her appearance in her compact mirror.

Ten minutes later, Toby, Aria, Keeley, Sarah from production,

Bertie, an actor called Darius, who reminded Lila of a young Jamie Foxx and who played the Bramertons' immoral but impressive arch rival and, of course, Sam, trooped onto the bus. They were laughing and joking with the air of, Lila imagined, lifers who had been unexpectedly released from prison. She hoped she wouldn't be heading there before the night was out.

'Here we are, folks,' Toby said. 'The venue for this evening. Lila has very kindly agreed to drive us down to the cove.'

'It's only ten minutes away by car,' Aria said. 'But it would be a long walk, and we'd have no shelter once we got there. The bus is perfect.'

'Gertie has a multitude of talents,' Lila said. 'And tonight will be her *Estelle* party bus debut.' She sounded confident enough, but now, with the cast on board, acting superstars who would all have heavy insurance policies, and Sam and Keeley, who she considered friends, it all felt very precarious. She thought of Charlie's confidence in her, trusting her with Gertie all the way from America.

She climbed into the driver's seat and took the keys out of her bag, then stared at the dashboard and tried to remember everything that Charlie had showed her. The other version of herself would probably not have worried too much and started the ignition anyway: the version of herself that Clara had torn a strip or two off that last day . . . She took a deep breath and slipped down from the seat.

'I'm so sorry,' she said to the assembled group, 'but we can't go anywhere.'

'Why not?' Toby asked.

She gave a nervous laugh. 'Because I don't have a licence to drive the bus. It's Charlie's, and she's entrusted it to me and although it would be lovely and the plan sounds perfect, I just—'

'So how do you move between locations?' Bert asked.

'Charlie arranged with Winston that Mike or Claude would drive the bus for me while she was away, so I—'

'Claude?' Toby asked.

Lila nodded. She felt embarrassed, but she couldn't risk everything her cousin had worked so hard for, with one act of total irresponsibility.

'I'll ask Claude if he'll drive us,' Toby said, standing up and flashing Lila a grin.

'He doesn't need to stay here?' Aria asked.

'We'll only be gone a few hours, and Sly can man the gate. Back in two secs.'

Once he was gone, the others started talking between themselves quietly.

'Lila, are you OK?' She hadn't heard Sam come up behind her. She turned and smiled. 'Of course. I mean—'

'Crisis averted,' Toby said, hopping back on board, Claude following behind. 'We have our driver.'

Sam gave Lila's arm a brief squeeze and sat back down.

'Are you sure, Claude?' she asked.

'It's more fun than standing guard for hours on end,' he said, giving her a warm smile. 'And I love driving Gertie. There's something very special about this bus.'

'You,' she smiled, handing him the keys, 'are a wonderful man.'

He waved away her compliment and settled himself in the driver's seat, then started the ignition.

Lila sat next to Keeley while Claude drove them away from the set, Aria hovering at his shoulder, directing him towards the cove. The atmosphere didn't seem dampened in any way, despite the change of plan, and when she caught Toby's eye, he gave her a mischievous wink.

131

The bus slowed, and she felt the incline as it travelled down a hill. Outside, the impenetrable black of a narrow, tree-lined road suddenly gave way to reveal a tiny, deserted cove, appearing, as if by magic, out of the gloom. The sea sparkled ahead of them, the sun having been replaced by a bold silver moon, and even in the dark, with the shadowy, hulking cliffs looming up on either side, it was breathtaking.

Claude drove Gertie onto a strip of concrete between the road and the sand, turned in a wide arc and brought the bus to a halt, allowing a view of the water out of the side windows.

'Bravo, Claude,' Toby said, while everyone gave him a smattering of applause. 'Now. Let's get this party started!'

Vodka, sparkling wine and pink gin in a curved, frosted bottle were produced from various carrier and tote bags. Lila found glasses in the cupboards, and released Marmite from his crate so he could mingle. She declined the alcohol and made herself and Claude a cup of tea, and Keeley helped her plate up a selection of sweet and savoury pastries, while the others moved to the top deck. Sam was last, shooting a quick glance in their direction before loping up the narrow staircase, his tan boots the last thing Lila saw before he disappeared.

'Are you sure you won't have any of Sarah's pink gin, since Claude drove the bus?' Keeley asked. 'Apparently you can only buy it online, and she's been going on and on about it. Liquorice and juniper or something.'

'Tea's fine. I've got to drive back to Porthgolow at the end of the night anyway, and even though I can't technically drive it, I still feel responsible for Gertie. Besides, I don't mind not drinking.'

'Because you're effervescent enough as it is,' Keeley chimed.

'What about you?' Lila asked. 'How are things with Jordan now?'

Keeley wrinkled her nose. 'Much better. Less frosty. It's just . . .' She glanced at her feet. 'I wish I was settling into it all better. I'm having fun, and the rest of the cast and the crew are all lovely, but . . . I didn't know it would be so *hard*, this long-term drama business. Everyone else seems to be taking it in their stride.' She pointed up, the sound of laughter drifting down from the top deck. 'And I feel out of sorts.'

'Is there anything I can do?'

Keeley shook her head. 'You're making it so much easier already. Knowing you're always on the bus and I can come and talk to you. And I'll be fine – I'm just having a moan. It's been a long week.' She smiled, but it looked forced. 'Let's go and join the others.'

Once on the top deck, Bert beckoned them over with his usual exuberance. 'Darlings, come and sit down! And bring some of those delicacies. This is better than pub grub.'

'And right on the beach, too,' Toby added. 'Near enough, anyway. Concrete's safer than sand, I expect.'

'But Gertie has a winch,' Lila said, 'so if we did get stuck, we'd be fine. It's already had one rather impressive use in its relatively short lifetime.' She slid into the seat next to Keeley, Toby and Sam opposite them. Lila felt a flutter in her abdomen as her knees brushed Sam's, and he caught her gaze. She'd put the fairy lights onto twinkle mode, and the light played across his features. He looked tired and energized all at once, and she wondered if any actor really needed caffeine, when the adrenaline of performing must run constantly through their veins.

'Hey,' he said.

'Hi,' she replied. 'I heard you had a big scene earlier?'

He gave her a lopsided smile, one eyebrow rising slightly. 'It was pretty big,' he admitted, shooting a quick glance at Aria.

'But it went well?' Lila didn't really want to know the details, but she couldn't seem to stop herself.

'I think so. Sometimes it's hard to tell. We had to do a lot of takes, but that was because Gregor was in hyper-perfectionist mode.'

'Due to getting there late?'

Sam nodded, sipping his drink. It looked like vodka and tonic, something clear and fizzing. 'It hasn't been the easiest day, let's put it like that. So this,' he gestured around him, 'is good timing. Great idea of Toby's to come on the bus, as long as you don't feel as if you're still working, playing host to a gaggle of arrogant actors? I see you're not drinking.'

'I need to get back to Porthgolow after this,' she said. 'And I'm happy to oblige, considering you've all had such a long day.'

Sam laughed. 'And you managed to fit in a nap this afternoon, did you?'

'Well no, but it's not the same, is it?'

He shook his head, lips parted as if he was about to reply, when Toby stood up and cleared his throat dramatically. The bus fell silent.

'Ladies, gentlemen, King Claude and Lord Bert,' he said, his deep voice rumbling, 'we have come together on this fine evening, on board this glorious bus, for a few drinks, and to welcome Sam and Keeley into the world of serious acting.'

'Good-oh,' Bert said. 'What's the plan, then?'

'Plan?' Keeley asked. 'Why do we need a plan?'

'This is the plan,' Toby said, bringing a bottle of tequila out from under the table.

'Oh, bloody hell,' Sarah murmured, but she was smiling. Darius whooped and clapped his hands.

Opposite Lila, Sam rolled his eyes. 'Come on then,' he said, 'do your worst.'

134

'Ah.' Toby held up a finger. 'Our hostess gets to control the size of the measures.'

'I do?' Lila glanced at Keeley, whose lips were pressed into a tight line. 'But I don't have any shot glasses or a jigger, so I'm going to have to guess. And I have salt, but no lime.'

'I am nothing if not prepared.' Toby reached beneath the table again and took four limes and a salt cellar out of a plastic bag. 'For you, Delilah.'

Lila hurried down the stairs and retrieved a chopping board, a sharp knife and more glasses. She resumed her place on the top deck and started chopping the limes into wedges.

'I assume we're not going to be left out of this tequila business because of our more mature years and wealth of experience?' Bert asked. 'That, young man, would be discrimination.'

'Not at all,' Toby said. 'But Keeley and Sam go first. One shot each, and make it generous, won't you, Lila?'

She finished cutting the lime, and handed wedges to Keeley and Sam. Then she turned her attention to the tequila. The glasses were tall and straight-sided. She had no idea what would constitute a shot, so she estimated. As she finished pouring, Darius whistled through his teeth.

'Oh God, Lila,' Keeley said. 'Seriously? That's about a quadruple.'

Toby grinned at her.

'It's not, is it?' she asked innocently, passing the drinks to the two victims, then putting the same amount in the other glasses and handing them out.

Sam rubbed his forehead and gave her a pained expression.

'It's perfect,' Toby said. '*Perfect*. You ready, chaps?'

To Lila's surprise, Keeley didn't hesitate. She knocked back her glass and winced, poured salt on her hand, licked it and then bit straight into the lime. Everyone applauded, and Sarah cheered enthusiastically.

'Good woman,' Toby said, clearly impressed. 'Sam?'

Sam was much more methodical. He poured the salt onto his hand, arranged the glass and lime in front of him, then took a deep breath and downed the tequila. He grimaced, waited a second and then licked the salt, finishing with the lime. As he sucked it, his eyes found Lila's. She felt hot all of a sudden.

'Excellent,' Toby said, slapping Sam on the back so that he almost choked. He poured salt on his hand and then waited while everyone else did the same, then raised his glass. 'A toast, to Keeley and Sam! Wet behind the ears, and quite possibly more talented than the rest of us put together. Welcome to the world of serious drama – let us always strive to make it as light-hearted as possible. And to Claude, stepping in at the last moment as chauffeur extraordinaire, and finally to Delilah, our generous and beautiful host for the evening!' He downed his drink, the rest of the group following suit.

Lila reached over and clinked her mug of tea against Claude's.

'Wonderful stuff,' Bert declared, after he'd discarded his piece of lime and held his hand out for the half-empty bottle. 'You don't need any of this guff, either.' He waved the salt cellar. 'Stands up entirely well on its own.'

'Seriously?' Keeley grimaced. 'I hate tequila.'

'Could have fooled me,' Sam said, through a mouthful of lime.

Lila laughed. 'You don't have to eat the whole thing.'

'I do,' he replied solemnly. 'I hate tequila too. And I am never trusting you to pour me a measure of anything, ever again, by the way.' He finally relinquished the forlorn piece of fruit and sipped his original drink.

'She did it on purpose, obviously,' Keeley said.

'We'll have to pay her back next time.' Sam shrugged.

'Definitely,' Keeley said, throwing an arm around Lila's shoulder and pulling her close. Lila laughed and hugged her back, trying to hide her delight that they both thought she was worthy of a 'next time'.

After Toby's tequila toast, the atmosphere mellowed. She was surrounded by funny, imaginative people, who all had stories she wanted to listen to, and with Marmite on her lap, Keeley at her side and Sam opposite her, she felt wholly contented. She was part of something here; she was valued. She hadn't been invited solely because Gertie was her responsibility, but because they liked her. The moon dusted the water outside, the fairy lights glimmered within and, as the drink and conversation flowed, Sam's gaze kept returning, again and again, to her.

Sometime around midnight, once the tequila bottle was empty and Lila was thinking of offering up a round of hot chocolates, and Keeley and Toby were deep in an animated discussion about his last television role, Sam's warm fingers touched her arm. When she looked at him he stood and held out his hand.

'Follow me,' he said quietly. 'I've got something to show you.'

It didn't occur to Lila, for a single second, not to take his hand and do as he asked.

Chapter Twelve

The air was colder than she had expected, but the feel of it against her face made her alive to their surroundings, the gentle lapping of the water against sand. The tide was going out, the sea further from Gertie's concrete plinth than it had been when they'd arrived. Sam was ahead of her, having let go of her hand to navigate the narrow stairs, and he walked away from the bus, down onto the beach, then turned towards her.

Gertie's windows glowed soft yellow, a beacon in the dark behind them, competing with the silvery moonlight. Lila took a step towards Sam and saw that he was still holding his drink. He was wearing a loose grey shirt and jeans, his hair ruffling gently in the breeze. He looked so at ease with himself; there wasn't a hint of the awkwardness she'd seen during their first couple of encounters. Of course, that could be due to the large tequila shot he'd drunk on top of several vodka tonics, or because today he'd spent ages – hours, probably – kissing one of the most beautiful women Lila had ever seen. Over and over again. Take after take. That must have been a huge ego boost. Lila swallowed.

'So, Lila,' he said. 'What is it you're thinking about this evening, then? Isn't this place magnificent, a true beauty?'

Her heart skipped. Sam turned and gestured at the inky water, but she couldn't take her eyes off him. His Irish accent was broad, but he spoke softly, in a low, melodious thrum. She had known when she'd asked him that it was rude – prying into his personal life, asking him to perform for her – and yet here he was, giving her a private viewing of the most toe-curlingly delicious voice, on a dark beach in the wilds of Cornwall.

'Sam,' she said. He grinned and walked backwards, towards the water. She followed. 'Sam,' she repeated, 'that was . . . lovely.'

'Lovely?' he asked, still in his Irish brogue. 'Pure lovely, was it?'

Lila giggled. '*Very* lovely. Thank you. Which part of Ireland does your dad come from?'

'Donegal, northwest. But I think I told you – I haven't been back since I was three, even though I've got a lot of cousins. I should really make the effort.'

'You've been busy being an actor everywhere else. Are you based in London?'

He took a sip of his drink and nodded. 'It's the easiest, for auditions and meetings.' He'd slipped back into his normal accent, just a hint of his heritage burring some of the words. 'And I've got a lot of friends there now. How about you? Keeley mentioned you come from London, but you can't be on holiday here, because . . . you're here. Unless this *is* your idea of a holiday?' He laughed gently.

'No,' she said. 'That's more Charlie's thing, working every hour available. I'm having a break, from London.'

'You've got a job to go back to?'

Lila shook her head, unable to hide the involuntary shiver.

'Are you cold?' Sam asked. 'We should go back in.'

'I'm fine.' Lila pulled at the collar of her leather jacket. 'You're the one in shirtsleeves. I don't want to go back in, unless you do?'

Sam glanced around and found a wide rock with a flat top at the edge of the sand. He patted it, then hopped up onto it and held his hand out for her. 'It's not damp.'

She accepted his hand to help her up, even though it was entirely unnecessary. His skin was warm and smooth, and if her body's response was anything to go by, shot through with electric currents.

'So,' he said, 'no job in London. This is your permanent gig now?'

'It's Charlie's bus, Charlie's business. I've sort of stepped into her life, because it was going a lot better than mine. And now she's off in America for a month with her boyfriend Daniel, I can pretend it all belongs to me. For a while, anyway.'

'Is your old life in London that bad?'

'I hurt my friend Clara.' She shrugged. 'I have a tendency to get overenthusiastic, to throw myself into things that don't always work out, and I end up bringing people down with me in the process. It's a habit I can't seem to break, and this time, I lost a friendship over it. Then I came to Cornwall and inadvertently got us this *Estelle* gig. Charlie was so cross to begin with.' Lila laughed. 'It was another Lila special, and it's pretty miraculous it's all worked out as well as it has.'

'I can't imagine, though of course I don't know the details, that what happened with your friend is completely unforgivable. What I *do* know is that the set wouldn't be the same without you. Knowing Gertie's waiting for me, with you on

140

board: the perfect coffee, one of those muffins – it's a highlight of my day.'

'And you've not even tried one of my hot chocolates yet.'

'Something special, are they?'

'Just as with everything Gertie has to offer,' Lila grinned. 'But I suppose when you have to fit into your costumes, those slimline jackets and breeches, hot chocolates with marshmallows are a no-go.'

'I think, on certain occasions,' Sam said slowly, 'hot chocolates can be allowed. And if they're as good as everything else on board Gertie then I'm going to have to try one.' The moonlight was lighting one side of his face as if it was a roaming spotlight that had found its target. She didn't blame the moon; she would have picked him out, too.

'Do you want one now?' Lila asked, trying to ignore the effect his gaze was having on her.

'Sounds great.'

They went inside and Lila found the cocoa powder, heated the milk, dug out a packet of mini marshmallows. Sam asked if he could help, and Lila tasked him with getting orders from upstairs. He returned with an order for five hot chocolates and a small bottle of brandy. He added a generous slug to every mug except Lila and Claude's. She finished them off with the marshmallows and a sprinkle of chocolate curls, and handed Sam a tray to take back upstairs.

'I'll meet you outside,' she said. 'Can you bring Marmite with you?'

'Sure.'

Lila returned to their rock, put Sam's mug on the flat surface and cradled hers in both hands. Gazing at the moonlit, restless sea, she crossed her legs, inhaled the sweet, rich scent of hot chocolate, and wished the night could last for ever. She turned at the sound of footsteps. Sam had Marmite in his arms.

'He's pretty sleepy,' he said, sitting next to her and holding the dog on his lap.

'I thought he might be, but I need to make sure he does his business out here before he settles down for the night.' Marmite squirmed, getting comfortable in his new, makeshift cradle. Sam gingerly removed an arm and picked up his drink to take a sip.

'Great hot chocolate,' he said.

'I told you.' She nudged his shoulder and he laughed.

'I didn't doubt it for a second. You've only been working on Charlie's bus for a few weeks, is that right?'

'I arrived in Cornwall on Leap Day, started working on the bus and then filming began two weeks later.'

'But what about all that stuff about coffee beans? You have a seriously good knowledge of coffee – and making the perfect hot chocolate – for someone who's only been doing this for a few weeks.'

'I worked in a coffee lounge before this, in London. We were *not* allowed to call it a café, or even a coffee shop,' she said, deepening her voice in a vague impression of her old boss, Giuliano. 'It was far too upmarket for that. The Espresso Lounge, to be precise.'

'No jelly beans in sight, then?'

'Not even a bubble-gum-flavour one,' Lila confirmed. 'We served lots of City high-flyers, and offered our barista expertise to corporate events.' Her voice trailed away as she pictured Clara's face, her horrified expression the moment everything had gone hideously wrong. She thought that if somehow fate had allowed her to resolve things with her friend and still end up working on *Estelle*, then she would have been messaging Clara about Sam. As it was, Marmite and Jasper were her audience every evening, listening to her wax lyrical about him, but with a severe lack of helpful advice to offer in return.

'Hey, Lila?'

She couldn't believe she was here, tonight, on this beautiful beach, sitting so close to him.

'Lila?'

But this was always how it was at the beginning, wasn't it? An initial spark of attraction, leading on to something heady and passionate that would run its course and then end, hopefully without acrimony on either side. And anyway, they barely knew each other.

His voice cut into her thoughts. He was singing, his tone lyrical and deep, his Irish accent pronounced again. He sang the first few lines of 'Hey There Delilah', which was one of her favourite songs, because it was romantic and complimentary, and not the usual one people serenaded her with when they learnt her name. She looked up at him, her eyes wide, a shiver of pleasure running through her.

'That got your attention, at least,' he said.

'Sam, that was . . . beautiful. You can sing in an Irish accent, too. Did you know you had such a good voice?'

His laugh was loud, and Marmite jerked up and scrabbled off his lap, padding across the sand until he was a few feet away. 'Sorry, Marmite,' he said. 'Shit. Come back!' He bent and held out his hand, but Marmite stared balefully at him and then turned away.

'He'll be OK,' Lila said. 'He needs to go and do his doggy business anyway. But Sam – your voice. Have you done any musicals?'

'They're not on the top of my to-do list,' he admitted. 'But

143

I don't shy away from the odd singsong, especially after a few.' He held up his drink.

'That's not the song I'm usually serenaded with.'

'We're talking the Tom Jones hit, I presume?'

'You presume right. Yours was much better. Much nicer.' It was just a few lyrics, he didn't *necessarily* think she looked pretty tonight. 'Can't you make Robert Bramerton Irish? All the female viewers – and no doubt some guys, too – would be falling all *over* themselves to buy the official Sam Magee calendar the moment it appeared on Amazon.'

'And they won't if I stick to my natural voice?'

'Of course they will! But with the Irish too, there would be hordes, Sam. *Hordes.* I would tell everyone: I *met* him, I served him coffee. He liked my muffins.'

Sam's laugh was more of a guffaw, and it set Lila off, too. Soon they were both laughing uncontrollably, Lila clutching her half-empty mug so she didn't upend hot chocolate all over her skirt. Marmite glared at them, his head cocked to one side.

'It's a bit more serious than coffee and muffins,' Sam said eventually. 'You'd have to tell everyone that we were friends. You could say: see that handsome man on the telly, we're mates. He's a great singer, even better looking in real life and genuinely humble, to boot.'

'Oh, *so* humble. Yes. None of that actor ego business, just a funny, warm, gorgeous man. And his Irish accent could melt a thousand hearts.' She turned to look at him, her smile faltering when she saw his had slipped. She had meant it to be amusing, light. She hadn't succeeded.

'Maybe I don't want to melt a thousand hearts,' he said.

'Not that greedy?'

He shook his head. 'Not nearly so greedy. I'd settle for one really important one.'

144

Lila swallowed. 'Right, so. Oooh, that sounded pretty Irish, didn't it? *Right, so. There, so.*' She put on her broadest Irish accent, desperate to dispel the tension, the way Sam was looking at her with eyes that were even more mesmerizing in the moonlight. She needed to stop her heartbeat trying to race out of her chest, as if it had decided it was the heart Sam wanted to melt and was making its own way towards him, ready to accept its fate. 'That's the kind of thing, isn't it?'

'Lila,' Sam said seriously, 'that is the worst Irish accent I've ever heard. The absolute worst.'

She grinned. 'I do try my very hardest, *so I do*.'

He rolled his eyes. 'Come on then, what else have you got for me? Scottish? Welsh? American?'

Lila jumped up, put her mug on the rock and stood in front of him, with the sea behind her. She thought of all the scripts she'd read, some of the lines etched into her mind as she'd absorbed the drama and the romance of it in quiet moments on board Gertie.

'We haven't known each other long, Mr Bramerton,' she started, trying her hand at a Welsh accent, and saw Sam's eyebrows rise in surprise, 'and not all our encounters have been amicable thus far—'

'That's Marianne's line,' he said quietly. 'How do you know it?'

'Toby let me see some of the scripts.'

He nodded, rubbing his jaw. He looked rattled, and she wondered if he thought she was intruding, inserting herself too much into his world. But a second later he seemed to snap out of it. 'Not the best Welsh accent I've heard, but not the worst. What else?'

She switched to Scottish. 'Not all our encounters have been

amicable, thus far, but there is . . . *something* about you. Something I can't . . .' she paused for effect. 'Forget.' She coughed lightly, clearing her throat.

Sam crossed his arms over his chest. 'Never, ever go undercover as a Scottish spy. But the emotion was convincing. Any more?' he asked, his voice slightly rough. Of course, he knew what was coming, which scene she had recklessly picked to parade in front of him on the beach.

Lila crouched to ruffle Marmite's fur, giving herself a moment to think. Could she really continue down this road? She stood up again, and this time put on her best hammy American Deep South accent, hoping that would break the tension. She picked up where she had left off. 'Your candour is appreciated, of course, though I can't see why you persist in seeing me when there is nothing more to discuss. Nothing *at all* between us.'

'*Estelle* does Vivien Leigh,' Sam said. 'That was impressive, though you're a bit on the dramatic side for Scarlett O'Hara.' He gave her a wicked grin, and Lila squealed in outrage.

'*Too* dramatic to be Scarlett O'Hara? That's not possible!'

He laughed. 'I think I just proved my point.'

Lila pretended to seethe. 'I've done enough.'

Sam took her hand, suddenly serious. 'Sorry – I'm sorry. I couldn't resist. You're good, Lila. Not all the accents are perfect, but you can deliver the lines, there's no doubt about that.'

'You don't need to butter me up, you know,' she said softly. 'We're just messing about.'

'I'm not buttering you up – why would I? I'm being honest. Take it again, from the top. No accent this time, just you and the lines: you being Marianne.'

Lila shook her head. 'We don't need to—'

'I know we don't, but I want to see it again, without the fooling about. Please, Lila. I'm not making fun of you.' He squeezed her hand and then let go, sitting back on the rock, watching her.

Lila chewed her lip. It was ridiculous, standing here on the beach in the middle of the night, quoting a TV series script to one of the professional actors starring in it, but she wanted, more than anything, to impress him. 'OK,' she murmured. 'Just once.'

The tension thrummed between them. They both knew where this scene ended. She took a deep breath.

'We haven't known each other long, Mr Bramerton,' she said again, enunciating the words, 'and not all our encounters have been amicable thus far, but there is something about you. Something I can't forget.'

'And that is?' Sam asked gently, picking up Robert's line. Just three words, but he said them so perfectly, with curiosity and a hint of amusement.

'Your candour is appreciated, of course,' Lila continued formally, knowing this part of the script off by heart, Marianne continuing as if Robert hadn't spoken. 'Though I can't see why you persist in seeing me when there is nothing more to discuss. Nothing at all between us.'

Now Sam stood, stepping in front of her, close enough that she could see the gold in his irises picked out by the moonlight. 'Nothing?' he echoed. 'Are you sure about that? If you appreciate my candour, I hope you'll listen to my next words. Because believe me when I say I've never been more certain about anything. Lila—' she registered that he'd used the wrong name as he brought his hand to her face, his thumb tracing the line of her jaw.

'Mr Bramerton,' she croaked out. She reached up on tiptoes,

her lips inching closer to his, and applause shattered the quiet. Lila stepped back, biting down on her bottom lip to stop the gasp from coming out. Sam blinked and dropped his hand.

Everyone had come off the bus. Keeley and Toby, Aria, Sarah, Darius, Bert and Claude. They were all standing there, clapping them. She felt herself flush bright red, but Sam smiled and put his arm gently around her shoulders. She could feel the tension in his body, and that his breathing wasn't quite as regular as it perhaps should be.

'Bravo,' Bert called, once the applause had died down. 'We came to see if you two were having a roll-about in the sand – bit cold for that sort of thing in these conditions, I would have thought, but Sam's a young, virile man.' Sam's fingers tightened around Lila's shoulder, but Bert continued, oblivious. 'It turns out it's even more entertaining than that. Lila, you've been hiding your talents from us.'

'That was pretty great,' Toby slurred.

'Perhaps I need to be worried,' Aria said, but she was grinning.

Lila shrugged. 'I was just getting into the spirit of things.' She felt a surge of pride that they were being so complimentary, even if it was mostly drunken hyperbole. She snuggled closer to Sam, loved how his tall, solid frame felt against her, his arm sheltering her from the wind.

'You can help Sam on Monday then,' Keeley said. Her pale skin was flushed, her blue eyes slightly unfocused. 'When I go back to Derbyshire.'

Lila tensed. 'You're *leaving*?'

'Just until Wednesday. I need to go and see Jordan.' Her lips were downturned in an exaggerated pout, and Lila would have laughed had her friend not sounded so sad. 'You can help Sam rehearse, 'cos we've got this scene coming up. Me and Sam and – and Toby, too. That's right. It's all three of us. And you know the scripts, Lila. You'd be perfect!'

'We don't need to—' Sam started.

'But Lila'll be *great*,' Keeley pressed. 'Promise me you'll help them.'

She was drunk and tearful, and Lila felt guilty for pouring her such a large slug of tequila. 'Of course I'll help.'

'Promise?' Keeley repeated, wrapping her arms around Sam and Lila, squeezing them together in a three-way hug.

'I promise,' Lila whispered into her hair. 'You don't need to worry. Go home and see Jordan. Everything will be fine here.' She exchanged a worried glance with Sam. 'We should be getting back now, anyway. It's nearly – ' she glanced at her watch – 'two in the morning.'

'Sure,' Toby replied. 'Don't want to spoil the magic by going on too long.' He flashed her a drunken grin.

'Come on, everyone.' Lila shrugged out of Keeley's embrace and flapped her arms, as if she was herding a flock of unruly sheep back into their pen.

Darius took Keeley's hand and led her back to the bus.

Soon only Sam and Lila were left on the beach. 'Poor Keeley,' she said. 'It's my fault she's so drunk and maudlin.'

'Hey.' Sam turned her gently to face him. 'She's homesick. She can sleep off her hangover on the train, and Jordan will be waiting for her at the other end. And the tequila was Toby's idea.'

'I'll get Max to cover for me on Monday, whenever you want to rehearse.'

'You don't have to do that.' Sam rubbed his eyes, looking tired all of a sudden. 'I shouldn't have made you act out the scene like that. I was just so impressed. I wanted to . . . to see you do it for real.'

'I started it,' she said, not pointing out that he had said Lila instead of Marianne at the end, because she was sure he'd noticed. 'But it is, essentially, your fault. If you hadn't sung "Hey There Delilah" at me so beautifully, I wouldn't have felt the need to compete.'

'Oh really?' He took a deliberate step towards her. 'Are you sure it wasn't something to do with my assertion that I wasn't after melting a thousand hearts? That I was, perhaps, looking a lot closer to home? Believe me when I say I've never been more certain about anything. *Lila*—'

'We need to get back on the bus,' Lila said, trying to ignore the thrill of anticipation as he repeated the lines, emphasizing his original mistake. 'Everyone's waiting.'

'You think they could wait a moment more?' He was close enough that she could feel his warmth contrasting with the cold night. She swallowed. She hadn't been exaggerating. He was gorgeous.

'Sam . . .' she murmured.

'Delilah.' He pushed a clump of hair away from her face and lowered his head to hers, and Lila had time to think that they probably had an audience again, inside the bus, but that she didn't care one tiny little bit, when a piercing animal wail filled the air.

'What the—' Sam started, stepping back.

'Marmite!' Lila shrieked. 'Oh, no! That was Marmite.'

Chapter Thirteen

'Where did the sound come from?' Sam turned in a circle, his eyes alert.

'Over towards the cliffs, I think. Oh God. What have I done?'

'Don't worry, we'll find him. Here.' He pointed to doggy paw-prints in the damp sand. 'This way.' He set off at a jog, calling for Marmite, and after a second Lila snapped herself back into focus and followed him. She couldn't lose Marmite; never mind Charlie never forgiving her – she wouldn't forgive herself.

'Marmite?' Sam called. 'Marmite!' He reached the edge of the sand and climbed up onto a rock. There was a jumble of them in front of the sheer cliff face. Marmite whimpered again, and Sam followed the sound.

'You can't climb up there, Sam!' Lila shouted. 'You've had too much to drink! Shit.' She followed him, pulling herself up onto the shiny, slippery surface. Sam was a few paces ahead of her and didn't respond. He was using the rocks as stepping stones, peering down into the hollows between them as he went. He made it look easy, but some of the gaps were huge. Lila hesitated, wobbling on her makeshift podium, looking for any signs of Charlie's Yorkipoo.

'What's happening?' Lila turned to see Aria and Claude hurrying across the beach towards them.

'It's Marmite,' Lila said, swallowing. 'He's missing. He was off his lead, but he's always fine on Porthgolow beach. We were watching him, but then—'

'Here!' Sam called, and she turned just in time to see him jump off a rock, the large spray of water as he landed in a rock pool. 'Bloody hell, Marmite,' he said, much more quietly. Lila took another long step, stretching her skirt to its limit, her foot skidding as it landed on the slick rock.

'Lila!' Aria squealed.

'Stay there,' Sam called, looking up briefly. 'Don't try and come over. I've got him. His collar's stuck.'

'Is he OK?' Lila shouted. Her bones seemed to dissolve with relief when Sam nodded.

'He's soggy, but he seems all right. Just a bit . . .' He leaned forward, disappearing from view, and then sat up again, holding a bedraggled Marmite close to his chest. 'There.' He grinned, and Lila decided that, skiddy surfaces or no, she had to get to that smiling man and the dog he had rescued.

But then Aria was beside her, offering a hand to help her down, and she couldn't really refuse. They watched as Sam hoisted himself back onto the nearest rock and, more carefully now, made his way towards them. Claude reached up to collect Marmite, and Lila and Aria each took one of Sam's hands as he jumped down.

Lila hugged him, hard.

'Steady,' he said softly, but he wrapped his arms around her. 'He's fine. A bit cold and damp, but otherwise OK.'

152

She stepped back and looked at him. 'I don't think Marmite's the only one. How deep was it?'

'Only up to my knees,' Sam said. 'Marmite was paddling, keeping his head above the water, but his collar was tangled up in seaweed. God knows how he got there in the first place.'

'You,' Lila said, taking Marmite from Claude's arms, 'are a terror.' The little dog blinked up at her, his fur bedraggled. 'Oh, it wasn't your fault. I should have been watching you. I'm so sorry.' She squeezed him tightly, and he whimpered.

The four of them trudged back to the bus. It was late, and cold, and Sam was drenched. 'I've got towels on board,' she said, 'but they're not exactly the huge, fluffy bath-sheet variety. Thank you for saving him.'

'I doubt we were going to leave him there, were we?'

'No, but . . . those rocks. Not to mention all the alcohol you've had. That could have gone so, *so* wrong. God, what a fuck-up.'

'Marmite's fine, and so am I. And we were both out there; you weren't the only one who lost track of him. But all's well, now.'

Once inside, Lila watched as Claude took his place at the wheel. She was proud that she hadn't, in the end, gone through with driving Gertie herself. Then she glanced at Sam, sitting with a very sorry-looking Marmite on his knees. She may have got some things right tonight, but, she thought as she sat opposite him and gave him a tired smile, she still had a way to go.

Over the weekend, the events of that night came back to Lila in snippets: Sam's Irish accent, her attempts at acting, him clambering over the rocks while Marmite wailed, his lyrical voice serenading her, and how exhausted he had looked as they'd started the journey home. Claude had driven Gertie smoothly back into place as if she'd never left her spot next to the catering tent.

Lila took Marmite to the emergency vet on Saturday morning, paying an extortionate amount to get the priceless reassurance that he was fine, and got an emotional message from Keeley on Saturday evening, apologizing for her outburst the night before, and saying she was sure Sam would be fine without an extra rehearsal. But by then, the idea was stuck in Lila's head, and she couldn't wait to spend more time with him. She told herself that she owed him after he'd rescued Marmite, and that she wanted to be more involved with the production. She'd got the bug, now – the performing bug. Not the love bug. Definitely nothing like that, she told herself: Lila had never been a swooning, hard-falling, hopeless-romantic kind of person, and she wasn't about to start now – especially not with the star of a TV show whose presence in Cornwall was likely to be even more impermanent than her own.

'Are you sure you're all right doing this?' she asked Max, late that Monday afternoon. She was already shrugging off her apron, smoothing down her blue silk top and wide-legged black trousers.

'I love Gertie,' Max said simply. 'Can I try one of these?' His fingers hovered over what was left of the display of mini doughnuts, some filled with chocolate sauce and some with jam. She and Amanda had cooked up a storm in Charlie's kitchen the previous afternoon, and Amanda had promised she would continue to keep the Cornish Cream Tea Bus fully stocked until Charlie came back. After the previous few months' success with SeaKing Safaris, they had been able to hire a trainee skipper, which meant that Amanda could take some time away from the business.

'You can have whatever you want,' Lila said to Max now. 'That's your reward for taking charge of the bus.'

'You're really going to rehearse with Toby and Sam?' He sounded awestruck.

'I am,' she replied, knowing she sounded equally stunned. But she couldn't think about it too much, or her nerves would stifle her. 'How do I loo—'

'Lovely,' Max said, grinning.

Lila gave Max a quick hug, picked up Marmite and hurried off the bus.

It was towards the end of the day, and neither Sam nor Toby was needed in the final scene, so they had agreed to meet at the edge of the backstage village, beyond the neat row of actors' trailers. The sun was bright but there was a strong wind, and Lila's hair whipped around her face. She skirted the edge of the final truck and stopped dead.

Robert and Henry Bramerton were standing on the grass, chatting easily in their frock coats, breeches and shiny boots. The sight of them together, their silky cravats emphasizing their strong jawlines, was almost too much. Marmite sat at her feet, unconcerned that she'd come to an ungainly halt.

Toby spotted her and raised a hand in greeting. 'Lila!' he called, and she forced her legs to move.

'Hello,' Sam said, giving her a sheepish smile. She wondered if he'd meant those things he'd said on the beach, or if he'd been drunker than she'd realized and was now regretting it. *Maybe I don't want to melt a thousand hearts.* She couldn't think about that, about him, right now. She had to concentrate.

'Hey,' she replied. 'You OK?' Marmite bounded up to Sam, and Sam lifted him up and rubbed him under the chin.

'We're grand,' Toby said. 'Even more so now you're here.'

'What scene do you need help with?'

He passed her a dog-eared script. *Estelle: Episode 4* was written on the front, and then, below it: *Strictly Private and Confidential.* She had seen this one already.

'It's where Henry sees the ghost of Estelle for the first time,' Sam said. 'Robert and Henry are together, they're having one of their more heated discussions and then – wham, there she is.'

'OK,' Lila replied, flicking through the pages, taking longer than she needed to find the right place.

'It doesn't matter exactly where you stand,' Toby said. 'We're not scheduled to film this scene until we get to Bodmin, so the landscape will be quite different. But Estelle has a monologue – it's as if she isn't aware of the boys' presence – and we need to make sure our lines and our reactions – our timing – is right.'

'Of course.' Lila scanned Estelle's words and felt a rush of satisfaction. She *loved* this part: it was so emotional.

'It was very kind of Keeley to offer your services,' Toby said, grinning.

'It's only us,' Sam added. 'And you were so good on the beach.' He caught her eye and looked quickly away, suggesting to Lila that it was still as much in his head as it was in hers. 'You'll nail it. And the shoot will go more smoothly if we're prepared.'

'I'm ready,' she said.

'Excellent.' Toby rubbed his hands together. 'Sammy, better put the dog down.'

'Oh . . . yes!' He put Marmite gently on the floor, and Lila clipped his lead to a nearby truck. She wasn't going to risk losing him again.

'If we start from your line, Sammy. We'll approach from this direction, Lila, and if you stand there looking all ethereal, we'll chance upon you and then you just follow our lines, then read out Estelle's part from the script.'

'Sure.' She watched as they turned and strolled away from her, Sam tugging at his cravat, his hair dancing in the breeze. She felt a pang of something that she put down to nerves and buried her nose in the script, reading through the words, suddenly terrified that she would be awful. Not that it mattered – she was only helping them rehearse – but she wanted Sam to look at her again as he had done on the beach.

'Stay for a moment, Henry. Can't we talk about this?' Sam was following Toby back towards her, their strides long, both of them looking manly and angry and determined, so that Lila's heart was suddenly racing.

'There's nothing *to* talk about. Not this time. You've made your thoughts on the matter perfectly—' Toby came up short, eyes widening as he saw her. Lila wondered for a second what was wrong, before realizing that this was the moment Henry saw Estelle.

Sam came to a stop alongside Toby, his gaze also fixed on her. 'You see her?' he said quietly. 'She's been . . . coming to me. Ever since we arrived. I thought it was the upheaval, I thought I was going mad, but . . .' he laughed humourlessly. 'You see her, don't you? Estelle.'

Toby opened his mouth to speak and Lila, knowing this was where she was meant to come in, cut him off. 'It wasn't supposed to happen this way,' she started. She didn't look at either of them but stared off to the side, holding the script at an angle so she only had to move her eyes if she forgot any of the lines. Every inch of her skin prickled with the awareness of being watched. 'It was my chance at a good life, one with purpose.'

'Is she—' Toby said.

'Brother,' Sam murmured, stopping him.

Lila, as Estelle, continued. 'I knew someone was watching me, almost as soon as we arrived. The moment we were husband and wife, and this house was my castle, the fear began working its way inside.' She pressed a fisted hand against her breastbone. She felt so sad for Estelle, for the young woman who had had her whole life ahead of her, but had lost it at the hands of some unknown – because Toby hadn't given her all the scripts yet – killer.

'A prickling at my nape,' she murmured, 'a sudden chill when the sun was still bright on the terrace. My things displaced, hardly noticeable, except to me, who had started with so little, and cherished each shawl and slipper and chain. There were unkind eyes on me. Planning. Plotting. Though I knew not why I was the flame to their moth. I had found love, a home. I believed that, at last, happiness was mine. But . . .' she swallowed, feeling the emotion rush through her like a tidal wave. 'It wasn't to be.'

Lila dropped her hand to her side, her head to her chest, waiting for Sam to say his next line. Or was it Toby? She couldn't remember. She glanced at the script, frowning when the silence continued. She risked looking up. Toby and Sam were staring at her as if she'd suddenly grown an extra head. And there was someone else standing behind them. Gregor. Lila almost dropped her script.

'Bloody hell,' Sam said quietly.

Toby started clapping.

158

'Was I . . . weren't you meant to come in? One of you?'

'It was me,' Sam said. 'I had the next line, but I was too busy watching you.'

Lila blushed. 'I—'

Sam was in front of her in a second, taking her hand. 'That was brilliant, Lila. The beach wasn't a one-off. You are . . . something else.'

'He's not wrong,' Toby said mildly. 'You dark bloody horse.'

'Delilah Forest,' Gregor boomed, making Toby and Sam jump. It was obvious they hadn't realized he was there. 'Coffee and cake aficionado, reckless abandoner of buses before the day's filming is done. What is the meaning of this?'

'She was helping us rehearse,' Toby said.

'She was not,' Gregor argued. 'She was stunning you, like trout.'

'She was incredible,' Sam said, laughing and rubbing his cheek. When he looked at her, Lila felt heat reach parts of her nowhere near her face.

'When we move to Polperro,' Gregor continued, 'Thursday morning, we need a Miss Trevelyan. It's only one line, but it's yours, Lila. I'll get Bethan to bring you a script, to tell you where you need to go and when. Carry on.' He turned and strode away.

Lila blinked. 'What just happened?'

Toby laughed. 'You auditioned yourself into the show. Your scene is with me on Thursday morning and, don't worry, Bethan's the assistant director, she's brilliant – completely on the ball. But whatever questions she can't answer, you have me and Sam.'

Lila inhaled, her mind whirring. 'What about Gertie?'

Sam's eyes were bright. 'You deserve this, Lila. Max or someone else from the catering team will pitch in to help.

159

You just need to focus on delivering your line, which isn't going to be a problem after what we've just witnessed.' He glanced at Toby, and Toby nodded.

'I'm going to be in *Estelle*?' She couldn't absorb it. The last twenty minutes felt like a blur. But then Sam's arms were around her, and he was pulling her against his chest and laughing softly into her ear, and even the prospect of being a small part of the BBC drama faded into insignificance.

'This ain't right, Mr Bramerton, sir, what you're doin' here.' Lila dropped the script onto the arm of the sofa. She didn't need it, but it felt like a talisman. She cast a wary glance at her audience: Juliette, Lawrence, Marmite and Jasper, sitting in a row in front of her. She waited, licking her lips. 'Well? What do you think?'

Lawrence rubbed his hand over his blond stubble. She didn't know Juliette's boyfriend that well, but he seemed so nice, so genial, and that was what she needed right now. 'That's it?' he asked.

Lila nodded. 'That's my line. I'm Miss Trevelyan, the schoolmistress. I'm part of the mob of angry villagers who don't like how Henry Bramerton is treating his tenants. But it's not really Henry's fault, you see; there's this other land-owner who—'

'And Henry Bramerton is Toby Welsh?' Juliette asked, slightly breathlessly. 'And you're speaking those words *to* him? You've spent actual time with him? You've acted in front of him already, and he said you were good?' Lawrence rolled his eyes good-naturedly.

'Yes,' Lila said, wishing Juliette would stop being so star-struck and give her some feedback.

They had turned up on Charlie's doorstep at half past

160

nine. Filming had finished early, as they had needed to move the entire production team over to Polperro, and Lila had been able to come home while Mike drove Gertie to her new position. The reality of what was happening tomorrow had been starting to sink in when there had been a knock on the door.

Apparently Charlie had told Juliette that Lila had seemed a bit frazzled last time they'd FaceTimed, and had asked Jules to check on her. Lila had let them in, made them hot drinks, and was now – after giving them a potted history of her time on set so far –, practising her line on them.

'Toby is lovely,' she continued, in response to Juliette's question. 'But he is a professional actor, and if I don't get this line right tomorrow, if I mess it up and have to do it hundreds of times, then he might not want to spend any more time on Gertie, and neither will anyone else.'

'But that . . . what you just said,' Lawrence continued, 'that was it?'

'Yes. That was my line.'

'It sounded great. But . . .'

Lila waggled her fingers. 'But what?'

'If that's *it*, what are you so worried about?'

'Because I've never done anything like this before! You understand, don't you, Jules?'

'If I was standing opposite Toby Welsh, I doubt I could make my voice work at all. I think you sound wonderful, Lila. Very Cornish, but still quite sultry with it.'

'Sultry? I don't want to be sultry. I want to be angry!'

'OK then.' Jules sat up straight and beckoned at Lila. 'Give it to us again. I want Cornish, sultry *and* angry this time. And we're not going to stop until you get it right. You will *not* be letting Toby Welsh down tomorrow.'

Lila managed a smile, wondered if enlisting their help had been wise, and then tried her line again. The dogs watched on impassively, their dark eyes shining with something that looked distinctly like pity.

The new filming village set up just outside Polperro was almost a carbon copy of the previous one, Gertie sandwiched between the catering tent and the other craft stalls, except that they weren't in a rural location and so everything felt more hectic. Lila's stomach danced with nerves when Bethan appeared in the doorway alongside the ever-cheerful Max, who was once again taking charge of the bus while she was gone. This time, she was going to leave Marmite with him too.

'We'll get you costumed up, take you for a brief stint in make-up, and then it's down to the set. Excited?'

Lila nodded, holding her script so tightly that she thought it might spontaneously combust.

The outfit she was given was heavy and uncomfortable: a dull brown dress, cinched in at the waist, with a short jacket in a slightly darker shade and sturdy, pinching boots. In the make-up trailer her hair was teased and pulled into a complicated up-do that, from her position in front of the mirror, looked deceptively simple and elongated her neck. Her shine and freckles were powdered into submission, her hair sprayed until it set.

While this happened, and Perry, the young, beautiful make-up artist chattered on, Lila's nerves slowly turned into excitement. She was here, getting to see how it all worked first-hand, experiencing what Keeley and Sam, Aria and Toby experienced on a daily basis. She was a genuine, bona-fide part of *Estelle*.

Once Perry had finished with her, a runner took her down to the set.

Unlike the lonely cliff-top scenes at their last location, this new set was a port town, flung centuries into the past. The narrow street had been stripped of all its modernity, shop fronts covered, benches hidden. It looked dusty and quaint, and there was already a crowd of extras milling about at its fringes, while a host of crew members chatted and scurried and moved cameras, lighting rigs, sound booms and bounce boards, getting everything into position. Lila was overawed.

'It's amazin', isn't it?' a young woman said, smoothing her hands down her simple white apron. 'Bein' a part of all this.' Her accent sounded genuine, and Lila's insides flipped.

'It is. It's going to be a wonderful series. It's—'

'Lila!' Toby, dressed impeccably as Henry Bramerton, was waving at her.

'Oh my *God!*' Apron Girl squealed. Lila gave her a quick smile and hurried over to Toby. She knew, from her several million read-throughs of the scene, that Robert wasn't in this one, but Sam had told her he'd be there. She hadn't decided if that made her feel better, or added to her nerves.

'You all prepared?' Toby asked. 'It'll be a cinch, honestly. You're a natural.'

'Yes, but look at all these people.' Her voice gave a perfectly timed wobble.

Toby squeezed her arm. 'There isn't an actor in the business who isn't daunted by the sight of a full set, however long they've dreamt of being part of one. Ride the adrenaline, turn it towards your performance, and you'll be fine. Gregor saw you taking Keeley's place as Estelle, and he wanted you to do this. Remember that. You're here because you're good.'

Lila swallowed. 'And it's only one line, right?'

'Every line is important,' Toby said, smiling. 'Don't think it isn't. I have to go and talk to Bethan. You'll be OK?'

'I'm grand,' she said, with more confidence than she felt. Once Toby had gone, Lila dissolved back into the crowd of supporting actors and waited for them to be called.

The waiting, it turned out, was the worst part. It seemed to take for ever for Gregor and his minions to set up the shot, to adjust the lighting, the camera angles, the props on set, check the doorways that would be opened or closed, check for stray pigeons, check . . . Lila didn't even know what else they were checking for – but it took *hours*.

And then her group, the angry mob, was called forward, and Gregor gave them instructions: how exactly the scene would go, at which precise moment to move forward, and where, specifically, to step. Lila nodded along with everyone else, but had the sense that they all knew a lot more than she did. They buzzed with energy, hiding their excitement under cloaks of professionalism.

'You good, Delilah Forest?' the director asked, just as Lila thought their briefing was over.

'I am. Very good,' she said, and then cursed under her breath. What kind of a response was that?

To her surprise, Gregor laughed. 'I know, otherwise I wouldn't have given you this part. Be my Miss Trevelyan, incensed and dutiful and intrigued by the Bramerton brothers. She knows she can get what she wants, knows she has the wit and cunning, but also that she has to take it one step at a time. That's all there is to it.'

Had he remembered she only had one line? She didn't think she should remind him, so instead she nodded and smiled and just about resisted giving him a thumbs-up, and hoped she looked as though she was absorbing his advice.

By the time they were moved into place, Lila's heart was beating so loudly in her ears she was convinced the person next to her could hear it. She breathed slowly through her nose, a yoga technique Juliette had taught her the night before. After a few deep breaths, it started working. Everything settled, her nerves and her pulse and her jiggling insides.

Toby strode onto the set, took up his mark alongside a reedy man who was playing the banker, to act out the end of a conversation that had started inside, and which would be filmed at an entirely different time, in a studio miles away from here, perhaps three months from now. Lila couldn't get her head around it, this discordance of story. But at this moment that was the least of her worries.

She focused as Gregor murmured something to Bethan, there was a shift of camera angle or another detail, and then he called, 'Action!'

Chapter Fourteen

Lila had thought that saying her line over and over the night before had been extreme, but compared to the number of times they had to shoot this scene, to say their lines and then reset everything, for Toby and his fellow actor to have a particular exchange, or end their conversation in a slightly different way, it felt like a few seconds' work. She supposed that with such a busy setting, so many more people, a hundred different things that could go wrong, it made sense that they would reshoot a lot. Besides, it was their first day at this location; they were still getting to know its quirks.

The first time she got to say her line, she hadn't been prepared for the look of pure scorn Toby gave her as he walked past. She had expected a quick smile to show her she'd done well, but of course, he had to be angry – their characters were opposed to each other. Here, he didn't know her. Here, she was against him.

After that, despite the long waits, the pinch of her boots and chill of the wind that found its way easily through her ill-fitting dress, she began to enjoy herself. She focused, harder than she had done in a long time, absorbing herself fully into the scene. Toby became Henry Bramerton and she was an impoverished, dedicated schoolmistress trying her best for her pupils and their families, outraged at being treated with so little respect by her new landlord, but still needing him to listen to her.

'This ain't right, Mr Bramerton, sir, what you're doin' here.' She injected anger and pleading into her voice, lifting her skirts and wringing them while Toby – Henry – strode past, again and again. She tried slightly different inflections, each time waiting while her fellow extras threw less distinct complaints and insults at Henry until he stormed out of frame, and she could give it another shot. She never wanted it to end. She wanted to keep going, keep trying until she felt she had got it exactly right. She was desperate for everyone to believe in Miss Trevelyan.

Lila said her line and watched Toby whisk past her again, staring after him in what she hoped was defiance, until she heard the familiar 'Cut!' and then Gregor added, 'Right everyone, that's a wrap!' There was an immediate change in atmosphere, people sighing and relaxing their postures, gentle murmuring as they made their way off set.

Lila was stunned. Was it really all over? Had she done the best she could? And then she felt a wave of emotion, of electricity, as if she'd been lit up with a thousand internal fairy lights. In a daze, she followed the young woman with the apron up the hill, back towards the costume trailer, and gasped when someone took her hand.

She turned to find Sam beaming at her. He was casually dressed, and she felt self-conscious in her unflattering outfit, so different to the silk gowns worn by Aria, or Keeley's floaty white dresses. She gave him a small shrug.

'You were amazing,' he said. 'And the Cornish accent was spot on.'

'At least they didn't ask me to be Irish. That would have been a disaster.'

He laughed. 'Your acting debut.'

'My acting debut and finale. I don't know how you do it. It was so stressful, rehearsing last night and then today – all that waiting. At one point I thought I might be sick with nerves.'

'But after you'd got your first take out of the way?' he asked, falling into step alongside her. 'Don't tell me you didn't love it, didn't get a thrill when Gregor didn't stop the scene or tell you to redo it, when it carried on after you'd spoken your line. When you realized how *good* you were. Because, believe me, Lila, you can do this.'

Lila chewed her lip, unsure what to do with his compliment. 'It was exhilarating,' she admitted. 'And I . . . after I'd done it once, I wanted to get it right. I wanted to be an authentic part of it.'

'There, you see. There's no other feeling like it.' He'd turned to walk backwards in front of her, his whole face alive, as if he'd just nailed the performance of his life. 'Hardly anything comes close.'

She grabbed his arm, moving him aside so he didn't back into a couple of PAs who had stopped in the middle of the path. She'd never seen him this animated. 'Hardly anything?' she asked.

He shook his head, but she could see the gleam of mischief in his eyes.

'So now I've done that, do you fancy working on board Gertie? Or, you could help me with some baking one evening in Porthgolow. I promise you, the adrenaline rush of taking your third batch of scones out of the oven and keeping them out of reach of Marmite and a German shepherd is the most thrilling thing you'll ever do.'

Sam laughed and took her hand again, stopping so that Lila had to stop, too. 'You were brilliant out there, Lila. I need to go and get into my costume, and I'm sure you're dying to take yours off, but I'll see you soon.' He lifted her hand and kissed it, and then turned in the direction of his trailer where, she thought, he probably had a whole Robert Bramerton wardrobe waiting for him.

She watched him walk away and then called, 'You didn't agree to help me with my baking!' But by then he was too far away to hear her.

It was Sunday morning, a bold sun filtering through the gap in the curtains, and Lila was lying in bed thinking about what she would do with the hours stretching in front of her. The production team was moving to Bodmin the following day. Mike would be driving the bus, and Lila didn't need to turn up until nine o'clock which, working on *Estelle*, was a lie-in. But it wasn't like *this* lie-in.

It was after eleven, she had a cup of tea and hot, buttery toast, and two dogs lying on her, Jasper across the very ends of her feet which, she realized, she couldn't feel any more. She had some baking to do later that day, but before then she was going to take the pooches for a long walk, and maybe have one of Hugh's famous fishermen's pies in the pub.

She reread Charlie's latest message; the course had gone well and Daniel had stacks of ideas about how to transform the hotel, and now they were off to Alcatraz on a day trip. Lila wasn't sure she would want to spend precious holiday time in a creepy, dank island prison, but each to their own.

She hadn't told Charlie about being an extra. That day in Polperro, ten days ago, was still a vivid, slightly unreal memory, and she wanted to tell her cousin in person, to see her face when she revealed she was actually going to be *in Estelle.* She took another bite of toast, shook her head at Marmite and Jasper when they raised their heads in unison, and closed her eyes against the crunchy, buttery perfection.

Charlie's doorbell rang.

Lila groaned. 'If I ignore it, do you think they'll go away?' Neither dog had an answer for her.

The bell rang again.

Lila wriggled herself out from under the dogs and duvet and, throwing a jumper on over her skimpy pyjamas, padded down the stairs. The figure blurred behind the patterned glass was tall, but she couldn't make out any other details. Lawrence, maybe? She pulled open the door, and her heart gave a little skip.

'I wondered if you had any baking to do today,' Sam said. He was wearing a navy wool coat, his hands deep in the pockets.

'How did you know where I was?'

'Well,' he said, leaning against the doorframe, his gaze flickering quickly over her bare legs, then back up again. 'I knew you were staying in Porthgolow, and I hedged. Turns out everyone knows everyone here. I spoke to a lovely woman called Myrtle.' His amber eyes danced with amusement.

'Oh God, Myrtle. She thinks I'm flighty.'

'She told me that very thing. Warned me, in fact, that I needed to watch myself around you, that you were nothing like Charlie, who apparently she adored from day one.'

Lila laughed and stepped back, inviting him in. 'Now I know *that's* not true. Come through.' She winced at the state

170

of the living room; dog toys, various items of clothing and at least three pairs of shoes littered the floor and sofas. At least the kitchen was spotless, Lila aware that everything to do with the Cornish Cream Tea Bus had to be kept to the highest possible standard. 'Sorry this is all a bit of a pickle. I've not had much time to clean. Have a seat.'

Sam perched on the edge of a cushion, and Lila sat on the other sofa, pulling her jumper as far over her legs as it would go. 'Did you really come to help me bake?'

'I will, if that's what you're doing with your day. I just thought we could . . . I was keen to see where you were staying, this magical village with its food market and its glamorous hotel.' He shrugged, looking uncomfortable.

'I was planning on doing a bit of exploring myself,' Lila admitted. 'You're very welcome to join me, though when I say *explore*, I really mean a walk on the beach and a fish pie in the pub.'

'That sounds pretty good,' Sam said. 'If you're happy for me to tag along?'

'I'm not going to send you away after you've come all this way. I can't believe you just hoped someone would give you my address – and they did! Seriously, can you imagine something like that happening in London?'

'No, but maybe that's part of the magic?'

'More like an invasion of privacy,' Lila muttered. But she was pleased Sam was here. More than pleased. 'I'm going to shower and dress. You stay here – oooh, and you can look after these for me. Jasper! Marmite!' she called up the stairs, and moments later, the dogs pattered into the room. Marmite jumped on Sam and buried his nose in his coat. 'Aah look, the victim and his saviour. He will be eternally grateful to you.'

'Not sure about that,' Sam murmured, trying to extract the small dog from inside his clothes.

'And this is Jasper. He shouldn't give you any trouble. Help yourself to a drink if you fancy – I promise I won't be long.'

'No worries,' Sam called as she hurried up the stairs, her Sunday looking even more promising than it had ten minutes ago.

Half an hour later they were walking the dogs on the beach. It was a feisty day, with small white clouds racing across a blue sky, the sea whipped into tufts and whorls. Marmite and Jasper scampered together and apart, delighting in the expanse of sand ahead of them, and a yellow SeaKing Safaris boat bobbed across the water in the distance, taking a group of passengers around the coast. Lila folded her arms across her chest, feeling Sam's warmth at her side.

'This place is beautiful,' he said. 'I can see why Charlie loves living here. I thought when I came down to Cornwall, I'd miss London. But so far, so good.'

'Being on the TV set is nothing like being here, though,' Lila replied. '*Estelle* is this huge community, this family. Don't you think if you lived here, as pretty as it is, you'd get bored? No action or adrenaline? Just the sea and the beach and a few nosy old villagers?'

'But if this was home, in between jobs – if I got to travel for work, then this place would be somewhere peaceful to come back to.'

'I thought you loved the pace of London, with all your friends, the ease of getting to auditions. Are you thinking about semi-retirement, Sam, at the ripe old age of . . .?'

'Twenty-nine,' he confirmed. 'And no, not at all. But there

is something mesmerizing about all that sea, the hidden beaches and towering cliffs. Days like this.'

'What, driving for miles to be pecked at by a belligerent old woman and then pounced on by two hounds and told to navigate an assault-course of a living room to make your own cup of tea? You've a warped sense of happiness, Sam Magee.'

He laughed. 'Well, when you put it like that . . .'

Lila watched Jasper run headlong into the waves, barking loudly. Before she could think about how wise it was, she grabbed hold of Sam's hand and dragged him towards the water.

He came easily, running with her, until they got to the edge of the sea. 'Oh no,' he said, pulling up short. 'I'm not going in after a dog again. My boots were close to ruined after the last time.'

'So take them off, then.' Lila was already yanking off her shoes and rolling up her jeans. 'This beach was made for paddling, and it's good to be spontaneous.'

Sam shook his head and bent to pull off the not-quite-ruined boots, jumping back when a wave lapped at his feet. He took them, along with Lila's shoes and his wool coat, and placed them in a neat pile further up the sand. Lila watched him from the shallows, the care he took, the way everything he did was calm and measured. Then he was jogging easily across the sand towards her, and she waited for him, until she realized he had too much momentum to slow down. She tried to move out of the way but it was too late. She screeched as he lifted her off her feet, hoisting her over his shoulder and walking deeper into the waves, his jeans, despite being rolled up, soon sodden.

'Sam!' Lila squealed, trying to turn her head so he would hear her.

'What?' he asked, all innocence. He changed her position, lifting her over his shoulder again, keeping tight hold of her until he had one arm under her knees, one supporting her back. She laced her fingers round his neck.

'Sam, I – what are you doing?'

'Paddling,' he replied.

'But it's so deep! I'm not as tall as you. Put me down!'

'Sure?' Sam asked, pausing, and Lila looked at the water, which was up to his knees.

'No. Don't let me go.'

'OK,' he said mildly. He turned and began walking along the beach, Lila in his arms as if she was no heavier than a bag of sugar.

She snuggled into his chest, feeling, after the initial shock, an unexpected rush of comfort. She giggled. 'What are you doing, Sam?' she asked again.

'Being spontaneous,' he said. When she didn't reply, he continued. 'You looked beautiful and vulnerable, standing there in the water, your hair loose around your shoulders. I had a sudden urge to grab hold of you and protect you from lurking sea monsters.'

'But we're still in the water. Couldn't the sea monsters get us both?'

'Not with me to take care of you.'

Lila didn't know if he was being wholly silly, or if some of what he said had a grain of truth to it, his feelings slipping out even while he tried to hide them in drama. She watched his Adam's apple bob, his gaze focused straight ahead as he waded through the water in the direction of the jetty. The beach was deserted apart from one other dog walker, and Lila could easily imagine that this was a scene from *Estelle*; the younger, more tolerant Robert Bramerton rescuing Miss

Trevelyan after a brush with a capsized boat – or a real-life sea monster. Estelle was a ghost, after all. Other things could be within the realms of possibility.

'Sam,' she murmured.

He looked down, his piercing eyes meeting hers. 'Do you want to know the real reason I came to find you today?'

'Yes,' she whispered.

He shifted her position slightly, and Lila thought how tired his arms must be. A muscle in his jaw moved. 'I came to see you, Delilah, because—'

'Lila! Lila, oh my goodness, are you OK?!' The words were screeched in their direction, cutting Sam's sentence in half.

Lila turned her head to see Amanda Kerr and Stella, who ran the bed and breakfast, running across the sand towards them.

'Do we need to call an ambulance?' Amanda shrieked.

'Seems your act of spontaneity has backfired slightly,' Lila said.

Sighing, Sam turned towards the beach and, after walking a few steps, slowly lowered Lila to the ground. The water was a shock of cold around her ankles. She reluctantly unwound her hands from round his neck.

'We're fine,' Sam called. 'Just . . .'

'Just messing around,' Lila finished, striding up the beach to greet the two women. 'Amanda, Stella, this is Sam. He's one of the actors in *Estelle*.'

'Oh God!' Amanda clapped her hands over her mouth. '*This* is Sam?' She gave Lila a knowing look. Lila had been regaling Amanda with news from the set whenever they'd baked together. She wondered, now, what she'd let slip about Sam.

Stella giggled. 'We're so sorry! When we saw you in the

water like that, we thought you must have fallen, or . . .'

'It was very dramatic-looking,' Amanda finished, holding her hand out to Sam. Greetings were made, both of the women staring at him for longer than was polite, which Lila couldn't blame them for.

'We were letting off a bit of steam,' Sam said, rubbing the back of his neck. Lila found his sudden awkwardness adorable. He could lift her off her feet without a moment's thought, be Robert Bramerton in front of hundreds of people watching his every blink, but the moment he was exposed as himself, with people he didn't know, she got the sense that he wanted to crawl under a rock.

'You were also *creating* a bit of steam.' Amanda flapped a hand in front of her face. 'We're so sorry we disturbed you.'

'Don't worry at all,' Lila said quickly. 'Sam and I were just taking the dogs for a walk.' She looked around, only to find that Marmite and Jasper were both close by, panting heavily and damp with sea water. 'And then we were going to the pub.'

'You could always join us for a drink, if you fancy it?' Sam said.

Amanda and Stella exchanged a glance. 'I think we've got time for one drink,' Amanda murmured. 'What do you say, Stella?'

'I can't think of anything more wonderful,' Stella replied, fiddling with a butterfly charm hanging on a cord around her neck.

'That's settled then.' Sam gave them a devastating smile. 'Lead the way, ladies.'

Chapter Fifteen

'W hy did you invite them to come with us?' Lila asked, giggling and sidestepping awkwardly round an uneven paving stone as they made their way back to Charlie's house from the pub. 'You didn't need to. You could have had me all to yourself.'

Sam slipped his arm through hers. 'Because you don't get to spend much time here at the moment, and I didn't want to monopolize you. Come on, Marmite, this way.' He pulled gently on the dog's lead.

'I still can't get over that they thought I'd injured myself when it was so obvious you were rescuing me from sea monsters!' She laughed again. She hoped she wasn't slurring her words. She had lost track of the glasses of wine, the hours they'd passed with Stella and Amanda. Stella's husband Anton had joined them, and Hugh, the pub landlord, had come to sit at their table for a while. Even the huge, delicious fish pie hadn't soaked up all the alcohol, and Lila knew she was drunk, that Sam, with the drive back to his accommodation ahead of him, was sober. She took a deep breath, trying to centre herself.

'I didn't mind that,' Sam said evenly. 'I was just frustrated about being interrupted.'

'Oh yes, you were going to say something, weren't you? It's this road,' she added, pointing to the sign that read 'Coral Terrace'.

'It doesn't matter now. It's been a fun afternoon, great to meet your neighbours.'

She dug in her handbag for her keys, then unlocked the front door. 'I have had too much wine, though.'

Sam followed her into the house, crouched to unclip Marmite and Jasper's leads, and steered her onto a sofa. 'I'm making you a strong coffee, seeing as I know my way around the kitchen and you need to be fully functioning and able to drive to set in the morning.'

Lila gasped. 'Oh shit, the baking!' She hid her head in her hands. 'I haven't done any of the baking I needed to do for tomorrow. Amanda does it during the week, but on Sundays I'm in charge. Fuck balls. Oh!' She looked up at him. 'Except we're not starting until nine tomorrow. I can get it done first thing. Yep, I'll do it in the morning.' She breathed a sigh of relief.

Sam leaned against the wall, his arms folded, the kettle bubbling behind him. 'You reckon you'll jump out of bed, fresh as a daisy, at six o'clock tomorrow morning and get it all done?'

'I'll have to,' Lila told him. 'I can't let Winston or Charlie down. I've done that to too many people already . . .' Her words trailed off as Sam took off his coat, folded it on the sofa and rolled up the sleeves of his jumper. 'What are you doing?'

He gave her a wide smile. 'You know how you wanted me to help you with the baking? I think that time has come.'

*

178

It was after midnight by the time they were finished. Lila, sobering up with strong coffee and copious amounts of water, had refused to simply instruct Sam and had worked alongside him. He was, as with everything, careful and diligent, measuring ingredients precisely and making sure the scones, Danishes, muffins and *arancini* were all evenly sized. When everything was done, Lila had a headache, and felt unbelievably guilty.

'I'm so sorry,' she said, when they had loaded the last of the scones onto the cooling rack.

'Why? I've had fun.' He had chocolate smudged across his cheek, his hair was dusted with flour and his fingers were stained blue from the blueberries they'd used in the muffins.

'You have toiled over my baking when you should have left hours ago. You didn't need to stay. I should have done it myself or faced the consequences. But,' she added, 'I am very grateful. Everything looks and tastes amazing, and you have made my life so much easier, perhaps even saved my job. I—'

Sam's fingers brushed her jaw and he tilted her chin up. 'I did this because I wanted to, because I was the one who turned up here and disrupted your plans in the first place. I wouldn't have stayed if I didn't want to be here.'

'Then you are an amazing man.'

He laughed softly. 'It's time I left, and you went to bed.' He dropped his hand, shrugged on his coat and walked past the sleeping dogs.

She followed him to the door. 'Thank you for today.' She reached up to wipe the chocolate from his cheek. Sam put his hand over hers.

'Sweet dreams, Delilah.' He bent his head and brushed his lips gently against hers. Sparks rushed through her; his touch was warm and soft and electrifying all at once. It only lasted a moment, and then he was gone. But she had caught a glimpse of his expression before he had turned away from her, his face lit by the pool of the outside light. She had seen tenderness and desire, and not a whisper of remorse. She shut the door, pressed her head against the frosted glass, and tried to slow her racing heart.

The Bodmin Moor location was wild and barren, a complete contrast to the coastal village and the cliffs. There were no acres of blue ocean, only miles of green; scrubland and fields, the first signs of spring dotting the landscape with fresh, bright colours. It was beautiful in an entirely different way and, even with her lingering hangover, Lila was looking forward to the day ahead.

She parked the old Volvo and Claude directed her to Gertie's new spot, still nestled next to the catering tent, but at the back of the sprawl of lorries and trailers, so that the windscreen gave her a view of rolling hills and a sky peppered with clouds. She settled Marmite in the driver's seat and carefully refilled the tins and display stands with the cakes and pastries she had made with Sam the night before.

She got the custard Danishes out of their box, and had a flashback to Sam standing at the kitchen counter, stirring the custard while she read him the instructions from Charlie's recipe book in her fake Irish accent. He had tried to keep his concentration, but a smile had tugged at his lips until he'd given up, started laughing and put a blob of custard on her nose. When she'd feigned outrage, he'd laughed even harder, the sound filling Charlie's kitchen and Lila's heart.

She wondered how soon he would appear, what his schedule was like for the day, and then chastised herself. She couldn't fall for Sam – that was the one, pressing thought she'd woken with, far too early and with a hammer pounding a rhythm behind her eyes. She was here to work. To look after Gertie and make Charlie proud. And all of this was temporary anyway. Soon it would be gone, and she'd have to go back to real life.

But when crew members came onto the bus and commented on how crunchy the *arancini* were, or that the sausage rolls were particularly herby, Lila had to resist telling them that it was because Sam had made them. It felt like a secret; as if every baked item had a little extra magic in it. She remembered one of Uncle Hal's sayings, one that had made her cringe when Charlie had first told her, but now made complete sense: They were made with love and extra calories. Those bakes held all her memories of the previous day and, try as she might, she couldn't help returning to them, to the way he'd said goodbye, the power of that one, brief kiss.

Em appeared on the bus, navy Puffa jacket zipped up to her neck. 'Everything OK, Lila? You've got all you need?'

'Yup. I'm all set up. Lovely view this time, too.'

'Good, good.' She tapped her hand on the back of the nearest seat, hovering as if she had something else to say.

'Can I get you a coffee or a tea? Help yourself to any nibbles.'

'A latte would be lovely,' Em said. 'Thanks. Have you seen Keeley recently? She seemed OK to you?'

Lila paused. It was unlike Em to discuss members of the cast; she was always so focused on her role, managing the catering squad to within an inch of its life. 'I saw her on Friday,' Lila said. 'She seemed fine.'

'That's good. You're close, aren't you?'

'Starting to be,' Lila admitted, frothing the milk for Em's drink. 'Is something wrong?'

Em frowned. 'A couple of guys in the tent said she'd been sharp with them – rude, even, which is so unlike her. And it's not as if we don't expect that. Cast members can be very . . . intense.' Lila could tell she was being tactful. 'But this is such a good-natured shoot, and Keeley's always been so sweet, and generous with her time.'

'I'll talk to her,' Lila said, 'as soon as I see her. I'll check everything's OK.' She handed Em her coffee and put a custard Danish into a bag for her.

'Thanks, Lila. You're a star.'

When she was alone, Lila pondered Em's words. Keeley had come back from Derbyshire a fortnight ago with a spring in her step. She had been so excited that Lila had been given the Miss Trevelyan role on the back of Gregor interrupting their rehearsal, and hadn't shown any signs of the tearfulness that Lila had seen on the beach that night. But she was a good actress: perhaps there was something wrong and – most of the time, at least – she was hiding it well.

The day was a quiet one, and Lila had a lot of time to rearrange her stock and try out some new coffee ideas, mixing various roasts with almond milk, adding vanilla essence and cinnamon syrup. She started to create a fresh, more versatile coffee menu, and then watched as everyone filed past Gertie to get to the catering tent for their hot lunch, her stomach flipping as she noticed Sam's sandy hair in the crowd. She knew their fixed breaks were short and precious, and that he was unlikely to have time to visit the bus as well, but at the last moment he stepped aside and jumped on board, distractingly handsome in his white shirt and breeches.

'I can't stay,' he said, 'but I wanted to check you were OK.'

'I'm fine,' Lila replied, discovering that any embarrassment at her drunkenness was obliterated by the joy of seeing him. 'Bit headachy, but it's my own fault. And the bakes are especially good today. You've got a busy schedule?'

'Yep.' Sam stole a halloumi bite from a cake stand. 'Lots of scenes with Toby. He's got another commitment for the rest of the week, so this day was always going to be a bit of a nightmare.'

'You didn't think you should have told me that when you were covered in flour in my kitchen at midnight? Oh Sam, you must be exhausted.'

'I'm grand. Honestly. I'll try and see you later, OK?' He turned to go, then noticed the empty mugs, syrup bottles and scrawled notes covering the tables. 'What's all this?'

'Coffee planning,' she said proudly. 'I'm going to make Gertie's menu even more desirable.'

'Oh? I think there are a lot of desirable things about the Cornish Cream Tea Bus as it is.' He squeezed her hand and hurried off the bus.

Lila closed her eyes. She couldn't fall for him. She *couldn't*. But her flush of pleasure at his final words suggested her heart might not be prepared to listen to her head.

The light was fading, and by the time Lila sneaked out, large, fat raindrops were splattering against Gertie's windows. She knew it wouldn't be enough to delay the shoot, and when she got to the set, the moor was lit up like a crime scene, tall lighting rigs spotlighting Sam and Toby, both resplendent in full period dress, facing off against each other.

A key thread of *Estelle*'s storyline was the two brothers and their differing opinions, and the way that both Estelle's presence and Aria's character Marianne came between them.

This scene looked as if it was an implosion – or explosion – of all that tension.

Lila tiptoed to the edge of the cluster of people watching the action, and folded her arms against the cold.

'It's unthinkable, Robert,' Toby was saying, his hands expressive, his dark hair twisting in the wind. 'There *is* no money for the house. Not if we want to get this new venture off the ground. We must take our chances while we can.'

'And what about good sense? Propriety?' Sam, as Robert, fired back. 'What about thinking things through for a change? You know why we're here, with this shell of a house our only hope, why we're unwelcome in London. Have you learned nothing, brother?' He clapped a hand to Toby's shoulder, his voice softening. 'We can never go back. I've come to accept it, but surely we should learn from it? Take our chances, yes. But only when we can be more certain of the outcome.'

Toby flung Sam's arm off forcefully. The rain was silvery flecks under the bold white light. 'You don't understand. *This* is what will make our fortune. If you knew what I know—'

'Then no doubt I would have walked away long before now.'

'When did you become so staid?'

'When I realized that one of us had to be, and it was never going to be you.' Sam jabbed his finger at Toby's chest, his eyes ablaze with anger. Lila held her breath. She was gripped, but she also had a creeping sense of dread, torn between watching them and running away before she heard it play out. She hadn't seen this particular script, so she hadn't been forewarned, and this drama, set centuries in the past, suddenly felt far too close to home.

'Robert,' Toby's tone was jovial, coaxing. 'Come now, you don't mean that—'

'I mean every word. No good can come of what you're doing. Those moments when you're not thinking? When you're carried away on the possibility of what *could* be? That's when disaster happens. I've seen you burn too many bridges. How can I – how can *anyone* – trust you, when you behave like this?' He took a deep breath, his handsome face flashing with pain. 'Sooner or later you'll hurt someone you truly care about, someone you love, and you'll lose them for ever.'

Lila swallowed, backing away as Gregor shouted, 'Cut!' and there was a smattering of applause. 'Very good,' the director said. 'Very emotional. Now I want to try it again, but this time with . . .' The words were lost to Lila as they began to reset the scene and she hurried back to Gertie.

There was nobody waiting for her, no one needing a coffee or a scone at eight in the evening, and she gave Marmite a distracted stroke and flopped into a seat. She had cleared away the detritus from her coffee planning, had felt such a sense of achievement at the new drinks menu she had put together. But now, none of that seemed to matter.

All of Sam's – Robert's – words had hit home. She knew it was fiction, a drama that was supposed to delight and unnerve and yank at the heartstrings, but it suddenly seemed to echo her own situation. And with Sam's character being the sensible one, too. How many bridges had Lila burnt? She didn't want to start counting for fear of never getting to the end. And those last words: *Sooner or later, it'll be someone you truly care about, someone you love, and you'll lose them for ever.*

She rubbed her hands over her eyes. She had explained to Charlie what had happened between her and Clara and, after hinting at it that night at the beach party, and with their friendship firmly established, she had since told Keeley the

185

whole story too. But her real feelings about the way it had ended, the finality of it and the devastation of losing her friend – she had kept those shut up inside. It seemed easier to pretend to others that it didn't matter: that way she might start to believe it, too.

She was spontaneous and impulsive and, sometimes, she knew, infuriating. When things went wrong, she bounced back. She took what was coming and moved on. But with Clara, it was different. She couldn't forget her friend's claims that she was irresponsible, selfish, a bad friend. That she was always flitting from one job, or one boy, to the next, avoiding anything that came close to commitment or responsibility. She couldn't be trusted – that was what Clara had said at the end. That's why she hadn't wanted her to work at her gala in the first place.

Being here, on *Estelle*, was throwing all that into sharp focus. Charlie putting her in charge of the bus, Keeley's friendship, and Sam. Sam, who set her pulse racing, who made her want to design a separate, delicious coffee *just* for him. But her time in Cornwall hadn't been without mistakes: committing the Cornish Cream Tea Bus to this job without Charlie's permission; leaving the set early; almost losing Marmite. Had Clara been right? Lila didn't want to believe it, but she wasn't convinced that any of her actions had proved her friend wrong.

She tugged her phone out of her pocket and, taking a deep breath, opened WhatsApp. She reread Charlie's latest update from America, and looked again at Daniel's recent message. He'd sent her a photo of an impressive, eco-friendly coffee machine at his course. *Hope you and Gertie are having fun. Thought you might like to see this!! Dx*

Lila had been touched that he'd thought of her.

Then there was her thread with Clara. One that scrolled up and up and up as they'd swapped funny anecdotes, moaned about work, sent holiday snaps and links to restaurant websites, planned nights and days out, either just the two of them or with Clara's boyfriend, Glen. There was a whole stream of photos of unicorn tattoos as they discussed which one to get, the excitement at their ridiculous plan obvious in the exchange. Years of friendship that Lila had taken for granted.

But then, at the bottom, after messages from Lila pleading with Clara to see her, to pick up the phone when she called, to at least let her know she was OK, was the one response Clara had sent. It had been as Lila was heading to the tube, in a daze after their argument on the street. Her phone had pinged and Lila had jumped on it, hoping it was an apology, forgiveness, a plea to return. But, when Lila had swiped open her phone, she had seen that it wasn't any of those things.

The tears started to fall as she read it again, even though she knew exactly what it said, more ingrained in her mind than her one line as Miss Trevelyan.

I will never forgive you, Delilah.

It was over. She hadn't been exaggerating when she'd said that to Charlie and Keeley, when she'd mentioned it briefly to Sam, brushing it aside as if it was just one of those things, a life lesson to be learned. From Clara's point of view, their friendship had ended.

But Lila missed her so much. She wanted to prove to her that she *could* be trusted, that she could be responsible and committed, that friends and family could open their hearts to her and she would guard them, treasure them, not do anything to betray them. She wanted, so badly, to get her friend back. She just had no idea where to start.

187

Chapter Sixteen

Lila didn't wait for Sam that night. The moment Em gave her the knock that filming was over, she locked up Gertie, took Marmite in her arms and hurried to her car. Amanda had let herself into Charlie's and left a pile of fresh bakes in the kitchen, and Lila collected Jasper and spent an evening on the sofa watching mindless TV, keeping the dogs close, unable to escape the fresh waves of sadness and guilt. She felt additionally guilty that she hadn't waited for Sam, sending him a brief, vague text saying she had to leave.

She woke the following morning feeling worse than she had the previous day, the scene between Henry and Robert Bramerton bringing everything back to her, as if the argument with Clara had happened hours, rather than months, ago.

The day was brisk and breezy, the backstage village bubbling with the usual noise and laughter, and Lila kept her head down and sneaked onto Gertie, switching on the coffee machine, fairy lights and oven. Everything was familiar and comforting, but she wished, for the first time since she'd gone off on her American adventure, that Charlie was with her.

Lila was glad when Keeley appeared on the bus, distracting her from her thoughts, and hugged her with a little too much enthusiasm.

'It feels like ages since we last spoke,' Keeley told her. 'How are you? What do you think of bleak old Bodmin Moor?'

Lila smiled, relieved. There was nothing off about her that she could see. 'It's beautiful, so different from the coast. It'll be perfect in *Estelle*. How are you? Busy?'

Keeley's smile faltered, something flickering behind her eyes, but she nodded. 'So busy. And it's nonstop now until the end of the shoot. You'd think with me only being the ghost I'd have a lot more time to myself.'

'Yes, but the show *is* named after your ghost, Keeley.' Lila turned to the coffee machine, loaded a portafilter with coffee, and poured milk into the jug to froth. She was going to add vanilla essence to Keeley's latte, to see what she thought. 'Didn't you realize it would be this hectic when you signed up? Surely you had the schedule months ago?'

Keeley collected Marmite and sat down with the dog on her lap. 'Of course I did. I knew all this, and at the time I couldn't have been more thrilled. This was – is – my big break! Thousands of women would *kill* to get this role.' She stroked Marmite's ears and sneezed three times.

'But?' Lila asked softly, bringing over Keeley's drink and sitting opposite her. 'You can't tell me that sentence doesn't have a "but".'

Keeley gave her a wan smile. 'But it's so hard.' Her voice cracked on the last word.

Lila reached a hand across the table. 'Tell me. If you have time?'

189

Keeley sniffed loudly, and nodded. 'Everyone is so kind and attentive, they're always making sure I'm OK, sheltering me from the rain with big umbrellas, eight hundred costume checks a day. The filming itself, I love. I *do* love acting, and I'm used to the waiting, the repetition, the cold. I don't mind any of those things, and nights like the one we had at the equinox, taking Gertie down to the beach – I'm here for those, even if they involve tequila.' They swapped a smile, and Keeley continued. 'But the rest of the time, I can't breathe. People are fussing over me constantly, and it's so well inten-tioned, which makes me feel like a bitch for hating it, but it's as if I'm trapped. I thought the weekend with Jordan would help, that it would be refreshing, but it just made me realize what I'm missing back home. I hoped it would get easier – that I would get used to it.'

'But you haven't?'

Keeley huffed a breath out between pearly pink lips. 'Not so far.'

'And you feel like you've given it enough time?'

Keeley shrugged, not meeting her eye.

Lila could see how close her friend was to tears, and she wanted more than anything to help her. But she had to tread carefully. She couldn't get this wrong; not if Keeley was trusting her to give advice.

'I can't claim to know how you feel,' she said gently, 'and I would never belittle it or tell you it doesn't matter, because you wouldn't be questioning everything if it didn't. But how long have you got left to go?'

'A couple more months, including the studio stuff.'

'So, two more months of this. It's stifling, and not quite what you were expecting, but you're with good people, you're making friends, and at the end of it, think what you will have accomplished. Think of how you'll feel when your series, the programme you have the title role in, is shown to thousands of viewers. It might be tough now, but don't you think it will be worth it when you're snuggled up with Jordan, watching *your* drama?'

Keeley sipped her drink and her eyes widened in surprise.

'I added some vanilla essence,' Lila said quickly, not wanting to lose her thread. 'Look, God knows I'm not exactly a role model when it comes to blossoming careers. But don't you think you owe it to yourself to see this through? Don't you think you'll regret it if you don't?'

Keeley peered at her. 'What is it?'

'What do you mean?'

'I've come here moaning about my problems, and there's something wrong. What is it, Lila? What's happened? Is Charlie OK? You've not had any news from America—'

'No, no, they're fine. It's all fine.'

'It is *not* fine! Did you message Clara? Did you try and speak to her?'

Lila shook her head. 'Nothing's happened, and we're talking about your future here.'

'What coffee do you like?' Keeley stood and put Marmite on the seat. 'I'll make you one.' She strode up to the coffee machine and stared at it, flexing her fingers.

'You don't need to do that.'

'Do I just need to put the – this thing, here. And then I can do this . . .' She started trying to attach an empty porta-filter to the group head.

Lila rolled her eyes and went to join her. 'You need to fill the portafilter up with coffee, and then press it down, so the grains are flat, like so. And *then* you can pop it here and press the button, but make sure you have a mug or cup under

191

it.' She demonstrated, frothing the milk and making a perfect cappuccino, the aroma of fresh coffee filling the air.

'Cinnamon or chocolate?' Keeley asked, holding up the shakers.

'Cinnamon,' Lila decided. She took the finished drink from Keeley and brought it back to the table.

'It's a complicated machine,' Keeley said.

'It's fine once you get used to it,' Lila replied, shrugging. 'Obviously, as with everything, that takes time. You can't be an expert straight away, and that first bit, when you're just starting out, can be very uncomfortable.' She knew she was shoehorning the metaphor in, but she was struggling to think of a way to get through to her friend.

Keeley sighed, her narrow shoulders dropping. 'I've given it loads of time. I have thought about this, you know.'

'Really?' Lila asked, careful to keep her voice soft. 'What will happen if you go now? Won't it destroy the entire shoot? Will they even be able to start again, with someone else in your role, or will the budget be blown? Think of all the people you'll be hurting if you decide, now, that this isn't for you. For the sake of a couple of months, Keeley.'

'Don't you think that's *all* I've been thinking about? I've started being horrible to people, snapping and shouting, wanting some space. What if I keep pretending everything's all right, and then I suddenly . . . explode!'

'That's not going to happen. And if it does, then you apologize. Everyone will understand. Won't they be able to sue you if you back out now?'

'But what if I lose it with Gregor or Winston? What if I get kicked off the show anyway? Isn't it better that I go on my own terms before that happens?'

'You're too important to the production to be kicked

off – and you're too important to so many people here. What about Sam? Sarah? Don't you owe it to them?' Lila sipped her drink nervously.

'Exactly!' Keeley said, her eyes brightening. 'I'm wasting their time, thinking that I'm cut out to be an actor, and it turns out I'm not. It's not my calling. I should get out while I can, be honest with everyone – including myself.'

'No, Keeley. You *can* do this – you're brilliant at it! You're just having a crisis of confidence. You need to stop and think—'

'I need to go. I need to talk to my agent.' Keeley stood and squeezed Lila's shoulder. 'Thank you so much for your advice, for the delicious coffee. This was exactly what I needed. You've made everything so much clearer. I'll let you know how it goes.'

'Don't you think you're being impulsive, Keeley?' Lila called as she lifted Marmite up and put him in the cab, then followed her friend off the bus. 'Keeley!'

Keeley turned and blew her a kiss, just as two crew members approached Gertie, rubbing hands red from the cold.

Lila cursed under her breath and led them on board. She made their drinks, her mind whirring. She had been intent on reassuring Keeley, convincing her this was too big an opportunity to throw away, that she was surrounded by friends, she could get through it and, Lila was certain, would be so happy when she had. Instead, what had Keeley taken from their conversation? That by making an early exit, she could avoid disaster.

Lila had got it wrong again, and this time it wouldn't only be Keeley and Lila that would lose their jobs, but everyone involved in *Estelle*. What would they all think of her, when Keeley told them that it was Lila who had encouraged her

193

to quit? What would Winston say? Oh God – what would Sam think when the truth came out?

And then there was the reputation of the Cornish Cream Tea Bus. Would Charlie and her business suffer the fallout if word got around that it had been Keeley Klein's visits to Gertie that had led to her dramatic change of heart?

On top of all that, Lila couldn't ignore the entirely selfish truth that she loved being here, spending her days on the set on board the bus. She didn't want to lose Keeley as a friend. She tried not to think about Sam, and how she would feel if she couldn't see him any more. If Keeley went ahead with her plan there would be no winners, just a long list of losers, with the actor herself firmly at the top.

Lila cleared away the used mugs with unsteady hands. She had to do something. There was no way she could let Keeley go through with this. She couldn't be the reason this beautiful, talented woman gave up her role and, quite probably, ruined her acting reputation for ever. Lila was not going to be responsible for another hideous mess, for someone else losing the trust of the people they cared about. All she needed to do was work out how to fix it.

Chapter Seventeen

Lila felt a wave of happiness when, pulling up outside Charlie's house that evening, she saw that the lights were already on. Charlie's suitcase sat in the front room, and Lila could hear the shower running upstairs. She went through to the kitchen and made a pot of tea, taking out Charlie's cherished narwhal-shaped teapot that never failed to bring a smile to her face. By the time her cousin came down, she had fed Marmite and arranged the teapot, two mugs and a bowl of *arancini* balls on the table.

'Lila!' Charlie skidded across the living room in her slipper socks and pulled her into a hug. 'How are you? How has everything been? It's so good to see you!' She released her cousin and lifted Marmite into her arms, burying her nose in her dog's fur while he barked excitedly and licked her face. 'And you, little guy. I have missed you!'

'It's been great,' Lila said, putting on her brightest smile. 'Gertie is popular on set, I've been experimenting with some new coffee ideas, and we're on Bodmin Moor now, which is beautiful in a desolate sort of way. But what about you? What about America?'

Charlie put Marmite on the floor, sat down and popped an *arancini* ball in her mouth. 'San Francisco is so vibrant, and the street food – Lila, you wouldn't believe it! I've got so many ideas about what we can do here. Daniel's eco-course was brilliant, too. He's so inspired.'

'You went on holiday and both came back desperate to get back to work. That is so typical of the two of you.' She rolled her eyes. 'Did you have any actual fun, or was it all research?'

Charlie rested her head on her hand. 'Oh yes. We had lots of fun.' She smiled dreamily. 'It was pretty much perfect.'

'So you and Daniel are even more loved up, then? Where is he?'

'He's gone to check in with Lily and pick up Jasper. He should be here soon.'

'Can't bear to be apart?' Lila poured out the tea and added milk, watching the mini whirlpool she had created.

Charlie put a hand on her arm. 'Are you all right, Lila? Sure everything's OK?'

'I'm fine. Gertie and the set – it's all gone really well. I'm just tired.'

'I left you with too much,' Charlie said. 'I'm so sorry. Has Amanda—'

'Amanda's been brilliant,' Lila rushed to assure her. 'And you didn't leave me with too much to do. I just . . .' she had an urge to confide in Charlie about her conversation with Keeley, but she wanted a chance to stop her from leaving without anyone else finding out. 'I'm glad you're back, that's all. I want to hear all about your holiday.'

Charlie stood and went to the fridge, smiling when she

opened the door. 'And I need to hear the gossip from *Estelle.*'

'I got some stuff in,' Lila said. 'I didn't want you to come back to a bit of dry old cheese and half a lemon.'

Charlie took out a bottle of white wine, poured them each a large glass and took the nibbles to the coffee table, gesturing for Lila to follow.

They sat on the same sofa, facing each other.

'How has it been with everyone on set?' Charlie asked. 'Keeley and Toby. Sam. Cheers, by the way. It's good to be home.'

Lila clinked her glass against her cousin's. 'It's been even better than I imagined. I've spent a lot of time with Keeley, and Toby and Aria. Sam, too. I've been an extra – sorry, supporting actor. That's the technical term.' She watched, grinning, as Charlie's eyes widened in surprise.

'What?' Charlie screeched. 'How did you manage that? Tell me *everything!*'

So Lila told her. Almost everything, anyway. Certain events, such as almost losing Marmite on the beach and Sam turning up in Porthgolow and sweeping her off her feet were too dangerous, or too close to her heart, to reveal.

Charlie gasped and laughed and squealed, and Lila embellished the stories, how over-dramatic Gregor was and her pounding fear, and then elation, when she'd said her one line as Miss Trevelyan. Any time she mentioned Sam she kept her voice neutral, hoping that there would be nothing for her cousin to pick up on.

'Oh my God, Lila,' Charlie said, when she finally took a breath and a big gulp of wine. 'Your month here sounds even more exciting than America!'

'Rubbish,' Lila protested. 'And I need to hear all about that right this moment. I can't believe I've monopolized the conversation. How was San Francisco?' She settled herself into the cushions, ready to be transported halfway round the world.

The bottle of wine was empty and both Lila and Charlie were all talked out, Charlie stroking Marmite's ears while he dozed, Lila scrolling through the photos Charlie had taken on her phone, when the front door opened.

Jasper trotted into the front room and sat in front of the coffee table. Daniel followed him in, looking happy and tanned.

'Daniel,' Lila said, getting up. 'Did you have a lovely time?'

'The best.' He gave her a tired smile. 'Jet lag's going to be a killer, though.'

'You don't have to go straight back to work, do you?' She hugged him.

'I'll pop into the hotel in the morning. I need to see what the state of play is. Everything been OK with Gertie?'

'It was grea—' Lila started, but Charlie talked over her.

'She was an extra, Daniel! A supporting actor. She's basically going to be starring in the series!'

Lila laughed. 'Charlie's exaggerating. How was your conference?'

'Enlightening. But you've been kicking back with the stars? I need to make myself comfortable. Hang on a second.'

He went into the kitchen and, as Lila sat back down, Jasper jumped up next to her. Charlie looked outraged. 'Jasper! Off the cushions! What on earth has got into you?'

Jasper slunk back onto the floor and put his nose in Lila's lap. She stroked his silky fur, hoping her blush wasn't too obvious, and was relieved when Daniel sat next to Charlie, opened a fresh bottle of wine and looked at her expectantly. Lila got ready to tell her story all over again, and silently prayed that her cousin wouldn't work out that she was the reason Jasper thought the sofa cushions were now an acceptable place for him to be.

Charlie came with her to the set the following day, saying she had to stay busy or she wouldn't beat the jet lag, and Lila felt as if she had a buffer between her and any ill-advised conversations she might accidentally start. She wondered where Keeley was, whether she'd spoken to her agent yet, or if there was still time to rescue the situation.

'Tell me all about these new coffee variations,' Charlie said, while they were piling up their sweet and savoury treats on the vintage cake stands. 'I'm always up for new ideas, and I'd hate to have you here and waste your expertise. Once the filming's done I want you back in Porthgolow with me as Gertie's personal barista.'

'You don't want me to go back to London?'

Charlie shrugged. 'Not if you're not ready.'

'Even though I'm staying in your house?'

'There's plenty of room, and I can go to Daniel's if I want to.'

'That would be wonderful, Charlie. Thank you.' She put her new, scribbled menu on the counter. 'This is what I was thinking . . .'

'Hello, anyone on board?' Sam looked scruffily delicious in a tatty blue shirt and jeans, his thick hair left to its own devices. His smile was instant, and Lila couldn't help but return it.

'Hey.'

'Hi, Sam,' Charlie said.

'You're back! How was America?'

'Amazing. About as far from sleepy Cornwall as you can get.'

'Apart from the food markets,' Lila said. 'Apparently they have these bonkers street-food places in San Francisco, and Charlie's going to use all her new knowledge to make the Porthgolow markets *even* better. She's a one-woman whirlwind!'

Sam laughed. 'I'm going to come to one, once they're back in full swing.'

'Porthgolow's such a special village,' Charlie said. 'You'd love it, Sam.'

Sam glanced at Lila and she shrugged. 'Charlie and Daniel only got back last night, so we haven't had much of a catch-up.' She realized that if she didn't let her know about Sam's visit, then someone else would. His presence hadn't gone unnoticed, and she was surprised Charlie hadn't had a text from Amanda or Stella, passing on the gossip.

Sam nodded, giving her such an intense look that Lila flushed. 'Actually,' she said lightly, 'Sam's seen Porthgolow.'

'Oh?' Charlie asked, her tray of scones momentarily forgotten.

'It was a weekend, so . . .'

'Sunday,' Sam prompted.

'Yes, it was a Sunday, and I didn't have any plans, and—'

'I decided,' Sam interjected, 'to come and see Porthgolow for myself. You and Lila have mentioned it so often, I was intrigued.'

Lila chewed the inside of her cheek. Charlie was frowning now. Would she mind that Sam had been baking in her kitchen? She didn't think so.

'So you spent a day in Porthgolow together?' Charlie asked, her frown dissolving. 'Just the two of you?' Her tone was curious, and Lila tried to think how to change the subject, to get her and Sam out of the spotlight.

'Have you heard?' a voice cut in, and Lila sent a silent prayer to whoever might be listening. But her relief faded when she saw that it was crew member Sarah standing in the doorway, and that she looked as panicked as Lila had felt the previous day.

'Heard what?' she asked, although she was sure she already knew.

'It's Keeley,' Sarah said, sounding choked. 'She just told me that she's going to quit. She's got a meeting with Winston and her agent next week, and she's going to give up the role. In the middle of filming.'

Charlie gasped, and Lila felt Sam go completely still beside her.

'What?' he said.

Sarah nodded vigorously. 'I promise you I'm not joking. She *just* told me. She seemed determined – a bit manic, if I'm honest. How can she do this? Does she have *any* idea what will happen? How much this will cost her, and not just financially? It's utter madness! Look, you can't say anything, any of you. Not to anyone. But—'

'She's going to do it next week?' Lila asked urgently.

Sarah nodded again.

'Then we've got time to change her mind. I mean, we can, can't we? We can save all of this.'

Sarah seemed dubious, Charlie still looked shocked and Sam . . . Lila could hardly bear to look at Sam. He and Keeley were really close, but she'd obviously kept this from him, hadn't considered what it might do to him.

'We can save this,' Lila said again. She took Sam's hand. 'Don't worry. I'll help to make this right. I promise.'

201

He lifted her hand to his lips and kissed it, then pulled her towards him, wrapping his arms around her and resting his chin on her head. 'We can do it together,' he said.

In that moment, Lila felt like it was possible. They could change Keeley's mind, save the shoot, get everything back on track. This was her chance to fix what seemed broken, to prove that she could be a force for good.

As Sarah hurried off to wherever she was needed, and Lila reluctantly pulled away from Sam and saw the questions in Charlie's eyes, she knew that fate had intervened again.

She had been sent down to Cornwall, to Charlie and Gertie, Daniel and Marmite, and the *Estelle* set. She was being given a chance to make up for her own disaster, by preventing Keeley from doing the same thing. The young actor might believe she had thought everything through, but Lila had seen from her body language, had heard in her shaky words, that she was simply reacting. She was rushing into a decision that would have consequences for the rest of her life, and would affect so many other people.

Lila would help her to see how much she meant to everyone – not just for the sake of the production and its budget, but as a friend. She would help her realize what she would be losing if she walked away. For the first time in a long time, and in part because she knew that her cousin, and this gorgeous, kind, inspiring man in front of her were with her, Lila believed she could make a difference.

She smiled up at Sam. 'You're right,' she said. 'We can do it together.'

Lila had come too far, and fallen for this new life too hard, not to put up a fight to save it. She didn't know how yet, but Lila, Charlie and Sam were going to save *Estelle*.

Part Three

My Tart Will Go On

Chapter Eighteen

'All we have to do is convince her to stay.'

'Yes, Lila. That is the obvious part. It's how we do it that's more complicated.'

Delilah sighed in frustration and kicked a pebble. It skittered along the smooth golden sand of Porthgolow beach and, a second later, was chased by a particularly boisterous Marmite, his tan and black body a dark smudge against the sinking Cornish sun. Lila glanced at Charlie, who was rubbing her forehead, as if trying to massage an answer out of it. But Lila knew she was trying to ward off exhaustion, staying awake as long as possible so as to keep at bay the jet lag that had been threatening her all day.

'Can't we just explain that she's sending *Estelle* to an early grave?' Charlie said. 'Not to mention the damage she'll be doing to her own career, just when she's at the start of it, too.'

'But her agent will have done all that,' Lila countered. 'And if she's having a really tough time, then the prospect of her career getting ruined isn't going to be a big enough carrot. It sounds like she wants to give up acting altogether.'

'So what do we do, then?' Charlie asked. 'Do we let her do it? If she's willing to risk so much, then maybe there isn't anything we *can* do.'

Lila squeezed her hands into fists. She imagined *Estelle* coming to an abrupt, unhappy end. She thought of how Keeley would be viewed by everyone who currently loved and respected her. She couldn't believe it was the right decision, not for Keeley or anyone else. Her gaze was drawn to the waves, and she remembered Sam hoisting her onto his shoulder, his arms around her.

'There has to be. Keeley's upset, but she's so good natured. If she's really thinking of causing pain to so many people, then she's not thinking rationally. She's unhappy because she's missing Jordan, and feeling isolated and lonely despite being constantly surrounded by people. Maybe she's started to believe that all the attention is false, because they *need* her to be there. Maybe, in a weird sort of way, she's trying to prove that by walking out.'

Charlie squatted and held out her arm, and Marmite came bounding towards her, a long trail of seaweed in his mouth. Lila thought it was testament to how much she had missed her dog while she'd been in America that she hugged him despite his slimy toy. 'That is some twisted logic,' Charlie said. 'But it actually makes sense. So, if that's the case, what are we going to do?'

Lila put her hands on her hips and looked out to sea. Porthgolow was such a beautiful place, with its quaint seafront, its curved, sandy beach and mellow water. Reenie's yellow hut jutted out on one side of the cove, Daniel's luxurious glass hotel on top of the opposite cliff. She hadn't spent a lot of time in the village since she'd moved here, but now, with the day's baking done and Charlie insisting that it wasn't just Marmite who needed a stroll in the fresh air, Lila realized how stunning it was. With Charlie back to help with the bus, Lila knew things would get easier, and she could stop taking her temporary home for granted.

She bit back a gasp as an idea popped into her head, as bright as a shooting star. 'I have a plan!' she announced. 'But I'm going to need your help. Yours and Sam's and . . . everyone's really. Everyone I know – and beyond.'

Charlie narrowed her eyes, but Lila could see she was excited. She was always, Lila knew, up for a challenge. And they would have to put their whole hearts into this one. The future of *Estelle* depended on it.

'A video?' Sam said, sitting on the edge of one of Gertie's tables and folding his arms. He looked gorgeous when he was confused, but Lila decided that now probably wasn't the time to tell him. Instead, she reached out and pushed his sandy hair off his forehead, unable to stop a giggle when his confusion turned to surprise.

'What?' she asked innocently. 'You looked too serious. This is not going to be a serious video – I mean, the purpose of the video is absolutely serious, but the video itself doesn't need to be.'

'I took a bit of convincing too,' Charlie said, from behind a cake stand piled high with muffins. 'But I do think Lila's idea makes sense.'

'Explain it to me, then.' He tugged at the bow of her apron, which she'd tied round the front due to the string being far too long.

Lila tried to ignore the spark of electricity. She reminded herself that he had simply touched her clothing, but her mind couldn't help taking it further: what if he'd tugged hard enough to undo the bow, and the next thing she knew they were ripping at each other's clothes – although somewhere a lot more appropriate than a bus in the middle of a television set.

'Lila?' Sam prompted. 'The video?'

'Oh – yes! The video. Keeley feels lonely here. Everyone's fawning all over her and tugging at her hair and—' Sam raised an eyebrow. 'That's different, I'm not part of the hair and make-up team. Anyway, she feels like none of it's real, that she would rather be with Jordan where she knows the affection is genuine. So I thought if we made a video, got everyone to say something about her – Toby and Aria, Winston, Bert, Darius, Sarah – all the crew. Maybe even people further afield. You know: "Keeley, we love you, we're so glad you're in this production", et cetera. We can show her how important she is – how much people care about her. Because they do, don't they? She's the first person I got to know on set, she took the time to talk to me when I knew nobody other than Charlie. You did too, of course, but—'

'I get it,' Sam said. 'Completely.'

'You do?'

He nodded. 'I think it's a great idea. And a very thoughtful one. I honestly had no clue she was struggling, or I would have done something sooner.'

'None of us did. It's as if she's been holding it in, trying to contain it and then . . . wham! She's decided the *only* thing she can do is leave, that there are no half-measures. I don't know if this will make a difference, but we've got to try.'

'And that, Delilah, is why everyone loves you.'

Her heart skipped a beat. 'They do?'

'Unquestionably.'

'Oh,' she said, taking a step towards him. 'But what if I don't want *everyone* to love me. What if I only want—'

Charlie cleared her throat loudly. Lila stepped back and Sam gave her a mischievous grin.

'So we've decided,' Charlie said. 'The video is happening. Now all we need to do is film it. What are you thinking, Lila? Borrow a camera from the team here? Find a good backdrop to shoot everything against? Sam, try one of these – it's a new recipe with chunks of dark chocolate.'

'Don't mind if I do.' He chose a muffin and took a bite.

'I am not thinking either of those things,' Lila said, taking her phone out of her pocket. 'This is my tool of choice and, in terms of backdrop, let's just see how it goes. We don't want it to be too polished,' she added, when she saw Charlie's exasperated expression. 'It has to be real, otherwise Keeley will think it's more of the same and it won't make any difference.'

Sam and Charlie stared at her.

'Trust me,' she said. 'I know what I'm doing.'

As Sam took his coffee and muffin back to his trailer so he could start his transformation into Robert Bramerton, and Charlie checked on the scones in the oven, Lila tried not to think about how those very words: *Trust me, I know what I'm doing*, so regularly preceded disaster.

'What does Keeley Klein mean to you?'

Daniel shrugged. 'I don't know her.'

'That, Daniel Harper, is not a good start.'

They were standing in the gardens of Crystal Waters, the sun a flaming orb behind them, the sea flat and shimmering beneath its sunset glow. The wooden hot tub, which Lila hadn't yet had a chance to sample, bubbled gently alongside them. It was a beautiful setting and, as long as she kept Daniel at this angle, he wouldn't be a silhouette. She had thought adding a bit of the Porthgolow magic to her video wouldn't do any harm, as it would remind Keeley that she was leaving Cornwall behind, as well as the people in it.

'I said I'd do anything to help you, Lila, but if I don't know Keeley, then what can I say about her?'

'Well, are you looking forward to *Estelle?*'

'Of course. I can't wait to see the end result, to get a taste of what you and Gertie have been working so hard on.'

'Excellent. So say that, but mention Keeley instead of me and Gertie.'

Daniel laughed and shook his head. 'Right.' He glanced at the floor, as if taking a moment to compose himself. When he looked back up, his expression was serious and tender all at once. Lila could see he meant business. She held her phone up and, giving him the *three, two, one* with her fingers, hit record.

'I don't know you, Keeley,' he said, 'but I've heard a lot about you from Lila and Charlie. This series, *Estelle*, sounds like a classy bit of drama, and I can't wait to see you in it.' Lila gave him a thumbs-up, her finger hovering, ready to end the recording, but Daniel carried on speaking so she kept filming. 'I may know nothing about acting, but I do know a bit about perseverance. I've been in the shittiest hotel jobs imaginable, where you work eighteen-hour days and, even though you're surrounded by people, you never have a meaningful conversation. It can feel isolating – pointless, sometimes – but you have to think of your goal. Do you want to be a part of something momentous? Do you want to be more in control, to have more say about your direction of travel? It seems impossible now, but look where those years of hard work, determination and perseverance have got me: running my own hotel on the Cornish coast. Don't give up now because it's tough, keep going because it's worth it and because, in the process, regardless of where you want to end up, it'll make you a stronger person.' He gave Lila and the camera a genuine, but slightly embarrassed, smile, and Lila hit stop.

'Wow, Daniel. That was—'

'Over the top? You can cut out the bits you don't want.'

'Oh, I'm keeping all of it. It was perfect! Thank you.' She hugged him, and Daniel put his arms briefly round her. 'And can I book the hot tub?'

'Any time. Just speak to Chloe on reception. In fact, let me know your next day off and I'll put a double session for you and Charlie in the calendar.'

'That would be amazing.' Lila checked the video had saved and put her phone away as they made their way back to the pristine, calming reception that Lila wished was the foyer of her own house. 'Right, I'm off. More videos to film, more inspirational words to capture. Thank you again, Daniel.'

'Catch you later, Lila.'

She waved goodbye and, as Daniel went to add an extra-long session for her and Charlie in the hot-tub schedule, she almost ran down the hill on her way to securing her next video contributors. She didn't have a moment to lose.

'Keeley, we are *desperate* to see *Estelle*,' Stella said, pressing her hand against her chest. 'From the moment we heard what Charlie, Lila and Gertie were up to, we've been utterly thrilled at the idea of it. It sounds perfect: A ghost story set in Cornwall, lots of drama and beautiful women, beautiful *ghosts*—'

'Not to mention delicious, strapping men wearing breeches,'

Amanda cut in, and Stella nodded eagerly. 'It has got so much going for it. Oodles of things. And it can't survive without its star! Lila loves you, and that means we love you too. Come and see us in Porthgolow when you have some time off.' They both raised their wine glasses to the camera, and Lila pressed the 'end' button.

'That was fabulous, ladies,' she said. 'Thank you!'

'Very happy to help,' Stella cooed.

'Though we would have been even happier if you'd brought Sam with you again,' Amanda added. 'Honestly, that vision of him carrying you out of the water was just magnificent. It deserved a drama series all of its own.'

'What's this?' Charlie asked, and Lila squirmed under her gaze.

She had joined them in the pub after her detour to see Daniel, intent on collecting as many snippets for her video as possible, and had forgotten that she hadn't told Charlie the whole story of Sam's visit to Porthgolow.

'We were paddling,' she said. 'And then . . . Sam was just being silly.'

'But we got the wrong idea and thought he was rescuing Lila,' Stella added. 'We intervened, and ended up having a fun afternoon in here. With a television star!'

'It seems like I've missed out on a lot of juicy details,' Charlie said, drumming her fingers on her glass.

'You've only been back a couple of days,' Lila protested, 'and we've got a very short window to get this video done. Speaking of which,' she pointed at Hugh, who was polishing glasses behind the bar, 'here is my next victim.'

'Need my help?' Charlie asked.

'No, you stay and catch Stella and Amanda up on all things America. I've got this.'

'OK, but later on I want to hear about this beach rescue.'

'We can tell you all about that,' Amanda said. 'Don't worry, Charlie. And let us know how the video goes down.'

'I will,' Lila replied, hurrying to the bar. 'Thank you for your contribution.'

Once she'd collected some rather stilted but very sweet words from Hugh, and accosted a holidaying couple in the pub and discovered to her delight that the woman had seen Keeley in one of her previous roles, a BBC3 teen drama, Lila stepped outside.

The darkness was almost complete, the seafront lit by the attractive, ornate streetlamps, the waves shushing backwards and forwards along the sand. She would go back to Charlie's, have a mug of peppermint tea and rest her aching feet. She was already looking forward to the weekend, and hoped that, by then, she would be editing the clips into a seamless video on her battered laptop. With all the footage she'd collected in this one evening, some from people Keeley had never even met, she believed her idea could actually work – that she would be able to change her mind and rescue the entire production. She didn't know what she'd do if they failed.

Chapter Nineteen

When Charlie and Lila arrived on set the following morning, Sam was waiting for them, leaning against the bus and staring distractedly into the distance. Lila spent a moment drinking him in before he spotted them. Charlie nudged her and added an eyebrow-waggle for good measure.

'Just because you now know what happened when he came to Porthgolow, doesn't mean you can use it against me.'

'Why would I do that?' Charlie asked. 'I think it's wonderful. You balance each other out.'

'What's that supposed to mean?' Lila hissed as Sam turned and noticed them. His smile was warm, but not entirely unworried.

'It means he's serious and you're . . . occasionally over-zealous.' She held her hands up when Lila glared at her. 'I know, I know, it's like the pot calling the kettle black. But at least I always have a plan behind my ambitious ideas.'

'This video has a plan.'

'And that is . . .?'

'To make it,' Lila shot back, and Charlie laughed. 'Nothing's gone wrong so far,' she added defensively.

'Hi, Lila, Charlie,' Sam said.

'Desperate for one of my coffees?' Lila asked. 'I don't blame you. They are pretty special. Can I tempt you to vanilla syrup, cinnamon sugar, maybe hazelnut cream? Whatever sort of day you've got ahead, I'm here to make it better.'

'I've no doubt you'll do that,' he whispered, then added loudly: 'Just a black coffee, please.'

Lila tried to make a disappointed face, but was too happy to pull it off. 'Sweet enough, are you?'

'Something like that. The reason I'm here so early is because Winston's on set today, checking in with Gregor, and I thought we could catch him before he goes, get him to say something for the video.'

'Oh Sam, that's brilliant! Let's go.'

'I'll get us opened up,' Charlie said, 'and have your coffee waiting when you get back.'

'Which way?' Lila asked.

Sam took her hand and led her away from the bus. 'Our line is that this video is for Keeley's birthday, right? But she mustn't know anything about it, because it's going to be a surprise.'

'And if it never gets back to her,' Lila said, hurrying to keep up with Sam's long strides, 'then she'll never be able to tell anyone it isn't actually her birthday, and it won't arouse suspicion.'

They wove through the trucks and vans, passing two grips helping to transport a lighting rig, and Gina and Erin who ran the costume department, their heads bowed together, deep in discussion. The sun was warmer than Lila was used to, a sign that summer wasn't far off, and she felt a surge of hope. Whatever else Keeley was worried about, there wasn't that long left on location. If they could just get her to hold on . . .

'Here we are,' Sam said, stopping outside one of the longer trailers. 'Are you going to take the lead? Or do you want me to?'

She squeezed his hand. 'I'd like to, if that's OK?' She took a deep breath and knocked boldly on the door.

Gregor opened it, his gaze sweeping behind Lila and resting on Sam, before returning to her. She'd noticed that he always seemed to be squinting slightly, as if he saw everything as a possible take, and was checking how it could be set up to achieve maximum atmosphere and message. She remembered how he'd stared – mesmerized – at the apple he'd knocked out of her hand when they first met.

'Sam Magee and Delilah Forest, aka Robert Bramerton and Miss Trevelyan. What can I do for you both this fine morning? If you've come to suggest changes to the script, to extend the role of the schoolmistress beyond her single, crucial line, then you are the most tenacious, strong-headed people I will have encountered since yesterday. But you wouldn't be entirely off the mark.'

Lila's planned speech disappeared, leaving her open-mouthed for a second. She quickly recovered her composure and smiled up at the director. 'We have a favour to ask you actually – and Winston, if he's still there?'

The man in question appeared behind Gregor, a coffee cup in hand. Lila felt a jolt of annoyance that he hadn't got it from Gertie. She would have to bring him one specially, and Gregor too.

'Sam! And Delilah, hello,' he said warmly. 'I trust everything is going well? I've been hearing good things – all good things – about the bus *and* your diversion into acting.'

'Thank you,' she said. 'Yes, it's wonderful. Gertie is popular, Charlie and I feel so at home here and . . . that sort of has to do with why we're here now.'

'I am on veritable tenterhooks,' Gregor replied. 'Your ability to build anticipation, to delay getting to the thrust of your argument, is startling. If you could make it there within the next hour, that would be incredible.'

Lila glanced at Sam, saw that he was suppressing a grin and decided he was too distracting. She turned back to Winston and the director. 'We're making a birthday video for Keeley, to show her how much we care about her. We wondered if you'd be happy to say a couple of things – not specifically happy birthday – but just . . . nice things.' She held her breath, hoping they hadn't got wind of Keeley being unhappy yet, that she was still holding out for her agent to come down from London before telling Winston why she wanted to meet with him.

'A video, you say?' Winston took a sip of his coffee. 'It sounds like a marvellous idea.'

'We could do that,' Gregor added, his gaze flicking between her and Sam.

'Great! Thank you. I'm using my phone,' she admitted. She waited for the award-winning, visionary director to shut the door in her face.

'Come on board,' he said instead, standing back to let them climb the three steps into the smart trailer. 'Let's see if we can't make this a mini masterpiece.'

Half an hour later, they left with heartfelt messages of adoration for Keeley – Gregor had surprised her by dialling down his eccentricity and giving such a warm, kind speech that Lila's throat had closed with emotion – and promises that they would visit Gertie more often.

'You were brilliant,' Sam whispered, as they strolled back towards the bus. 'It's not easy to cope with Gregor sometimes, and you managed to avoid either of them saying happy birthday.'

'I could have edited that out, but it's easier if they don't say it in the first place. Keeley's going to be confused if our plea to her to stay is littered with birthday well-wishes. Think we can do the same with Toby and Aria?'

Sam nodded.

'Bert and Darius, too?'

'I spoke to them yesterday, and they're all going to come to Gertie at some point today, in between scenes. You're going to use the top deck?'

'Hardly anyone goes up there,' Lila said, 'and I can ask the crew who come on board to say something, too. At this rate our video will be feature length! God, I hope it works.'

She came to a stop a few metres from the bus, not wanting to relinquish Sam quite so soon. He took her hand and pulled her behind the catering marquee.

'I have total faith in you,' he said. 'The fact that you're even trying to help – and I know you're doing this for Keeley, but also for the rest of us, for *Estelle* and all who sail in her – is beyond generous. You and Charlie could take Gertie back to Porthgolow and carry on as you were. The Cornish Cream Tea Bus doesn't need this gig to be successful.'

'I know that,' Lila replied, 'but my motives aren't entirely unselfish. I don't want this to end, Sam. I want Keeley to see this through, to realize what she's going to lose. I have, and I don't *want* to lose it. There are too many important people here.'

218

His Adam's apple bobbed. 'I feel the same. The other sets I've worked on have been like a family too, but here . . .'

'Everyone's particularly lovely.'

'Yes, but—'

'And Cornwall is beautiful. You couldn't be working anywhere more picturesque.'

'Will you please let me finish my sentence?' He bent his head towards hers. 'It's not always about the camaraderie or the scenery. Sometimes, you find a connection. And I say that as someone who is finding that connection for the first time.' His lips were inches from hers, his breath warming her face.

'So you don't always choose a member of the catering crew to seduce, then? Because for a moment it sounded like—'

'Be quiet, Lila.' His lips found hers, and desire flooded her senses as he kissed her with purpose; with definite, unrestrained intent. She wrapped her arms around his neck, pushed up onto tiptoes so she could return the kiss more thoroughly, felt his hands flat and warm against her shoulder blades. When they parted, he looked into her eyes, his golden gaze almost as electrifying as his touch.

'That was what I was trying to say,' he murmured.

'Well said.' She pressed a finger to his bottom lip. 'I'm glad I let you speak eventually.'

'I need to go and get changed.'

'Robert Bramerton awaits?'

He nodded, his perfect lips curving into a smile. 'Yes. And he's going to have to work extra hard not to be distracted today.'

Lila laughed. 'I might get a few coffee orders wrong, too.'

'I'll come and see you later.'

'And I'll get on with the stealth video recording.'

'I can't wait to see the finished article.' He grazed his thumb over her cheek and gave her a swift, bold kiss. Lila watched him go and then drifted back to Gertie, her head full of Sam, unable to prevent herself from looking like the cat that had got the cream.

On Sunday afternoon, Lila was in Daniel's office in Crystal Waters, using his powerful computer to thread all her clips together into one, complete video. Charlie had offered to help, but it was such a fiddly process, not to mention one she hadn't done for a while, and she thought it would be best to do it on her own. Besides, she would see Charlie in a few hours for their hot-tub session, timed so it could be their reward for getting the video ready to show to Keeley, on set, the following day.

Lila downloaded her video snippets onto the Mac and started organizing them. She had Toby and Aria together, their beautiful faces smiling at the camera as they told Keeley how she was perfect on set, funny and professional, a dream to work with and – more than that – a close friend. She had Sarah, who of course knew the real reason behind the video, flat-out pleading with her to stay, for her own sake and for her future sanity. Winston talked about her uniqueness, how everyone knew they had found a star-in-the-making when she auditioned, before going into a ramble about Cornwall and how they were trying very, *very* hard to make this the *ultimate* Cornish production. Lila should have taken that part out, but it had made her laugh so much that she thought Keeley might find it funny too.

Gregor talked about her grace and luminescence, his thoughtful words choking Lila up all over again, and the hair and make-up crew had given her a chorus of James

Blunt's 'Beautiful', which sounded as though it had been sung by a professional *a cappella* band. There was Claude, hardly the most talkative person on set, but who had real tenderness in his eyes when he told Keeley she was a delight, and that he wished her the best – Lila had had to cut off the part where he said 'birthday', so it was a bit abrupt, but she hoped Keeley wouldn't notice.

Bert and Darius laughed their way through their message, and Darius told a funny story about when Keeley had thought she'd been locked out of her trailer and, not wanting to bother anyone, had climbed in through the window wearing her white shift dress. Lila hadn't found the story so funny: if Keeley was feeling isolated, she was probably, in turn, shutting herself off from people, and creating a vicious circle from which she couldn't escape.

It made Lila even more determined to get it right. She kept working, adding in clips, splicing and editing them, changing the filter if any were too dark, her face getting closer and closer to the screen. When Daniel appeared in the doorway with a glass of champagne, Lila jumped and let out a little squeak.

'I did knock,' he said, amused. 'Half an hour until hot-tub time. I thought this might help.'

'Really?'

'You've been in here for over three hours. I would have brought a coffee earlier, except I've been tied up with house-keeping. You must be parched.'

She held up the empty jug, which had been full of water at the start of her editing session. 'You've looked after me brilliantly. Especially considering I've stolen your office for the entire afternoon.'

'How's it going? Can I see?'

'Give me ten minutes,' she said, splaying her hands over the screen. 'Then you can view it in all its technicolour glory.'

'You know, you're as bad as Charlie for failing to relax.'

'Says the man who is *always* working. How much hot-tub time do *you* ever have?'

He gave her a sly grin. 'Oh, I get my fair share. Sometimes I convince Charlie to join me, too.'

'And you're telling me this thirty minutes *before* I get into it?' She made a face, and he laughed.

'I'll be back in ten.'

'It'll be ready.' She thanked him for the champagne and, turning back to the screen, took a long and very welcome sip.

True to her word, half an hour later Lila lowered herself into the hot tub, her tired, stiff limbs singing out as they met the bubbles, her eyes drinking in the sight of the sun just beginning its descent over the sea. Lit windows in the houses in the village began to wink in the dimming light, and the air around her was sharp and fresh.

It had reached that time of year, close to the start of May, when the sun warmed the air during the day but the temperature dropped sharply as soon as it set. Lila didn't mind: she loved the contrast; the way a cutting wind or the scent of something on the breeze inspired new emotions or brought back memories. Now, though, she was too frazzled to do anything except feel joy at no longer being in front of a computer, snipping and splicing and reformatting.

'You've earned this,' Charlie said, sliding in opposite her and holding the bottle of champagne up, refilling Lila's glass. 'That video is a masterpiece. It's funny and thoughtful; it strikes just the right balance and it's so moving. Never mind convincing Keeley to stay, it's going to earn you a job on the editing team.'

'I just combined everyone's clips. They all said those things.'

Charlie gave her a warm smile, then sank lower into the bubbles. 'You need to stop downplaying your part, Lila. What you've achieved, in only a few days, is miraculous. The concept, the filming, the editing. Getting Daniel and the other villagers involved was inspired – it means it's not the same message over and over. If someone presented me with something like that, I'd feel like the most loved person in the world.'

'Really?'

Charlie nodded. 'And what it says, most of all, is how much *you* care about her. The fact that you've gone to all this trouble . . .'

'I don't want it to end,' Lila blurted. '*Estelle* or us being there with Gertie, everyone eating your delicious cakes and trying my coffees. Compared to The Espresso Lounge it's a blast. It's one of the best things I've ever done. It's for me as well as Keeley.'

'What's wrong with that? Why can't you put a lot of love into yourself, your own wishes and desires, as well as your friends'? You're so hard on yourself, when you're doing so much good. You ran Gertie single-handedly while I was away, you're trying to protect Keeley and *Estelle's* future. We can't always get everything right in life, but now, Lila, you *are*. You're doing what Hal always said—'

'Forgetting the mistake, remembering the lesson?' Lila said.

'Exactly. And there's this one from me, too,' Charlie added. 'Live in the moment, rather than the past. Take time to stop and look at the view. Tonight, I think you'll agree, we've hit the jackpot.'

They both turned towards the sea, leaning their arms on the side of the hot tub. It was spellbinding; unreal, almost. As if God had got hold of Instagram and knew his way around the filters. But, despite that, Lila couldn't be entirely captivated by it. And it wasn't just because she was worried about Keeley's response to the video. It was because the last clip she had added was Sam's.

He had been sitting on Gertie's top deck, wearing his pristine white shirt and a blue and gold waistcoat that brought out the amber in his eyes. His message to Keeley had been generous, heartfelt and funny. He had spoken without any self-consciousness. He had been wholly Sam – a man who, Lila was coming to realize, she cared deeply for, and was starting to think about in terms that went beyond flings or holiday romances. Those thoughts scared her.

After they had recorded it, with Charlie talking to people downstairs, Sam had kissed Lila as if his life depended on it. She had just about had the brainpower to wonder whether he'd ever had kissing lessons, if that was one of the sessions at drama school, because she had never *ever* been kissed like that, feeling it all the way through her, right to the tips of her toes.

Tomorrow, they would show Keeley the video and she would make up her mind whether to stay or go. Lila had no control over the outcome; she could only prove to Keeley that people cared about her, that she mattered as a friend and a colleague, as well as an actor with a bright future. But if the answer was no, Lila would have to make a decision about Sam.

She had so much more to learn about him, so much more to feel. But was she prepared to accept everything that came with those feelings? The potential for her to give all of herself to him, and for it to end, anyway, when the *Estelle* juggernaut rolled out of Cornwall? Clara had told her she couldn't be trusted with anyone's heart, and maybe that was in part because she couldn't reciprocate – she wasn't brave enough to trust anyone with hers.

'Did I ever tell you about the time Daniel coerced me into this very hot tub?' Charlie asked, breaking into her thoughts.

'Do I want you to?' Lila asked, screwing her face up.

Charlie laughed. 'It was a defining moment in our relationship,' she said dreamily. 'And not for the reason you're implying.'

'Go on then,' Lila said, turning away from the pink and golden hues of the sunset, deciding that it was too showy, that it didn't deserve all her attention. 'Tell me.' She sipped her champagne and listened to Charlie, and tried to put Sam to the back of her mind.

Chapter Twenty

A whole colony of frogs was performing circus tricks in Lila's tummy when she stepped into Keeley's trailer first thing on Monday morning. There had been a discussion about who would show the video to her, and conscious of not wanting it to feel like an ambush, Lila had been prepared for anyone to do it, to hang back and keep everything crossed for a positive outcome. But Sarah, Sam and Charlie had all decided that she should do it; she had thought of the video, and created it, and was the right person for the job.

So, armed with Charlie's iPad, she had made her way through the sea of trucks to Keeley's trailer, her name and 'Estelle' written on a sign stuck on the door. The morning was grey, and the sea as they had left Porthgolow had been tumultuous, expressing perfectly how Lila felt. She had stood, steeling herself, before raising her hand to knock. A moment later Keeley had answered, and Lila had seen the flare of happiness in her eyes before her face set in a neutral expression.

'I'm meeting them later,' she said, standing back to let Lila in. 'Winston doesn't know what it's about yet, but it's all going ahead.'

'What did your agent say?' Lila asked, looking around the smart space: leather sofas, a television flush against the wall, a polished coffee table with a bowl of fruit on it. There were scripts flung onto sofas, a framed photo of Keeley grinning with a handsome, dark-haired man, and another of a sheepdog, its tongue lolling out, standing in a field. The smell of rose-scented perfume and coffee filled the air.

Keeley sat on one of the sofas and gestured for Lila to do the same. There was something different about her, haughty, almost, as if she'd decided to banish all affection towards anyone else and to think solely of herself.

'My agent has tried to discourage me, of course. She's laid everything out, what I stand to lose if I go through with it. She's not happy with me.'

'But she's still coming down?'

Keeley shrugged. 'She has to. She's my agent, and this is what I want. She can advise me all she likes, but in the end she has to accept my decision, to make everything right.'

'It's not going to be all right though, is it?' Lila shifted, pulled out a pale pink cardigan from under her bum and set it to one side. 'Not for you, or for anyone else on *Estelle*. This far into filming, you could kill the production completely.'

Keeley frowned, her pretty features hardening. 'I know that. But what am I meant to do?' There was an edge of pleading in her voice. 'I'm so miserable, Lila. Without Jordan, I . . . None of it's real.'

Lila couldn't help but laugh. 'You're working on a fictional series. Surely the point is that it isn't real?'

'I don't mean that. I mean all *this*.' Keeley flung her arm wide. 'Fresh fruit every day, stuck in this trailer most of the time, people pandering and simpering and pretending to be nice.'

'Is anyone really pretending, though?' Lila said. 'Charlie and I certainly aren't. I know Sarah is a good friend, and think about Sam.' Her voice softened. She found it far too easy to follow her own instruction. 'His friendship, his affection, isn't false. I know you miss Jordan, and that must be shit, but it doesn't mean this isn't part of your real life, too. That these aren't genuine, worthwhile relationships you're making. If Jordan could come down for a few days and spend some time with you here, rather than back home, would you consider staying?'

'I don't know, Lila. I . . . I don't know anything any more. I'm so confused.' She pressed her hands over her eyes, and Lila saw that cold, haughty Keeley was gone. Hope flared in her chest.

'Then maybe this will help.' She got up and sat next to Keeley, opened Charlie's iPad and navigated to the video. She squeezed Keeley's arm and waited for her to emerge from behind her hands. Her eyes were red, her cheeks tear-stained.

'What is it?'

'Just watch,' Lila said quietly. She pressed play.

The first shot was of her, standing in the gardens of Crystal Waters, the afternoon sun dancing over the waves behind her. She had realized, when she'd gone to stitch the video together on Sunday afternoon, that she had no kind of introduction, so she'd hastily gone outside to film one. It was rough and ready, but she didn't think that mattered. She watched herself in classic selfie pose, grinning inanely into the camera.

'Hi, Keeley. Welcome to your own, personal love-fest. Nobody wants you to go, everyone adores you and . . .' She squinted, despite the sun being behind her. Lila thought how strange it was, watching herself. 'Anyway. Sit back, relax, and bask in the waves of adulation that are *all* genuine, and all entirely deserved. Take it away, folks!' She remembered turning her phone, disappearing from view in place of the sea, the hot tub sliding into shot before the scene cut to Darius and Bert, standing on the top deck of Gertie, their faces serious but not entirely without mischief.

Keeley was rapt. She didn't take her eyes off the screen, her chin in her hand, fingers pressed against her mouth. She laughed at Bert and Darius's antics, squeaked when Toby and Aria turned on the charm, and blushed at Claude's kind words. She was entirely silent for Winston and Gregor, and also Sarah's plea, and flicked Lila a questioning look when some of the Porthgolow locals appeared, Stella and Amanda's insistence that they couldn't wait to see *Estelle*, with its beautiful ghost and strapping men. She gasped when the woman in the pub mentioned her role in the BBC3 drama *Outfoxed*, and grew quiet again when Daniel gave his speech about perseverance. Charlie was second to last, with Sam's emotional entreaty saved for the end.

The video stopped, reverting to the first frame of Lila's face, ready for its replay.

Lila held herself perfectly still, breath in her throat, watching Keeley closely.

Eventually she sat up, rubbed her eyes and then turned towards Lila. 'You did this – you *all* did this – for me?'

'Nobody wants you to go,' Lila repeated. 'Although, for discretionary purposes, some people think it's about to be your birthday. But the sentiment's the same.'

Keeley laughed, her cheeks flushing. 'It's not until November. They all . . . that's what they really think?'

'I know you're in show business, but did any of that look faked to you?'

Keeley shook her head.

'I – we – want you to know that we all care about you. That while it might be hard, being on location this whole time, it's not all empty flattery. You're my friend, Keeley. I don't want to see you go, or lose this incredible chance. It's your decision in the end, of course, but . . . I would never forgive myself if I didn't try to show you the other side of things.'

'Thank you,' Keeley whispered. 'It means a lot.'

Lila nodded, both desperate and reluctant to ask the obvious question.

'Give me to the end of the day,' she said, as if reading Lila's mind. 'My agent will be here at lunchtime. We're going to talk things through.'

'Of course.' Lila rubbed her hands down her trousers and stood.

'Can I hold on to this?' Keeley asked, pointing at the iPad. 'Just for today. I'll bring it to the bus later on.'

'No worries. The passcode is one, two, three, four.'

Keeley gave her an incredulous look.

'Only because of this,' Lila clarified. 'We thought you might want to watch the video again. Charlie's got a *little* bit more sense than that.'

They exchanged a smile and, even though Lila didn't have the answer she wanted, at least they were parting on good terms. She left Keeley's trailer, wondering how on earth she was going to get through the day.

Sam and Sarah were on board when she got back, Sarah tucking into a rosemary scone, Sam sitting at a table with Marmite on his lap. They all turned to look at her.

'Well?' Charlie asked.

'Did she watch it?' Sarah blurted. 'Has she changed her mind?'

Her eyes locked with Sam's as she spoke. 'She watched it, and it definitely affected her. She asked if we could give her to the end of the day. Her agent's coming down at lunchtime apparently, so . . .'

'So she didn't fling herself into your arms and tell you she was staying?' Charlie asked. 'Bollocks.' She gave Lila a resigned smile. 'But remember, you did a really good thing. Whatever decision she makes, at least she knows how much she means to everyone here. That should give her confidence, if nothing else.'

'It has to work,' Sarah muttered, picking up crumbs on the end of her finger. 'It just has to.'

Lila's stomach grumbled and she picked a scone off the pile, sliced it in half and buttered both sides. She held one out to Sam and he took it.

'Thank you,' he said quietly. 'You know if, after this, Keeley does decide to go, we have to respect it, whatever the consequences.'

Lila opened her mouth to speak, to rail against it all, but it was pointless. They had been round these same circles so many times.

'All we can do is wait,' Charlie said.

Lila decided that waiting was the hardest thing in the world.

For the rest of that day, Gertie was a refuge for the people waiting for Keeley's answer. Sarah spent time there in between jobs, sampling a wide range of cakes, and becoming a keen recipient of Lila's coffee experiments. She was a location assistant, the walkie-talkie attached to her belt crackling regularly with requests or questions, sending her to check something or help reset a particular scene. Every time it went off, Marmite bounced in his seat and barked uncontrollably. After the fourth time, Sarah hid the transmitter inside her fleecy jumper to muffle the sound.

Sam returned after the hot lunch in the catering marquee, his Robert Bramerton costume in a state of disarray, the white shirt stained and the waistcoat ripped. He had a smudge of a bruise on his right cheekbone, blood crusting his hairline.

'Sam!' Lila shrieked, almost dropping her jug of milk. 'What's happened?'

He grinned. 'I got into a fight with Henry. Don't worry, all planned. This is my dishevelled look. What do you think?'

'I wish you'd warned me,' she said, discarding the milk and pressing her hands flat against his chest. 'I thought for a second that you'd fallen off Gregor's scaffolding or been attacked by a rabid dog. Don't worry me like that!'

'You were worried?' he asked softly.

Lila nodded, any further response deserting her.

'Any news from Keeley?' he asked.

'Not yet.'

'OK, I have to go and be tidied up so Toby can pummel me all over again.'

'Be careful,' Lila rushed out.

'It's choreographed to within millimetres. I'll be fine. I'll be back later, though.'

'You'd better be. And in one piece, too.'

'Understood.' He gave her a determined nod and walked off the bus.

'That was *very* adorable,' Charlie said, giving her an indulgent grin.

'Shut up.' Lila felt the blush from her neck to her ears.

Charlie turned back to the dishwasher, humming a tune that Lila couldn't quite make out.

They had all reconvened on Gertie when Keeley appeared, half an hour after filming had finished for the day. Sarah was sipping a caramel flat white, and Sam, while back in his civvies, still had fake blood in his hair, the remains of his black eye too convincing for Lila's liking.

Keeley had her hands shoved deep into the pockets of her cream hoody, a tote bag slung over her shoulder. Lila could tell that she'd been crying.

'Keeley,' Sarah said affectionately. 'How are you doing, girl?'

'I'm good,' she said. 'Really good. Much better. I spoke to Matty, my agent, and . . . that video. I mean . . .' She glanced at Lila, took her hands out of her pockets and folded them tightly over her chest. 'I'm staying.'

At first, nobody reacted.

'You're not leaving the production?' Sarah asked, after a moment. 'You're still Estelle?'

'I'm going to stick it out,' Keeley said. 'I was so resistant to it, so closed off. I'm going to change my mindset. I'm sorry I've caused you so much trouble.'

'Shit, Keeley!' Sarah blurted. 'That is *great* news.' She stood and wrapped the young actor in a hug.

Sam was next, pulling her against his chest. 'I'm so glad you're staying,' he murmured. 'And you're sure you're OK? If you're ever unhappy, you need to tell someone. Don't bottle it up.'

'I know,' Keeley said, pulling back to look at him. 'Matty and Winston met up this afternoon. Winston didn't know I was planning on going, but Matty spoke to him and they're changing a few things, just to make me feel more comfortable. And I've spoken to Jordan – he's taking some time off and I'm going to go home and see him again this weekend.'

'That's great news, Keeley,' Charlie said. 'We would have missed you so much, felt so sad for you, if you'd gone.'

Keeley nodded. 'It was selfish, I know. But your video, Lila! I must have watched it a dozen times already.' She laughed. 'And I need to return this. Thank you for lending it to me.' She opened her tote bag and handed Charlie her iPad.

'I'll send you the video so you can keep it,' Lila said. 'We're all so pleased you're staying.'

'Was that your Daniel?' Keeley asked Charlie. 'The one with the hotel, talking about perseverance?'

'That's him. He can get a bit preachy when he wants to – he's very sure of himself.'

'What he said was great,' Keeley said quietly. 'It really helped. It all did.' She smiled, then waved at Marmite who was watching them from the cab. 'And you, Lila. I was convinced that you thought I should leave, that you were encouraging me to get out before it all went wrong. But I guess I just listened to the parts I wanted to hear.'

Lila held her breath.

'When was this?' Sarah asked.

'A little while ago.' Keeley waved a dismissive hand.

'You *knew* Keeley was planning on leaving?' Sam asked, turning to look at her.

'I hadn't quite made up my mind,' Keeley explained. 'But Lila and I had this heart-to-heart, and I told her all my woes, and after that I decided I was going to quit. And then she presents this video, and that's what convinced me I was overreacting, reminded me what I'd be giving up. Thank you for helping me see things clearly.' She gave Lila a hug, then walked to the door. 'I have to say goodbye to Matty. I'll see you all tomorrow, though. Are you doing muffins, Charlie?'

'I'll be doing them,' Charlie said. 'See you later, Keeley.'

Once she'd gone, all eyes swivelled to Lila.

'You knew before Keeley told me?' Sarah asked.

'I didn't know for sure,' Lila said. 'She told me that she was unhappy, that she was thinking of leaving, and I tried to explain what a mistake it would be, but . . . I somehow gave her the opposite message. She thought I was agreeing with her. I had already planned to fix it, but then Charlie came back from America, and the next thing I knew, Keeley had spoken to you and made it sort of official.' She sank into a seat.

'What a mess,' Sarah murmured, shaking her head. 'At least it's all worked out for the best. I have to love you and leave you, but thanks for the cakes, the coffee, the support. I will sleep easier tonight.'

'Why didn't you tell me?' Sam asked gently, once Sarah had gone. 'If she'd come to you with these concerns, and Charlie was still away, why didn't you talk to me?'

'Because I wanted to change her mind before anyone else found out,' Lila admitted. 'I felt like I was partly responsible, for accidentally talking her into it, and I wanted to make it right.'

'You're not on your own, Lila! What have you just spent four days trying to prove to Keeley? That you're entitled to ask your friends for help if you need it.' Sam's eyes were hard, his jaw clenched. He ran a hand through his hair. 'Sorry. It's late, and I'm knackered. Can you at least be proud of yourself now? *Estelle's* safe, Keeley's staying and, more than that, she seems happier.'

Lila gave Sam a weary smile. 'I'm pleased it has all worked out.'

'That's not as effusive as I was hoping for, but it'll do for now.' Sam held his hands out and Lila took them. He pulled her to her feet and into a hug, his lips brushing the top of her head. Lila accepted his embrace, and wished that it could go on for ever.

Chapter Twenty-one

After Charlie's return and the scrabble to make Keeley's video, Lila relished the relative calm over the next few days, and tried not to think how soon it would all be over. *Estelle* had one more month shooting on location before moving to the Bristol studios. Charlie had told Lila, after her most recent talk with Winston, that the production team would be back in Cornwall for a few days in early July. They were filming at a stately home that could only accommodate them while it was closed for repairs, but by then summer – and Gertie's other commitments – would be in full swing, and Winston didn't expect the Cornish Cream Tea Bus to be available.

So Lila had a month left to enjoy life on set, the new friendships she had made, and being with Sam. She was looking forward to spending more time in Porthgolow, to helping Charlie with the food markets and tours, and knew she should feel lucky. But only a few more weeks with Sam, when their time together was so limited anyway, seemed like nothing. There had been no declarations of affection, no labels applied; they were simply edging their way closer together, like pebbles pushed by the tide. Lila told herself this was for the best, that the countdown meant she couldn't get too attached, all the time ignoring the fact that she already was.

'This one,' she said to Darius one morning, lining up three espresso cups in a row, 'is an arabica bean medium roast. This one is made from liberica beans, and the third one,' she pointed at the final cup, 'is an Italian roast made with excelsa beans. I've added a shot of gingerbread syrup to each one.'

'To *espresso*?' Darius peered into the cups as if he might be able to see tiny gingerbread men hiding beneath the coffee's murky depths.

'Yes. I'm not sure it works with the excelsa beans, though.'

'But syrup in espresso?' He looked immaculate in a black velvet waistcoat and coat, white shirt and cream cravat, a silver watch chain hanging across his chest. Lila felt dowdy in her apron, liberally smeared with chocolate smudges from the brownies that had begun to melt in their window position before being hastily relocated to the fridge.

'I don't see why not,' Lila shrugged. 'It's just like adding a sort of smoky sugar. I've never understood why only milky coffees have syrups added to them. You get those flavoured coffee grounds but they're pathetic. I'm trying to enhance the richness of the beans and create something a little bit different.'

'Right,' Darius said, frowning.

'But you do need to actually *try* them. They all look the same – though of course, smell is a big factor. Did you know that you shouldn't leave your lid on a cup of takeaway coffee, because the smell is as much a part of the experience as the taste?'

'I did not know that! Do all your customers get this treatment?'

'Nope,' Lila admitted. 'You just turned up at exactly the right moment to be my guinea pig.'

'Lucky me.' Darius picked up the first cup and sipped. His frown lifted.

'Good, huh?'

'Lila, wow. That's—'

'Right, we've got approval!' Charlie said, jumping into the aisle, her cheeks flushed.

'Approval for what?' Darius asked, sinking the second espresso.

'Next Friday. We're taking Gertie to Porthgolow at lunch-time.'

'What?' Lila asked.

'You're leaving?' Darius said. He downed the third coffee and looked ruefully at the empty cups.

'Just for an afternoon – not for ever. But it's the Cornish Cream Tea Bus's one-year anniversary, so we *have* to do some-thing, and Winston said they can cope without us on Friday afternoon, so we'll drive back to Porthgolow and get everything set up in time for Saturday.'

'What's the plan?' Lila asked, trying to hide her relief that Charlie wasn't pulling them out of the catering team early.

'We have a party on the bus, of course! Fingers crossed for some good weather.' She beamed, and Darius held one of the espresso cups out to Lila.

'More, please,' he said.

Lila gave him a smug smile and refilled his cup.

The day of Gertie's anniversary, the heavens opened on Porthgolow. But the village was in a jubilant mood, and the pounding rain couldn't dampen the spirits inside the bus.

The day before had been a bank holiday – unusual for a

239

Friday, but changed from Monday to coincide with VE Day. Charlie had driven Gertie back to Porthgolow as promised and, after spending the afternoon baking, they had joined most of the villagers in the Seven Stars, complete with local music and Hugh's excellent buffet food. Lila, Charlie and Daniel had left at a reasonable time, conscious of the next day's early start, and not wanting to feel jaded for their own celebration.

'All this partying,' Amanda said, coming on board with Jonah and her two young daughters Flora and Jem, and starting to peel off raincoats. 'I'm going to be the size of a house, soon. I won't be able to fit on the boats.'

'Actually,' Jonah said, 'those RIBs can take a weight of up to—'

'Jonah,' chided his mum gently, 'I don't need a target to work towards. I need to exercise more, and possibly eat a little less.' She eyed the wonderful display, and selected a pecan plait and a couple of red velvet cupcakes for the girls, while Jonah chose a cheese and bacon scone.

'How's the filming going?' Amanda asked. 'How is the delectable Sam?'

'Good and good,' Lila said, smiling. 'Though we've only got a few weeks left. It'll feel strange asking people to pay for things when they come on board.'

'I'm going to make us a sign,' Charlie added, getting out the tub of mini marshmallows to sprinkle over hot chocolates. 'Otherwise all the profit we've made from *Estelle*'s generous fee will have to bolster our lost takings.'

'And Sam?' Amanda prompted.

'Who's Sam?' Jonah asked, taking a bite of his scone. His hair was flattened to his forehead; Lila was unsure if it was because of the rain or because, on the verge of teenager-dom,

240

he'd discovered hair gel and hadn't quite learnt how to make the best use of it.

'Sam is the actor I told you about,' Amanda said. 'The one we thought was rescuing Lila from a near-drowning.'

'The one who can't seem to stay away from Porthgolow.' Charlie grinned and pointed out of the window.

Lila's heart thudded, but she tried to remain outwardly calm as she watched the familiar figure, head down, hood up against the rain, hurrying across the sand towards them.

'Happy anniversary,' he said, bursting onto the bus just as regulars Jeremy and Delia came down the stairs. Delia shrieked in alarm. 'Sorry,' Sam rushed. 'Sorry, I didn't mean to startle you!' He held out a hand and helped the old woman down the last few steps.

She soon got over her surprise, and looked at him with an adoring expression. 'Thank you, young man. Very kind.' Jeremy scowled behind her, and Lila tried not to laugh.

Once the older couple had paid and left the bus, Sam slid into a chair.

'What are you doing here?' Lila asked. 'Not that I'm complaining. It's lovely to see you.'

'Can't keep away, can you, Sam?' Amanda said gleefully.

'You're the actor?' Jonah cut in. 'The one they've all been going on about?'

Sam gave him a bemused smile and held out his hand. 'Possibly. I'm Sam Magee.'

'Jonah Kerr,' Jonah said, giving his hand a firm shake. 'So you're in the drama that's being filmed for the BBC, and you're doing all the location shoots in Cornwall, and then moving on to the studios? Isn't it unusual for there to be a random bus as part of the craft services? How many days do you get off, or do you just not have any scenes today?'

241

'Uhm . . .' Sam looked to Lila with pleading eyes, and she grinned at him.

'Jonah, love,' Amanda said softly, 'let the man catch his breath. Perhaps order a hot chocolate before you start on the Spanish Inquisition.'

'This is an interrogation,' Jonah said. 'The Spanish Inquisition was actually—' Amanda placed a hand gently on top of his head and gave him a look, and Jonah's cheeks went pink. He mimed zipping his lips.

'I don't know if anyone fancies it,' Sam said, 'or if it's even allowed, but I bought you a gift.'

He pulled out a bottle of champagne from inside his coat, just as Reenie Teague, village matriarch, dweller in the precarious yellow hut that Lila still hadn't visited and, according to Jonah, secret-mermaid, stepped onto the bus.

'It looks as if I've turned up just at the right time. Congratulations, Charlie.' She walked down the aisle and embraced her, her long grey hair swinging behind her. She came up to Charlie's shoulder. 'One year of this brilliant, village-saving bus, and of you. I had to come and celebrate the best thing that's happened to Porthgolow in decades.'

'Thank you, Reenie,' Charlie said, obviously touched. 'And thank you, Sam, for the bubbles. As long as we're not selling it, it's most definitely allowed.'

'Sam, eh?' Reenie gave Lila a penetrating gaze. The two of them had met briefly when Lila first arrived in Porthgolow, and Charlie had described Reenie as one of the most honest, and one of the kindest people she knew, with a killer Instagram page to boot. Lila couldn't help being intrigued by the woman, who was clearly in her sixties at the very least, but who seemed much younger, everything about her fizzing with energy. She could see why she and Charlie were friends, and why her cousin had some of her photos on her living-room wall.

'You're making yourself useful, Delilah, I see?' Reenie said now. 'Letting Gertie have a break from playing host to the stars?'

'It's not up to me,' Lila murmured, heat rising up her neck. 'But being on set has got its perks.'

'And Sam is one of them?' Reenie stared unashamedly at him, a wry smile on her lips.

Sam opened his mouth, then shut it again.

'Sam is one of *Estelle*'s lead cast members,' Charlie said, crouching to get glasses out of a cupboard, 'and a good friend, who has very generously turned up on his day off to bring us a bottle of champagne, and is probably regretting it already.'

Sam gave a nervous laugh. 'I'm not, honestly.'

'Good-oh,' Reenie said, sitting opposite him. 'I can't say I recognize you, but then you are a spring chicken. What else have you been in? Maybe I'd know one of your earlier projects.'

'Do you even have a TV?' Lila asked.

'I'm not a dinosaur, young woman. Now, Samuel, don't worry about the interruptions. I want to hear all about this glitzy acting life of yours.'

'You haven't answered my questions yet,' Jonah protested.

'What do we do?' Lila asked Charlie in a panicked whisper.

'First, we make sure Sam's glass is the fullest,' Charlie replied, picking up five glasses at once, 'and then we go in and rescue him.'

'Good plan.' She followed her cousin to where Sam was slowly shrugging himself out of his coat, a cute worry-line forming between his brows as Reenie and Jonah jostled for

243

position. It might not have been the full-on Spanish version, but the Porthgolow Inquisition was looking like a pretty close-run thing.

'What made you want to become an actor?' Lila asked later that afternoon, jumping as a wave threatened to engulf her shoes. 'Sorry – you've probably had enough questions to last you a lifetime, but I'm curious. Are you prepared for people to be that interested in you for the rest of your life?'

Sam laughed and slid his hand into hers. 'It's what I've wanted to do ever since I was little,' he admitted. 'To be on stage or in front of a camera.'

'But you're not always vying to be the centre of attention. You're not naturally . . . dramatic. You're calm and thoughtful, you don't bluster or make everything about you. So . . . why?'

'I've always been fascinated by stories. I remember reading *Treasure Island* and wondering what it would be like to be involved in that kind of adventure. I thought acting would let me do that, let me explore all those different scenarios – what emotion and circumstance can drive you to do. Then I was cast as the innkeeper in a school Nativity, and that was it. I just wanted to act. I had one line – "There's no room at this inn" – and it decided my life for me.'

Lila laughed. 'But it took you a long time to get here? Not that you're old, or that this is your first role, but those tales about people being spotted on the street and getting instant Hollywood careers, aren't they a bit of a myth?'

'It certainly wasn't how I got my break. I've done the hard graft, faced opposition from my parents who didn't think it was a stable enough career. They're both secondary-school teachers, and my older brother is an engineer. I've had to work to get to where I am, and I'm not naive enough to think it's all plain sailing just because I've landed this gig.'

'You were genuinely worried about Keeley, then? Bringing the whole thing down like a house of cards?'

Sam turned to face her. The waves crashed close by, the sea tempestuous after the earlier rainfall, the sand damp beneath their feet. He looked pained, his jaw, with its smattering of stubble, tight. 'I was terrified,' he said. 'The thought that it could end midway through, and in such a devastating way, too. It would have tainted everyone associated with it – been known as "doomed production, *Estelle*". It wouldn't have been a good look.'

'I'm sorry, again, that I didn't tell you I knew she was thinking of going. I wanted to change her mind before anyone else found out.'

'And you did change her mind. Keeley's happier now, more settled than I've seen her. You did that, Lila.'

'You could have told me how worried you were. I feel like . . .' She sighed, changing tack. 'I love spending time with you. I'm so happy that you're here, that you've taken the trouble to come back to Porthgolow, to celebrate Gertie's first anniversary. How long is your drive back? Can you stay for the drinks at Crystal Waters, too?'

'I've been playing it by ear, but I'm pretty sure I won't go back tonight.'

'Oh?' Lila tried for nonchalance, but her heart thrummed.

'I knew you and Charlie wouldn't do things by halves, but I also didn't want to be presumptuous about being a part of it. If you're happy for me to stay, and if we're going to be up at the hotel, then I might see if they've any rooms available. I've got a bag in the car.'

'I'm sure Daniel will be able to accommodate you but,

even if he's fully booked, we'll be able to find you a bed somewhere.' Lila stood on tiptoes to kiss him. Sam wrapped his arms around her waist and deepened the kiss, and Lila let sensation take over, the feel of his lips and his strong arms, the sea breeze hugging them in its own embrace.

Sam had chosen to spend the weekend with her – he had nowhere else he wanted to be. The thought that he could be feeling about her what she was beginning to feel for him both thrilled and terrified her. But, for the moment at least, she was going to enjoy it. Lila kissed Sam with all the intensity she could muster, holding nothing back, giving all of herself to him.

The private function room at Crystal Waters was set snugly in the corner of the building, at the back of the restaurant, and had glass walls on two sides. Lila had never seen it before, and with its neat ceiling spotlights turned down low and the table decorated with a vase full of sea glass, the cutlery and glassware gleaming, the sight made her catch her breath.

'Bloody hell,' Sam whispered. 'Are you sure you want me here for this?'

'I'm wondering if Daniel and Charlie want *me* here. It looks so romantic, doesn't it?' She smoothed her hands down her blue, daisy-print dress, glanced at her comfy worn wedges, the chipped varnish on her toenails, and wondered if she'd made enough effort. Sam was effortlessly stylish in the black shirt and dark jeans he'd turned up in, but this looked like a location suited to proper evening wear – slinky gowns and kitten heels.

She turned at the sound of laughter. Charlie and Daniel were walking down the corridor towards them. Charlie waved, her eyes sparkling. 'Lila . . . and Sam! Thank you so much for staying.'

Sam cleared his throat. 'Are you sure, Charlie? This looks so—'

'We should get out of your hair,' Lila cut in, giving Charlie a quick hug and taking Sam's hand.

'What do you mean?' Charlie said. 'I thought we were going to celebrate together!'

'But shouldn't you be doing that with Amanda or Stella? What about Reenie? I've only been here a few months, and this looks so—'

'Perfect?' Charlie said. 'Yes, well that's Daniel's fault.' She gave him a kiss, silencing his objection. 'He has high standards. But I've been on the bus all day, every villager has been in to see us, and now I want to have a fun dinner with you and Daniel. And you, Sam. You brought champagne, and . . .' she flicked Lila a knowing look, 'you're very, *very* welcome here. I would be gutted if either of you left. I've even sorted out a dog-sitter for Marmite.'

'In the form of Lily, my next-door neighbour,' Daniel said, 'who is getting a spa day in return. This is an opportunity not to be wasted. And neither are these.' He strode over to a silver bucket, where two bottles of Moët nestled among ice. 'If Charlie and I have these between us, tomorrow will be a write-off.'

'Have we convinced you yet?' Charlie asked, taking Lila's hands and dragging her further into the room.

She glanced at Sam, who shrugged. 'OK, then.'

'This is very generous,' Sam said. 'Thank you.'

'We will, of course, be expecting tickets to the *Estelle* premiere,' Charlie replied, grinning wickedly. 'There's no such thing as a free dinner.'

*

Two delicious courses and several glasses of champagne later, Lila was convinced this was one of the best nights of her life. The Cornish scenery beyond the glass was like a painting, the sky shifting from pink to purple, turquoise then midnight blue, as the golden sun scorched the surface of the sea before dipping out of sight.

The food was mouthwatering, with delicate flavours and work-of-art presentation. Her veggie main course, a wild mushroom risotto with slow-roasted tomatoes and a goat's cheese crumb, looked like a miniature garden, garnished with delicate red and purple edible flowers.

But despite the surroundings, the luxury of it all, it didn't feel stuffy. Charlie and Daniel were as relaxed as ever, and after a brief awkwardness when Sam and Daniel were introduced – Lila got the sense that Daniel was mildly protective of her – they were getting on famously. They found common ground in hard work and dedication, as well as a love of cricket that Lila hadn't known either of them had.

'I try and get to Lord's if I can, when I'm in London,' Sam was saying. 'I'm not based too far from there, and it's a great way to relax on days off.'

'It's been a dream of mine to follow the Ashes tour one year when it's Down Under,' Daniel replied. 'Drinking beer and watching us pummel the Ozzies in thirty-five-degree heat, followed by evenings on the beach.' He shook his head, a faraway look in his eyes.

'I can't imagine either of you spending an entire day sitting around watching a load of blokes hit a ball and then catch it,' Lila said, forking in another mouthful of risotto. 'You're both too energetic for that.'

'You'd be surprised how engrossing it is,' Sam replied.

'Pretty sure I wouldn't think it was,' she said, smiling. 'But I would be happy to spend one day, *one day*, watching it, just to see. Except not this summer, because I'm going to be busy on board Gertie, helping Charlie with her Cornish Cream Tea tours.'

'Tours?' Sam asked. 'You take Gertie on tours as well as everything else?'

'It's one of my most popular offers during the summer,' Charlie admitted. 'We're already booked up throughout July, and I've only got a few spaces left at the beginning of June. Seeing the sights of Cornwall while indulging in a Cornish cream tea is a lot of people's idea of a good time.'

'Of course it is,' Lila said. 'I can't wait for my first one, even if I'll be serving. What do you think, Sam? Do you want to come on one? We could see if Keeley wanted in, too.'

'I'd love to,' Sam replied. 'You miss out on so much when you're tied up on set, and I wouldn't know the best places to visit without some local advice. I'm sure Keeley – and maybe some of the others – would be keen.'

Lila sipped her champagne, her brain suddenly working overtime while the conversation carried on around her.

'Hey, Lila?' Sam put his hand on her leg, and Lila drew in a breath.

'Sorry – what?'

'Are you OK? You were a hundred miles away.'

'Not a hundred,' she said. 'Perhaps not even one.'

'What do you mean?' Charlie asked her cousin, her glass paused inches from her lips.

'I'm thinking about the Cornish Cream Tea Bus sitting down there on the sand, primed for hosting tours over the summer, and I've had the most brilliant idea – or, to be more specific, Sam has given me a brilliant idea.'

'Oh?' Daniel said, raising an eyebrow. 'What's that?'

Lila took another swig of champagne and, giddy at the thought of putting her plan into action, took a deep breath, and told them.

Chapter Twenty-two

'A tour of Cornwall, with all the *Estelle* cast on board Gertie?' Charlie rested her elbows on the table. 'Why?'

'Because,' Lila said, 'the main reason we ended up as part of the catering team was so that Winston could show the series was authentically Cornish, and used local companies and suppliers. We're the crowning glory of that particular angle, and what better way of getting publicity for them, and for Gertie, than doing a tour? We could ask someone to film it, invite the local press along. We could visit the parts of Cornwall where filming has already taken place, so it promotes those beauty spots without sending hordes of fans to disrupt the rest of the shoot.' She sat back, waiting for the reaction.

'You think Winston would be up for it?' Charlie asked.

'I think he would be overjoyed.' Sam laughed, and Lila felt the weight of his hand on her thigh.

'And you, Sam?' she asked. 'You'd be part of it, but it would be work as well as fun.'

'I think it's a great idea,' he said. 'A spark of genius. I'm happy to do a bit of extra work if it involves a Gertie tour around Cornwall.'

'Genius, eh?' Lila said, the warmth of his touch spreading to every part of her.

'That's going a *bit* far,' Daniel cut in, grinning when Lila shot him a cross look. 'But I can see how it could help you both. You, Charlie, and the publicity for the production. What do you think?'

Charlie chewed her lip. 'It's brilliant,' she murmured. 'A spark of genius isn't, actually, far off. God, think of everything that's happened since you arrived in Porthgolow, Lila. Think how unexpected – and amazing – these last few months have been. I was able to go to America with Daniel, there's *Estelle*, you, Sam. I know what happened in London was a really low point, but sometimes good things come out of bad.'

'They do,' Lila said, nodding. 'It has all been rather monumental.'

Charlie stood and topped up their glasses. 'So let's have a toast. To Delilah Forest and all her hare-brained ideas. May they continue to make our lives better for decades to come!'

'To Delilah,' Sam and Daniel echoed, their glasses clinking.

Lila dipped her head, blushing, but Sam put his finger under her chin and guided it up again. 'Embrace it, Lila. Soak up the praise. You deserve it.'

It was close to one in the morning when Charlie stretched her arms up to the ceiling and yawned. They had moved on to a bottle of Daniel's fine single malt, and while Lila wasn't usually a huge fan of whisky, it gave her a warm glow and cemented the evening's status in her mind as memorable for all the right reasons.

'Let's call it a night,' Daniel said. 'Sam, you've got one of the sea-view rooms on the lower floor. I've put your bag in there already, I just need to collect your key from the office.'

'It's very kind of you to find me a room.'

Daniel stood. 'No problem at all. Tonight's been great – we should do it again soon.'

They made their way down the plushly carpeted corridors, Daniel and Charlie walking ahead. Lila slipped her hand into Sam's. 'Thank you for coming. It's been so much fun.'

'I should be the one thanking you,' he said. 'For letting me hijack your family's celebrations.'

'I'm getting used to being a spare wheel when it comes to Charlie and Daniel, but having you there was perfect.'

'Perfect?' He raised an eyebrow. 'I think that's the champagne talking.'

She laughed. 'I don't.'

The foyer was mostly in shadow, a few discreet lights above the reception desk and the double doors guiding the way. The gold pattern in the centre of the floor shimmered subtly, and beyond the glass Lila could see solar lamps marking the walkways through the gardens.

'Here you go.' Daniel handed Sam a key. 'Room twelve. It's through those doors and then down the lift or stairs. I can show you, if you like?'

'I could do that,' Lila said quietly.

There was a pause, and then Charlie strode forward and gave first Sam, and then Lila, a hug. 'Goodnight. Thank you for a lovely evening.' Then, whispering in Lila's ear, added, 'See you sometime tomorrow?'

There was another round of hugs and handshakes, then Daniel unlocked the glass doors and he and Charlie stepped into the night.

With them gone, the place was deathly quiet.

'They didn't wait for you,' Sam said.

'No. I wasn't sure, on this occasion, that it was necessary.' She looked up at his handsome face, the way his eyes seemed to glimmer like the gold stones in the floor. The smile that whispered across his lips was all she needed. He held out his hand and she took it, and they walked quietly along the deserted corridors, their steps almost in time with Lila's heartbeat. When they reached room twelve, Sam unlocked it and held the door open for her.

Lila stepped inside, taking in the details of the luxurious space. The bedside lamps glowed softly, picking out the earthy, natural colours of the walls and furnishings, the gold and gunmetal grey details – on picture frames, twisting light stands and the expensive-looking coffee machine. Thick, floor-length curtains covered what she knew was a glass wall with the sea beyond. The bedspread and pillows on the king-sized bed were pistachio green, a rug on the floor a muted lilac. She wanted to touch everything, to run her hands over the different textures. But there was something she wanted to touch far more than any of the room's features. She turned.

Sam was standing with his back against the closed door. 'Lila,' he said. She stepped up to him and put her hands on his shoulders, and then slid them up around his neck. He brought his head down to hers, his arms circling her waist and pulling her against him. Lila ran her hands though his thick hair and let him guide her, gently, to the bed.

'This room is beautiful,' she sighed, sliding her hand lazily up and down Sam's chest, the golden dusting of hairs on it.

'Is that why you wanted to stay? For my hotel room?'

They were lying in the giant bed, the curtains partially open so that the sea, visible beyond only a sliver of cliff, felt almost close enough to touch. It was a pale blue this morning, flecked with white horses, the sun giving everything a hazy glow. The coffee machine gurgled hopefully on the sideboard, the smoky aroma permeating through the room – Lila had been overjoyed that Daniel had taken her advice and changed his coffee order to a better brand.

'That's exactly it,' she said. 'When I found out you were staying here, I knew this was my chance. It's not as though Daniel would give me family rates if I wanted to book a room myself, so I had no other choice but to let you seduce me.'

'Your hotel lust is my gain,' Sam said. 'How I got you and your unicorn tattoo here is inconsequential.' He was twisting a lock of her hair around his finger, tugging at all Lila's nerve endings.

'It isn't just lust, though,' she said cautiously. Could she really be so open, so declaratory, after one night together? Would Sam think she was being over-dramatic if she told him she'd never felt like this about anyone before, that she wasn't used to wanting to hold on to any relationship as much as she wanted to hold on to him?

'No?' he glanced at her and shifted slightly, his warm foot finding hers.

'It goes deeper than that. I mean, sure – it's a truly stunning room, the decor is breathtaking. But it's got so much more going for it – a great coffee machine, the glass wall showing off the view, a claw-foot bath *and* a drench shower. It's . . . thoughtful. Generous. It's a room you want to spend time in, get to know intimately.'

'Delilah Forest, are you saying you like me for more than my body?' He slid his arm out from under her and turned on his side, so he was facing her. His smile mirrored hers, his morning hair tufty and adorable.

'I might be,' she admitted. 'But your body is pretty good too.'

Sam laughed and kissed her, and Lila let herself be overwhelmed by him all over again.

Sam had been right about Winston's enthusiasm for her '*Estelle* meets Cornish Cream Tea Tour' idea, and it took place a fortnight later, on a Sunday morning. The filming had moved to a stretch of rugged coastline not too far from Porthgolow, so the cast wouldn't have to spend too long travelling to reach them. June was only just over a week away, and the weather was ahead of the game, supplying high temperatures and burgeoning sunshine that prickled the back of Lila's neck.

She watched the gleaming black people carriers drive into the car park, and felt a rush of excitement. She was looking forward to the tour and, mostly, spending time with Sam. Over the past two weeks they'd had stolen moments on the bus, hurrying up to the top deck when the coast was clear – though Charlie had been strict about what was and was not considered appropriate bus behaviour, and Lila wasn't about to disobey her cousin when she'd been so generous.

The previous weekend Sam had returned to Porthgolow, and cooked a delicious vegetable curry for her, Charlie and Daniel in Charlie's kitchen. Then they had all watched a disaster movie about an implausibly large earthquake destroying California.

Lila had felt so utterly content – snuggled up to Sam on the sofa, laughing and pointing out plot holes – that she believed, for the first time in her life, settling down could be in her future. It was a terrifying thought, both the speed with which it had appeared in her and Sam's relationship, and the strength of it. She'd taken him up to her room at the end of the evening, not caring that she hadn't made a huge effort to tidy up. She wanted him to get the real her, not a curated version. He seemed to like what he'd seen so far.

'Toby Welsh,' said the beautiful brunette beside her. 'And Aria Lundberg. On Charlie's bus, no less.' She clicked her tongue. 'What a coup.'

'It is a bit, isn't it?' Lila agreed. 'Thanks so much for coming, Josie.'

Josie was a reporter for the local paper, who Daniel knew quite well and who had done a profile of the food markets when they'd first started. Charlie had admitted that she and the journalist hadn't got off to the best start, but they had been able to get over their initial misunderstanding, and now Josie was a firm fan of the Cornish Cream Tea Bus.

'A bus tour round the Cornish coast with a cast of delicious actors and a cream tea thrown in?' Josie said now. 'It's days like these when I love my job. I owe Charlie one after this. Shall we go and greet them?'

'Lila!' Toby bounded out of the car with his usual enthusiasm, hugged her and then shook Josie's hand, dipping into an elaborate bow. 'I'm Toby Welsh. It's lovely to meet you.'

'Josie,' she replied, her calm exterior melting under his charm. 'It's a real pleasure to meet you, too.' Lila had never seen anyone so obviously flutter their eyelashes. 'I'm looking forward to covering this for the *Cornwall Star*. I can't wait to hear about *Estelle*.'

'And I'd be lying if I said I wasn't looking forward to telling you about it.' He winked and jumped onto the bus, and Lila heard him greet Charlie just as effusively.

She said hello to Aria, Darius, Bert and Winston, who had said he wanted to be there to keep an eye on everyone, though

Keeley had told her that he had been talking nonstop about the tour since the moment they suggested it.

Keeley came next, and Lila gave her a tight squeeze. 'This is going to be epic,' she said, her blue eyes shining. She was a different person – she had a new energy and commitment, was spending more hours rehearsing than anyone else, and had asked Aria to be her mentor, to help with the aspects of the job that weren't in front of a camera. Lila felt slightly guilty that she hadn't confided in her about Sam, but they had decided to keep their relationship under the radar for now; there was hardly any time left before they moved the filming to Bristol, and she wanted to hold on to him as tightly as she could until then.

Keeley introduced herself to Josie and then, when she was on the bus, it was only Sam left.

'Hey,' he said. 'Good Saturday?'

'Very nice, thanks. We took the dogs on a five-mile walk along the coast, so my feet are aching, but I feel refreshed and full of the joys of life.'

'Glad to hear it.' He smiled. 'I'm fairly happy with how things are going, too.'

He gave her arm a discreet squeeze and greeted Josie, while Lila pretended to tie her shoelace so she could watch him. She had begun to recognize Sam's moods and mannerisms, and had noticed that, despite his assertion that he was happy, his smile hadn't quite reached his eyes.

'So this is where you started the shoot?' Josie asked, peering out through the windscreen as Charlie brought Gertie to a stop. They were on a familiar road, and the view was breathtaking. The coastline stretched out before them, glittering water beyond the grass-topped cliffs. Lila remembered the very first morning they'd arrived at the *Estelle* set, Claude standing there with his clipboard, waiting to take their names, her amazement and anticipation as they'd driven down to the rows of trucks and trailers.

'This is it,' Toby said smoothly. 'The first few days, when you're getting to know each other – though of course you've done read-throughs together first – it's somehow doubly difficult because you have to forge real relationships with your colleagues, and also work out how your characters will interact. You're getting to know your fellow cast members on two separate levels.'

'I hadn't thought about it like that,' Josie said, her dark eyes rapt.

Lila brought teapots full of Assam, Earl Grey and English breakfast tea to the top deck, along with coffees for Darius and Aria. The actors murmured thank-yous as she served them, and Winston gave her a grin and a thumbs-up. She tried to catch Sam's eye but he was staring out at the water, his fingers pressed to his lips, deep in thought. Lila took her tray downstairs.

'Mini sandwiches here,' Charlie said as she appeared, 'then we'll have the cakes at the next stop, and save the scones for the end. Everyone seem happy up there?'

'It's all going swimmingly.'

Charlie narrowed her eyes. 'You said that like it was scripted.'

'What do you mean?'

'What's wrong? I know Josie's disarmingly beautiful and confident – believe me, I *know* – but honestly, you don't have to worry about her and Sam. He's as loved up as a puppy dog,' she said, laughing.

Lila tried and failed to join in. 'I'm being paranoid. There's just something . . .'

'Today was always going to be tough,' Charlie continued, 'because you can't be outwardly affectionate in this group of people, but give it a couple of weeks and all that will change.'

'We'll be out in the open but hundreds of miles apart.' She shrugged, trying for unconcerned.

Charlie wrinkled her nose. 'Dramatic, much? Bristol isn't *that* far away. And when Gertie's back in Porthgolow, the pace won't be so relentless. We'll mix it up – tours, days on the beach, food markets. You'll have time to go and see him.'

'You're right,' she said. 'Anyway, enough about that – I'm holding up our sandwiches. You lead the way.' She gestured at the stairs and picked up a tray.

'Fingers crossed they get a good reception,' Charlie murmured.

As Lila followed Charlie up the staircase, she could hear Josie's silky voice. 'What about you, Sam? This is your big, on-screen break – I know you've done a lot of theatre work too. How important is it to you that *Estelle* does well? And what are your plans after the shoot's over?'

Lila tiptoed forwards, putting sandwiches on tables as quietly as she could. She didn't want to interrupt, or even disturb the air. She waited for Sam's answer.

He sighed and gave a low, quick laugh that did delicious things to Lila's insides. 'Of course we all want *Estelle* to be a success, and the scripts are great. Cornwall's popular at the moment, and the producers have used it to its full potential.' He gestured to the landscape. 'Hopefully the combination of impressive locations, interesting characters and plenty of action will see that it's a ratings hit.'

'I agree, it has all the elements of the perfect autumn drama. But what about *you*, Sam? What are your personal goals?'

Josie's gaze was intense, and Lila could see Sam was uncomfortable, twisting his mug back and forth on the table. 'It's too early to be talking about a second season,' he glanced at Winston, 'but I'm hoping this will be a stepping stone to . . . other things. I feel very lucky to be in this position, but I've also worked hard to get here. I'm looking forward to what the future holds.'

'Sammy's probably the most dedicated of all of us,' Toby said. 'Won't let anything get in the way of his career. And good on him, I say. This is such a fickle business, you've got to grab the opportunities when you can.'

'Nothing to tie you down at the moment, then?' Josie asked. 'You're fully focused on making your star rise?'

'I wouldn't say that,' Sam replied. 'It's not about fame for me, but about getting good roles, trying new things, challenging myself. I think that *Estelle*, while teaching me a lot, is also going to open up doors.'

'It'll open up *all* the doors,' Keeley said passionately. 'Wait until you see him as Robert Bramerton, Josie. He's incredible! This time next year he'll be in Hollywood. Nothing's going to stop Sam Magee now he's got the bit between his teeth.' She reached over and ruffled his hair. Everyone laughed, and Josie nodded and looked pleased, her recording device winking on the table next to her.

Lila risked a glance at Sam and saw the muscle working in his jaw, his smile plastered on. Lila wondered what had happened since the last time she had seen him, because that smile was one bit of acting that wasn't going to win him any awards.

Chapter Twenty-three

'That,' Charlie said, as she added delicate ribbons of icing to a tray of cupcakes, 'was a triumph.'

'I can see why Josie's an excellent journalist.' Lila poured milk into the metal jug and held it under the steam wand. 'She squeezes information out of people like you and that piping bag. She had them all eating out of the palm of her hand.'

'I think you'll find that they were eating our wonderful Cornish cream teas,' Charlie corrected.

It was early morning on set, the penultimate week of filming, and the *Estelle* tour had gone off the previous day without a hitch. Unless you counted the fact that Lila hadn't had any time alone with Sam, and he had seemed pensive, and not quite himself. Lila counted that as a very private hitch, and one she planned on rectifying as soon as possible.

'Josie says it'll be in the Entertainment section on Friday, a double-page spread with lots of full-colour photos. Lila, have I ever told you that you're invaluable, and that I might have to hire you permanently as my ideas guru?'

Lila laughed. 'Hardly. It was one suggestion.'

'What about the video for Keeley? Not to mention that without your intervention we wouldn't even be here. Can you imagine if we get hired by other TV crews further down the line? Cornwall's always going to be an idyllic filming spot, and Gertie can be on hand whenever she's needed. Another string to her bow.'

'Those cupcakes look ace,' Lila blurted. She didn't like the idea of other sets, other casts — anyone beyond Sam. It might be a temporary gig for them all, but Lila hoped it would have lasting ramifications.

'Big day ahead,' Keeley said, walking onto the bus, 'so I've decided a cupcake is just what I need.' Her hair was professionally styled into Estelle's elegant curls, but her face was bare of make-up and her faded peach T-shirt was definitely not nineteenth century.

Charlie held out the tray. 'I started icing them while they were still warm, so they look a bit forlorn.'

'They look delicious.' She took one of the cakes and bit into it. 'I also came to say thank you for yesterday. I know it was a publicity stunt, but I had a great time, and the others did too. I'm worried they're going to turn Gregor green with envy talking about it this morning. I'd love to come on one of your regular tours, Charlie. I want to see some of Cornwall's other beauty spots.'

'You're back for a few days after Bristol, aren't you?'

'Yes, at Striker Manor in July. That's not too far from Porthgolow, is it?'

'Only about ten miles,' Charlie said. 'I'll let you have the schedule, so you can pick a day to come.'

'Amazing, thank you! I'd better go and submit to the make-up wizards.' She wiped crumbs from her lips.

'Who are you filming with?' Lila asked.

'I've got scenes with Aria and Toby first, and then Sam later on, so I'm hoping the weather holds. It's not looking particularly summery today, is it? But Gregor likes a bit of atmosphere, so he'll be pleased.' She shivered dramatically, and Lila laughed.

'Say hi to everyone for me.'

'Of course! I'm sure Sam'll be by later. He can't live without at *least* one Lila coffee these days. I'm worried he's addicted, that once we zoom off to Bristol he'll get withdrawal symptoms.'

I hope so, Lila thought. 'Did he seem OK to you? Yesterday, I mean?'

Keeley's pretty brows knitted together. 'I think so. Maybe a little distracted. Why? Is something wrong?'

'No, I just . . . I got that impression, too. That he had something on his mind.'

'I'll see what I can find out,' Keeley said, tapping her nose. 'Catch you later, girls!' She planted a sugary kiss on Lila's cheek and hurried off the bus.

When Sam appeared later that day, his smile reached all the way to his eyes; his arms, when he pulled Lila onto his lap on the top deck of the bus, locked tightly around her.

'I'm sorry we didn't get to talk yesterday,' he said. 'It was so hard, not being able to do this.' He kissed the tip of her nose, then her chin, then each of her fingers in turn.

Lila wriggled happily, relief rushing through her. 'I was worried something was wrong. You seemed a bit . . . down.'

'Nothing was wrong, other than having to stay away from you.' He ran his thumb over her cheek, as if clearing off a smudge. 'Which is why we need to make the most of these moments. Except this one has to end almost as soon as it's started, because Robert Bramerton has to go and have an angry confrontation with a cruel landowner, and if I spend any more time with you, I'm not going to be able to manage a single scowl.' He kissed her, and Lila wished she could keep him there indefinitely, on the top deck of Gertie, with the fairy lights dancing around them.

'Do you want to do something this weekend?' she asked, hovering at the top of the stairs, wanting to eke out their last seconds together.

'I have to go to London. I haven't been back for so long, and I have a couple of people I need to catch up with. I'm sorry.' He took her hand.

'Then it's the last week of filming. I can't believe it.'

'The end of filming doesn't mean the end of us,' Sam said. 'We can find a way to make it work.'

She swallowed down the lump in her throat and followed him to the lower deck.

That Saturday evening, Lila left Daniel and Charlie to their own devices and took Marmite and Jasper to Porthgolow beach. The dogs made the most of the open space and chased each other through the shallows, finding sticks and seaweed and, in Marmite's case, a dead jellyfish that was at least as big as he was. Lila dragged him away from it, her hands trembling with terror at the thought that, even dead, it could still harm the little dog.

'You shouldn't ever, *ever* do that,' she said, trying to inject anger into her voice while he looked up at her with large, sorrowful eyes. 'Be safe, puppy dog. What would Charlie say if anything happened to you?'

Marmite barked at her and ran off, ignoring her pleas for

him to come back. She turned to find Charlie hurrying towards her, waving. Lila frowned and jogged up the beach to meet her.

'I thought you and Daniel were spending the evening together,' she said, reaching her a few seconds after Marmite, Jasper plodding happily along behind.

'Something wonderful's happened,' Charlie replied breathlessly. 'Something which needs celebrating immediately. Come with me to the pub. Daniel will meet us there.'

'What . . .?' Lila started, but Charlie pulled on her sleeve and, laughing at her cousin's enthusiasm, Lila went with her.

The Seven Stars was full to bursting with familiar faces. She waved at Amanda and her husband Paul, who had all three kids in tow. Stella and Anton were there, as were Myrtle and Reenie, and Hugh was in his usual place behind the bar. Juliette and Lawrence stood at a table in the middle of the pub, a bottle peeping out of a bucket in front of them. Charlie's slight friend was wearing a grin that threatened to split her face in half, and solid, stoic Lawrence looked flushed and smug, his arm tightly around Juliette's waist.

'You're all here,' Juliette said. 'Good. I think you can guess what this is about, but we wanted to let you know in person.'

There were whistles and cheers, and as Lawrence poured champagne into his and Juliette's glasses, Hugh and another barman handed out full flutes to everyone else. Lila accepted hers and turned back to the couple, marvelling at the unadulterated joy on their faces.

'So,' Lawrence said, 'in case any of you *haven't* guessed – and if you haven't, then who knows how your brain is wired up – last night I proposed to Juliette. And she said yes! We're getting married!' He raised his glass and the room erupted into applause and squeals of delight. Everyone took turns to clink glasses with the happy couple, and Juliette held out her hand to show off her sparkling diamond ring.

'Isn't it amazing?' Charlie said, with tears in her eyes. 'Obviously, they were always meant to be together, but this is . . . I'm so happy for them! And Juliette wants the wedding on the beach, and for Gertie – for us – to do the catering. They want it as soon as possible – at the beginning of July. Isn't that *amazing*?' she said again, and sniffed loudly.

'Wow, that's . . . are we going to host Gertie's first wedding?' Lila asked.

'We are! For the most deserving of couples. Once *Estelle* is done, we've basically got a month to plan it. Still,' Charlie added, laughing, 'it's not as if we don't like a challenge, is it? Oh, Lila. I'm so glad you're here! I'm so glad we get to do this together.' She wrapped her arms around her, laughing and crying at the same time.

'How much champagne have you actually had?' Lila asked, which only made her cousin laugh harder.

Lila woke on Sunday with a pounding headache, Marmite lying across her feet and her clothes from the previous day dumped unceremoniously on the floor. Juliette and Lawrence's engagement celebrations had gone on well into the night, and Lila had experienced some more of Porthgolow's community spirit. Aside from the rock band pounding an entirely unhelpful beat in her head, she had also awoken with a strong conviction that she couldn't let the important things get away from her, that she wanted a taste of the happiness that Juliette and Lawrence, and Charlie and Daniel had.

She leaned over the bedside table, waited for the room to stop spinning, and reached for her phone. She checked her messages, relieved that she hadn't sent any to Sam the previous night, and saw a name at the top of the list that made her freeze. *Glen.*

Clara's boyfriend was the last person she expected to hear from. Expelling a long, slow breath, she clicked on the message, which had been sent the previous night, and read it through.

How is this still going on, L? You and Clara are the most stubborn people I know! I don't care what you said to each other, you need to get over yourself and sort this. If you don't, then I will! And then, because he was one of the sweetest people she had ever known and being threatening was not in his nature, he had signed it: *Glen. Xx*

Lila was stunned. She wanted to reply, to find out if his message meant Clara was thawing, that a part of her was as desperate to make amends as Lila was. She wanted to tell him that she was trying to be a better person, and she hoped, one day, that Clara would forgive her. But Glen's text suggested Clara still wasn't ready to talk – not if he was threatening to sort things out for them. She didn't know where to start, how a few sentences would be able to convey all that she felt and meant. And she wasn't up to dealing with it when she was so hungover she could barely think straight. She closed the app and rolled onto her back, staring up at the ceiling.

Pushing Glen's text to the back of her mind, thoughts of Sam inevitably drifted to the front. They had made it clear that they cared about each other, but Lila had a sudden urge to be explicit. She needed to tell him that she was done with short-term relationships that were fun but risk-free, her heart staying safely away from the action. She wanted him to know that she'd never felt this way about anyone, that she wanted him in her life and was prepared to work at it, to be flexible

– to move back to London if she needed to – in order to make that happen. Somehow, hearing from Glen made her even more resolved. It was time for her to be responsible, to own her feelings and her relationships, to put her heart on the line and admit how she felt. Maybe if she could do it with Sam, she could do it with Clara, too.

The realization was both thrilling and daunting, and she spent Sunday in an excruciating state of hungover restlessness, with her, Charlie and Daniel all nursing their sore heads, eating too much junk food and napping on the sofas in the afternoon.

On Monday Sam's visit to the bus was sweet but fleeting. He was sympathetic about her two-day hangover, and kissed her forehead before rushing off to get into costume. His presence on Tuesday was even briefer, as Gregor squeezed all he could out of his actors in their last few days.

On Wednesday the sun was bright, the clouds gathering in the distance too far away to be threatening, and the bus was full of delectable goodies that Charlie and Lila had spent hours making the night before – compensating for their somewhat lacklustre offerings on Monday and Tuesday. Lila felt a renewed determination, and when Sam came on board in white shirt, navy breeches and boots, his nose and cheeks bronzed from spending so much time outside, her stomach knotted with desire and anticipation.

'Can I have a double espresso?' he asked, glancing at the production assistants Charlie was serving.

'Which beans?' Lila said.

'Bubble-gum flavour, please.' He grinned, and Lila rolled her eyes. 'Arabica.'

'Syrup?'

He shook his head, and Lila forced herself to turn away

269

from him to make his coffee, wondering how to get him upstairs without it looking suspicious in front of the assistants. She didn't know how long he would stay; all she knew was that she couldn't hold it in any longer.

'Here you go.' She handed him his takeaway cup.

'Thank you.' His fingers brushed over hers and lingered there, before he took the cup. 'I'll see you later.'

'Sam . . .'

He hesitated.

'Have a good day,' she said and, not knowing what else to do, watched him walk off the bus.

When lunchtime arrived and people began drifting towards the catering marquee, Lila decided she would have to risk it. Surely there wouldn't be anything *too* unusual about her going to Sam's trailer? Their friendship wasn't a secret, after all.

'Can I have ten minutes?' she asked Charlie.

'Of course.'

'Thanks.' She pulled off her apron and hung it up, then jumped down from the bus and made her way through the backstage maze, smiling at people as she went, her palms slick with sweat. She passed Toby's trailer and then Aria's, saw the light was on inside Keeley's and wondered if she should nip in for a pep talk first, then chided herself. She wouldn't have long to talk to Sam, and what she had to say was important.

She saw his name, his character's name underneath, in bold black font on the door in front of her. She took a deep breath, pushed the loose strands of hair behind her ears and—

'Lila! Delilah?'

Her first sensation was confusion. The voice was familiar,

270

but completely out of place. A voice she hadn't heard for months.

'*Delilah!*'

She turned slowly, and there he was. Tall, with stocky shoulders, chestnut hair curling on top of his head, familiar square-framed glasses.

'Glen,' she croaked out. 'What are you doing here? How did you get in?'

'Claude,' he said simply. 'We had a good chat. I told him I needed to see you, that it was urgent. I showed him photos on my phone to prove we knew each other.'

'But you can't be here . . .' Her words trailed uselessly away. 'How did you even know I *was* here?'

'I have my sources,' he said. 'One of whom was your mother.' He shrugged, unsmiling. She heard a door opening behind her, but she was frozen to the spot, as if the ground beneath her had swallowed her up to the ankles.

'I don't know why you've come, but—'

'I had to, didn't I? This has gone on for far too long. I told you that if you didn't sort it, then I would. Enough is enough.'

'Don't you think it's too late to fix anything?' It was as much a question as a statement: she had no idea how Clara felt after all this time.

He shook his head. 'I don't believe that, L, no. Not for one second. There's too much history to give up on it now.'

'Lila?'

It was Sam. He knew what had happened between her and Clara, but she hadn't had a chance to tell him about the message Glen had sent on Saturday night.

'Sam,' she said, forcing herself to turn. 'This is Glen, he's—'

'Come to see you, all the way from London.' Sam's jaw

was set, his eyes not angry, but full of hurt. 'He thinks there's too much between you to give up on.'

'No – Sam! Glen is Clara's—'

'She's here, in the car,' Glen cut in, and Lila's sentence died on her lips.

'Here?' she whispered instead, her body turning to ice, her attention back on Glen.

'I've only got half an hour for lunch,' Sam said. 'Perhaps we could talk about this later?' He slammed the door of his trailer and walked away. She knew she should go after him, she *needed* to go after him, but she couldn't. Clara was here. In Cornwall.

'Does she want to see me?' Lila asked, and Glen's expression softened.

'I don't know.' He shrugged. 'I brought her here on holiday as a pretence. She doesn't know anything about this.'

'I do now.'

Lila took a step back, aware, suddenly, that a few crew members had paused on their way to the lunch tent to watch the unfolding drama. But she couldn't focus on them because her best friend was standing in front of her. The friend she had failed all those months ago, the friend who wouldn't forgive her.

'Clara,' she managed, her mouth dry.

'Delilah.' Her voice was devoid of warmth.

'Well, then.' Glen rubbed his hands together nervously. 'Don't you two think you've a few things to talk about?'

Lila closed her eyes, praying that this was a nightmare, but when she opened them again the scene was the same. Clara was here, in Cornwall. Lila's stomach twisted as she thought of the way they had left things. But perhaps they could get past that. They could talk, make things right, and then Lila could go and find Sam, explain who Glen was, tell him that he didn't have anything to worry about and that she was entirely, wholly his.

As a plan, it was simple. Now all she needed to do was put her brain, and her mouth, into action.

She stared at her best friend and tried to think of something to say.

Chapter Twenty-four

'Clara.'

'This is a bit of a situation, isn't it?' Clara said, her arms folded across her chest. 'How long have you been plotting this intervention?'

'A few weeks,' Glen admitted. 'I don't care if you're pissed off with me. It needed to be done.'

'So . . . what? We hug and make up?'

'Once you've had a chance to talk, I'm hoping that will be the outcome, yes.'

'I'd love to talk,' Lila said, and Clara turned her icy expression on her. Lila cleared her throat and tried again. 'There are things we can clear up, aren't there? We can go . . .' She glanced at the crew members who were still lingering. 'Let's go to Gertie.'

Clara frowned. 'Gertie?'

'Charlie's bus. I told you about her.'

'I honestly think it's better if we just leave. Glen's paid for this expensive hotel, and I thought I was coming here for a relaxing holiday. Not to dredge up the past.'

Lila winced. She had still hoped, despite all that had happened, that she hadn't been relegated to Clara's past.

'Ten minutes,' Lila said. 'Everyone will be in the catering tent having lunch. We'll have it to ourselves.'

She started walking, not waiting for the others to follow but praying that they would. She glanced behind her and saw that Glen was remonstrating with his girlfriend. A moment later, they were following. Lila led them to Gertie, beautifully glossy among the sea of white trucks and tents. She felt a flush of pride and turned to watch the others' reactions. Glen laughed, and Clara's eyebrows shot up towards her hairline.

'Meet the Cornish Cream Tea Bus,' Lila said, 'otherwise known as Gertie. Come on.' She jumped on board, and Charlie looked up from her phone. 'Charlie, Clara's here.'

'What?' she gasped.

'Glen's brought her here, and I—'

'Wow!' Glen said, his gaze roaming over the interior of the bus.

'Bit different to The Espresso Lounge,' Clara added.

Lila closed her eyes. 'Why don't we go upstairs?'

'Hi, Clara,' Charlie said. Charlie had met her once, but a long time ago. 'I'm Charlie, Lila's cousin. Hello, Glen.' She shook their hands, doing her best 'friendly host' routine. Lila wanted to hug her. 'What can I get you to drink?'

'Tea, please,' Clara said.

'Same for me,' Glen added.

'You go ahead. I'll bring them up.'

Lila shot her a silent 'thank you' and climbed the narrow staircase to the top deck which had, over the last few weeks, become her and Sam's sanctuary. She was itching to talk to him, to clear the air, but she had to do this first.

'Clara,' she said, as soon as it was just the three of them. 'You know how sorry I am, for everything, but don't you think we could put it behind us? What I did, what . . . what happened, between us?'

Clara stared at her. She had always had a thick skin, and was ambitious and dedicated and approached everything in a proactive way. But whereas Lila threw herself into things without looking both ways first, Clara had every eventuality planned out. They complemented each other in that respect, and Lila's impetuousness had often been a source of good-natured hilarity between them – when Clara hadn't been on the receiving end of it. Lila thought she must be furious with Glen right now: surprises were not her thing.

'If I could take everything back, get you your job back, I would. You know that.'

'It's not as simple as that though, is it?' Clara said quietly. 'Good intentions aren't enough – it was your good intentions that got us into this mess in the first place.'

'I'm trying really hard to be better,' Lila said. 'I listened to what you said, that day.' Clara winced, but didn't interrupt. 'I'm trying to be more responsible, to think things through. I *do* care about the future, and I want you to see that . . . that you can trust me, now. I want, more than anything, to make it up to you.'

'Some of those things . . .' Clara started. She looked away and shook her head. Lila felt a surge of hope.

'You were angry. You had every right to be. And I'm sorry I said you were too focused on work. You must know I didn't mean it, that I was just reacting. I was hurt to begin with, by what you told me, but I've tried my best to learn from it.'

Clara rolled her eyes. 'I've heard that before. Before my gala, before it all went wrong. You've said, *so many times*, that you'll try and be more prepared, but I don't think you can be, Lila! It's just how you are.' She was suddenly animated, the stone façade cracking to reveal the emotion beneath.

'So . . . what, then?'

'I lost my *job*. I'd been there five years, graduate scheme straight to junior assistant. All that time, all that effort and energy, completely wasted because I made the stupid decision to allow *you* to come to my event. I knew it was a mistake the moment you suggested it. But then you kept trying to convince me, saying how everything was planned out this time, and—'

'It *was*, though,' Lila said, exasperated. That was one of the worst things about this whole situation. On this one occasion, for Clara, she had planned everything meticulously. She just hadn't known it would be a different coffee machine. She hadn't even thought to ask, because they'd been working with the same model ever since she'd been there. 'I had planned it,' she added miserably.

'But you hadn't considered all the outcomes. You never do. You never, *ever* do. And look what happened.'

Lila heard footsteps on the stairs and gave Charlie a forlorn wave when she appeared with a tray bearing steaming drinks and a plate of mini Danishes. There were custard whorls, pecan plaits, cinnamon buns and chocolate twists. Lila wanted to tell Clara she'd helped make them – she wanted to find something her friend could be proud of her for. Instead, she waited while Charlie put the tray down and retreated downstairs without saying a word.

'How have you been?' Lila asked, once they were alone again. She realized, when she saw Glen's frown, that she should have asked that question earlier. 'Have you got another job?'

277

Clara nodded, eyeing the treats on the table. 'Slater gave me a good reference, but that was more about protecting their reputation, minimizing the fallout from what he called *the little incident*. He managed to patch up the relationship with the US partners, smooth things over, do some serious ass-licking. I heard all this from my friend James in the events team while I was updating my CV and peddling myself round the agencies.'

'You got something fairly soon, though, didn't you?' Glen said. 'Not long after you and Lila spoke that last time. And it's better. Closer to our flat, better pay, better chance of promotion.' Clara glared at him, but Lila's heart lifted.

'So something good came out of it in the end?' She picked up her mug, cradling it in both hands.

It was Clara's turn to shrug. 'But it doesn't alter what you did, what . . .' She inhaled, and it sounded like a sob. 'Fuck, Lila. That was one of the worst moments of my life, and I know that I was harsh, but you understand why, right? I was *so angry,* and I needed time to get my head around it, to work out what I was going to do. And then you were there, every day, phoning and texting and pleading with me. I just needed you out of my head for a bit, to think clearly, but you couldn't leave it alone.'

Lila stared out of the window. The clouds were rolling in, choking the sunshine.

'Because I didn't want to lose you,' she said. 'I knew how badly I'd messed up. For you, for your company and the US partners, for The Espresso Lounge as well. How many people I'd let down. I know how much that job meant to you; how much making a good impression with that event would help your career. I couldn't believe I'd ruined it in just a few minutes, and at the same time, of course I could.'

Clara picked up a cinnamon bun and bit down, chewing angrily.

'So if you thought it was going to be an unmitigated disaster,' she said, when she'd finished eating, 'why did you convince me to let you be a part of it in the first place?'

'Because I wanted to prove to you that I could do it! Come on, Clara, you've had enough time to learn my contradictions – you reminded me of them all that day outside your flat. I was desperate to help you make the event a success. I wanted you to be proud of me, for it to be something we could talk about for years to come, down the pub or on spa weekends.'

Clara laughed and brushed at her cheek. 'It's definitely a talking point,' she said. 'And I see that, despite everything, you're all right. Working down here in Cornwall, on a swanky television set, trusted with what looks like a rather impressive coffee machine.' She raised an eyebrow. Lila couldn't get used to this angry, bitter side of her friend. She had been stunned by it after their last meeting. This time, she hoped Clara would blow herself out.

'Charlie's been very kind to me,' Lila admitted. 'I am lucky to be in this position, but if you think that means I've forgotten what happened, that I don't think about it every day, then you're wrong. Can't we put it behind us? I get that I tried too hard, that I pressured you straight after it happened, but now? It's been months.'

'And this was your plan, was it? Getting Glen on your side?'

Glen's surprised mirrored her own. 'Lila had nothing to do with this. I only got in touch with her at the weekend, and I didn't tell her we were coming. You have too much history to give up on it,' he added, choosing a pecan plait. 'I don't regret what I've done.'

'But I immediately assumed you were involved, Lila,' Clara said. 'That this was another one of your ridiculous schemes. I just . . . I can't do this. Not now. Not when it's been sprung on me like this.' She stood up abruptly and, wiping her eyes, hurried down the stairs.

'Shit.' Glen shoved the rest of the Danish in his mouth and stood up.

Lila was quicker. She followed her friend down the staircase and off the bus. Charlie called her name but she paid no attention, seeing the flash of Clara's berry-coloured jacket and following it, weaving through the vehicles, not heading in the direction of the exit but down towards the cliffs, close to where they were filming. Lunch was over, they would be starting again any moment.

Lila picked up her pace.

'Clara!' she shouted. 'Clara, please wait!' Her wedge sandals were comfortable but not ideal for running in. She skidded and slipped in the mud that had been churned up by the hundreds of journeys made by the production team. She heard Glen breathing behind her, hot on her tail.

Lila rounded a corner and stopped, the sea a grey mass ahead of her, the dark clouds above promising rain. Clara had come to a halt, and over to her right Lila could hear Gregor's brisk, commanding voice.

'Clara.'

Her friend turned. 'This is . . .'

'It is a bit,' Lila admitted. 'Even when the weather's shit, Cornwall puts on a good show.'

She saw her friend swallow. 'I can't do this right now, Lila. I thought I might be ready to let it go . . . I accused you of some *horrible* things, I know that. And I know you didn't plan what happened, but it's your assumption that everything will turn out OK, that your enthusiasm will carry you through. If I just say that it doesn't matter, that all is forgiven, then I'm not doing justice to myself *or* to you.'

'I know you can't forget what I did,' Lila replied, 'and believe me, I can't either. But I have tried, *so hard,* to be better. And I miss you so much. I have loads to tell you. About Porthgolow, where Charlie lives and where I've been staying, about Toby Welsh and Aria Lundberg; about working on Gertie, the Cornish Cream Tea Bus tours, this amazing hotel that Charlie's boyfriend owns and is better than *any* of the spa days we've ever had . . .'

Clara's eyes widened, and Lila could see that she was at war, that a part of her wanted to let go of her anger.

Lila took a deep breath. 'I want to tell you about Sam.'

'Sam?' Clara asked. 'Who's Sam?'

Glen cleared his throat and Lila closed her eyes, hiding her frustration. 'I think it might be this guy,' he said apologetically.

Lila turned round. Sam was standing next to Glen, dressed in his Robert Bramerton finery. He looked so commanding in his navy waistcoat, frock coat and breeches, but his expression was softer than the last time she'd seen him, and Lila made a silent wish that this meeting, this unexpected foursome, standing on the cliff while the Cornish June uncharacteristically growled around them, would fix everything. This, she decided, could be one of those moments of perfect alignment. Of fate. She looked between Sam and Clara, and let the hope blossom.

Chapter Twenty-five

'I should leave you to it,' Clara said, walking past her. 'Come on, Glen.'

'No, wait, Clara – please stay. I'd love to introduce you to Sam.'

'This is Clara?' Sam flicked Lila a questioning look and then, ever the gentleman, held out his hand. 'I'm Sam Magee. It's lovely to meet you.'

Clara faltered, then shook his hand. 'You're one of the actors? I mean, obviously.' She gestured to his outfit and laughed nervously.

'I'm a PA, actually. I just have a thing about Regency outfits.' His eyes flashed mischievously, and Clara's laugh was louder, unforced.

'You're friends with Lila?' she asked.

'We're . . . close. And you're Glen? Great to meet you, too.' The two men shook hands and Lila wanted to dance with joy. 'I've got to head to set, but are you hanging around? Maybe we could get a drink together, now you've had a chance to sort things out with Lila.'

'No,' Clara said hurriedly. 'We're not hanging around, and we haven't sorted things out. I didn't know Glen was bringing me here, and I . . . it's a bit more complicated than simply hugging and making up.' She shrugged, clearly embarrassed at giving the details to a man she didn't know, but as forthright as ever.

'Clara—' Lila started.

'Are you sure?' Sam said, frowning. 'I would have thought it was exactly that simple. I know Lila's sorry for what happened, but I also know she's tried her hardest to make it right between you. Do you really think it's worth losing your friendship over?'

Lila felt a swell of affection for him. 'Sam, you don't need to—'

'Look, Sam,' Clara said, the edge back in her voice. 'I've only just met you, and you seem very nice, and it's great if Lila has found someone to confide in, but I'm not sure this is any of your business.' She spun to face Lila. 'This is a low move, getting your actor boyfriend to make me feel like *I'm* the one in the wrong.'

'I didn't! He's just . . .' She shot him a look. 'He's just trying to help. He knows how much I care about you.'

'So you let him emotionally blackmail me? Make out like you've done all you can to fix this, that I'm the heartless bitch for refusing your apology?'

'I never said that.' Sam held out a placatory hand.

'Clara, he wouldn't—'

'I'm going back to the hotel. Glen?' She turned and strode away. Glen gave Lila an apologetic look and hurried to catch up with his girlfriend. Lila watched them until they disappeared behind the video village, and then looked at the space where her best friend had been.

283

The waves were pounding somewhere behind her, the wind tugging at her hair. She had come close to reconciliation. She had watched Clara mellow, seen her desperation to hear Lila's news and catch up on the gossip she'd missed. And then Sam had shown up.

'I'm so sorry,' Sam said. 'I had no idea that was Glen, Clara's boyfriend.'

'No,' Lila sighed. 'You assumed he was an ex, maybe even a current boyfriend I'd left behind in London.'

'What I overheard, Lila—'

'You thought I'd do that to you?' she blurted. 'Thought it would make total sense that I hadn't just left one mess behind, but a whole series of them? That that's who I am?'

'You know I don't think that. I was surprised, that's all, when you were outside my trailer and so was he. I didn't know—'

'Chaotic old Delilah. What has she gone and done now?'

Sam took a step towards her, holding out his hands. 'I have *never* thought that. The way I feel about you . . . Lila, you have no idea.'

She folded her arms over her chest, ignoring his outstretched hands. The wind bit into her neck, howling between the vehicles like a phantom wolf. 'Do you want to try and fix all my mistakes, the way you just tried to fix things with Clara? Well, you didn't exactly get that right, did you? You're not as perfect as you think you are.'

Sam dropped his hands. 'Lila, come on. I'm sorry, I—'

'If you wanted to help me, then this was not the way to go about it! As much as it may sometimes appear to you, I'm not a complete idiot. But maybe that doesn't matter. Like you said to Josie on the bus, you don't want anything to get in the way of your career, and you've realized I'm too much trouble.'

'Sam!' A voice called from somewhere. 'You're needed on set!'

He didn't move. 'Of course I don't think you're too much trouble,' he said gently. 'I love who you are. Haven't I shown you enough?'

I love who you are. The words bounced around Lila's head, and she tried to swallow the lump in her throat. She was so angry with herself; she knew Sam had been trying to help, but her fury needed a direction. 'Saving Marmite on the beach,' she murmured.

'What? I can't hear—'

'When I lost Marmite on the beach that night, you had to rescue him. We went to the pub and I got drunk, so you had to step in and do my baking. Just now, with Clara, you thought you could swoop in and make all those months of hurt and upset go away, that she would listen to you because you're so much better than me.'

'That is the most ridiculous thing I've heard,' Sam said, anger edging into his voice. 'That's not why I'm here – why I come to see you in Porthgolow, why I come to the bus *every day*. Why I can't get enough of you. You really think all that is because I've decided you need rescuing? For fuck's sake, Lila. I come because I have fallen for you, completely.' He ran a hand through his hair. 'And I am very, *very* far from perfect. I'm just fumbling through and trying to make the most of things. You think that you're the only person entitled to get things wrong? You cannot have a monopoly on self-pity.'

She shook her head.

'I know how much you miss Clara, and I wanted to help you, I admit it, even though it wasn't my place. But my intentions were good.'

285

'The road to hell is paved with good intentions,' Lila said. 'I can't count the number of times my mum has said that to me.'

'Sam! We need you here now!'

'You should go,' Lila said. 'Go to set.'

'I don't want to leave you when you're like this.' He stepped closer, his brow lowered in a frown. He looked so good, smelt so good. Lila wanted to wrap herself around him, to press herself against his chest, but she was too fired up.

'What about what you told Josie, on the bus?' she said. 'About all those opening doors? What are we even doing here, Sam? The shoot will be over in two days, and then you'll be off to Bristol and, after that, who knows where? You *are* going to leave me, whatever you say now.'

'Now you're just being self-destructive,' he said, but suddenly he wouldn't meet her gaze.

Lila's insides shrivelled. It was the same look he'd had on the bus tour. Evasive – not wholly present. At that moment, the rain started. Fat drops that sounded like hail as they hit the roofs of the vehicles close by.

'Where are you going?' she asked softly. 'What aren't you telling me?'

Sam pulled at his cravat, as if it was suddenly too tight.

'Has anyone seen Sam Magee?' a voice called, and his name rang out over and over, like an echo.

He turned to go and Lila, desperate, clutched his hand.

'No,' she said firmly. 'You told me you would stay, that you didn't want to leave me like this. So tell me. Tell me where you're going when shooting wraps up here.'

He hesitated, then looked straight at her. 'I've been offered a film role in the States. It starts as soon as this is over, shooting until Christmas. I was invited for a final audition in London – the director had flown over, so that's where I was—'

'This weekend,' Lila finished for him. 'And what about on the bus with Josie? Something was definitely on your mind.'

He sighed. 'My agent had called the night before, told me I'd made it through to the final stage. I was pleased, of course, but—'

'Congratulations,' she cut in. 'That's great news.'

He grabbed her hand. 'Lila, this doesn't mean we—'

'Of course it does!' She pulled her hand away and he stepped back, shocked. 'You're so optimistic,' she continued. 'You think that as long as you have a plan and stick to it, everything will work out. Life doesn't follow the rules like that. You can't beat the odds every time, just as you can't iron out my rough edges and fit me into your perfect little mould.' She took a deep breath. 'But I don't know why I'm bothering with this. It's over, isn't it? You're going to America. I'm staying here.'

'You think it's easy for me to go? I've been battling with it ever since I found out. My agent put me forward for the role before I'd even met you, and I honestly didn't think I'd get it. But I did, and it's the biggest opportunity I've had, but I can't enjoy it because of *you*.'

'Me?'

'Yes, you!' He flung his arm out. 'I've been working towards this for years, and suddenly everything's falling into place. I'm getting good roles, being noticed, heading in the direction I want, but now here *you* are. With all your . . . ideas and energy and determination, and your beautiful laugh, and the way you kiss me. And suddenly I can't think straight because I've got this path ahead of me, to the US and . . . who knows where else? And I can't embrace it, because I can't bear the thought of going without you.' He took a step towards her. 'I don't want to be apart from you, and it's . . . impossible. This. Right now. I don't—' He ran both hands through his hair and Lila's heart thudded, hating to see his anguish, knowing there was one way she could take it away. She could do this one, decent thing and not fuck up the life of someone she cared about.

'That's OK,' she said. 'I know exactly what to do.'

'You do?' He looked up, the hope on his face so innocent somehow.

She gave him one of her brightest smiles. 'It's over, Sam. Go and do your thing in America. Don't let one little fling get in the way of all your dreams.'

'Fling? I—'

'Did you really think it was more than that? I had a great time, honestly, but . . .' She shrugged, putting on the perform-ance of a lifetime. 'We went into this knowing it was temporary. A bit of a distraction for both of us. And now filming's nearly done. It's come to its natural end.'

'Delilah, this is so much more than—'

'Sam, Jesus Christ!' It was Gregor, storming towards them, hood down, snarl visible below it. 'I thought you were a professional! We've been waiting for you for ten minutes. And look at you! You'll need to change, go back to hair and make-up. This is not on. Come with me.'

Sam barely seemed to notice him. He stared at Lila, his hair plastered to his forehead, his heavy jacket sagging as the rain continued to fall.

'Go,' Lila mouthed, smiling at him, glad the weather could hide her tears. 'Be brilliant.' She rushed up and kissed his cheek, felt his hand on her waist, his lips brush her jaw as Gregor took hold of his arm and dragged him away.

A fitting ending, Lila thought, as she watched them for a moment and then turned her back on them to stare out at the raging sea. She had done the right thing. They had no future and, at least this way, she wouldn't be responsible for him turning down the greatest opportunity he'd ever had. By letting him go, she was saving him. Lila thought it might be the most selfless thing she had ever done: it turned out she *was* learning, after all. She took a deep breath, held herself together and, hardly feeling the rain as it pounded down on her, made her way back to Gertie and Charlie, Marmite's soft affection and a hot, soothing coffee.

It wasn't as if she could trust Sam's almost-declaration, said in the heat of their argument. He couldn't possibly love her, not after such a brief time together. And what she was feeling wasn't love, either. It was the drama of it all, the whirlwind, the heightened tension of the television set. It didn't matter, anyway, how deep their feelings had been. She would be in Cornwall, he would be in America – they would have an ocean between them. Whichever way Lila looked at it, this was for the best. Another one of her impermanent relationships, no commitment, no heartbreak.

Except this time, her heart wasn't unscathed, and it was telling her that she was making the biggest mistake of her life.

There were two days left on the *Estelle* set and Lila, feeling like the world's biggest bitch, faked a migraine for both of them.

'You sure you don't want to come?' Charlie asked. 'You could sit in the back, see how you feel. We can fold the pull-out bed down on the top deck, so you can have a nap if you're still feeling rough. It would be such a shame to miss the last couple of days.'

'I really don't think I can,' Lila said, pushing her head under the pillow. At least Charlie believed her sadness was to do with Clara, and not because she had ended things with Sam. She thought if she could just get to the end of Gertie's association with *Estelle*, then Charlie couldn't try and patch them up. Sam would be gone and her life would move on, as it always did.

He had tried to get in touch with her on Wednesday evening, presumably when Gregor had finally released him, but she had ignored all his messages and calls. She had got him in trouble with the director, but that small aberration seemed better than ruining his entire career. Then Keeley had called her, sometime after nine o'clock that night, as she'd been sitting on Charlie's sofa, burying her head in Marmite's soft fur and trying to hold back a fresh wave of tears. Lila had considered not answering her call either.

'Hello?' she'd said, warily. She'd had every reason to be wary, it turned out.

'What the hell, Lila? You and Sam?'

Lila had lifted Marmite off her lap, so she could go up to her room.

'What's he told you?'

'That you were together, and that you've ended it. I only managed to get it out of him because he was so hopeless on set this afternoon, so angry and upset, and Gregor was pissed off at him for missing the call. It was the worst day I've had on *Estelle*, and remember that I used to be *miserable* here, so that's saying something! I've never seen Sam like this.'

'It's for the best,' Lila had said.

Keeley's laugh was humourless. 'In whose world?'

'His. I promise you, Keeley. He's going to America, did he tell you that?'

'Yes, of course! We're all over the moon for him, but it's only for six months.'

'He told me he couldn't enjoy it because of me.'

Marmite had appeared in the doorway, pattered over and jumped on the bed, then curled against Lila's thigh while she stroked his silky fur.

'Because he's been so focused on his career,' Keeley said quietly, 'and suddenly he's got other priorities. It's because he cares about you, Lila. If he didn't, he wouldn't be so torn.'

'Exactly. He needs to do this, to enjoy every second. If he can't make that decision, then I need to be the one to do it for him.'

'You don't think you're worth his affection?' Keeley had asked. 'Lila, that is the most ridiculous—'

'It wasn't ever that serious. Not for me.' The lie stuck in her throat, but she thought the more people who believed it, the less likely Sam was to try and get her back. 'You know this is what Sam needs, what's best for him. Promise me you'll help.'

'Help how?'

'He's been texting, calling. Please tell him you've spoken to me, that it's definitely over. Tell him I don't want to talk to him, that this needs to be a clean break, for both our sakes.' She'd swallowed, squeezing her eyes shut. 'It's been a couple of months, if that. He'll get over me, just as I'll get over him.'

There had been a long silence, before Keeley eventually spoke. 'This is horrible. I love you both. And you're perfect together, by the way, like salt and pepper, sweet and sour, Napoleon Solo and Illya Kuryakin.'

'Please don't,' Lila had said, laughing through her tears. 'This is the way it has to be.'

'You're not coming back, are you? To set?'

'Come to Porthgolow if you get a chance. A day off when you're in Bristol, or when you're back in Cornwall for that last location shoot. We'll stay in touch.'

'You can stay in touch with me, but not with Sam?'

'You know it's different,' Lila had said. 'I have to go now, Keeley. Thank you for helping with this.' She'd said goodbye and hung up before her friend had a chance to respond.

On Friday afternoon, after spending the day in bed, Lila forced herself to walk down the hill to Porthgolow beach. Wednesday's rain had cleared, and the sun was beating down, turning the water to a blue and golden shimmer. Reenie's yellow hut sat perkily on its precipice, and Crystal Waters gleamed on top of the cliff. Lila felt dull, heavy-headed, as if she really was recovering from a migraine. She took her shoes off and walked in the damp sand, close to the edge of the water, remembering Sam hoisting her up on his shoulders and striding deeper into the waves.

She couldn't help dwelling on the irony of how she had gone from being determined to tell him just how much she cared for him on Wednesday lunchtime, to severing everything between them less than an hour later. It wasn't Clara's appearance, the reminder of how royally she had screwed up her friend's life – although that had something to do with it. No, it was America that had changed everything, Sam's admission that she was the one standing in the way of his dreams.

She knew he was simply trying to convey the strength of his feelings for her, but he had inadvertently put the ball in her court. And her decision hadn't been impetuous. She and Sam had always been on borrowed time, and she would not be responsible for someone else losing out on something that mattered, even if it meant *she* had to lose *them* in the process.

Lila stood and faced into the wind, letting it buffet her face and twist her hair. She wouldn't think about the last afternoon on set, what Charlie and Keeley would be doing: the celebratory atmosphere; bottles being opened and hugs given. She wouldn't think about whether, now Sam had had a chance to cool down, he had decided that she had been right to break things off, and was looking firmly to the future, to new opportunities, new acquaintances, new lovers.

It was summer and she was in Porthgolow, one of the most beautiful places she had ever been. She would help Charlie on board the Cornish Cream Tea Bus, throw herself into planning Juliette and Lawrence's wedding, running tours and food markets. She turned in the direction of Crystal Waters, wondering if there was a free massage slot where, for half an hour, she could empty her head of all the perfect, taunting memories of their time together. She would bury herself in her work, she decided, and she would stop thinking about Sam Magee.

That way lay nothing but heartbreak.

Part Four

Muffin Compares To You

Chapter Twenty-six

It was summer in Porthgolow, and Delilah Forest was trying very hard to embrace every glorious moment, which wasn't easy when, only three days before, she had given up the love of her life.

Charlie's Yorkipoo looked up at her questioningly, and Lila rolled her eyes, brushing away fresh tears that she couldn't seem to keep at bay. 'I'm not being over-dramatic, Marmite,' she told him. 'That's exactly what's happened. But I had to let him go; it was the only option.' Reaching the beach, she crouched and undid the dog's lead, and he took off across the sand in the direction of the water.

It was early, the light still had a shimmering, ethereal quality to it, but even so, there were already a couple of food trucks parked close to the Cornish Cream Tea Bus. Lila was about to take part in her first Porthgolow food market. She had arrived in the village in the midst of one, intrigued by the brightness of the beach on such a dull February day, but since then, and with them only happening once a month in the low season, Lila hadn't been to another one.

Filming for the television drama *Estelle* had concluded its Cornwall shoot – for the time being, at least – and had moved to studios in Bristol. Lila hadn't been there for the last two days of filming, but Charlie had come home last night, bringing Gertie back with her, full of details about the final day – the jubilant feeling on set, the goodbyes and well-wishes she had received, and how many people had asked after Lila, and been disappointed not to be able to say goodbye to her, too.

'Toby and Aria got us this,' Charlie had said, hefting a large tote bag into the living room. Marmite, and Daniel's German shepherd Jasper, had started sniffing it while Charlie reached in and pulled out a beautiful gift set full of cheeses, chutneys and expensive crackers, along with a bottle of raspberry vodka. There were small plates with a swirling red and blue pattern, a cheese knife with a gilt handle and two gold-rimmed shot glasses.

'Wow!' Lila had said, nursing a cup of peppermint tea. 'That looks like something from Fortnum & Mason.'

'They said they didn't know what to get us, but that we might fancy something a bit different after spending so much time up to our elbows in baking.'

'I love cheese,' Lila had admitted, and Charlie passed her the gift set so she could look at it more closely.

'Keeley said she'd be in touch,' Charlie had added, folding the tote bag slowly, avoiding Lila's gaze. 'Apparently she knew you weren't well.'

'We spoke on the phone the other night.'

'Ah,' Charlie had said. And then, after a pause, 'Winston and Gregor were there, too. They thanked us for all we've done.'

'That's good,' Lila had replied, reading the tiny print on the chutney jar.

'And Darius and Bert, especially, were sad to miss you. They said they had fond memories of that night on the beach.'

Lila had looked up, her cheeks flushing. 'That was . . . while you were away.'

'I figured,' Charlie said. 'I certainly don't remember a night on the beach. But they wanted me to pass on their love. We'll get tickets to the London press launch later on this year.'

'Ace.' Lila had tried her biggest, brightest smile, and hopped up from the sofa. 'I'm feeling a lot better! I'm so full of peppermint tea I smell like a toothpaste factory. Do you want a glass of wine to celebrate, to mark the end of an era?' She had opened the fridge and pulled out a bottle of rosé she had bought on her way back from the beach earlier that afternoon.

'He was gutted not to see you, Lila,' Charlie said softly. 'He looked awful. Miserable. What on earth happened?'

Lila had turned to her cousin, the tears spilling from her eyes even before she'd had a chance to realize what was happening. 'He's going to America. He's got this amazing film gig, and I . . . I didn't want to stand in his way.'

'So you ended it? Oh, Lila. Relationships have survived more than a few months of long-distance.'

Lila shrugged into Charlie's embrace. 'It seemed like the best thing to do,' she'd mumbled into her shoulder. 'A clean cut.'

'If only love was as simple as a freshly baked cake,' Charlie had said. 'You can't just slice yourself down the middle and throw one set of feelings away.'

Now, as Lila watched Marmite racing in the shallows, she tried hard not to think about Sam Magee on this beach with her, or stealing kisses on the top deck of Gertie while Charlie served below. She tried fervently not to think about their night at Crystal Waters, surrounded by luxury, or the night in Lila's bedroom, how they had snuggled up together, laughed and talked and made love. He had accepted all of her, had cherished her, and she had thrown it back at him.

She winced as she remembered what she'd said to him down by the cliffs, flinging her anger at him like sea spray, hoping he would take the hint and turn away. But he had hung on, and so she'd been left no choice but to sever it herself. She knew, in her head, it was the right decision. She just had to convince her heart.

Collecting a soggy Marmite and clipping his lead on, she started making her way up the sand. Myrtle was standing outside her Pop-In shop, adjusting the position of the newspaper stand which, instead of displaying the day's headline, had a bold sign announcing the food market on the beach.

'Glad to see Gertie's back for the summer,' she called, giving Lila a thumbs-up.

'Me too!' Lila shouted back. 'I'm going to eat myself silly today.'

'That, cheel,' Myrtle continued, her voice lowering as Lila approached, 'is a rookie mistake.'

'What do you mean?'

'We've all done it. Got overexcited by what's on offer, gone round samplin' and buyin' and tryin' to fit three lunches in. You'll be sick as a dog come this evenin'.'

'That's not a very good advert for the food markets.' Lila wrinkled her nose.

'The markets are wonderful,' Myrtle protested. 'My nephew Bill runs the vegan truck, which is one o' the best additions we've ever 'ad.'

'I'm a veggie, so he'll be right up my street.'

'But,' Myrtle continued, holding a warning hand in front of Lila's face. 'You must treat it responsibly. You've got the whole summer ahead of you, Delilah. No need to fit everythin' in today.'

'Thanks for the advice,' Lila said, touched by the older woman's concern, hoping it wouldn't set off a fresh wave of tears. 'I'll be sure to pace myself.'

'So,' Charlie said, as she and Juliette both turned to face Lila. 'We were thinking . . .' They were standing in Gertie's kitchen, and their smiles were definitely complicit.

Lila narrowed her eyes. 'Thinking what?'

'That instead of majoring on Cornish cream *teas* today,' Juliette said, 'though of course Gertie will always major on Cornish cream teas, what with it being the Cornish Cream Tea Bus . . .'

Lila waited, but Juliette didn't elaborate. 'Yes?' she asked.

'Oh, right!' Juliette slapped a hand to her forehead, her engagement ring sparkling in the light. 'I've got wedding brain.'

'Isn't it baby brain?' Charlie corrected, laughing. Then her laughter stopped abruptly, and she turned to her friend with wide eyes. 'Unless you—'

'No!' Juliette said hurriedly. 'No, no. That isn't the reason we want to get married so quickly. Also, we're not living in the Dark Ages, so even if I was pregnant, I wouldn't feel the need to hurry into the wedding. All I'm saying is that wedding planning, especially when you're working to such a tight deadline, makes your brain hurt. I'm all dress designs and vows and playlists. But *anyway*, that's not important right now. What is important is making this day yours, Lila.'

'What?' Lila's mind had started wandering in the direction

of what she would wear at her own wedding, were she ever to have one. It would be something entirely unconventional, in animal print or neon blue. 'What do you mean, making this day mine? It's a food market, isn't it? We're serving Cornish cream teas.'

'Yes, but today . . .' Charlie said, and she and Juliette moved away from the counter, and Lila saw packets of different coffees and bottles of syrup laid out on the top. 'We're going to specialize in coffee.'

'We *are*?'

'I had planned to do this anyway,' Charlie said. 'Make more of your skills on the bus this summer, but then . . .' She shot Juliette a quick glance.

'Char told me about Sam,' Juliette continued, her dark eyes full of empathy. 'I am so, *so* sorry. That it had to be that way.'

'His star is rising,' Lila said past the lump in her throat. 'I don't want to be the weight that keeps him tethered to earth.'

Juliette smiled. 'You couldn't keep anyone tethered. You're too full of sparkle for that. But, whatever has happened, today is about coffee.'

'I ordered a load of stuff and got it sent to Crystal Waters,' Charlie explained. 'It all turned up yesterday. Daniel said it smelled as though a Starbucks had exploded in reception.'

It did smell wonderful, and as Lila looked at the display on the counter, she saw that they had got everything. Every type of bean and roast she could think of, and a syrup pack with ten different flavours, including the more unusual lavender and rosemary. There was a mini electric grinder and three tall, polished cafetières. 'This is amazing.'

'I know we have the coffee machine,' Charlie said, 'but it's

302

not so easy to keep swapping the different beans in and out. I thought this way, if anyone wanted a speciality coffee, this could be your work station. We've got an hour before the market officially opens. Do you want to draw up a new menu?'

'I don't think so,' Lila replied, a smile forming on her lips. 'I think we just write out all the options – bean and roast, coffee style, and then the additions – full fat, soya or almond milk, cream, sugar, syrup – and let customers decide. If they want advice or suggestions, I can help them, and we'll go from there.'

'OK then,' Charlie said. 'Juliette and I will take orders, serve and clear tables. You're in charge of the coffee emporium. Deal?'

'Deal!' Lila and Juliette said in unison.

Lila started to organize her new coffee paraphernalia as if it was unearthed treasure.

Within half an hour of the Porthgolow food market opening, they were all rushed off their feet. Visitors to the bus – locals, regulars from further afield and newcomers – were all intrigued by the 'build your own coffee' idea, and Lila had been creating concoctions she hadn't ever considered before. A flat white with rosemary syrup and cinnamon sprinkles; a latte with medium-strength liberica beans, hazelnut syrup and some of the marshmallows usually reserved for hot chocolates. Stella and Anton sat at one of the downstairs tables and had a Cornish cream tea for two, with Americanos instead of tea, a shot of vanilla syrup making Stella's order even sweeter.

Lila spent her time beavering away in the kitchen and talking to customers, explaining the different strengths and qualities of the roasts, suggesting which cakes would go with which drink. She created a bus-shaped stencil out of cardboard, so she could dust the cappuccinos and lattes with a unique, Cornish Cream Tea Bus design. Charlie introduced her to everyone she knew, and Lila was greeted warmly by people with thick Cornish accents, and heard so much praise for Charlie and her bus that her pride mingled uncomfortably with a growing sense of guilt.

'I underestimated your reputation,' she said, looking up from the Marmite-shaped stencil she had moved on to.

'What?' Charlie leaned on the counter alongside her, her forehead glowing with perspiration. 'What do you mean?'

'This place – Gertie. She's so loved. I'm wondering if kidnapping her to work on *Estelle* was the right thing to do.'

'You can't be serious,' Charlie said. 'Working on *Estelle* was wonderful. We got to meet all those amazing characters, and got paid handsomely for our time, so all my plans for repaints, outdoor chairs and tables and a new sound-system can go ahead. Also, you were in your element surrounded by thespians, which meant I felt able to go on my American adventure with Daniel.'

'You wouldn't have felt OK doing that if Gertie had been here?'

'Of course I would have,' Charlie said. 'But . . . I don't know. I liked thinking of you there. It made me happy, knowing you were happy.' Her voice softened when she added, 'And would you really rather have never met Keeley? Or Sam?'

Lila stared at her stencil, the little doggy ears alert. 'No, of course not. I'm not saying I wish it had never happened, but—'

'But your heart feels like it's breaking into a million splintered pieces?'

Lila forced out a laugh. 'I thought I was the melodramatic one.'

'So you're not heartbroken?' Charlie asked. 'I shouldn't have been flippant, I'm sorry. But I can see . . . well, you're hiding it pretty well. That's what I think. Hiding it from other people, but not from me.'

'Does this look like Marmite to you?' Lila held the stencil up in front of Charlie, seeing portions of her face through the cut-out shape.

'It doesn't have to be over with Sam if you don't want it to be.'

'Maybe it looks more like a hippo. Do you think people will mind having their chocolate sprinkles hippo-shaped? Perhaps they'll think hippos are a feature of Porthgolow Bay, like the dolphins.'

Charlie huffed in frustration. 'OK, I get it. Now is not the time. But I am going to talk to you about this later. I know what it's like to be unsure, to come up with a hundred different reasons why a relationship might not work. But if your gut is telling you it's right, then—'

'Charlie, how's the cream tea coming on for table five?' Juliette asked, slightly breathlessly. 'We're getting a queue! How cool is that?'

'Five minutes, Jules,' Charlie said, turning away from Lila and setting out a tray. 'I'll be right there.'

Despite the day continuing on its relentless trajectory, and Charlie having no more time to ambush Lila with her concern, she couldn't entirely escape the spectre of Sam. He hovered in her thoughts, popping up between customers and coffees, filling every available space she had. And it wasn't just her mind conspiring against her, but the outside world, too.

She had gone upstairs to deliver a tray of gingerbread cappuccinos and brownie slices to two women, and couldn't help overhearing their conversation.

'It's just finished apparently, only this last week. It's a shame, because Maria wanted to go down there and ogle Toby Welsh, you know, from that hospital drama? I told her it was probably a good thing. The security would have been intense, and she'd only have been disappointed after driving all that way.'

'They were on this very bus!' the other woman exclaimed. 'Didn't you see it in the paper? All those beautiful people. And the bus was on set – I'm sure I read that – though what a double-decker bus is doing in a period drama, even if it *is* a vintage Routemaster, I honestly have no idea. Talk about anachronisms.'

'Here you go,' Lila croaked. She cleared her throat and put the drinks down. 'I hope you enjoy them.'

'Do you know anything about this *Estelle* series, then?' the first woman asked. 'Was the Cornish Cream Tea Bus really on the set, or did it just do the tour with all those lovely young things?'

'We worked on the set,' Lila admitted. 'We were part of the location catering, offering something a bit different to the cast and crew.'

'My word!' the second woman said. 'So you met them all, Toby Welsh included?'

'I did. He's very nice.'

'And his brother – oh, what's his name? That's who my Maria really took a fancy to, once she saw some of those long-lens shots on the *Sun* website. Sam something. Tall, dark-blond fella. All angles and cheekbones. Very handsome.'

'Sam Magee,' Lila managed.

'You met him too?'

'I met everyone. It was a brilliant place to work. A real privilege.'

'And I suppose you have loads of spoilers, don't you? Know the whole plot and everything.'

Lila smiled. 'I might do. But I'm sworn to secrecy, of course. I wouldn't want the producers to come and shut our bus down because I've been a bit too free and easy with the on-set gossip.' She tapped the side of her nose, realizing that she had so much to be grateful for, so many happy memories. It was a time in her life that she would never forget; she should embrace all the good that had come of it, then move on to whatever came next.

'Good heavens, no!' gasped one of the women, her brownie momentarily forgotten. 'Shut down the Cornish Cream Tea Bus? They wouldn't get away with it – it's a local treasure. I should think they'd cancel the television series first, if it came to it. Close this beautiful bus, I ask you!' She shook her head and her friend patted her hand, as if what Lila had said had been a personal affront rather than a joke. She didn't need to be smack-bang in the middle of a showbiz set to find pockets of drama – they were everywhere.

As the afternoon morphed into evening, Lila felt the satisfied exhaustion of time well spent, working hard and making people happy. It had been so much busier than any of the days on *Estelle*, an entirely different kind of thrill. She couldn't even begin to count how many coffees she'd made and served, or all the different combinations. But she'd accepted all feedback gladly, and was going to use it to create a tailor-made coffee menu for Juliette and Lawrence's wedding, complete with some alcoholic options. Juliette had floated around as if on a cloud, working without pause, smiling and laughing, her eyes sparkling. Lila was so pleased for her.

She pressed her hands against the counter, stretched out her fingers and arched her back, loosening the tension. Beyond the window, the food market was still in full swing, the vibrant trucks selling burgers and burritos, fish and chips and curries, candyfloss and cocktails. Lila wondered what she would try: she was going to head straight to Bill's vegan truck, and maybe pick up some fudge, too. Her gaze wandered over the busy scene and then drifted down, beyond the market, to where people thronged on the sand, playing games or lying on beach towels reading books, a fair few still in the water.

One person stood at the edge of the waves, boots in his hands.

Lila's breath caught. It looked so much like Sam. The tall frame and wide shoulders, thick hair dancing in the breeze. The way he stood so still, making no hurried movements. But the sun was behind him, lowering towards the horizon, and he was little more than a silhouette. Of course she couldn't be sure, but a part of her was. She could feel that it was him.

She turned away, her heart thudding as Charlie came down the stairs. 'Do you mind if I head out for five minutes?' she asked, trying for nonchalant.

'Go,' Charlie said. 'We're close to shutting anyway. You've worked like a Trojan, and Juliette and I can do the clean-up.'

'You're sure?'

'*Go*, coffee queen,' she said, laughing. Lila was already untying her apron, hurrying down the aisle. She ran out, weaving through people eating ice creams and chips, drinking beer out of plastic cups. She passed them all, her shoes pounding against the hard sand and then, as soon as she reached the softer part of the beach, digging in, puffing grains up around her ankles. She stopped to catch her breath, and dragged her gaze along the length of the beach.

The silhouette was gone. There was no sign of a tall man carrying his shoes, walking close to the water or anywhere else. Her imagination had conjured him up. She had wanted to see him so badly that suddenly, there he was. She turned away, her shoulders sagging, and trudged back to the bus.

Chapter Twenty-seven

The days in Porthgolow settled into an easy rhythm. The Cornwall holiday traffic was picking up and, in contrast to Lila's time on Gertie when she'd first arrived in the village, there was a healthy stream of customers coming on board for Cornish cream teas, a vanilla cappuccino or a sausage roll, before heading to the beach or boarding a SeaKing Safaris boat from the jetty.

And the first Cornish Cream Tea Tour was only days after Lila's coffee-themed food market, Charlie not wasting any time getting back to her summer schedule now that *Estelle* was over. They picked up customers from Padstow and headed north, skirting the coast in the direction of Tintagel and Port Isaac. Charlie drove and kept up a steady stream of information over the speaker system, and Lila served the cream teas, arranging mini sandwiches and cakes on trays, warming scones and refreshing teapots.

She loved seeing the delighted faces of the customers when she appeared on the top deck with a tray laden with golden, fluffy scones, or they bit into a mini raspberry doughnut, the jam oozing out. But her mind wandered, inevitably, to the first tour she'd been a part of, when the bus was full of *Estelle*'s cast, and Sam had been subdued, his usually bright eyes cast towards the table. And the figure on the beach. She had been replaying it since Saturday, wondering whether it had really been Sam, or simply someone who resembled him. Perhaps there had been nobody there at all, just Lila's longing and regret.

'Excuse me, love,' said a deep, booming voice, 'but you're rather covering the floor in tea, there.'

Lila brought herself back to the present and saw that the man was right, and the teapot she was holding was listing dangerously, leaving a trail of hot, wet tea at the top of the staircase. A health-and-safety executive would probably condemn Gertie for this one act alone. 'Oh no! I'm so sorry. Let me— I'll get a fresh pot.'

'It's no bother,' said the man. 'I'm sure there's still enough in there.' He beckoned her over, and Lila topped up his and his wife's cups, noticing that there was nothing left on their plates save for a couple of crumbs.

'Did you enjoy it?' she asked.

'Oh, it were wonderful,' said the woman, who had grey hair and a smattering of freckles across her nose that made her age hard to guess. 'I could fair live on a bus like this. Just give me a little camp bed, offer me one of these meals every day and I'd be happy.'

'You'd miss the TV though, love,' her husband replied. 'All those soaps. How would you cope without your dose of *EastEnders*?'

'I'm sure we could get a television installed,' Lila said. 'After all, it has a dishwasher and an oven, and I'm not even sure how they work! A telly can't be beyond the bounds of possibility.'

'We've got a deal then, dearie.' The woman patted her arm. 'Now, you'd better go and get that tea mopped up before we all break our necks getting down those stairs.'

'Of course,' Lila said, flushing. She stepped carefully over the spill and went to grab a roll of kitchen towel.

'Goodbye, thanks for coming! Goodbye, lovely to meet you, thanks for coming. Yes, they're my favourites, too. Lovely to see you. See you again soon!' Lila and Charlie waved their customers off and Lila felt suddenly exhausted, as if she'd endured an extended family gathering with relatives she only vaguely knew but still had to be polite around.

'Right,' Charlie said. 'We need to load the dishwasher and pack up the leftovers, and then you and I have a date with Daniel's swimming pool.'

Lila tipped her head back, stretching her neck. 'Sounds glorious.' She ran upstairs to begin clearing tables, double-checking the pool of tea was no more, even though all the tour visitors had made it safely off the bus. She could hear Charlie talking to someone downstairs – probably Marmite, who had sat patiently in his crate the entire time – but then Charlie laughed, and Lila heard footsteps on the stairs.

'Lila?' Charlie popped her head above the balustrade. 'Just bring that lot down and I'll sort the rest.'

'Why?'

'Because you have a visitor.'

Lila's heart missed a beat. 'Oh. Right.'

Charlie frowned. 'It's not Sam, I'm afraid.'

'Oh,' Lila said again. 'Of course not! Not that I – I didn't expect . . .' She couldn't bear the pity in Charlie's smile. 'I'll be down in a second.' She turned away, stacking mugs and plates on her tray, giving herself a moment while Charlie retreated.

Laden with her precarious stack of crockery, she stepped gingerly down the narrow staircase and almost dropped the whole lot when she saw that her visitor was Clara, sitting at one of the downstairs tables, her hands clasped tightly in front of her.

'Clara. What are you doing here?'

Her friend turned and gave her a weak smile. 'I thought that . . . it's our last day in Cornwall and I . . . some of the things I said to you, that day on the set, and before . . . In London. I've been so horrible.'

Charlie beckoned for the tray, and Lila passed it to her, before sliding into the seat opposite Clara. 'I deserved them – and more. You know how sorry I am for what I did. And it's been killing me, not being able to talk to you. I know you can probably never forgive me, but—'

'Lila, shush. Let me say a few things.' She smiled, and Lila felt the tension she had been holding on to start to crack.

Charlie appeared at their table with two takeaway cups and a paper bag. 'I'm closing up. Two caramel lattes – I hope I've followed your recipe right, Lila – and a custard Danish each. Go and sit in the sunshine.'

Lila accepted them, gave Charlie a grateful smile, then she and Clara strolled across the sand.

'Have you enjoyed your time in Cornwall?' Lila asked.

'Honestly? It's been brilliant,' Clara replied. 'I know Glen booked it to try and sort the two of us out, but I've had the best holiday. The Eden Project, a boat trip along the Helford river, fish and chips in Rick Stein's in Padstow. I've eaten *so* much food, but we've done loads of walking, too, along cliffs and beaches, and sea swimming – I haven't done that since

I was a kid! You picked the perfect place to escape to, Lila. I'm gutted we're going home tomorrow. It's given me the chance to have a bit of perspective.'

'You've done more than I have,' Lila said, laughing. She picked a dry bit of sand and sat down, Clara doing the same. The sun was beginning to sink, its bold rays forcing Lila to squint, but she didn't want to turn away from its warm glow.

'Done more than you?' Clara replied scornfully. 'You've been working on a television set, hobnobbing with film stars! Which, by the way, entirely suits you.'

'What do you mean?'

'You're too full of fire for the barista life. Wow, this latte is delicious. Your recipe?'

Lila took a sip. 'Yup.'

'You're good at coffee, but it's not where you're going to end up.'

'Because of what happened?' she asked tentatively.

'No.' Clara shook her head, her short hair bouncing. 'No. *Not* because of that. Shit, Lila.' They both scooted round so they were facing each other, cross-legged, like they had done countless times before, on beds and sofas and living-room floors. 'I know you didn't mean for any of it to happen. And that should have been the end of it – you made a mistake.'

'But you lost your job,' Lila said. 'Your new promotion, all those years of hard work, and—'

'It was for the best,' Clara cut in. 'Glen mentioned my new job, didn't he? It's ten times better – a hundred times. I am so much happier. There's less pressure, more opportunity for me to be creative with my events. I can put my own stamp on things. My boss, he . . . respects me. It's the best thing that could have happened. And so, in a way, I have you to thank for that.'

'I wish I could say that was my intention all along.'

'You don't have to,' Clara said, taking a Danish when Lila offered her the bag. 'You're always banging on about how things happen for a reason, and in this case, I think they have. I just wish I had done *this* earlier. I am so, *so* sorry for what I said to you that day. I was still so angry, I needed time to breathe and think, to get over it, but you were always there and I . . . I flipped. But I didn't mean any of it.'

'But you were right,' Lila said. 'In lots of ways. I do avoid responsibility; I'm always looking for the next thing. Maybe I didn't want to hear it all, especially not from you, but it was good for me.'

Clara shook her head. 'I was a bitch. And that day on your set, I couldn't even make it up with you then! I was so stubborn, still so entrenched in the things I'd felt before. I was shocked that Glen had intervened, and it caught me off guard. I've done a lot of thinking while I've been in Cornwall and I *don't* feel like that any more. Life is too short to hold grudges, and you're one of the most important people in my life.' She held out her hand.

Relief and happiness rushed through Lila, so that she felt almost dizzy with it. She took Clara's hand. 'You're my best friend,' she said. 'And I never meant to hurt you.'

'I know. It's done – finished. All behind us. If . . . if you're prepared to forgive *me*? For what I said to you?'

Lila pulled Clara towards her and held her in a tight, welcome hug. 'Of course I am,' she said. 'You massive weirdo.'

Clara laughed and sniffed, then wriggled out of the hug. 'Now I need to hear all your news, every detail of this TV show, what Aria Lundberg is like, and about this Sam bloke. I've been thinking about him a lot – about the way he defended you. I owe him an apology, too.'

Lila shook her Danish, watching the flakes fall onto the foam on her coffee.

'Lila?' Clara said. 'What is it? You and Sam – you're more than good friends, aren't you?'

She nodded. 'We . . . had a thing. For a little while.'

'It's over?'

'It had to be.'

'Why?'

Lila ran her fingers through the sand. She had wanted this so badly, this reconciliation with Clara, the person she could tell absolutely anything to. But she was reluctant to talk about Sam.

'Come on, Delilah. This is me we're talking about. I know things have been – that I've been awful—'

'I lost you your job.'

'And you lost yours too, and I didn't even stop to consider that when I was shouting at you, so I think we need to put it all behind us and start again. Caramel lattes to seal the deal!' She held her cup out, and Lila tapped it with her own. 'Good. We're done. Now, tell me about Sam, because I have never seen you so misty-eyed over a man, and I'm worried that this might be serious.'

Her friend's voice was so solemn that Lila laughed, which opened the gate on her feelings. She told Clara everything, about meeting him and thinking he was a bit awkward, being much more interested in the prospect of having Toby Welsh come on board the bus, about the way Sam had slowly worked his way into Lila's thoughts, and the night on the beach when she'd deflected their sudden closeness with ridiculous accents that in the end had brought them closer. She told her how he had come to find her in Porthgolow, about the night at Crystal Waters and then, after Clara had left, her anger and his admission that he was going to America.

'So this is my fault,' Clara said. 'You never would have picked a fight with him if I hadn't shown up and failed to forgive you?'

Lila shook her head. 'And then what? We would have been happy for three more days, then he would have gone to Bristol and I would have found out about America further down the line, when I was even more—'

'In love?' Clara finished softly. 'This is not a side of you I've ever seen. You're not blasé about Sam. He matters.'

'He was an amazing summer fling during a crazy time in my life, and I will never forget him.' She worked hard to keep her voice level. 'None of it was real, though. Being surrounded by those stars, being an extra, that night at Crystal Waters, draped in all that luxury. We were never in the real world, so it was never going to last.'

'Delilah Forest, that is the most ludicrous thing I've ever heard. Of *course* it's real. Just because he spends his time being other people, doesn't mean that off set, between the two of you, it wasn't genuine. He seemed lovely, thoughtful, even if I didn't say it at the time. Fuck,' she rubbed her forehead. 'I was a bitch to him. I probably got his back up, and you were shocked that I'd appeared suddenly, and weren't thinking straight.'

'So? What does any of that matter?'

'It means you need to have your last conversation with him again. You can't leave it like you did.'

'If I hadn't broken it off, he might have turned down the film in America for me.'

'Did he actually say that?' Clara asked, tearing off a strip of Danish. Lila had never understood how her friend could savour her food like that, keep it going for ages while Lila wolfed everything down within about two minutes of it appearing in front of her.

'No, but he said I was making it hard. That it was all exciting and brilliant to start with, and then there I was, complicating everything.'

'Because he *cares* about you, L.'

Lila hugged her knees against her chest. The sun was still warm, the waves gentle and placatory, the perfect summer's evening. Lila had her best friend back, and Clara was doing what she always did, reasoning with her, finding sense when Lila had lost it. She was drawing out the conclusion that Lila had already come to but was trying her hardest not to think about. That she'd made a mistake.

'He wouldn't have said that if he'd seen it as a fling,' Clara continued. 'To be honest, he doesn't sound like the fling type of person and, even though you've had a fair few in your time, I can tell from the way you're talking about him that this was more than that to you, too. If you care about each other that much, then you need to work at it, because – despite the obstacles – it will be worth it.'

'I don't know, Clara. I've done it now. Told him to go off and live his life.'

'Do you remember when Glen and I first got together?'

'Of course,' Lila said. 'You were insufferable, loved up beyond belief. I had to walk around with a sick bucket.'

Clara hit her on the knee, laughing. 'Don't you remember, two months in, his dad suddenly got very ill and he had to go back to Yorkshire. I'd just moved up at work and was trying to prove myself. It was so hard. Glen was emotionally exhausted, trying to come to terms with his dad being so poorly, and I wanted to be there for him, more than anything.

I was close to giving up my job – I wrote a resignation letter and had it sitting on my desk for over a week. But then I told myself, this is just one part of my life. One short time out of so many. So what if I'm running on Red Bull and chocolate brownies, getting the train up to Yorkshire late on Friday night and coming back on Sunday afternoon? So what if I've given up even a whiff of a social life? Things will change.'

'I remember,' Lila said. 'I didn't see you for about six months, and we'd text nonstop on your train journeys to make up for it. I had limitless texts in my mobile package but that still didn't seem enough.'

'Exactly,' Clara replied. 'But my job was important to me and, even though I didn't know him that well, so was Glen. I made it work, and eventually things changed. His dad slowly improved, and they got some carers in, so it wasn't all on him and his mum. He could come to London to see me, and things evened out.'

'So you're saying I can make it work with Sam, despite America?'

'I'm saying it doesn't have to be this dramatic, cliff-edge ending, which is what you've turned it into.' She smiled gently. 'Always with the drama, Lila. Why don't you go for a love story instead this time? Get in touch with Sam. See where you stand. If he's still in Bristol, then what's stopping you?'

Everything, she wanted to protest. What she'd said to him, the way she felt about him, the possibility that he would reject her. The possibility that he wouldn't. Everything about Sam scared her, and she realized, as she peered out across the water to where a speedboat was bouncing over the waves with the apricot sun behind it, that the reason it scared her so much was because she cared so deeply.

Her feelings hadn't miraculously disappeared, as she'd hoped they would. She wasn't bouncing back, throwing herself into Gertie and the tours with as much gusto as she should be. Sam was always there, hovering in her thoughts.

'I don't know,' Lila said, instead.

'Well.' Clara stood up. 'Whenever you want to talk it through, call me. Are you thinking of coming back to London anytime soon?'

Lila took her friend's outstretched hand and let her pull her up. 'Not yet.'

'I didn't think so. So, using up our unlimited texts again?' Clara grinned.

'And FaceTime. And come back here, soon. I'll organize a spa day for us at Crystal Waters.' She pointed and Clara turned, looking up at the hotel, its glass walls glinting gold.

'And *you* have to think about what I've said.' Clara hugged her. 'If Sam is that important to you, and I think he is, give the two of you another chance. Don't think that by letting him go you're doing him a favour. Be open with him about what you're scared of, and see what he says.'

'Stop being such a wise old bird,' Lila said, squeezing her friend. 'And thank you, for coming to find me.'

'Yeah well, you're all right, most of the time.'

'You too.'

They walked up the beach together, the sun behind them. Lila had got her best friend back – all was right with the world. Except that it wasn't, really, because she'd let Sam go and, regardless of what Clara said, he might have banished every thought of her, put all his energy into the end of the *Estelle* shoot and his trip to America, and moved her firmly into a box marked *The Past*. She might have already lost him.

Chapter Twenty-eight

As soon as Clara left it was as if a switch had been flipped, and nothing was of any importance except Juliette and Lawrence's wedding.

In between serving customers on the bus, Charlie was making lists and looking up bunting and table decorations and decorative glasses online, talking to wholesalers about bulk orders of champagne. In the evenings, they trialled new recipes. The happy couple wanted a buffet with an elaborate, unique Cornish cream tea at the centre, and so Charlie and Lila concocted different sandwich fillings together: crayfish with a lime dressing, peppered beef with a local plum chutney, the silkiest egg mayonnaise with slices of a French cheese which, Charlie declared, originated in the village that Juliette's family came from. It was fun and exhausting, and it gave Lila an excuse to avoid making any decisions about Sam.

In the middle of a particularly hilarious cake-making session, Lila came to the conclusion that she was never, ever going to be as good at baking as Charlie. She was attempting a batch of raspberry custard tarts, and even though the custard mixture was a bit too soft when she took the tarts out of the oven, she was still keen to see how the edible flowers and pearlized jelly sweets would look on top. She started arranging them, using Charlie's catering tweezers, her tongue protruding in concentration. She was on tart number three when she heard Charlie's guffaw.

She looked up to see her cousin, about to put a tray of white chocolate and pecan muffins into the oven, with lips pressed firmly together.

'What?' Lila asked, defensively.

'Nothing,' Charlie said, and then snorted.

'What?' Lila looked down at her tarts. Her decorations had sunk into the reddish-brown custard. 'Oh.'

Charlie's laughter erupted, and Marmite, who had been behaving himself on the sofa in the front room, ran into the kitchen, desperate to be part of whatever was going on.

'It's not funny,' Lila said, abandoning her tweezers. 'They were going really well up to that point.'

Charlie put her tray down and clutched her sides, tears streaming down her cheeks.

'God, Charlie, get over it.'

'They look like . . .' She gasped in a breath. 'They look like swamps.'

'Swamps?'

'Swamps where someone's been murdered and bled out, with limbs and . . . and bits of dying foliage.'

'Oh,' Lila said, her own laughter bubbling up. 'Oh, well. Perhaps not ideal for your best friend's wedding then.'

Her lips twitched, and soon she was laughing along with Charlie, leaning against the counter, her ribs aching. Marmite bounded up and down, yelping, and Lila had to sit down until the moment had passed. Charlie slid down the kitchen cupboards until she was sitting on the floor, and Marmite jumped onto her lap, his paw jabbing into her crotch so she yelped in unison with her dog.

Daniel found them five minutes later, his mild expression turning quickly to concern. He put three large cardboard boxes on the sofa and hurried into the kitchen.

'What's happened? Are you both OK? Charlie? Lila?'

Charlie pointed in the vague direction of Lila's creations. 'She made crime-scene swamp cakes,' she stuttered, 'for Juliette and Lawrence's wedding.' Lila couldn't help it, she was off again, both of them giggling helplessly and wiping tears from their cheeks while Daniel shook his head pityingly.

When they'd finally stopped laughing, Daniel held his hands out and pulled them effortlessly to their feet. 'Come on. The latest delivery arrived today. Come and see what it is.'

'The bunting!' Charlie gasped. 'Gertie will be as dressed up as the rest of us.' She peeled the Sellotape off the first box, peered inside and then, with wide eyes, reached in and took out a pale green satin bag. Putting it on the sofa, she began loosening the drawstring. Marmite jumped onto the cushion next to it and Daniel picked him up, cradling him against his chest.

'Oh wow,' Lila murmured, as Charlie took out a string of the most beautiful bunting she had ever seen. The pennants were pastel coloured, made of a delicate, lacy material, and with a faint shimmer running through them: cream, then pistachio green, pale pink, pale blue, buttery yellow, coral red, lilac and back to cream. 'That is beautiful.'

'And then this one,' Charlie said, undoing the next box, 'should be . . .' She pulled out a fuchsia pink bag this time, the bunting inside much brighter – the colours bolder versions of the pastel set, and again, faintly shimmering.

'So lovely,' Lila murmured. She'd never been so enamoured by scraps of material before – unless they came from Victoria's Secret and cost a small fortune.

'And this last set – this is the really celebratory one.' Charlie opened the final box, and inside that the drawstring bag was silver, the fabric metallic but, when Lila touched it, impossibly soft. The bunting inside was of the same material, the pennants alternating between white, silver, gold, bronze, gunmetal grey, black and rose pink, and sparkling so much that Lila had to squint.

'Bloody hell,' Daniel said. 'The Rolls-Royce of bunting.'

'Juliette and Lawrence deserve nothing less, and we can use this again and again – different sets for different events. It's an investment in the Cornish Cream Tea Bus. What do you think?' Charlie draped the metallic bunting over herself and then, when there was still acres of it on the floor, over Lila, too. They turned to face Daniel, who was restraining a scrabbling Marmite.

He rolled his eyes and grinned. 'I think that, whatever anyone says, bunting is a universal crowd-pleaser. And this particular bunting,' he added, reaching out to rub the fabric between his fingers, 'is going to knock everyone's socks off.'

Charlie laughed and shook her head. 'I never thought I would see the day, Daniel Harper, when you were impressed by a bit of bunting.'

'Neither did I,' he admitted, his grin softening to a smile. 'What have you done to me, Charlie?'

Charlie stepped towards him, and wrapped the end of the bunting around his shoulders. She kissed him, and then began unwinding all three of them, her movements slow and careful, as if the coloured flags were part of a centuries-old, priceless tapestry. Lila felt a sudden ache of sadness, and took Marmite from Daniel's arms, holding his warm, wriggling body against her.

The Saturday before the wedding, and after the food market had finished for the day, Lila was sitting on the middle shelf in the Crystal Waters sauna, and Keeley was opposite her. Lila had been counting down the hours until her friend's visit, the interest and vibrancy of the market failing to hold her attention. When she'd met her outside the doors of the hotel, it was immediately obvious that Keeley was still thriving – her blue eyes were bright, her renewed confidence impossible to miss. They had picked the sauna as their first destination.

'Where's Charlie?' Keeley asked, leaning back against the wooden slats.

'She and Daniel have gone for a meal in Padstow.'

'Oooh, Rick Stein?'

'I don't think so – some other posh restaurant. They got a taxi in, and I'm picking them up later on.'

'And you're loving Porthgolow?'

'It's great. Working on Gertie is pretty similar to being on set, but without the familiar faces – though I am getting to know the villagers now. Then there are the tours, and we're right in the middle of wedding planning. It's fun.'

'It's fun, *but* . . .'

'No "buts". It's fun. It's different.' Lila shrugged. 'Tell me about Bristol. What's it like being in the studios? Is Bert still swanning around like he owns the place? What about Toby?'

'They're all well,' Keeley said, 'and no different, really. Gregor seems more relaxed – he can control everything much more easily; he isn't at the mercy of the weather, or the locals in a village he's commandeered. Most people are really enjoying it.'

'Most people?' Lila bit her lip.

Keeley sighed. 'I'm so pleased you've sorted things out with Clara. I knew it would all come good in the end. Friendships like that are too important to lose, and you're a *good* friend. I'll never forget what you did for me. That video – making me see the sense of what I was doing – or lack of it. Being honest, and kind, and taking all that time.'

'You sound like you're working up to something.'

Keeley flashed her a smile. 'I'm meant to be good at this. I'm really that transparent?'

'I hope you're not acting now,' Lila said. 'Not with me.'

'No. Which is why I have to tell you, even though I'm sure you don't want to hear it.'

'Hear what?' Despite the relaxing heat, Lila's shoulders tensed, the wooden boards of the sauna digging into her flesh.

'Sam is miserable, Lila.'

It was a moment before she could reply, and what came out was, 'Oh.'

'It's terrible,' Keeley continued. 'The worst thing about *Estelle* at the moment. And I know he's trying. He's super professional on set, he's getting everything right, but when we've wrapped every day he's just . . . so down. I did what you said, I told him that you didn't want to talk to him, that what you had wasn't serious, and he got angry. He said you didn't mean it, that you were trying to protect him or something. I had to plead with him to not send you any more messages.'

'Shit,' Lila whispered.

'And Gregor knows he's feeling bad. He's working him extra hard, getting him to rehearse more than anyone else just to keep his mind occupied, which means he's miserable *and* exhausted.'

Lila squirmed on her bench and glanced at the sand-timer to see how much longer they had left. 'I thought I saw him,' she said. 'A few of Saturdays ago, at the food market – walking along Porthgolow beach, anyway.'

Keeley looked at the floor.

'What?' Lila asked.

'You did see him.'

'*What?*'

'I tried to dissuade him, but he left before I could stop him. He got back late that evening, threw himself a bit too vigorously into our Saturday night drinks in Bristol, and admitted he'd been here. He wanted to convince you that you could still be together, that it didn't need to be over.'

'I didn't get a chance to talk to him,' Lila said. 'I thought it was him, but I couldn't see properly against the sun. But then he didn't come to the bus, and by the time I got to the water's edge, he'd disappeared.'

Keeley sighed. 'He told me you looked so beautiful, chatting and laughing with the customers; he felt sure you must be over him and he couldn't bear to risk being rejected again. And he only confessed all this because he was drunk. He said the main thing was that you were happy, and if that meant leaving you to get on with your life, then so be it. He was resolved, determined, but since then . . . I guess it's been harder for him to put you out of his mind than he thought.' She laughed sadly.

'That's so . . .' Lila put her head in her hands. 'God, I have messed this all up.'

'What did you say? I can't hear you when you're hiding your face like that.'

'Let's go to the Jacuzzi,' Lila said. 'Our time's up in here and I don't want to boil completely.' They left the sauna, showered, and walked round the side of the indoor pool to the Jacuzzi. It wasn't as luxurious as the outdoor hot tub, but that had been booked when Lila had enquired about it. She would have to bring Keeley back another time.

'So,' Keeley said, once they were settled in the bubbles. 'What were you saying? About Sam?' The pool was quiet, with only a couple doing slow lengths and an older woman lying on a lounger, engrossed in a hardback book with a sinister cover.

'That I have messed everything up. All those things I said, that last day I was on set. Hiding away in Porthgolow so I didn't have to face him again before the end of the shoot. I really thought I was making the right decision. If he believed I had never seen us as long-term, then he'd be able to move on more easily.'

'You're saying breaking up with Sam was a mistake? That you *did* care about him as much as he thought? *Seriously?*' Keeley's voice was loud, and Lila winced.

'But I can't tell him that. He's this amazing, gorgeous man with a bright future ahead of him, and I've treated him like crap. I can't dump him, leave him to be miserable and then, just when he's beginning to get over me, tell him I've made a mistake and want him back. It wouldn't be fair.'

Keeley shook her head. 'You don't think he'd run straight into your arms? He loves you, Lila. I'm sure of it.'

'So I've already broken his heart and now I'm going to swoop in and try to mend it, only to ruin his career in the process? He's got this film, hasn't he?'

'And he'll go and do that and be brilliant, and you'll be waiting for him when he comes back. Either it will work, or it won't. But you shouldn't run away – you shouldn't *have* run away – just because the path ahead looked a bit choppy.

328

If you love him too, then you owe it to yourself, and to Sam, to try.'

Lila slunk further into the bubbles, submerging her chin. Her heart was racing, which probably wasn't a good thing when Jacuzzis were supposed to raise your heart rate anyway. 'Relationships and me. Subtitle: Disaster Zone.'

'Not true. Clara forgave you because, despite what happened at her event, she cares too much to lose you. Nothing about our friendship has been a disaster, except when *I* was about to make the most stupid decision of my life, and you pulled me back from the brink. Charlie loves you enough to let you live in her house, and respects you enough to want you involved in her business. You're focusing on the wrong things. What you need to be concentrating on is what you're going to say to Sam, when you're going to meet him.' She clapped her hands together. 'Oh Lila, this is amazing! I thought you didn't care about him; all that stuff you said about it just being a bit of fun.'

'Don't remind me,' she whispered. 'I was trying—'

'To protect him, I know. But you can explain all this to him, not me. Now, when are you going to do it? We have the weekends off, of course, then it's pretty relentless during the week. But you should come to Bristol for one of our Saturday-night sessions. They're so much fun – I hope you realize what I've given up to spend time in this luxury hotel with you.' She laughed.

'I need to think,' Lila said.

'You need to seize the moment. There are only a couple more weeks of filming in Bristol, then we're back in Cornwall for that last location, and then we go our separate ways. Sam heads off to America, and probably won't be back until the pressers just before Christmas.'

'I've got Juliette and Lawrence's wedding,' Lila said. 'There's no way I can fit in a trip to Bristol before then – I don't have the time. But . . .' She turned to stare out of the window, tapping her finger against her lips.

'Look at you,' Keeley said. 'A portrait of emotional conflict. Are you *sure* you haven't considered being a professional actress?'

'Why does everyone always say that? I'm not acting!' Lila shot back, grateful for the change of subject.

'But you can,' Keeley replied. 'You knocked it out of the park delivering one line as the schoolmistress – Gregor is always mentioning you, and Miss Trevelyan's coat will have its own Twitter account once that episode has aired. When you wanted me to see sense you made a *video*, Lila. A whole video full of talking heads, stitched together perfectly, with an intro and a middle and the most poignant bit at the end, as if it was a mini feature film.

'And what about being Marianne on the beach that night – the personal performance you gave to Sam? You hadn't even had any tequila. Then you lost Marmite so there had to be this ridiculous rescue: Sam, all handsomely soggy and dishevelled, clambering over rocks, carrying the cute puppy in his arms.' She shook her head. 'You may not *mean* to be a drama queen, but it sure as shit follows you around.'

Lila gazed out at the hotel gardens, the sun almost out of sight below the cliffs, the sky around it shades of pink, purple and orange, so bright they seemed unnatural. 'Drama queen,' she whispered to herself. And then, something about the beauty of the sky, the sun sinking over the sea, the romance of it all, kick-started her thoughts.

She turned back to Keeley. 'When are you in Cornwall again – at that stately home?'

'Uhm . . . for a couple of days in the middle of July. I'll have to look up the dates.'

'After the wedding,' she said. 'That's good.'

'Why? What are you planning? We're not going to be there long. A few large-scale interior scenes with most of the cast, and a couple of night shoots in the grounds.'

'Everyone's going to be there?'

'There's a big party at the halfway point in the series. It's Darius's character – Lord Mosenby's – residence, and the brothers get invited, and Marianne, and of course Estelle shows up. You know the middle of any story has to be dramatic: it keeps the viewers hanging on.'

'That sounds . . . perfect.'

'Perfect for what?' Keeley asked, her gaze drawn to the view beyond the glass. 'Wow. Would you look at that?'

'Cornwall has the best sunsets,' Lila said, distractedly. 'Keeley, will you help me with something? And when I explain what it is, will you promise not to laugh? Will you just tell me, honestly, whether you think it can be done?'

'I promise,' Keeley said, dragging her eyes away from the sky. 'I'm here for you, Lila. Whatever you need.'

'Good. Because I've just thought of a way to let Sam know how I feel, but I'm going to need a lot of help.'

Her grin was mirrored by Keeley and, in that moment, Lila was more thankful than ever that not only had she and Clara fixed their relationship but, in the aftermath of her calamitous mistake, she'd made another friend for life. She just hoped that, once she'd explained her plan, Keeley wouldn't declare their friendship null and void, tell her she was mad, walk out of Crystal Waters and leave Lila to slowly boil to death in Daniel's expensive Jacuzzi.

Chapter Twenty-nine

The day of Juliette and Lawrence's wedding dawned bright and blustery, and by the time Charlie and Lila had driven down to the beach with all their boxes of cakes, sandwiches and pastries, the sea was whipping up into white crests, the breakers bigger than Lila could remember seeing them. Porthgolow looked beautiful in the early July sunshine: the day had a golden hue with yellow accents – the sand, the cliffs rising up either side of the cove, the SeaKing Safaris sign fixed to the jetty and the bobbing RIBs moored there. There was Reenie's buttercup-coloured house, and marigolds in Myrtle's hanging baskets. Lila even spotted a vase of yellow roses in the window of Stella and Anton's B&B.

'We need to load everything onto Gertie,' Charlie said, piling Lila's arms full of cake tins, 'then you can take the car back up, and walk down again.'

Lila nodded. 'I hope Juliette won't be too chilly on the beach. Her dress is strapless.' She hadn't seen it in person, but Charlie had shown her a photo on her phone, taken on the day of the last fitting, and then deleted it in a fit of paranoia in case Lawrence somehow got hold of her mobile.

'At least it's not raining,' Charlie said. 'That was the main worry, because as much as Gertie is totally up for hosting a wedding breakfast, the aisle of a bus is not an ideal substitute for the aisle of a chapel or registry office.'

'What would we have done then, do you think?'

Charlie grinned. 'We would have had it at Crystal Waters, of course.'

'Ah, of course.' Lila leaned back to accommodate her tower of tins, putting her chin on the uppermost one to clamp it in place. Charlie was equally laden down, and they made their way slowly across the car park and onto the beach. Charlie unlocked Gertie, and they put everything on the tables.

'Do you want me to bring Marmite when I come?' Lila asked.

Charlie shook her head. 'Marmite is coming for the celebrations, but not the ceremony. He and Jasper will be fine at home, making some kind of mischief together, no doubt.'

Lila left her cousin to it, drove her car back up to the house and then walked back down the hill.

The sea stretched ahead of her, and she filled her lungs with the fresh, salty air. The last week had been manic, hilarious and happy, with all hands on deck because even a small wedding breakfast on a vintage Routemaster took quite a bit of organizing. As Gertie's section of the beach came into view, Lila stopped. Charlie was attaching the metallic bunting, securing the strings of pennants along the outside of the upper deck. They were dancing in the breeze, adding an additional, sparkling touch to the Cornish Cream Tea Bus, and Lila felt a jolt of excitement for the day ahead. By the time she reached the bus she was grinning.

'What's up with you?' Charlie asked, taking the pastel bunting out of its box.

'Nothing. Just this.' She gestured around her. 'I'm so happy for Juliette and Lawrence.'

'Me too,' Charlie said, her eyes glistening. 'And I am beyond proud we get to host it on Gertie. I sometimes wonder what would have happened if I'd stayed at home, with Mum and Dad and the Café on the Hill. No Porthgolow, no Daniel. Being Juliette's friend from afar. My holiday to Cornwall last spring worked out way better than I'd hoped.' She laughed.

'It's got a little bit of magic, this place, hasn't it?' Lila said, taking the other end of the bunting and walking slowly backwards, the shimmering pastel pennants unravelling.

'No,' Charlie said. 'It's got a lot.'

Once they'd laid out the food on the tables and in the fridge, ready to serve or heat or assemble, they went over to the Seven Stars to pick up the chairs that Hugh had lovingly polished. Lila hoped they wouldn't suffer too much from spending an afternoon on the sand.

'How are you getting on, Lila?' Hugh asked. 'Coping with the monotony of village life after all the excitement of that TV set?'

'It's not exactly been boring,' Lila said, lifting her two chairs higher, feeling the stretch in her shoulders. 'The Cornish Cream Tea Bus has a reputation to uphold, and I've loved being a part of that. Not to mention helping to host its first wedding.'

'But definitely not the last,' Charlie said, arranging her chairs to face the sea.

Lila gasped, but Charlie shook her head. 'I'm not talking about me and Daniel. But I have had an enquiry about whether we can be hired for weddings. A young woman whose grandma is getting married again at the age of seventy-eight, to a lifelong bus driver. She wanted to know if she could hire Gertie to serve cream teas in the grounds of the venue.'

'That sounds like so much fun,' Lila said. 'You're going to say yes?'

'I'm meeting her next week.'

'There are no ends to Gertie's skills.' Hugh patted her red paintwork. 'Tour bus, showbiz caterer, wedding venue. You'd better not turn her into the Cornish Bar Bus, or I'll be out of business.' He grinned mischievously and strolled back towards the pub.

'That's fabulous news about the other wedding,' Lila said.

'I just need to make sure we're not too stretched. I can do a lot with Gertie, but I don't want the quality to suffer or it's not worth it.'

'Everything you turn your hand to will be a triumph. You care too much about it not to do it justice. I mean – look! I know this is your best friend's wedding, but even so. Look at the bunting, the chairs. Have you seen the towers of cakes and sandwiches inside? You've done all of this.'

Charlie put an arm around Lila's shoulders. 'We've done it together. Are you doing OK? After . . . Sam? Weddings aren't the best place to be if your heart is tender.'

'I'm fine. Really.' She hadn't told Charlie about her brain-wave, because they'd been so busy and she was still mulling it over, but once the wedding was done she would ask Charlie's advice – maybe even Daniel's – and see what they thought. This was one occasion where she wanted to break the habit of a lifetime and plan for every eventuality.

'If you need to go off and kick something,' Charlie said, grinning, 'then do it discreetly.'

'I don't want to kick anything,' Lila laughed.

'Come on, you two.' Daniel was walking across the sand, looking striking in a grey suit and white shirt. His top button was undone, a brightly coloured tie sticking out of his jacket pocket like a tongue. 'I'll finish getting the chairs set up with Hugh while you go and do your maid-of-honour duties.'

'You look gorgeous.' Charlie wrapped her arms around his neck and Lila turned away while they kissed. 'And I'll only need ten minutes. Juliette knows I can't get ready with her because I have to make sure everything's sorted here.'

'What's left to do?' Daniel asked. 'It's looking pretty good to me. And I'm here now, I can put the flowers on the tables, finish off whatever's left on your impeccable to-do list.'

'And I can stay,' Lila added. 'You should go and get ready with Jules, Charlie. She would want you to, more than anything.'

'I've just dropped a bottle of champagne off at her house,' Daniel said, 'and you're both going. I'll stay here with Gertie. Get your asses up that hill.'

'You, boyfriend, are the best.' Charlie squeezed his hand, then whispered something in his ear. When she turned around, her eyes were shining.

'I agree,' Lila said. 'You're the dog's bollocks. And I love how your tie matches the bunting.' She pulled it out of his pocket, admiring the colourful pattern.

'It's a wedding.' Daniel shrugged. 'Now piss off, both of you. Take your minds off baking and organizing for a couple of hours.'

Charlie and Lila ran up the hill, Lila's breath ragged by the time they reached Coral Terrace. They collected their outfits, grabbed handfuls of make-up and their chosen shoes and shoved them into a weekend bag, then ran to Juliette's house. The good thing about Porthgolow, Lila thought as she tried to keep up with Charlie while holding the two dresses – still on their hangers – up above the pavement, was that it was so compact you could get anywhere in about five minutes.

A tall, dark-haired man opened the door and gave them a wide smile. 'Charlie,' he said, in a French accent. 'Lovely to see you. You're looking so well.'

'You are too, Marc. This is my cousin, Delilah. Lila, this is Juliette's dad.'

'Great to meet you,' Lila said, shaking Marc's hand.

Juliette appeared behind him wearing her bathrobe, her hair half pinned up. Her eyes widened in alarm. 'What's wrong? Is Gertie OK? Has—'

'Shhhh,' Charlie said, stepping inside. 'Everything is perfect. And it's even better now because I can help you do your hair.'

'And I can do your make-up if you want,' Lila added. 'I'm a dab hand with liquid eyeliner.'

'But I was . . .' Juliette stammered. 'I didn't think you could come. Mum's just getting changed in the spare room.'

'Daniel's looking after the bus,' Charlie said. 'He told us to get our asses here. If you want our help, that is? If you'd rather it was just you and your mum—'

'No, of course not. I would love you to stay. And the champagne! I thought it was a wedding present for me and Lawrence. Daniel just dropped it off and said he had to run.'

'It's for now,' Lila said. 'And we need to get some music on. Where's the sound system?'

'The living room. Charlie, Lila, this is wonderful! I didn't want to ask you, because I've already asked you to cater our entire wedding. I thought you'd be too busy.'

'This is where being organized, and having a helpful boyfriend, pays off,' Charlie said. 'Do you want me to do your hair? Tell me what style you want, and we can give it a go.'

'What's all this?' called a voice from the top of the stairs. It belonged to a plump, cheerful-looking woman with russet curls. 'Charlie! You're here!'

Charlie introduced Lila to Juliette's mum, Elaina, and Marc slipped his jacket on and opened the front door. 'I think that's my cue to go to the pub. I'll leave you ladies to it.' He kissed Elaina, gave Juliette a tight hug, and stepped out into the sunshine.

'I'll get glasses and champagne, and sort the music,' Lila said. 'And then I'm going to give you the best wedding make-up you've ever had.'

Juliette laughed through happy tears. 'I've never had wedding make-up before. This will be my first and only wedding.'

'That's a very good point,' Lila replied. 'It's still going to be the best, though.'

An hour and a half later Juliette looked like a goddess, and Lila had only had to reapply her eye make-up twice.

'We're going back to the beach,' Charlie said, gently embracing her friend. 'You look stunning.'

'Is your car coming soon?' Lila asked.

'In five minutes.'

'Marc is on his way back,' Elaina said, kissing Charlie, then Lila, on both cheeks. 'And ready to deliver my princess of a daughter into the arms of her future husband.' She dabbed at her eyes with a tissue.

'I can't thank you both enough,' Juliette said. 'You have already made this day so memorable.'

'We've not even started yet,' Charlie said, laughing. 'See you down there, beautiful bride.'

Lila and Charlie left Juliette's house and strolled down the hill. They weren't the only ones on their way to the beach, and Lila waved and smiled to everyone, soaking up the happy atmosphere, even though she didn't recognize half of them. The sun was higher in the sky, the wind gentler, as if it had been hurrying to blow itself out in time for the ceremony. The beach was full of people, lots of the chairs already taken, and Lila spotted the entire Kerr family, Jonah looking much older than his age in a navy suit, and Stella and Anton achieving peak-1960s glamour, Stella's golden dress and perfectly coiffed curls like something out of *Mad Men*.

Daniel and Hugh were greeting the guests, and Lila bit down a laugh as Daniel noticed Charlie, his mouth falling open. The lavender-coloured dress hugged every inch of her tall frame, and Lila had applied her make-up: nothing too bold, but enough to accentuate her features. Her cousin was a knockout and Daniel, it was clear, was entirely at her mercy.

'Charlie,' he said as they approached. 'You look—'

She silenced him with a kiss, and then, with the last few stragglers reaching the sand, they took their seats.

Lawrence was handsome in a charcoal grey suit and sky blue waistcoat and cravat, his best man – someone called Martin, who he worked with – patting him on the shoulder and giving him some final words of encouragement. The guests murmured excitedly until a loud car horn blared, and everyone swivelled to watch as the multicoloured VW camper van drove onto the beach and turned elegantly, so it was side-on to the congregation.

A Pete special, Charlie had told Lila a few days before. The man who had converted Gertie also worked on old VW vans, which were popular with Cornwall's surfing community. This one was vibrant, its paintwork swirls of yellow, red, blue and purple, with a shining white roof and gleaming hubcaps. A lithe man dressed in a jaunty, chequered suit jumped down from the driver's seat and came round to open the sliding door, helping Juliette onto the sand.

She looked like a mirage. Her ivory ballet pumps were the perfect accompaniment to the cream silk dress with an intricately embroidered bodice and straight, plain skirt. Charlie had piled her hair up in an expertly tousled design, thick tendrils falling to her bare shoulders, tiny white flowers dotted throughout standing out against her dark hair. Lila had helped her get ready, yet she still had a lump in her throat.

'Bloody hell,' Lawrence muttered, and everyone stood as Juliette, on Marc's arm, made her way slowly towards them. The smile she gave Lawrence was both tender and excited, an acknowledgement of the beginning of this next chapter in their lives. They held hands and turned to face the wedding registrar.

The ceremony was simple and beautiful, and when Lawrence and Juliette exchanged their vows, Lila was sure there wasn't a dry eye on the beach – even the seagulls went quiet. Charlie and Daniel had their hands clasped tightly together in Daniel's lap, and Lila hoped there might soon be another wedding on the horizon, that all this romance was contagious. Once the couple were pronounced man and wife, everyone stood and cheered. The applause seemed to go on for ever.

Lila and Charlie quickly moved to the bus, putting their aprons on over their finery, and started assembling the wedding breakfast cream teas. They were more elaborate than usual, with finger sandwiches and sausage rolls, Lila's *arancini* balls and halloumi sticks, and mini salmon quiches. The delicate cakes included raspberry doughnuts, passion-fruit cheesecakes, the custard tarts that Lila had continued to practise and finally got right – no swampish murder scenes in sight – and tiny chocolate mousses.

There were fluffy, golden-crusted scones with clotted cream and jam, and several of Lila's new coffee creations on offer, as well as the usual tea varieties. Buckets held bottles of champagne on ice, and with the windows open wide, music filtered out from Gertie's onboard sound system.

The guests drank champagne and filled their plates from the displays that Charlie and Lila had arranged inside the bus and on Hugh's trestle tables outside. The weather was so good that nobody chose to eat on board, instead clutching plates and glasses and mingling under the sun's constant gaze. There were appreciative moans and exclamations of pleasure, and Lila felt a swell of pride that she had created some of the food, and that Juliette and Lawrence had wanted her and Charlie to cater for one of the most important days of their lives.

Once people had eaten, Charlie caught Lila's eye and nodded. They went on board and, slowly, reverently, took the *pièce de résistance* out of its box: the wedding cake.

'Goodness,' Amanda said when they emerged, inching down onto the sand. 'That is nothing short of magnificent.'

Daniel smiled as he cleared a space on one of the tables. 'My girlfriend is a culinary genius.'

'It's my first wedding cake,' Charlie admitted. 'I hope it passes muster.'

'It passes *all* the musters,' Lila said, as they lowered it gently into position.

It was a three-tiered lemon sponge covered in buttercup yellow icing and decorated with pale pink icing roses. Charlie had created icing versions of Lawrence and Juliette for the top, and Lila knew how much work, how many hours of trial and error, had gone into bringing those tiny people to life: crafting Juliette's long dark hair and yoga mat, a mini marquee to stand alongside Lawrence. She didn't like the cake being anywhere near the sand – it belonged in a display case.

'This is ridiculous, Charlie,' Lawrence said as he hugged her, unable to take his eyes off the cake. 'You made this – for us?'

'Char,' Juliette added, her bottom lip wobbling again, 'it's stunning. Look at us! Oh, Lawrence, how are we supposed to eat them? Can we save them?'

'I'm not sure how long they'll last,' Charlie said, laughing. 'Come on – come and cut your cake.' She held out the knife, and the newly married couple took it and, once everyone had been called over to witness the moment, sliced into the top tier to a round of jubilant applause.

As the afternoon wore on, and with Porthgolow beach busy, it seemed like the wedding party extended for miles. Their small area, with the food tables, bus and chairs was cordoned off, but only by a thin silver rope. Visitors to the beach spotted the happy couple, or noticed the sign Charlie had put outside Gertie announcing the wedding and apologizing for the bus being closed, and there were shouted congratulations from strangers, and a few expressions of mild disappointment that the Cornish Cream Tea Bus wasn't open for business as usual.

Lila spent hours talking and circulating, chatting to familiar faces and new. With the buffet decimated and the cake cut, coffees and teas served to those who wanted them,

Lila kicked off her shoes, refilled her champagne glass, took a piece of wedding cake and slipped under the cordon. She strolled towards the far cliff, below where Crystal Waters sat, enjoying the feel of the sand between her toes, the light breeze caressing her skin. This part of the beach – away from the jetty and closer to the car park – was quieter, as if visitors wanted to get as far from their cars – and the thought of going home – as possible.

She found a space, sat on the sand and took a bite of cake. She closed her eyes in appreciation, relishing the moment of calm.

'Lila!'

She opened her eyes.

Jonah was hurrying towards her. He had discarded his jacket and tie and was clutching a sausage roll. 'Can you tell me about the TV set?' he called.

Lila patted the sand next to her. 'What do you want to know?'

'Everything,' he said, flopping down beside her.

'OK then.' She recounted her impressions when they'd first arrived – the endless rows of lorries and trailers, the hubbub, the security; what it was like when Sam and Keeley had come on board, her and Charlie's excitement at meeting some of the actors, and then the added thrill when Toby Welsh and Aria Lundberg had visited them. She told him about reading the scripts, sneaking down to watch the filming, her terror at being a supporting actor, and the exhilaration she'd felt once she'd discarded her nerves.

Jonah was more interested in the technical details – cameras, lighting and sound tricks, editing suits – than in the showbiz side of things, though his eyes lit up when Lila got to the part about being Miss Trevelyan.

'My school are doing a production of *Hamlet* when we go back in September,' he said, tearing his sausage roll in half. 'I'm going to audition for the lead, but I'm not sure how to do it. Mum already told me that you were an extra. She keeps going on about it – you being in the show, and how nice Sam was, and how he answered all my questions on the bus that time. He *was* nice, but I don't see how that's going to help me get the part.'

Lila was hit by a surge of longing for Sam that was so overwhelming, she had to pause and take a deep, steadying breath before replying. She picked carefully around Jonah's comments about him, and focused instead on the acting. 'When I was an extra, I only had one line. But I think a lot of it is down to confidence – and talent, of course, though I'm not sure I have heaps of that. You can go to drama school and learn how to do it properly, if you're really serious about it.'

'I don't have time to go to drama school between now and September,' Jonah said.

Lila grinned. 'That's very true.'

'How did you do it, then? If you don't have all the skills?'

Lila resisted the urge to laugh, and considered Jonah's question. 'You have to put yourself in the place of your character. You have to believe, entirely, that you're them. That you live in that time period, with that specific background and circumstances. How would you behave if that was you? You have the script, so you don't have to come up with the words yourself, but how would you deliver them? What would you be feeling at that precise moment? You are going for the role of Hamlet, aren't you? Not Horatio or one of the players?'

'It's Hamlet all the way,' Jonah said.

'Good man.' Lila held out her clenched fist and Jonah

humped his against it. 'OK, so, Hamlet is very tortured. He's just found out that his dad has been killed by his uncle, but – for a whole host of reasons, not least because it was his dad's ghost who told him – nobody believes him. And his mum has gone and married his murderous shit of an uncle, so she's even less likely to come round to the idea.'

'Wow,' Jonah murmured.

'So what you could do,' she said, warming to her theme, 'is imagine you've discovered something huge, and it's torturing you. Maybe someone at school is being mean to one of your friends, but the teachers don't believe you. Or you've found out a devastating weather event – a tornado or a tsunami – is about to descend on Porthgolow and you need to evacuate everyone, but they think you're exaggerating. Or someone you really care about is going to America and leaving Cornwall behind for good, and there's nothing you can do about it.'

'You'd never get a tsunami on this part of the coast. Not right now. But I guess with climate change—'

'It was just a silly example,' Lila said, laughing.

He grinned at her. 'OK. I need to imagine it's something that I would hate?'

'Yes. Something that you can't live with, but that no-one else believes or wants to help you with.'

'Like I'm ready to pilot the boats. I know I am, but Mum says I'm not old enough.'

'There you go, then. Start with that, channel all the anger you feel, the conviction that you're right and she's wrong, and put it into your audition. You'll be brilliant.'

They sat in silence for a few minutes, watching as the sun started to descend, the calm water a perfect, glittering backdrop for Juliette and Lawrence's wedding.

'It's Sam, isn't it?' Jonah said quietly.

'What?'

'You said I could imagine someone I cared about is leaving Cornwall for good, going to America, but that's what Sam's doing. Charlie told my mum.'

'Yes, Jonah.' Lila felt her throat thicken. 'Sam's going to America.'

'And that's what's torturing *you*. That's why you used it as an example.' He looked at her, his face open and unembarrassed.

'I am sad that he's going,' she admitted.

'It's going to be OK,' Jonah said brightly. 'You're too nice for it not to work out.'

'Jonah, that's—'

'And I'm glad you came to Porthgolow,' he continued. 'I don't think you're a handful at all or, if you are, you're a handful of something good. Like the bunting Gertie's covered in. That's it! You're a handful of brightly coloured bunting!' He grinned at her and Lila smiled back, thinking that, as descriptions went, it was pretty complimentary.

'Come on,' she said, jumping to her feet and holding out her hand, 'let's go back. I don't want to miss the first dance.'

'Do you know why there's always a first dance at a wedding?' Jonah asked, taking Lila's hand and letting her pull him to his feet. 'I looked it up.'

'Go on then,' Lila said. 'Give me all your knowledge so that one day I might be as wise as you.'

They walked along the beach, Jonah telling her what he'd discovered about first dances, Lila's bare feet sinking into the cool sand and Gertie ahead of them, her celebratory bunting glistening in the evening sunshine.

Chapter Thirty

When Daniel hugged her and Charlie on the doorstep of Charlie's terraced house, close to midnight ten days after the wedding, Lila felt as if he was sending them off to war.

'Be safe,' he said. 'And Lila, break a leg.' He gave her one of his cocky, nonchalant grins, and Lila punched him gently on the arm.

'I will,' she replied, trying to keep her voice steady.

'There will be no broken limbs tonight,' Charlie said, kissing him.

'Only broken hearts,' Lila mumbled. She lifted Marmite up and stared into his dark eyes, wishing she could take him with her. He licked her cheek, and she felt instantly better.

'There is to be none of that talk, either,' Charlie said. 'This is going to go amazingly.'

'He would be a fool to turn you down,' Daniel added. 'Even if you weren't making all this effort. Do you know where you're going? Sure you don't want to take the Beamer so you get there before dawn breaks?'

'This car has got me through a lot of long drives,' Lila said, patting the rusty Volvo. 'I'm not abandoning it now. It would be like when Mildred Hubble replaces her silver cat, Tabby, with Ebony, just because Ebony is a better witch's cat.'

Daniel stared at her. 'I have no idea what you're talking about.'

'*The Worst Witch*,' Charlie clarified. 'We can discuss tragic moments in children's literature after this is over, but now we need to get going. We don't want to be late.'

Lila walked round the bonnet of the car, but Charlie got there first. 'I'm driving, you are not. Not tonight.'

'Any more rules you want to tell me about?' Lila asked as she climbed into the passenger seat and handed over her keys. Charlie grinned at her.

Daniel stood in the lit doorway with Jasper and Marmite and waved them off, a beacon of warmth and comfort compared to where Lila was heading – very possibly a dark abyss.

'It's so good of them to do this,' Charlie said, as they drove out of Porthgolow in the direction of Striker Manor, the impressive stately home being used as the final location of the *Estelle* shoot. 'Especially when the filming schedule must be so tight for these last few days.'

'I know.' Lila chewed her lip. 'But is it the right thing to do? Should I have called Sam and asked him to meet up, just the two of us? What if he hates that I've done this?'

'I don't think Sam could find it in him to hate you. I know you, Lila, and I've seen the two of you together.'

Lila stared out of the window. The landscape was an inky black, the sky a blanket of stars, bright enough to be visible through the windscreen. She had never thought about anything so much in her life. Ever since she'd conceived her master plan, she'd been going over and over it, weighing up the pros and cons but struggling to come to a conclusion. She decided that, on balance, and especially when it came to matters involving her own heart, she preferred the '*not thinking things through*' approach – though of course she would never admit that to anyone, and definitely not to Clara.

'Is it too dramatic?' she asked.

'What do you want to do, Lila?' Charlie indicated left and turned onto the A road, the occasional headlights and tail-lights winking at them as they headed north. 'You have to be true to yourself, too. There must have been a reason you came up with this idea in the first place?'

'I want Sam to know how sorry I am,' Lila said. 'Keeley told me how miserable he's been, how much it's affected the end of this shoot for him. I want to admit to my mistakes, make a declaration, let him know I got it wrong, and . . .' She paused, smoothing down her top. It was dark blue, a scattering of stars picked out in silver thread, mirroring the sky beyond the glass. She'd accompanied it with skinny jeans and silver sandals. Despite the late hour it wasn't cold, the heat of the sun lingering long into the night.

'And?' Charlie prompted, shooting her a quick glance.

'And that night on the beach,' Lila continued, 'the one that happened when you were in America. I picked this scene from *Estelle* and I was doing all these different accents, and Sam was giving his verdict on each one. It was so silly, but then it . . . it got serious. That was when I fell for him, and I thought that I could recreate it, somehow.'

Charlie nodded. 'It's very dramatic and wildly romantic.'

'If it works,' Lila said. 'Otherwise it will be very embarrassing and wildly upsetting.'

Charlie laughed gently. 'Positive thoughts, Lila.'

They drifted into silence, the dark countryside passing them by, the gentle thrum of tyres against tarmac lulling Lila into a calmer state. Her phone buzzed with a text from Keeley.

All set. You on your way? followed by lots of clapping hand emojis and a couple of kisses.

Nearly there, Lila typed back, adding three shocked-face emojis for good measure.

Keeley's next message read: *We're all buzzing. It's a wonder S hasn't picked up on anything! Xx*

Shitting hell! Lila replied, and Keeley sent back a laughing face.

'All good?' Charlie asked. 'Next turn-off.'

'All good,' Lila croaked.

Charlie turned right and slowed her pace. The long, narrow road was lined by tall bushes that loomed up on either side of the car. The view of the sky was lost, and Lila's anxiety stepped up a notch, prickling her palms and dancing a jig in her stomach. Then a soft, low light appeared in the darkness, and there was Claude, fluorescent jacket on, standing next to an ornate iron gate. As they neared, he grinned and doffed an imaginary cap.

'Claude!' Charlie said when she'd rolled her window down. 'We're back.'

'Without the bus, I see,' he replied jovially. 'Bit of a shame that, but this approach road is particularly tight. We had enough trouble getting the trailers in. You might have had issues in the daylight, let alone the dark. You good, Lila?' he added, peering down at her. 'All set?'

'As I'll ever be,' she said. He gave her a warm smile.

'Down to the end, turn right. Keeley should be waiting for you.'

'Right you are,' Charlie nodded. 'Thanks so much, Claude.'

The hedges beyond the gates were manicured boxes, the sky once again opening up, a light source somewhere ahead of them, further into the grounds. Charlie drove at a snail's pace along a track edging the house's neat lawns and formal gardens.

'This is a bit special,' Charlie said. 'Fitting, really.'

'Oh God.' Lila shoved her hands between her knees.

Then Keeley appeared in front of the car, looking every bit the ghost in the headlights, white lacy frock visible beneath a thin navy cardigan, scuffed trainers on her feet. She waved and grinned, then pointed. Charlie swung the Volvo into the space that Keeley had indicated, turned off the engine and handed Lila her car keys.

'I've done my bit. The rest is down to you.' She squeezed Lila's arm. 'OK?'

'Let's do this.' Lila pushed open the door and was engulfed in Keeley's sweet-smelling hug.

'You look wonderful. We're all so excited! Come and see the house. Charlie, hi.' Keeley embraced Charlie and then led them along a tall, ivy-covered wall.

Lila gasped as Striker Manor came into view. The handsome, golden brick façade, the dormer windows and gabled roof were all dramatically lit from below, gleaming against the darkness. There was a gravel driveway leading up to the front door, and a circular lawn with a rose bed in the centre, the pale flowers just beginning to bud.

'It's a picture, isn't it?' Keeley said. 'It's equally impressive inside, but I'm not sure I can get you in there without our cover being blown.'

'Are they filming inside right now?' Lila asked.

'No, over by the pond. It's a beautiful spot, Lila. We've got about fifteen minutes until you're on! Come and see everyone.'

351

As Keeley led Lila and Charlie down the side of the house to a very familiar catering marquee, Lila felt a pang of sadness that that part of their life was over. Had she appreciated it enough while it was happening? She wasn't sure.

'Well, look who it is!' Toby grinned expansively. He was sitting with Aria, Darius and Bert, and they all abandoned their chairs as Lila and Charlie walked in. Lila accepted hug after hug, feeling more detached with each passing moment, as if she was watching a scene rather than participating in it.

'This is so brave,' Aria said. 'I never guessed about you and Sam. He's become a miserable bastard, but I didn't realize this was the reason. After that night on the beach, when Bert made those jokes, I assumed it *wasn't* true. I'm so happy it is!'

'Depending on how the next half an hour goes,' Lila shrugged.

'Don't be ridiculous, Delilah,' Bert said. 'The man's besotted. He'll be back in your arms before you can say "denouement"!'

Lila was given a cup of coffee and a chair, and she sank into it while everyone chatted around her. Keeley sat next to her. 'Ready for your performance? You've got this, Lila.'

'I should never have suggested it. Never have even *thought* of it. Once again I have concocted a stupid plan that has "disaster" written all over it.'

'Don't be defeated before it's happened. Look, here's Gregor, coming to give you some direction for your moment in the spotlight.' She nodded at him, then slunk off to join the others.

'Delilah Forest,' Gregor said, dropping into the chair Keeley had vacated and turning to face her. 'Glad to have you back.'

'Glad to be back. And thank you. I know this is a huge ask, and possibly the most idiotic thing that has ever happened on one of your sets.'

He gave her an incredulous look. 'I have worked in this industry for fifteen years. You would not believe some of the things that I've had to deal with. But I have something to ask you before we move to the next scene. We've imprisoned Sam in hair and make-up, by the way,' he added. 'It felt like that was the best place for him until everything's in place.'

Lila nodded, trying to ignore the twinge she felt every time someone mentioned Sam's name.

'Your character, Miss Trevelyan,' Gregor started.

'My one-line schoolmistress?' Lila tried to hide her surprise.

'The part you won that day rehearsing with Welsh and Magee on the cliff top.' His stare was so direct, Lila struggled not to squirm beneath it. 'We've started to consider the possibility of a second series. We've not aired yet, of course, but the buzz around *Estelle* is positive, and we want to be ahead of the game in case we get the green light. And so, to Miss Trevelyan. We all believe the character could come into her own, could fuel the fire that is building in the village and be a new strand of consternation – among other things – for the Bramerton boys.'

'She's going to become a proper character?' Lila said. 'So you need to reshoot the scene, with the new actress playing her? I understand. It was fun being an extra, but I don't mind if I don't actually appear on screen.' She did a bit, but she wasn't about to tell Gregor that. She wondered why he had picked this moment, when her insides were already in knots, to tell her she was being cut.

'You misunderstand me, Delilah. We can't go back to Polperro and reshoot.'

'Oh,' Lila frowned. 'So you're cutting that scene altogether?'

'Not that, either.' His smile widened, his expressive hands gesturing towards her. 'Would you consider playing Miss Trevelyan again, if we're green-lit for series two?'

'Me? Play her again? For more than just one line?'

He nodded.

'But I . . . I'm not an actor. I've had no training. I've never done anything like this before.'

'You impressed me, on the cliffs and in Polperro. And not just me. I've been in this game long enough to spot talent, and you, Delilah, have it. We'd need to give you a screen test, to see that you have the range required, but I have no concerns about that. There's a lot to consider, of course. But I'd like to sit down and discuss it, meet up once filming's over. There's a real opportunity here, and I want you to think seriously about it. Now, we need you in the gardens in five minutes.' He tapped the arm of his chair, then stood and strode away, leaving Lila flummoxed and even more agitated than she had been before.

'Did he tell you?' Keeley asked, reappearing at her side. 'I suggested he should leave it until afterwards, that you had enough to think about now, but you know Gregor. What do you think? Do you want to do it?'

'*Acting*, Keeley? Me? I make coffee!'

'You're not a human espresso machine,' Keeley said, laughing. 'Just imagine. We'd be working together in Cornwall. You, me, Toby and Aria. *Sam*. But it's only if we get another series, and if you decide it's right for you, of course. Filming wouldn't start until next year anyway, so . . .' She waved a hand dismissively. 'Stand up and let me look at you.'

Lila did, and Keeley smoothed her hair over her shoulders, brushed something off her sleeve.

'Perfect. Are you ready?'

Lila nodded, although she wasn't sure she could even speak.

'God,' Keeley said, as they left the catering tent, accepting winks and pats on the back from the cast and crew. 'I'm so nervous! I can't imagine how you're feeling.'

'Like I might throw up,' Lila admitted, and they both laughed, which cracked the tension a tiny bit.

'Wait a second, Lila.' It was Charlie.

Lila turned, and saw tenderness in her cousin's eyes. 'Pep talk?'

Charlie nodded. 'Just a quick one.'

'Go on, then.'

'Uncle Hal,' Charlie started. 'He had his words of wisdom. He knew exactly the right thing to say at any given moment. But you, Lila, you show people how to make the most of things. You are generous in your heart, and you don't let life faze you. You take everything that it has to offer you. I've learnt a lot from you over these last few months, and I'm so proud that you're my cousin, and my friend. Now.' She squeezed her shoulder. 'Go and get your man.'

'Charlie, I—'

'Go now,' she said.

Keeley gently took Lila's arm and led her through more formal gardens. She stopped in front of a topiary archway and pulled her to the side.

From her position Lila could see bright, artificial light through the gap, could hear the familiar mumblings, the movement of equipment as they set up the scene. Gregor was shouting instructions and laughing with his colleagues, and then there was another voice, belonging to the person who had started this whole thing off by walking on to the Cornish Cream Tea Bus and talking loudly on the phone.

'All set?' Winston said. 'Can't believe we're down to the last couple of days. What a production! You doing OK, Sam? Coping with these night shoots?'

Lila's breath stalled, and Keeley gave her a sympathetic smile.

'I'm good,' came the reply, and Lila heard that subtle lilt she loved so much. 'I quite like the night shoots. These clothes are bloody hot, and in daylight it's stifling. Not that I'm complaining about summer.'

'Damn sight better than March,' Winston said. 'I thought my fingers might drop off on at least three occasions.'

'Yup,' Sam laughed. 'If it's not one thing, it's the other. Still, I've had some great times down here in Cornwall. Really, really special.' Lila could hear the emotion in his voice, but that was entirely understandable – coming to the end of a long shoot like this was bound to provoke strong feelings among the cast and crew.

'Right then,' Gregor said, clapping his hands. 'Aria's in position beyond the yew. On your mark, Sam, and we'll get the cameras rolling. I want agitated pacing, a couple of seconds and then we'll bring her in. And . . . *Action.*'

Everything fell silent except Lila's heart, which was pounding loudly enough to wake the whole of Cornwall. Bethan stuck her head through the gap and nodded.

'Your cue,' Keeley whispered. She positioned Lila in the archway, and then pushed her gently through it.

Lila didn't have time to think. She stepped into the small garden, blinking in the harsh light. She saw Gregor's subtle gesture and, head down, she walked forwards and placed her silver-sandalled feet on the mark directly in front of Sam. She heard his steps falter as he half grunted, half gasped his surprise, and her ears also picked up, from somewhere behind her, the rustle and patter of people arriving, slowly siphoning through the archway and into the space. They all knew what was happening, had all agreed to her subterfuge, and were coming to watch it play out.

Not a drama queen, my ass. Lila took a deep breath and looked up, right into the eyes of the man who, she had come to realize, she loved. They burned brightly, gold and green, confusion and hurt. His jaw was set, his hair styled into perfect dishevelment, his body dressed impeccably in fawn breeches, navy jacket and waistcoat, white shirt so bright it reflected the light.

She loved everything about him. Every single hair on his head, every fleck of amber in his eyes, every note of his beautiful voice. She loved him, and this was her last chance.

'Sam,' she said, hoping with all she had that he would at least hear her out. 'I've got something I need to say to you.'

Chapter Thirty-one

Lila waited for him to reply, to say her name – anything – to give her a moment to compose her thoughts. But Sam didn't speak. He simply stared at her, his face a blank mask, only his eyes betraying any hint of emotion.

'OK then,' she said, running her palms down her jeans. 'Sam, I got it wrong.'

Still, he didn't say anything.

Lila swallowed, and kept going. 'I have got so many things wrong, and it always seems to be the important ones. With Clara, of course. We've made up now, by the way, and I think that was partly down to you, but . . . that's not why I'm here. I'm here because . . .' She closed her eyes and sent a wish to the stars twinkling high above her. 'I'm here because I made a mistake when I broke up with you. But I didn't know how to make us work. Almost as soon as we got together – even after that night on the beach, when you spoke to me in your Irish accent and rescued Marmite from the rock pools,' she thought she heard Charlie make a noise somewhere behind her, but she couldn't think about that now, 'I knew I was on to a good thing. But I don't do serious, Sam, and so it was easy to tell myself, even when I started to fall for you, that it wouldn't last. That I could have fun with you and then let you go, and my heart would stay intact.

'This whole thing – working on the set, getting to know everyone, you turning up on Gertie looking like Mr Darcy,' she gestured towards his outfit, and thought his eyes softened slightly, 'it has never felt entirely real. And in some respects, it's not. It's fiction. For someone who isn't used to this lifestyle, it felt like I was living a fantasy.

'When you showed up in Porthgolow and carried me into the sea, drunken-baking in Charlie's kitchen, dinner at Crystal Waters with Daniel and Charlie and then . . .' She stalled, cleared her throat, continued: 'All those stolen moments on Gertie's top deck. It was as if I was starring in my own, personal romance film.'

'What's wrong with that?' Sam asked quietly, and Lila was so relieved that he was talking to her, she almost flung herself at him.

'Nothing was wrong with it – that was the problem. It was great, the best . . .' She trailed off, realizing how trite she sounded. She had to be honest with him. Regardless of the setting, who was watching, and how exposing it was, she had promised herself that she wouldn't hold anything back. 'It was the best time of my life,' she said. 'And it was terrifying. Because it quickly became precious to me, what we had. You're so important to me, Sam. I didn't want to lose you.'

'So, why . . .?' he started, and she nodded.

'I was angry, after Clara turned up on set and you tried to fix things between us. You were only trying to help, but it made me feel like even more of a failure. I thought Clara

359

was gone for good, that it was my fault, and so when, after all that, you said you had this film in America, I knew that if you stayed for me – and you told me I was making it harder for you to accept it – I would be doing it again. Hurting someone else I cared about. I thought the only way I could stop that happening was to walk away. To let you go.'

He didn't reply immediately, but she waited. She could see the muscle working in his jaw. She had more to say, but she needed to hear him speak, to know that he had heard her.

'You didn't give me a chance,' he said, his voice hard, his Irish lilt more noticeable, as if his control was slipping. 'You didn't discuss it with me, didn't give me any time – give *us* any time to come up with a compromise.'

'I know, but—'

'It felt like there had been an "us". Strong and happy, and at the beginning of something good. And then, that day with Clara, you wouldn't even talk about it. You told me it was over, that it had all been a bit of fun, and I had no say.' He stepped forward, brushed his hand through his hair, entirely focused on her.

'I did it because—'

'At first I thought you just needed time to cool off. I expected to see you the next day, but you didn't show. And then Keeley told me that I wasn't to call you, that you didn't want to speak to me. It was so cold, Lila.'

She dropped her head. 'I know. I got it wrong, Sam. *So* wrong. But I thought a clean break was the only way. Cold is the opposite of what I feel about you, but I thought I had to slice—' she swiped her hand through the air. 'Slice it. Slice *us*.'

'And now, here you are.'

She nodded, tried to subtly clear her throat. She could see, from the way Sam was standing, the way he was looking at her, that it wasn't working. He was angry – he had every right to be. But still, she had to say everything. This was her last chance to say it, regardless of the outcome.

'I didn't want you to give up your career, to feel reluctant about another part, because of me. I believed I was doing the right thing. I believed that, this time, I had thought it through.'

Sam laughed humourlessly. 'You broke it off three minutes after I told you I'd been offered the role.'

'But the moment I met you, the moment I started to like you, I decided that I wouldn't hold you back. It just turned out the end came more quickly than I'd anticipated. You have so much ahead of you, Sam—'

'And you didn't consider that I never saw you as holding me back? You didn't think that we could at least try to make it work, that we could do and be all we wanted to be together? I thought we made each other stronger.' His eyes had narrowed, and his voice was wavering in a way that made Lila, in turn, feel unsteady. 'God, Lila – you are *so* infuriating. Because you make out you're this free spirit, flitting from one thing to the next like some sort of butterfly, but it's really because you're scared to properly grab hold of anything. You believe you're always one step away from fucking it up, so better to move on before you do.'

'And this proves that I still can!' Her voice was louder, her bubbling emotion needing somewhere to go. 'I've changed, I've learnt so much, but with this one, crucial thing, I have still managed to get it so wrong. Because I thought what I had done was for the best, but every moment since, I've been regretting it more and more. And I . . . I just needed to tell you that.'

'Tell me what?' Sam asked. 'You've said a lot of things, but I'm struggling to find a conclusion in it all. Are you saying that you never should have broken up with me? Or that you're a hopeless case and not worth a moment of my time?' He rubbed his forehead. 'You've turned up here in the middle of the night, sabotaged the filming which, I'm assuming, was not entirely down to you – ' he flicked a glance in Gregor's direction, then looked back at her – 'and I'm still not sure what you want. Is there a point, here, in all this?'

Lila took a deep breath. It was too late. He had too much anger, frustration, weariness. But she had to finish this – she was so close to the end.

'I wanted to tell you that I'm sorry, Sam. That I never should have hurt you the way I hurt you. I never meant for any of it to happen.'

'Any of it? Not that evening on the beach. Not Porthgolow. Not Crystal Waters. You truly wish that none of that had happened, and you came all this way to tell me?'

'No, I—'

'Lila?' It was Charlie, stepping in, trying to save her. She didn't turn around.

'Sam.' Lila screwed her eyes shut and opened them again, forcing herself to meet his gaze. 'Sam Magee, you brilliant, warm, generous, *amazing* man, what I am trying – and so far, failing – to say, is that I have royally messed up and that, regardless of what happens next, or what your future holds, I want you to know that . . . that I love you. I think I have done since that night on the beach. I never wanted to hurt you. I know now that it's too late, that I can't just decide to let you go and then, weeks later, have you back again. That's selfish and unfair of me. But

I needed to tell you that you have my heart, that you will *always* have a piece of it, and I wish you all the happiness in the world.'

There was a beat of silence.

Another one.

'Lila . . .' Sam stammered, his eyes wide.

Her breath faltered at the look on his face. Her declaration had shocked him. She had been acting under a misapprehension the whole time. He didn't feel as strongly for her as she did for him, and he had certainly never come close to loving her. He had been pissed off with the way she'd ended it, was pissed off all over again now that she'd turned up to disrupt the night shoot, but that was all. He hadn't been distraught, as Keeley had suggested; or, at least, if he had been at the beginning, he was over her now. She had come here and embarrassed him in front of his friends, his director and the entire production team.

Her cheeks burnt with the shame of her big, emotional confession ending in stunned silence.

'Sorry, Sam.' She stepped forward and reached up on tiptoe to brush her lips against his cheek, feeling his hot skin, the graze of stubble. His fingers, warm and familiar, grasped hold of hers, but she tugged free and turned away, keeping her head down as she started running.

She ran past Gregor and Winston, Keeley and Charlie, Toby, Aria, Darius and Bert. She ran through the thick yew archway, and on.

'Lila – wait!' It was Sam, but she didn't stop. She didn't want his pity.

'Lila?' Was that Keeley or Charlie calling her? She couldn't speak to them right now. She ran faster, pulling her car keys out of her pocket as she went, hurrying back to the Volvo.

The car park was full of cars but deserted of people, everyone still at the scene of Lila's latest disaster.

She scrambled into the driver's seat, started the car and reversed swiftly out of the space, turning the wheel hard, the tyres squealing as she drove down the hedge-lined avenue towards the exit. She glanced in her mirror and saw a tall figure, sandy hair flying as he ran after her, shiny boots pounding the gravel. She put her foot down, sickness swirling in her stomach. The dark gates loomed ahead of her and she slowed, but then Claude walked across and pushed them open, and she sped up again. She raised her hand in a wave, and the security guard mirrored it, his face creased in confusion as she drove past.

Lila risked one last look in the mirror and saw Sam, bent double in the middle of the path, hands on his knees, head hung low. She pressed the accelerator, driving far too fast down the narrow road, twigs and leaves reaching out to scrape the Volvo's paintwork. Her phone buzzed and she tried to ignore it, to focus her attention on the road ahead, blocking out all sound and feeling, shame and embarrassment mingling with the heartbreak. But what, honestly, had she been expecting? Sam to fall at her feet and tell her he'd been desperate without her, that he'd been waiting, every day since their fight, for her to come and say those words?

She shook her head, idling at the junction. He phone rang again and she pulled it out of her pocket. It was Charlie. She closed her eyes, realizing only now that she had stranded her cousin at Striker Manor.

The road was deserted. She turned off the engine and answered the call.

'I'm sorry, Charlie, I didn't mean to leave you—'

'What were you thinking? Come back here right now!'

'I can't.'

'You have to, Lila! For God's sake. You didn't give the man a chance!'

'I saw it, on his face. I said what I needed to – now it's over.'

'No – wait a second.'

She heard the bang of car doors in the background, feet crunching on gravel. 'I have to go. Can you get a lift home?'

'Don't worry about that, but—'

'I'm so sorry, Charlie. I'll make it up to you, I promise.' Lila ended the call. She switched off her phone and started the engine, the pinprick of another set of headlights, a long way behind her down the endless, hedge-lined road making her heart race.

She drove through the darkness, trying desperately not to replay what had just happened, the look on Sam's face, the anger in his voice when he'd said: *Is there a point here, in all this?* She pressed her lips together, trying to bottle up the tide of emotion that was threatening to overwhelm her.

She kept her pace steady, her eyes firmly on the road, the white lines down the centre, the occasional flash of light as she passed a farmhouse or petrol station, the rest of the world in darkness. When she got close to Porthgolow, she thought of Daniel in Charlie's house, waiting with Marmite and Jasper. Perhaps he would be asleep and wouldn't hear her come in. Or maybe he was waiting up, expecting a jubilant Lila and the woman he loved, only to discover that not only had Lila failed, but she had abandoned Charlie too, not thinking to wait for her, even after all her kindness and support.

'Fuck.' She slammed her hand against the steering wheel.

When she got to the top of the hill, she slowed the car. Porthgolow Cove was lit by a thin, crescent moon, the dark shapes of the houses rising up the cliff, a few lights glowing softly behind curtains. She thought about driving down to the beach, sitting in the car and looking out at the sea. She thought about driving somewhere else, somewhere nobody would be able to find her. But then she saw the sign for Crystal Waters, and something about its serenity, the honey-coloured bricks and the light over the entrance, drew her in. She turned into the car park, parked her Volvo in a space at the back, and got out.

The wind was brisk on top of the cliff, and she wrapped her arms tightly around herself. Instead of heading for the main doors, she went to the side gate that led to the hotel's gardens, where sunken spotlights lit up the meandering paths like fairy trails. She walked slowly, quietly, not wanting to wake anybody.

After a few moments she stepped out from behind the building. The sea stretched ahead of her, cast almost entirely in shadow, the moon giving it the faintest, slender shimmer. Lila kept walking, down towards the garden's edge, past night-scented jasmine and evening primrose yellow in the gloom, past tufty, low-slung herb bushes. She walked past the wood and glass globes of the alfresco dining pods, and continued down to where the outdoor hot tub stood, still and silent, its surface a mirror. She sat on the bench that ran around the wooden structure and rested her elbows on her knees. Sunrise couldn't be far off, now.

Had she been naive to think that Sam would take her back? She had known it was a long shot, had told herself over and over again in the days before that – even once she'd poured her heart out to him – he might not want her any more, not after the way she'd ended it. But when it had actually happened, when she'd told him that she loved him and he'd done nothing more than stutter her name, a hollowness had opened up inside her. She wasn't sure how she would ever fill it.

Lila pulled her legs up to her chest, wrapped her arms around them and rested her chin on her knees. As the new day slowly began to show itself, she sat in the deserted gardens of Daniel's hotel and wept, her tears soaking into her jeans and the sparkling, star-covered top she had put on the evening before, when everything had seemed so much brighter.

Chapter Thirty-two

Lila watched the sun come up, the way it transformed the sea from a bottomless, colourless nothing into a glittering ocean, blue and inviting. The silence also lifted. She heard cars passing on the road into the village, the cries of seagulls as they started searching for breakfast, the sounds of the hotel and its guests waking behind her, the crunch of soft footsteps on gravel. She sat and hugged her knees, her bum numb beneath her, her shoulders stiff. She was cold too, and grateful for the early sun's weak warmth. She should go home and have a shower, see whether Charlie needed her to work on board Gertie.

She winced, thinking of how she'd left her cousin behind in her haste to flee from yet another mess. She wasn't sure whether Charlie would still want her in her house and, even if Charlie was forgiving, she wasn't convinced Daniel would be. She fantasized briefly about returning to London; getting in her car, leaving everything else behind and going back to her mum's flat and the warm embrace of her resurrected friendship with Clara.

But she couldn't. She needed to face Charlie, to apologize, to do what she could to make it up to her and then decide what her future held. Her mind flashed back to her conversation with Gregor. She had been shocked, of course, but also thrilled at the thought of being part of *Estelle*, being on set again, this time as a member of the cast, with lines and costumes and *cut* and rehearsals, instead of cappuccinos and *arancini* balls. Surely that chance was gone now, too.

Lila inhaled, filling her lungs with the salty coastal scent she had come to love, and closed her eyes.

'I think you're supposed to get *in* the hot tub, not just sit on the edge.'

Lila almost fell off her bench. She turned, disbelieving, but her ears hadn't betrayed her – the voice belonged to Sam. He still had his costume on, or some of it, at least. His jacket and waistcoat were gone, his shirt open at the neck above his breeches. He stood behind the Jacuzzi and dipped his hand in the water. 'Except it's freezing, so you've probably made the right decision.'

'Sam?' she said, still not entirely sure this wasn't a dream. 'How did you find me?'

'Trial and error.' He came to sit beside her. He was warm and solid and smelt faintly of aftershave, and Lila resisted the urge to snuggle into his chest. She had no right to do that.

'You've been looking for me?'

'You turned your phone off.' There was reproach in his voice, but he didn't sound angry.

'I'm sorry,' she said. 'After what happened, I—'

'Legged it. I know. I was there.'

'But you still came to find me? Did you go to Charlie's first?'

'I did. I dropped her off. She told me to tell you she's not mad, by the way. She thinks you're impetuous and melodramatic, but she's not upset you drove off without her. Not *too* upset, anyway.'

Lila nodded. 'And what about you?' She could see how tired he was. There were dark smudges under his eyes, his stubble glinting in the morning light.

'I think you're impetuous and melodramatic, too.'

'Sam, I—'

He swivelled to face her. 'You didn't give me a chance to respond. You stood there, in front of me – which was a big enough shock in the first place, considering it was getting to the end of a very long shoot and I was expecting to see Aria, have a brief argument with her character, and then get some sleep. Then you told me that what you'd said that day was a lie. And I get it, Lila, I do . . . I knew you'd broken up with me out of some sort of twisted sense of loyalty – letting me go off to America in this big fall-on-your-sword moment, but I still thought . . .' His voice hitched, and he rubbed his jaw.

'You thought what?'

'I thought part of the reason you'd done it was because for you . . . what we'd had wasn't as important. As it had been to me.' He reached out and took her hand. 'Bloody hell, you're like ice. How long have you been here?'

'Since I drove back,' she whispered, desperate for him to continue.

He gathered her to him, his strong arms circling her back, bringing her against his chest. She let herself sink into his embrace for a second. But she didn't know what this meant. He was talking to her, but was that it? Reluctantly, she pulled away. 'You believed me when I said that it was just a bit of fun?'

'I didn't see you again after that. You ignored my calls and texts. You asked Keeley to tell me not to bother getting in touch with you. So when you turned up last night – early this morning – in front of the entire production team, and said all that – that it was selfish of you to dump me and then want me back. That you loved me. *Loved* me. Can you understand why I didn't have a ready-made answer?'

'I could see you were shocked.'

He laughed. 'Of *course* I was! All these long days and nights, and I've not been feeling my brightest anyway, since . . . And you were suddenly there, after I'd been wishing you to be, declaring your love for me like it was part of the drama. I was off-kilter. I wasn't sure if it was real.'

'It was real,' Lila murmured. 'But now I know that—'

He pressed his finger to her lips. 'It's my turn to talk. You've had your chance, and now I've had time to think about what you said – I am someone who usually thinks before I act, after all – I have a response for you.' He took her left hand in both of his and rubbed it, warming her skin. Then he did the same with her right hand. She felt a small, internal glow return, felt her limbs start to relax, the sun warmer on her face, somehow, now that Sam was here.

'Are you going to—'

'Give me a minute,' he said. 'I have to get this right.' He gave her an embarrassed smile and ran a hand through his hair.

Lila scooted backwards slightly, as if she wanted to give him space. Really, it was so he couldn't hear her heart pounding out of her chest.

'Lila,' he started, and her name alone, the way he said it, made her want to melt into him. 'Delilah Forest, this last month has been torture. I've always prided myself on being a resilient person, able to take knock-backs, to look at things logically. But when you ended it with me, I realized the only reason I've been resilient up until now is because I have never cared about anything, anyone, as much as I care about you. I was devastated, desperate to talk to you, but I knew I should respect your wishes. I couldn't, though. I came to the food market. I was going to speak to you, but you looked so happy, working on Gertie, and I thought you'd already put me behind you.'

'I saw you,' Lila said.

'You did?'

'Walking down by the sea, holding your boots. I thought I'd conjured you up, that my mind was playing tricks on me for ending it the way I had. I wasn't happy, I was miserable. I regretted it so much by then.'

'If you regretted it, then why didn't you contact me?'

'Because I still thought it was best for you. You're going to America, Sam. For six months.'

'Have you ever heard of these things called aeroplanes? You don't have to spend weeks crossing the Atlantic in a ship any more.'

'You're going to be a big star, and I—'

'Couldn't possibly love someone like that?'

She hesitated, biting her lip. It all felt so different, away from that huge stately home, the cameras and the lights. Was she brave enough to say it when there was no drama to hide behind, when it was just the two of them? But then she looked into his eyes, and it was the only thing that mattered.

'I love you, Sam. I love who you are right now, who you're going to become. But I'm just me. I make coffee, I'm chaotic and I get things wrong. I'm—'

'You are all I want, Lila. If you love me even half as much

as I love you, then an ocean is insignificant. An ocean is a raindrop.' He cupped her jaw, tilting her face up to meet his. His eyes searched hers, and they were so full of warmth that Lila felt the prickle of tears. 'Hey there, Delilah,' he murmured.

Then he kissed her.

Lila wrapped her arms around his neck and kissed him back. All her worries and her tension, the coldness in her limbs, her fear and her regret, melted away. In Sam's arms, she was invincible. She *was* chaotic and impulsive, and she didn't think things through nearly enough, but Sam didn't mind. Sam loved her anyway, and he had forgiven her.

'I'm so sorry I ran off,' she said, once they had stopped kissing. He put his arm around her shoulders and pulled her close. Lila watched the sea rippling, the sky turning a gauzy blue with clouds drifting across it. 'Both times.'

'You really need to learn to stick around,' he said softly, his breath tickling her hair. 'The good things hardly ever happen right at the beginning. You wouldn't leave the cinema an hour into the film, would you? Not unless it was *Star Wars: The Phantom Menace*. Mind you, if you'd stayed that long then you might already be asleep.'

'I quite liked that one. All that weird *Ben Hur* stuff.'

'I wish you'd admitted that before I told you I loved you.' He kissed her forehead.

Lila grinned and snuggled closer to him. 'Do you have to go back to the set? I assume you've still got that last scene to film with Aria, seeing as I usurped her and then you came chasing after me.'

'Gregor knew about your plan, obviously, so that's built into tonight's schedule. He also made me aware of something else.'

'What's that?'

'Miss Trevelyan?' Sam raised an eyebrow. 'What do you think? I know it's out of the blue, and it's dependent on *Estelle* getting a second series, but if you want to do it, then you should.'

'It wouldn't be weird, having me on set? Possibly being in the same scenes?'

'Spending time with my girlfriend, watching her outshine everyone else, getting to kiss her in her trailer afterwards? Oh yeah, that would be awful.'

'I wouldn't have a trailer,' she said, laughing.

'You might. But seriously, think about it. These chances are pretty rare, and even if you didn't know you were interested before Gregor spoke to you, you might decide it's exactly what you want. I can introduce you to my agent, and I'll answer any questions you have – Keeley, too.'

Lila nodded. It was an exciting prospect, something she would have to consider properly, but right now she didn't want to think about *Estelle* or what future career might be calling to her, or about America or aeroplanes or coffee. She wanted to savour this moment with Sam.

'You said I was your girlfriend.'

'I'm pretty confident that's what you are. Unless you've got another name for it? Partner, lover, significant other.'

Lila wrinkled her nose. 'I think I like girlfriend best.'

'Girlfriend it is, then.' He leaned down for another kiss.

'Do you think we should face the wrath of Charlie and Daniel and go back to mine? If you don't have to be at work until later.'

'Aren't you needed on the Cornish Cream Tea Bus?'

'We don't open until ten on weekdays, and it's still early.' She looked at her watch. 'God, it's so early.'

'Come on, then.' Sam stood and took her hand. 'I could do with a few hours' sleep.'

'Me too,' Lila sighed, as they strolled along the path, the sun shining down on them. 'I don't know how you cope with your crazy schedule.'

'It doesn't usually include a mad dash across the countryside.'

'So I definitely make your life more exciting, then,' Lila said, laughing.

'That you do.' Sam squeezed her hand.

'Where's your car?' she asked, once they'd reached the car park.

He pointed at a Land Rover. 'I borrowed Gregor's.'

Lila thought for a second. 'Let's leave them both here – we can come and get them later. I could do with the fresh air.'

'You've been sitting out here since three in the morning. I can't understand how you're not chilled to the bone.'

'I know that you're going to warm me up when we get back to Charlie's, and I can survive until then. Besides, my joints are stiff, and this hill is a workout whether you're going up or down.'

'Porthgolow is beautiful,' Sam said, as they walked slowly towards the cove. 'I keep saying Gregor needs to book in some scenes here if *Estelle* does get a second series. Do you think the villagers would mind being overrun by the production team for a couple of weeks next year?'

Lila thought of Amanda and Stella's breathless excitement whenever Sam or the filming was mentioned, and Jonah's questions on the beach at Juliette's wedding. She wondered if Sam would be happy to give him a few pointers, and her heart skipped at the sudden realization that he was hers. 'I think they'd love it,' she said.

'Especially if one of their own was the new star.'

'I'm probably going to have about three scenes.' But even that thought was beyond exciting. Three scenes in a television series destined for the BBC, in which her boyfriend, the talented and utterly desirable Sam Magee, just happened to be one of the leads. Suddenly, she couldn't contain her elation.

'The three best scenes then—' he started, but she flung her arms around him and kissed him for all he was worth, nearly toppling them down the last few feet of the hill together. A passing car honked its horn, and Lila heard the familiar scrape of the newspaper stand being dragged outside the Pop-In, ready for a new day.

'Good grief,' Myrtle exclaimed. 'What on earth is all this about? You comin' back from a night in that hotel at stupid o'clock in the mornin' with this . . . this *man*? I've a good mind to tell Charlie! We don't want any walks o' shame in this village.'

They pulled apart, and Lila saw that Sam's cheeks had gone pink.

'Myrtle,' Lila said, 'this is Sam Magee. You met him a few months ago, when he came looking for me here? You gave him Charlie's address. And this is not a walk of shame, it is a walk of pride. Sam is my boyfriend, and I love him, and we haven't been canoodling in the hotel.'

'Oh,' Myrtle mumbled. 'Well then I'm truly—'

'We've been canoodling in the hotel *gardens*,' Lila corrected, watching as the old woman's expression went from contrite to horrified in half a second.

'Good Lord, maid—'

'It's very nice to see you again, Myrtle,' Sam said, holding out his hand. 'And Lila was joking. We've been doing a night shoot for *Estelle*. I don't know if you've heard of it? Neither of us have had much sleep, so we're a bit giddy with exhaustion.'

Myrtle softened instantly, and Lila had to stop herself bursting out laughing. 'Oh, well then. That *Estelle,* you say? I've heard a fair bit about that. You're the star, are you?' She peered up at him, then nodded approvingly.

'I'm one of the actors,' he admitted. 'You have a stunning village. I hope I'll be spending more time here in the future.' He said goodbye and pulled Lila across the road and on to the beach.

'Did you see her?' Lila asked. 'She was actually simpering.'

Sam grinned. 'You're incorrigible.'

'Oh, to be sure,' she said, in her terrible Irish accent. 'But that's why you love me, ain't it?'

Sam dropped her hand.

Lila laughed, feeling a rush of happiness that they were here, on Porthgolow beach, together. She had got one thing right, at least. She had accepted the job on *Estelle* and dragged Charlie and Gertie there, exposing them to new people and new possibilities, to stunning locations and drama. To Sam.

'Good to see your Irish accent hasn't improved at all.' His eyes danced with amusement as he took hold of her waist.

'For you, Sam Magee, it will stay perfectly awful. *A pure terror.*'

'That's good then,' he murmured, looking at her with those mesmerizing eyes.

'Oh? Why's that?' she asked, revelling in the solid warmth of him, the summer breeze and churning waves at her back.

'Because I don't want you to change. Believe me when I say I've never been more certain about anything. *Lila . . .*'

She smiled as he spoke Robert Bramerton's line, swapping Marianne's name for hers, just as he had done on the beach that night. 'Yours is the only heart I ever want to come close to melting.'

'Ah, so it *was* my heart you had your sights on that evening,' she said softly. 'I thought as much.'

'And? Has it melted? Because if I need to spend more time on it, then I am entirely dedicated to the task.' He bent his head and, before Lila had a chance to reply, to tell him that, yes, in fact he had pretty much succeeded, that it would only take a few more words in that sultry Irish accent, perhaps another rendition of 'Hey There, Delilah', he took her words and her thoughts away with a kiss.

Lila wrapped her arms around Sam and committed, finally, to her own happy ever after.

Chapter Thirty-three

It was not the day to be wearing a thick wool dress, that was for sure. Lila pulled at the fabric around her waist, then tried to get a bit of air between her boobs, while Perry touched up her make-up. She blew a breath up towards her forehead and he gave her a sharp look.

'Nearly done,' he said.

'Jolly good,' Lila replied brightly.

The door to the make-up trailer opened and Keeley flew in. 'How's it going? All set for your big moment?'

'Do you mean, have I had my lines going round my head constantly for the last fortnight? Yup. Yesterday, instead of asking what Amanda wanted to go with her latte, I said "It's good to see you, Mr Bramerton." She almost fell off her chair in hysterics.'

Keeley threw her head back and laughed. She looked happy and relaxed – much more relaxed than Lila felt – in her denim shorts and white camisole top.

'I can't believe you're here,' Lila said. 'I can't believe anyone is. You don't need to be, do you?'

'Well, no. But I couldn't miss your first major scene as part of the *Estelle* cast. Besides, Jordan and I have booked into Crystal Waters for a few days. Didn't Daniel mention it?'

'No, he didn't! I am going to give him a serious talking-to when I see him.'

'You'd better not. You'll spoil your first take.'

Lila's mouth dried out. 'He's not here, is he?'

'Of course he is! Everyone is – your whole village, by the looks of things. I was worried Gregor might have a fit – he's only got Striker Manor booked for this weekend, after all, but he seemed quite taken with the interested faces. He's showing a young boy how the cameras are set up.'

'Jonah,' Lila said, rolling her eyes. 'It has to be. Even Jonah's here? Fucking hell!'

'*Estelle*'s going to go out to millions of people on a Saturday night. It's too late to get stage fright.'

'Yes, but I won't see any of them, will I? This is . . . this is *real*,' she whispered, realizing it was a ridiculous thing to say when it was, in fact, entirely fictional.

'We're done,' Perry said with a flourish. 'Go and knock their socks off, Lila. Though if anyone's wearing socks in this weather, then they're insane.' He gave her a sparkling smile, and Lila glanced down at his three-quarter-length trousers and polished brogues with no socks.

Keeley pulled her outside, and Lila put up her hand to shield her eyes from the sun, her make-up instantly starting to melt. 'Bloody hell,' she muttered.

'Don't worry, Lila. You're going to be wonderful. We all know it.' Keeley squeezed her hand and Lila smiled back, feeling instantly calmer.

Ever since the second series of *Estelle* had been approved, and Lila had made the crazy decision to accept Gregor's offer to be a part of it, Keeley had been her right-hand woman. She had gone through everything with her: setting up a meeting with her agent, accompanying her to the screen test – which Winston assured her was just a formality – and answering all her questions. The scriptwriter had written a new scene into the last episode of series one, introducing her character, Miss Trevelyan, more formally, and an additional two days' filming had been hastily scheduled.

Which was how she found herself, in the middle of August, wearing a corset and a dress thicker than the Crystal Waters curtains, walking through the formal gardens of Striker Manor, the place where, only a month before, she had poured her heart out to Sam in front of the entire production team.

Sam. She grinned at the realization that, any moment now, she would see him in the flesh for the first time in three weeks. He had gone to America to start working on his film, Lila accompanying him to Heathrow Airport, waving him off and then, as prearranged, spending the weekend with Clara and Glen in London, catching up on what seemed like years, rather than months, of news, and keeping her mind off the fact that her new, perfect relationship was going to have to be conducted via Skype for the immediate future.

But not now. Miss Trevelyan's scene was with Robert Bramerton, and so Sam was flying back for the weekend, truly living the jet-set lifestyle, already an actor in high demand.

'It's not hard to guess what you're thinking about,' Keeley said. 'Looking forward to seeing him?'

Lila nodded. 'And I'm sure once he sees me in this seductress outfit, he won't be able to keep his hands off me.'

Keeley laughed. 'It sounds like he's doing well.'

'He is,' Lila agreed. 'He's loving it.'

'And you're still happy here? Working on the bus? I guess it's busy in the summer.'

'It's so frantic I barely have time to think. What with Charlie and her San Francisco-style changes to the food markets, and Daniel starting to plan the eco-upgrades for Crystal Waters, it's all work and no play in Porthgolow.'

'How can you say that? You've got the beach, not to mention instant access to the spa and hot tub at Daniel's hotel.'

'Oh, I don't mean me,' Lila said. 'It's Charlie and Daniel. They're both obsessed, and even when I go up to my room to talk to Sam, I come back down and they're discussing outdoor furniture for Gertie or the merits of solar panels over wind turbines.'

'That's what floats their boat, I guess.' Keeley shrugged.

'They're mad,' Lila said. 'I need to come up with a way to switch their brains off for a bit, give them a holiday that doesn't involve green living courses or food fair research. I don't know what yet, but I'm working on it.'

They turned the corner and Lila faltered. Gregor and the crew were waiting for her in front of the house's impressive entrance, the bright sun glinting off the windows. Beyond them, standing in a cluster, were her friends and neighbours. The Porthgolow Massive, she thought with a grin. Charlie and Daniel were there, Marmite scrabbling in Charlie's arms, no doubt waiting until the moment action was called so he could break free and disrupt the shot. Juliette and Lawrence were back from their Mexico honeymoon, Juliette looking tanned and glamorous, Lawrence resembling a cheerful lobster.

Amanda and Stella, Jonah, Hugh and Myrtle were there too, all whispering excitedly. Jonah gave her an enthusiastic wave, his young face eager, and Lila thought he would have a job transforming into a tortured Hamlet, even if Sam did give him some pointers. Even Jordan, Keeley's boyfriend – she recognized him from photos Keeley had shown her – was part of the assembled crowd, chatting amiably with Daniel.

No backing out now, she thought.

And truly, she didn't want to. Despite the fact that she was about to do something terrifying, something that, only a few months ago, she would never even have considered, she felt strangely calm. She didn't know what the future held, all she knew was that coming to Porthgolow had opened up doors for her. She had escaped here at a low time in her life, had continued to act rashly and make mistakes despite her best intentions, and had discovered that she was accepted, and loved, in spite of it.

'Ready, Lila?' Gregor called.

'Coming!' Lila watched Keeley join Jordan and the others, and then walked to her mark.

She stood on it and smoothed down her skirt. Her lines were like a mantra, repeating over and over in her head. Gregor gave her a reassuring smile and glanced at his watch. He muttered something inaudible into a walkie-talkie, and Lila was briefly taken back to that night by the pond, waiting beyond the yew hedge to deliver her own words to Sam.

'Sorry, everyone,' Gregor said, 'it seems that—'

'Sorry sorry,' shouted a familiar voice, 'I'm here!'

Lila's heart leapt as Sam appeared, pulling on his jacket and shoving his white shirt roughly into his breeches. Perry followed behind, looking aggrieved and waving a foundation brush.

'If it isn't our Hollywood superstar,' Gregor said, slapping Sam on the back.

'Good to see you, Gregor.' Sam returned the gesture and looked around distractedly. 'Traffic was shit, but I'm here.' His eyes fell on Lila and immediately softened. He strode over to her, while Gregor mumbled something about wardrobe.

'You're a sight for sore eyes,' he said. He kissed her deeply and wrapped his arms around her, seemingly oblivious to their audience. 'I have missed you.'

'I've missed you too,' she replied. 'So much.'

'Let us never do that again.'

'What? I . . . how can we not? Your film . . . you're—'

'Come and join me, in America. Forget what I said about oceans being raindrops. They're bloody huge, and I can't bear to have one between us. Come and explore LA, we'll have time together when I'm not working. It's a few months, up until Christmas, then we'll come back here.'

'Sam, you need to be straightened out by wardrobe,' Gregor called. 'Time's ticking.'

Sam kept his eyes on Lila while Gina and Erin smoothed down his jacket, checked his collar and his boots, tugged and pawed at him like he was a mannequin about to go on display.

'OK,' Gregor said. 'Perry?'

Perry swooped in and dusted Sam's face with a brush. His skin had bronzed since he'd been away, and he looked even more gorgeous than when Lila had watched him walk through the gate into the departures lounge. Could she go? Could she leave Charlie and Daniel and Porthgolow behind, have her own adventure in America with Sam, and be back in time for Christmas? She had been working hard on the Cornish Cream Tea Bus, had made more than she'd spent, and along with her share of the money they'd got for bringing Gertie to the *Estelle* set, it meant she had savings. Savings and opportunity, plus an agreed fee for her part in the drama when series two started filming in the spring.

She stared at Sam, waiting for the anxiety to kick in, the little voice that said she was being too reckless, not thinking things through, as always. But instead, she felt a growing sense of elation.

'Right, I need you both on your marks,' Gregor called, as Perry stepped away.

Lila took up her position, her back to the grand house, with Sam, as Robert Bramerton, opposite her.

'Think about it,' he murmured, low and quiet so nobody else could hear.

'Camera one good to go?' shouted Gregor.

'I don't need to,' Lila whispered back.

Sam's eyes widened and his lips twitched, struggling to suppress a grin.

'OK everyone,' Gregor said. 'I think we're set.'

You're coming? Sam mouthed it this time.

'Aaaaaand in three, two, one—'

I'm coming, she mouthed back, and then stood up tall and straightened her shoulders.

'Action!' Gregor called.

After a beat, Sam Magee walked towards her, and she smiled serenely up at him.

'It's good to see you, Mr Bramerton,' she said, in a Cornish lilt that Myrtle had spent hours helping her with. Miss Trevelyan nodded a welcome to Robert Bramerton, and for the next few minutes, Lila and Sam were strangers once more, feeling their way around each other, Lila's happiness and excitement contained by a thick wool dress and a level of self-control she hadn't known she possessed. But she was learning a lot about herself, discovering new strengths.

And this time, she wasn't running away. She was running towards something – towards hopes and dreams, adventure and happiness. And, as soon as Gregor had shouted cut on this first, imperfect take, she was going to run straight into Sam Magee's arms and hold on to him until the scene had been reset and they had to start all over again. This wasn't a rehearsal, this was the real thing, and Delilah Forest was ready for her starring role.

Acknowledgements

As always, writing *The Cornish Cream Tea Summer* has not been a one woman show. These are the people who have helped me with this book in practical, and other, ways.

Kate Bradley, my wonderful editor, who gets me and my writing completely, and always knows how to make my books shine. She puts up with a lot from me, and I am so lucky that she does!

My brilliant agent Hannah Ferguson, who is hugely supportive and reassuring, and supports me every step of the way. Thank you, also, to the rest of the team at Hardman and Swainson.

The whole HarperFiction team for their dedication, and for turning my words into beautiful, polished books that readers want to buy. Thank you to copy editor extraordinaire Penny Isaac, to proof reader Sarah Bance, and to designer Holly MacDonald and illustrator May Van Millingen for the gorgeous covers I want to dive right in to.

I didn't know a lot about filming on location, or the world of television, before I started writing this book – other than watching endless 'behind the scenes' videos of my favourite series on YouTube – so one of the biggest thank you's must go to Ross Bambrey, who patiently and thoroughly answered all my questions, gave me hilarious anecdotes and made me want to be a supporting actor. I have twisted some of the information he gave me to fit my story, and any mistakes or implausibilities are mine alone.

I cannot write these acknowledgements without mentioning the BookCampers, who this book is dedicated to. Isabelle Broom, Kirsty Greenwood, Cesca Major, Cathy Bramley, Rachael Lucas, Alex Brown, Holly Martin, Jo Quinn, Katy Colins, Emily Kerr and Liz Fenwick. They are the most supportive bunch of writing friends, and I don't know what I would do without them.

To David, husband and coffee provider – though that is the very least of all he does for me. No other romantic hero comes close.

To Mum, Dad and Lee, the best family a girl could hope for.

And, finally, to all the readers. I wouldn't be writing books if you didn't want to read them, and I love hearing from you. Thank you for making this job everything I hoped it would be when, all those years ago, I was staring at that first blank page, wondering if I could write a novel.

Discover more delightful fiction
from Cressida McLaughlin.
All available now.

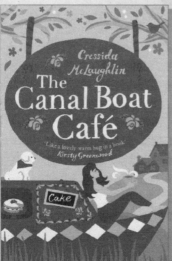

'A wonderful ray of reading sunshine' - Heidi Swain

The Cornish Cream Tea Bus

Bestselling author of *The Canal Boat Cafe*

Cressida McLaughlin

Haven't read how it all started?

The wonderful journey begins here . . .